A COLD COPPER MOON

PRAISE FOR THE COOPER SERIES

A COLD COOPER MOON

Action doesn't stop! From beginning to end, Cooper, a private detective specializing in finding missing persons, and his band of off-center friends, go in search of a man missing in the Florida Everglades. In the process, Cooper uncovers illegal operations spanning the globe from China through Cuban waters to Boston. In the midst of it all, Cooper's increasingly detailed nightmares bring his son, kidnapped seven years ago, into vivid reality. A great read!

DAVID HARRY TANNENBAUM, AUTHOR
(UNDER DAVID HARRY), THE PADRE PUZZLE
SERIES

PRAISE FOR COOPER'S MOON AND BLOOD MOON RISING

The novel is so richly cinematic that I read it while simultaneously imagining each of the chapters and scenes playing out on the silver screen, the suspense high-tension from beginning to end.

JACK DRISCOLL, AWARD-WINNING
AUTHOR, *LUCKY MAN, LUCKY WOMAN*

If you like vigorous adventure blended with high profile issues, this book – and most likely the series – is for you. (Conrath's) elevated prose is raised to poetry.

Cooper, our protagonist, is the smoothest customer you'll ever meet – complete with a sharp tongue and a sharper mind, not to mention his fir share of faults and demons. Relentless in pursuit of justice and closure, "Coop" is the best combination of DeMille's Daniel "Mac" MacCormick (The Cuban Affair) and Connelly's Harry Bosch. Pick it up. Buckle up. And read it like you stole it!

Lovers of the genre will find much to keep them engrossed. Readers will root for Cooper in his search for victims and the identity of the ruthless and mysterious killers. The author successfully raises tension with gripping descriptions and emotional dialogue.

ALSO BY RICHARD CONRATH

Cooper's Moon
Blood Moon Rising

A COLD COPPER MOON

Best wishes from Sanibel! Enjoy your stay. Richard Conrath June '22

RICHARD CONRATH

AWARD-WINNING AUTHOR OF THE COOPER MYSTERIES

GULF SHORE PRESS
ST. PETERSBURG, FLORIDA

COPYRIGHT

A Cold Copper Moon is a work of fiction. The names, places, and incidents are the product of the author's creative imagination and, as such, are being used fictitiously. Therefore, any resemblance to persons, living or dead, businesses, companies, events, or locales is entirely coincidental. See Author's Note.

A Cold Copper Moon,
Copyright © 2021 by Richard C. Conrath

Published by Gulf Shore Press, 2021, St. Petersburg, FL. Gulf Shore Books are available on Amazon and most book stores near you. If the bookstore does not have the book, you may order it through them.

FIRST EDITION

Library of Congress Control Number: 2020925880

ISBN: 978-1-946937-04-9

ISBN: (e-book): 978-1-946937-05-6

Cover Design & Book Layout by Laideebug Digital

"Yesterday, upon the stair
I met a man who wasn't there!
He wasn't there again today,
Oh how I wish he'd go away!"

WILLIAM HUGHES MEARNS,
ANTIGONISH, 1899

As always—
To my wife, Karyn

THE SWAMP

He was having trouble with the motors. They were catching on some seagrass. So he raised the twin Yamahas and cleaned out the propellers from the grass they had been hauling. Then he lowered the Yamahas back into the water and started them up again, the motors now back in tune, purring like a cat when you gentle its fur. *I should have headed home hours ago,* he thought, but he had stretched his luck, the fishing was too good.

Then, thump, thump, thump. Not the sound from the Yamahas idling. Another sound, echoing off the water, maybe emanating from it. He could feel the noise in the sides of the Grady White, faint, but steady. Thump, thump, like the beating of drums—but the Seminoles had put those away decades ago—or like the loud thumping of a gator's tail, but it was too steady for that, or like the throb of his heart against the sense of danger, but he knew better. He had been in these waters too long not to recognize familiar sounds, and this was not familiar. But he headed for it anyway, guessing in his guts that he shouldn't.

So, he idled his boat toward the thumping and it grew more

distinct as he moved back into the sea grass at the southeastern edge of the Everglades. He watched the evening grow even darker as he did, knowing that he should be heading the other way, back toward the open water and safe harbor. But what the hell, it was just thumping, just a curious, persistent hammering in the water. *Was it hammering now?* And it was. And it was coming from the near distance, from some moving forms in the distance. *Machinery? A boat?* And voices carried quietly over the waters, but he couldn't make them out. And *What were they doing out here in the dark? In the Everglades with heavy equipment?* He didn't like it, but he realized too late that he shouldn't be here because a single voice sounded an alarm, over the water, through the dark, and in his direction. *Oh*, he thought.

And he decided, too late, to turn the boat and urge the Yamahas on, because he heard the roar of another boat, churning the water. He knew it was a fast boat because he could see it outlined against the feeble light of the night sky, but he couldn't get his boat going fast enough because the roar was on him like a swarm of disturbed bees. Only there was no way to escape them. Like jumping into the water to avoid the sting. He saw it bearing down on him now, two men standing and pointing, fire erupting from their hands as they pointed, and he felt the boat slip from his control, his hands losing the wheel, and his legs giving way as he felt the pelting on his body. Like sleet or hail from an icy sky. And a darkness spread through his brain, the night perhaps? *No*, he realized. Something much worse than that...

PART ONE

THE ZHI ZHU NU

CHAPTER ONE
OCEANSIDE, FLORIDA

Monday Morning, November 28

I love the big window in my office. It overlooks a wide street lined with palms and live oaks. With buttonwoods thrown in to fill the spaces left by storms. And the oaks don't lose their leaves. This is Florida. Paradise. With heat and sun and all the birds that fly here from the north where there is no heat and sun. I grew up in Cleveland and would watch the birds swarm and head south and wished I could join them. After all, who wants to be in Cleveland in the winter? When the 'lake effect' turns off the sun, and grey, ugly clouds push in from Lake Erie. And the night. There are few stars in the night sky in Cleveland, Ohio. It's just cold, damn cold...and windy, raw and windy.

Up the street a man was leaving the police station. He passed an adult video store with a sign over it that read, Shhh. Don't tell Mama. I've never been in there. Honestly. Next to the video store is a compounding pharmacy where I get my drugs—legal ones I mean. Between the pharm and the video store is a pawnshop. You can't see through the front window—

it's darkened—but go in and you'll find Jorge, sitting behind a cage, his hand on a gun. You won't see his gun though.

As the walker got closer, he looked less like a *him* and more like a *her*: short hair, jeans, shirt, sleeves rolled up. She stopped across the street from my office, looked up at my window— there's wording on it—in big black letters:

COOPER INVESTIGATIONS

Then she crossed the street and walked toward the bakery below me.

I wondered why she was alone in this neighborhood. It's dangerous for a young woman—for anyone actually. That's why I'm here. The rent's cheap. Maybe that's why she was dressed like a guy. Or maybe she was just lost.

I rented this space a few weeks ago figuring it was about time I put Cooper Investigations on firmer ground. *Get an office, for Chrissake, Cooper!* Tony DeFelice, a cop friend of mine from Miami PD, had said. *Nobody's gonna trust a private dick, don't got an office.* So I'm listening to someone coming up the stairs to my office. There's a small entryway at the top of the stairs—and just one door: *Cooper Investigations* painted in black across a smoked glass pane. I could make out a woman's form through the window.

"Hello?" the woman said, opening the door and looking through the reception area into my office. I closed my computer and went out to meet her. She was young—late twenties, maybe early thirties, brown hair, marks on her face—acne maybe—but pretty, despite that.

"Mr. Cooper?" she said, standing now just inside the door, tentative. And when I nodded, she introduced herself. "Cynthia Hayward," she said, extending her hand. She stared at the empty desk in reception.

"That's where my secretary will be when I find one," I lied. She nodded.

I led her into my office and pointed to a wicker chair next to my desk.

"Coffee?"

She looked around.

"My coffee pot's in the bakery downstairs," I said.

"I'm fine," she said. "You don't have much furniture, do you?" Observant.

"I just opened this office. I'm getting new furniture," I lied again, looking around at the bare walls. "I practice minimalism."

She smiled, then settled into the chair, moving around in it, trying to get comfortable. After she found the right spot, we stared at each other for a few moments, me leaning back, waiting, she studying me. I hadn't shaved. It had been a long night. It's been a month since I closed a missing persons case. I should say several cases: one about a young woman who showed up in the Ohio River with missing body parts; another, about a coed from the University of Miami who turned up on a Russian trawler in the Caribbean—she was still alive. Her boyfriend wasn't so lucky—I found him in a bathtub in an apartment in Sunrise (near Miami), dead—some of his body parts missing. There's a lot of money in that business—selling arms and legs on the black market—even skin. So that was really three missing persons, wasn't it? I saved one. One out of three. Is that a good result?

"I need you to find someone," she said and put her hand up to her mouth as if to think about what she had just said. I hoped she didn't know my record.

I waited.

"My father disappeared four days ago."

"Four days ago? Thanksgiving."

She nodded. "That's right."

"Jack Hayward?" I said. There was a story about him in the *Herald*.

"That's him," she said, steadying her voice.

"The Coast Guard and Park Police are already looking for him. Why do you need me?"

"They're not getting any-freaking-where," she said, pissed, and crossed her legs. "I need to do something."

"Uh-huh. But why me?"

"Tony DeFelice gave me your name. He said you're good luck...in finding missing persons," she added.

I thought of my son. Missing now for eight years. He was taken from our home when he was seven. And I've spent every moment of my life since then thinking about him, wondering if he was alive or dead, my former wife, Jillie, doing the same thing. It's why she's my former, and why I'm a private cop. I left my job, teaching at a small college in Ohio, left my wife, and in reality, left my life. So, don't talk to me about luck. I've had no fucking luck finding Maxie. And no life since then.

"Are you okay?" she asked, uncrossing her legs and leaning forward.

I nodded. "How do you know DeFelice?"

"I was a reporter for the *Miami Herald*. I had the crime beat before I went freelance," and she sat back, crossing her legs again, her foot bouncing like she wanted to run. Tense. I wondered if she ran in her jeans—the pant legs were frayed.

"*Miami Herald*?" I paused and stared, thinking. "Didn't you interview me my first day on the job?" I was trying to picture her. She was younger then—early twenties.

"That was me. You made a good story. My first Saturday feature, 'From Prof to Cop.' It got a lot of response."

I had been teaching philosophy at a college in central Ohio when Maxie was kidnapped. After a year of fighting about whose fault it was, I left, worn out by the pressure from the newspapers, from the lack of progress by the local cops, and from my own guilt at not finding him. So, I quit my job and left my home and Jillie. I think she was happy with that. No more staring at each other over morning coffee waiting for the next round of angry accusations. No more early risings, looking out over the front porch at the lawn where Maxie had been playing, no more getting up in the middle of the night after the hundredth nightmare about his disappearance.

I had a friend in Miami, Tony DeFelice, a detective with the MPD, who said he might have a clue about Maxie's disappearance—a gang working the Magic City—and why don't I come down there? So I did. I joined the department and after a year was working homicide. Fast, huh? And when I was off duty, I tried to find my son. So, that's what that story was all about: "From Prof to Cop."

She was nodding, maybe thinking back on it. "I went freelance shortly after that," she continued. "Now I'm working on a series of articles about Big Oil in south Florida. As a matter of fact, Jack..." and she hesitated. "My father...was helping me. I'm hoping his disappearance didn't have anything to do with my stories," she hurried on. Gazing into the distance, she continued, almost confessing, "I upset a lot of people with those articles."

"Tell me about your father's disappearance." I sat back to listen.

"Jack—that's what he wanted me to call him instead of dad —made him feel old, I guess. He was supposed to come to my house for Thanksgiving dinner. It's been a tradition since my mother died. Charles and I —that's my brother," she added, seeing as I was going to ask, "we traded off having the meal. It was my turn." She looked away. Then, "He never showed..."

She hesitated, looking worried, maybe puzzled. Like maybe it was her fault. "I mean, he's usually late, but..."

"But he was late, late, I guess," I said, trying to help. "And you never heard from him after that?"

"That's right. Around 11:00 p.m. we gave up. We waited until early Friday morning to call the police." She was staring into the empty space on my walls. I realized I needed to hang some pictures.

"Was he planning on going anywhere that day?"

"Fishing. He always went fishing on Thanksgiving morning. He's out there early, before the sun rises. It was a tradition for him."

"Any idea where he might have gone fishing?"

"Sure. In the Keys. Maybe the Ten Thousand Islands." She paused. Then, "But just exactly where he went?" She shrugged. "I have no idea. Jack was a loner. Didn't share a lot." Then she looked over at me—as if I might help.

Of course, I couldn't. What did I know? So I just nodded—like the cops did when Jillie and I told them about Maxie. They didn't know anything either.

"I'm still not sure what you think I can do," I said. "The Coast Guard and Park Police are already looking for him—and you want me to...?"

"Look. They think my father either got lost in the Everglades or had an accident. I'll tell you this," and her leg was bouncing again, "my father knows those swamps like the Miccosukees who live there. He wouldn't get lost. An accident maybe. But he's got a phone—and a radio. What kind of accident would prevent him from calling? I can't imagine. My worry, something bad happened to him out there and I want you to find him," she said, pulling away some strands of hair that had fallen across her face. I noticed some scarring on the outside of her left arm. A burn? Oddly enough, it wasn't disfiguring.

"Can you start today?" she said, pausing like she was holding her breath.

"Wow," I said, "let me see," pulling out my phone like I was checking my calendar. "Okay, looks like I'm clear." Actually, my schedule was non-existent.

"How about now?" she said, sitting forward, hope written in large letters across her face.

"Now?" Then, "Sure. Why not? I'm good," I said, holding up my hands.

"That's great!" she said, settling back in her chair, relieved. "Now I just need to know your fee," and she was reaching for her purse.

I told her and she wrote out a check. It covered a whole week.

I called Huxter Crow, a Seminole who grew up in the Everglades and is a skilled tracker. I filled him in on Cynthia and asked if he would meet us at the Pilot House Marina. "Noontime," I added. It was 10:00 a.m.

"Let's get your car," I said, locking the door to the office. There's nothing in there...yet. No files. A couple of desks, three swivel chairs I picked up from St. Michael's used store, and a tiny airplane-size bottle of Captain Morgan. The bottle was there for someone who wanted to burgle the place.

CHAPTER TWO
WHAT HAPPENED TO JACK?

We headed back the way Cynthia had come, toward the video store and police station.

"Where did you park?" I said, trying not to look at the sign over the porn shop. "And, by the way, why *were* you at the police station?" Curious. This was not an Oceanside case.

"Checking up on you. I'm a reporter, remember?" she said, a smile forming at the edges of her mouth. "So, I talked with a friend of yours, Detective Neumann. He said you're okay. But I got the feeling he didn't like you," she added quickly, looking at me for a reaction.

I nodded. Sandy Fatso Neumann. I liked his partner even less. Randall Flagg. The guy with the horrible acne. I wondered if he had taken medication for it as a kid.

"Was Flagg there?" I couldn't get those pockmarks out of my mind.

She stared at me like I had read her mind. "You mean the guy with the bad teeth?"

I had forgotten about the teeth.

She nodded. "Yeah. But he didn't say much. He let Neumann talk."

That was Flagg all right. "How do you know them?"

"When I worked homicide with Miami PD. They don't have a gang unit so we supplied it," and I thought about Louise Delgado, the detective who headed up that unit and I thought of the grief that Neumann and Flagg had given us on two missing person cases. Cops are territorial and we were in their territory. They piss on every lamppost.

"You don't like them," she said.

I shrugged. "They're assholes." Then quickly, "Don't quote me."

She smiled.

"Ah, go ahead," I said. "Quote me."

She kept smiling. "Yeah, they're assholes."

"Uh-huh," I said. "Anyway. Where'd you park?"

"In the lot behind the station."

"You'll drop me off at mine and I'll follow you, okay?"

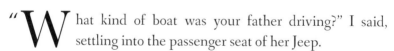

"What kind of boat was your father driving?" I said, settling into the passenger seat of her Jeep.

"He has two boats," she said, forcing the manual gear stick into reverse. "A Grady White 376 Canyon for larger groups, and a Canyon 306 for just a few people or when he wants to go out alone. The 376 is still in dock at the Pilot House Marina in Key Largo. He rents out space there for his 'fishing fleet' as he calls it." She paused as she checked the street for cars. "So, in terms of what he took, the dock-master said he went out on the 306."

"Okay. We'll need a boat. It would help with expenses if

we could use your father's. My boat won't take us where we need to go."

"We?" she said, surprised, taking her eyes off the street. "I was hoping I could..."

"I'll need you," I said. "You must know some of his favorite fishing spots."

"Great," she said, her smile spreading like the sun just rising. "I need to stop by my father's house. I could meet you at the marina."

"I'll follow you," I said. "Maybe we'll find something you missed."

"I already went over the whole house looking for anything...whatever...but I didn't find a thing," Cynthia said, shaking her head.

"I'm sure. But..."

"You think...?"

"Who knows. Funny how small things turn into big ones," I replied. "You mentioned Jack might have been working on your story?"

"He said he was going to help me. I told him *no*, but..."

"He still might have...?"

She nodded. Looking sad, maybe like she did this thing to him.

"Jack have anyone didn't like him?"

She did a double-take.

"Enemies?" Like it was a crazy question. "None that I can think of, other than..." She paused as she pulled against the curb underneath my office window.

"Other than what?"

"You know, other than the trouble my articles might have gotten him into if he was nosing in their business. But besides that, no. I can't think of a thing. I mean, he's a fishing captain for God's sake. How do you get into trouble doing that?" she exclaimed, throwing up her hands.

A massive shadow was building in the street and creeping up the side of the building as clouds rolled over the hill behind the police station, burying the sun.

CHAPTER THREE
WHAT DREAMS MAY COME

Cynthia's Jeep was just ahead of me as we hit the bridge that crosses Florida Bay. Coming off that bridge into the Keys is like descending into a whole new world. It's 113 islands of coral and limestone linked by forty-two bridges and surrounded by the deep blues and greens of the waters of Florida Bay (on the continental side of the United States) and by the Florida Straits (on the Caribbean side). And somewhere in that chain of islands, Jack Hayward got lost and all I had to do was search those islands, the whole southern end of the Everglades, the waters surrounding them, and the Florida Straits to see if I could find him. And, so far, the Coast Guard and the National Forest Rangers had not been successful. And I'm the guy that's supposed to be so lucky—in finding missing persons, that is—the guy who hasn't even found his own son. Wow! One lucky guy.

And my mind drifted into memories of dreams. I have them nightly now. Nightmares are what they really are:

The screen door slammed after him as he ran across our porch, down the wooden steps that front our house, an old colonial, and into the yard, freshly green from the recent rains.

He threw a baseball into the air and caught it—he always did that—then he ran in circles as he tossed the ball, scuffed from falling into the dirt, watching it into his mitt, laughing each time he threw it into the sky, a little higher each time, and he would do this until I would come home—Jillie would tell me—and then we would play catch. But he would have to practice in the meantime.

I was watching him now as the ball sailed higher and higher, floating into a cloud and then dropping out of the white, Maxie losing it momentarily, then reaching for it when it appeared once again, and missing it.

It hit the ground and rolled toward the road, slowly at first— and I held my breath—but, as he chased it, the ball caught the edge of an incline and continued its descent more rapidly, Maxie after it quickly, laughing at the ball as though it were something living, playing hide-and-seek, his hair blowing in the wind like the wheat in the nearby field, the mid-morning sun bright on his face, and he took the incline quickly—I tried to stop him—and hurtled down after the ball until it came to rest in a ditch bordering the road, settling in some mud and stones at the very bottom of the incline, where he reached for it, rubbing the ball against his pants to wipe it clean of the grime from the ditch, but a man stooped down, and said, "Let me help you with that"—and I tried to warn him!—and Maxie looked up at him, a stranger with an odd voice, not at all like the voice of Anthony who owns the antique shop on Main Street nor like mine, nor like anyone he had ever heard. The man took the ball from him and said, "Let's go to my car and get a rag and clean this ball up for you, eh?" And he took the boy's hand before he could answer and led him to a black car, opened the door, and said, "Now let's see if we can find that rag, shall we?"

Then he asked Maxie to look in the back seat to see if he could find it because his eyesight wasn't that good any more.

And Maxie did, felt a shove, and fell forward into the seat, the car door slamming at the same time as his mother called out, "Maxie...Maxie, where are you?" And I tried to call out, too. But the car was already moving quickly ahead, too late for him to see the door of our house opening as he looked out the back window of the car. But I could see him. I could see the fear rising in his eyes and choking him. I could see him look into the front seat where a second man was rising up and reaching for him, while Maxie was trying to call out... for me. And I reached for him again, and called him, but fear must have closed his ears.

And I watched helplessly as they passed Anthony's Antique Shop.

CHAPTER FOUR
JACK'S HOUSE

I shook my head violently to drive out the memory of the nightmare, one I was having almost nightly these days. Getting to bed at 4:00 a.m. to avoid them. Hoping to be so tired that my mind was as dark as deep space. Because if I tried to turn in earlier, I would spend hours watching the red numbers on the clock on my dresser move so ponderously that I wanted to pick a fight with them. I had no idea, none at all, where those damn dreams came from, nor if they offered any clues about my missing son. Or if I was indeed dreaming about my son. Maybe just some boy burned in my imagination from my constant obsession about the kidnapping.

We had picked up US 1 just north of Florida City and took it south to the bridge that crosses Florida Bay. Once we hit the bridge, we passed Long Sound on the right, then Little Blackwater Sound, before we came to the first large piece of land that constitutes the Keys. We passed over Lake Surprise— I always wondered how it got that name—and finally descended into the Keys proper and the beginning of Key Largo where US 1 is more commonly termed the Overseas Highway. Here the road makes a sharp turn to the right heading west-southwest toward Key West, forming what is one of the longest, if not longest, ocean highway in the world: 127 miles of road and bridges, the longest span being the seven-mile bridge built by Henry Flagler, the railroad tycoon, in 1938.

We wouldn't cross that bridge. We would stop in Key Largo, and I would think of Bogart and Bacall as we passed the Caribbean Club that claimed to be the site where Key Largo was shot. Who knows? Maybe it was. Maybe not. At any rate, it's a fun place to drink and it's just a short distance from the point where you leave the bridge and enter the Keys.

Cynthia turned left off the highway at Transylvania Avenue and headed for the ocean side of the Keys. The avenue dead-ends at Shoreland Drive that looks out over the Atlantic. She turned left at Shoreland and pulled into an old Florida ranch, sitting on the right. The house was situated sideways on the lot, the front entrance facing the neighbor's house. The back yard sloped to a dock where a small motorboat rested on davits.

"It's Jack's runabout," Cynthia said as she looked out at the boat, then turned and opened the door. It was unlocked. "Nobody locks up around here," she said, noticing my surprise. "Neighbor carries a shotgun. Would shoot anybody who tries to get in. It's one of the reasons Jack built here. It's remote."

"Nice neighbor," I said, looking around to see if I spotted him aiming at us.

The entry way was to the far left of the house where there was a small living room facing the door. To the right was the kitchen, separated from the living room by a waist high bar and several stools. A good place to drink and watch the large flat-screen TV mounted on the wall in the corner of the living room.

"Jack is a big Marlins fan," she said. I was thinking of a beer and looked towards the fridge. "It's Jack," she said. "He eats peanut butter sandwiches—that is, unless I make him something. Which is all the time since Mom died."

A corridor ran off the kitchen to the right, past several rooms, and emptied into a fireplace.

"That's his den," she said, as she watched me stare down the long, narrow hallway at the room with the fireplace. It made me feel claustrophobic. I felt like I was elbowing my way past doorways and must have shown it.

"Jack liked it that way," she said. "Narrow and dark."

Some model boats lined the mantel above the fireplace. "Your dad collect those or did he make them?"

"He made them. He also made wood models," and she pointed out a menagerie of finely carved, intricately painted miniature animals resting on a table situated under a window that faced the road. I had noticed that the dining room table in the living room held some more.

"Where's his office?" I asked.

"Right here," she said, pointing to an old-fashioned roll-top at the far end of the room.

"Do you mind?" I asked, nodding at the roll-top.

"Be my guest. As I told you, I've already searched the whole house, including the desk," and she watched as I slid open the roll-top.

It took me a few minutes to go through the desk. I pulled out the center drawer. It was a mess: pencils, pens, erasers, paper clips, white-out, some spare change in an ashtray, rubber bands, glue—everything scattered haphazardly in the drawer. I found a Captain's Log in the back of the drawer. I pulled it out and paged quickly through it. The latest log was entered a year ago.

Some small pay envelopes were stuffed into one of the cubbyholes lining the inside of the desk. The others were empty and full of dust.

"Does Jack keep his logs on board?" I yelled to Cynthia who was rummaging around in the kitchen.

"Yes," she yelled back. "The log for the 376 is on board." I nodded—to nobody.

"You find anything?" she shot back.

"Not yet," I said, trying to break free a drawer on the right side of the desk. Something from inside was jamming it. By pushing my fingers through a narrow space I had created perforce, I was able to manhandle it open and felt a package wedged up against the top frame of the drawer. I forced the culprit down and away from the frame and was finally able to pull the drawer free. It was an eight-and-a-half by eleven brown envelope that had been originally taped to the bottom of the desktop. That's why it got stuck. The tape gave away, dropping the envelope partially into the drawer and blocking it. I looked around for Cynthia but she was still in the kitchen making a lot of noise.

"He needs to dump some of this food," she yelled, irritated.

I called her into the den.

"What did you find?" she said, hurrying in and seeing me turn the package in my hands.

"I found this taped to the bottom of the desktop. You want to open it?" I said, offering it to her.

"No, go ahead." Like she didn't want to touch it.

The envelope was several inches thick. I unloosened the string that held the flap down, reached inside, and pulled out a stack of photographs, most of the ones on top were 8x10 black-and-white images. We sat down, spread-eagled, on the wooden planking of the den floor and began to sort through the pictures one at a time. The first photograph was of an oil rig, enormous, two cranes extending from either end, one reaching for the sky, the other hanging over the water.

"My God, he's taking pictures of that damn rig. Why in the

hell was he doing that?" Then she paused. "I had taken him out one afternoon to see it, and he got all upset—about foreigners drilling in American waters."

"Maybe wanting to help?" I said looking over at her as she stared at the photos. She held up a plate where the name of the rig stood out in large letters:

ZHI ZHU NU

"Wow," she muttered to herself as she continued to stare, then reached for a few more plates, the shots all taken from different angles but of the same rig. "This is one of the largest oil rigs ever built, did you know that?" she said, holding up another picture.

I shook my head and leafed through a few more prints. I wondered how the men on the platform would have reacted to a man in a motorboat taking pictures and circling their ship. Because that's what the rig looked like—a ship—a ship on four giant pontoons.

"You know the story?" she pressed on.

"Not really," I said, only remembering the ongoing fights between the environmentalists and Big Oil over drilling rights in and around the Everglades.

"Well, a Chinese firm has purchased the rights to do off-shore drilling in Cuban waters, and in May of this past year our government had given the CNOOC" (she noticed I was looking for a translation), "that's the Chinese National Offshore Oil Corporation, the leasing rights to drill for oil in the Gulf." She hesitated. "Didn't know that, did you?" I shrugged. "Didn't read my articles, did you?" she said, shaking her head. I shrugged again.

"Should read my articles," she continued, playing with me. "I feel like I'm fighting a losing battle—intelligent guys like you don't read my articles. How can any of us make a difference if nobody listens or reads!"

I'm sure I looked guilty as hell to her because I was, and I hated to admit it.

"And several Russian firms are ready to jump in as well," she added. I wondered when we would see Chinese and Russian submarines offshore in the Straits.

"Don't be surprised if you see a Chinese aircraft carrier in our waters sometime in the near future," she said, almost as if she were reading my thoughts. "They're building one of the largest in the world even as we sit here looking at their derrick," and she was nodding her head like I was a willfully uninformed idiot just like all the other unconcerned Americans she was trying to bring her story to.

"Moreover," she continued, "there are now over 125 leases to drill in the Eastern Gulf—all the way down to the Keys and north into the Florida Straits. That covers over 700,000 acres of Florida water. And that's what I'm talking about, Cooper."

Lesson for today.

"And eventually,"—another lesson—"that will do it for the Everglades and for our ground water. And," pausing, "our children will inherit all the chemicals that the oil companies are pouring into our swamp and you can kiss our paradise goodbye," she complained, tossing her hand like she was throwing it all away. *Paradise Lost*.

"So, go back and read my damn articles, Cooper."

And then she stopped—thank God—picked up the photos and began to page through them, laying them out so we could both study them.

She puzzled over one of them. "This one..." she said, picking up one of the plates, "this one is different," and she held it up to the lamp next to the desk. "It's smaller," she added, studying it carefully. "I wonder where this picture was taken?"

It was a mere shadow of the *Zhi Zhu Nu*. No heavy cranes leaning out over the water. And the deck was no more than maybe fifteen feet, twenty max, above the surface of the water. The sun was setting behind the derrick, so Jack was looking from east to west when he took the picture. I picked up several more photos as Cynthia continued to stare at the one she was holding. The ones I turned over were of the same rig, only Jack must have been circling it now, much like he circled the *Zhi Zhu Nu*. In all there were six shots of this rig, catching the structure from every angle, even some of the workers who were staring at the camera—in one shot a man was pointing a rifle at him.

"The Feds have ceased issuing drilling leases in the eastern Gulf. But...," she continued, holding up one of Jack's photos of the smaller derrick, "the state of Florida—now that's a different matter. State waters extend from seven-and-a-half to ten statutory miles from the coast into the Gulf." She paused again, still studying the photo. "I wonder where in the hell this baby is?" she mused, mostly to herself, looking closely for a landmark.

"Had he ever supplied you with material for your articles?"

"He told me he was working on something but never what it was." She paused to wipe sweat from her forehead. "It's hot in here," she said, handing the photo to me.

"It's certainly not in the deep part of the Gulf. See how close the shoreline is in the distance?" I said, pointing to a vague stretch of land behind and to the right of the derrick.

Cynthia sighed and shook her head. "I sure hope Jack didn't get himself killed because of me."

CHAPTER FIVE
THE PILOT HOUSE

I t was not far from Jack's house to the Pilot House Marina
—a little over four miles. A ten-minute drive. It was early
afternoon when we left his place. I retraced my steps
back to US 1, passing streets that were named after fish: Bass,
Bonefish, Jewfish, Snapper, and Marlin and finally came to
Transylvania Avenue—oddly out of place among the fish
streets—and turned right. In a few minutes we were back on
the Overseas Highway and heading south toward the Lower
Keys.

On the left we passed John Pennekamp Coral Reef State
Park, a large expanse of green that extends out into the Florida
Straits. I turned off the highway at Laguna Avenue near the
Holiday Inn where there are some famous shrines: Bogie's Cafe
and the African Queen. From Laguna, I turned onto
Homestead Avenue—Cynthia right behind me—passed an
Office Depot and a Bank of America, and finally hit Ocean Bay
Drive, a two-lane road, lined on both sides by scrub palms and
sea grape all growing wild, and by telephone lines trying to
fight their way through the branches. I was looking for
American Legion Post #333—my landmark. It came up quickly

on my left: a two-story, cement block building painted yellow years ago. It was now faded and dirty. The surrounding area was pretty much the same: run-down buildings with tired paint jobs, and dusty. Just past the American Legion building was a post office sitting on the corner of Seagate Boulevard and Ocean Bay. And directly behind that was the Pilot House Marina. I turned left onto Seagate.

The marina is located on the north end of Lake Largo. But don't think of the lake as a large body of water. It's maybe a football field across. And Seagate is hardly a boulevard. When I think of a boulevard, I picture a wide street overhung with trees on both sides and a wide green space running down the center with traffic running only one way on each side. No, that's not Seagate. It's a crowded narrow street jammed with boats lining the side near the marina, and parked helter-skelter, like the owners had just gone into the restaurant for a drink and would be right back.

Just past the marina, I turned right onto North Channel Drive (a short street) and then made an immediate right into a parking lot that constitutes the marina's main entrance. The Pilot House is a two-story structure, painted the same pale yellow as the American Legion Post, the second floor sitting on top of the main structure like the top deck of a battleship, set in and squared off. The roof was tin, painted a dull sea green, the sheen worn off by the storms that beat down on it. I parked under a large sign that rose almost as high as the roof of the marina. On it was a large ship's wheel and to the right of the wheel were the words:

PILOT HOUSE

I looked for Huck's truck. I didn't see it, but I heard his voice even before I got through the door. He was wearing a rawhide jacket and pants, his Florida cattleman outfit, tassels and all, and talking in an elevated voice to a man behind the desk. We headed his way.

"What took you so long, Cooper?" he said. "See my new transportation outside?"

"No."

"Red Ford pick-me-up. A V-8 with a 3.5 liter engine," Huck explained proudly, his thumbs tucked like a cowboy in his belt. Huck is a descendent of Florida's original Seminole cowboys, not to be confused with the Florida crackers, so-called for driving their cattle with a whip rather than a lasso. The Florida cowboys actually predate their western counterparts.

"Nice!" I said, wondering how he paid for it.

"The money you gimme for the last job," he said, reading my mind.

I introduced him to Cynthia, and then he introduced us to Sam something or other, the blond guy behind the desk.

I said "Hi" to Jimmy, because his name was Jimmy not Sam, and he had been behind that counter for years, as testified by the lines on his face. Too much time on the water. His skin was dark, a fair complexion compromised by the Florida sun. The only thing that didn't tan was his hair. And the sun had bleached that blond.

He knew why we were there and told Cynthia—probably not for the first time—how sorry he was to hear about Jack and no he couldn't figure out what happened to him.

"Jack knows these waters," Jimmy continued. "It don't figure," and his voice was partially drowned by the sound of a chopper flying too close to the marina.

"Coast Guard," he said, chewing at the end of his mustache —it was blond too. "They've been searching most of the day," and he glanced at Cynthia—hesitated, then, "They'll find him," he said quickly. I knew that was a lie.

Then I pulled out the photos Cynthia and I had found and showed them to him. "These were in Jack's house. We're trying to locate the site of this smaller rig," I explained, holding up the photo of the oil platform.

"Lemme see the picture of that big one again," he said. I flipped back to the *Zhi Zhu Nu.*

"That there's the Chinese rig," he said, staring at the photo. "Now you tell me what in the livin' hail are they doin' out there in U.S. of A. water?" Jimmy's a Florida redneck. He carries a loaded shotgun in the back of his pick-me-up.

"It's in Cuban waters," I said. "Nothing anyone can do about it. Did Jack ever let on that he was taking pictures out there?"

"Never did. He always said he was goin' fishin'. Said it was his way of relaxing: fish and drink beer."

"What about this?" I held up a print of the smaller rig again. "Any ideas?" I was trying to hold the picture against some sunlight that had sneaked through a window behind the desk.

"Nope, sure don't," he said, studying the picture. Then he picked up several more, turning each one so that it would catch the light and finally coming back to the same print. "It ain't in the Straits. That's for sure. Lookee here." He was pointing at the hint of a shoreline on one of the plates. "It's off the west coast somewheres...maybe up around the Ten Thousand Islands," and he kept studying the prints as he talked. "Why don't you leave one of them photos with me and I'll study on it a while longer." Then he turned to Cynthia. "Anyway, if I can help, Miss Cynthia, you know I will. Jack was a special friend and we're all prayin' he's okay."

Cynthia took Jimmy's hand, held it and thanked him. "No need to cry," Jimmy said when she began to tear up. "Ol' Jack'll show up sure as I'm standing here. He knows these waters. If he's lost, he'll get hisself back here. You can take that to the bank."

I pushed Jimmy one more time before we left. "Look, I know you've been over all of this before with the Coast Guard and the Park Rangers but is there anything more you can tell us about where Jack might have been headed? Into the Gulf? The Glades?"

He shrugged. "The Straits maybe. But he usually went fishin' up Ten Thousand Islands way. Like I told the Rangers, he went that way," he added, pointing toward the channel that leads to the Straits. "Said he was goin' fishing. I asked him if he was gonna take the 376. He said, No. Just the little boat. And that's the last I seen of Jack."

CHAPTER SIX
THE SEARCH

I t didn't take long to get Jack's Canyon ready. The boat was in dock and the fuel tanks were full. "Just like Jack," Cynthia said as I started the motors and she and Huck cast off the lines. "He's always ready for clients."

"Did he have any scheduled?" I said, suddenly realizing he probably did.

"Of course," Cynthia said. I eased back on the throttle to hear what she was saying. "He was booked solid for the next few weeks. But most of his clients had read the newspaper article and called the marina. The ones I didn't hear from, I called," and she cast the last of the lines onto the dock.

I eased the Canyon out into the lake at idle speed until we escaped the No Wake zone. The three Yamaha 350s churned and growled like a cougar trapped under water. In several minutes we were in the channel that leads into the Florida Straits.

"Did Jack keep a gun on board?" I asked Cynthia, who had one foot on the step that led below.

"Yes. He never went out without one." She paused. "Why?"

I had packed my Glock and Huck had stowed his alligator gun, but I was hoping for another weapon. "We don't know what Jack ran into out there."

"Pirates?" she asked, surprise in her voice. "I never thought..."

"There are pirates in the Caribbean—as you must know—so..." I was focusing on steering through the channel, the open water of the Straits just ahead.

"I wouldn't think pirates got Jack—but that depends on where he went."

"I wouldn't count 'em out," came a voice from below. Huck. "I never run into one, but my friend has," he added, coming topside. "That was over by the Bahamas."

Cynthia looked worried.

"Don't think the worst," I said. "I checked Noonsite."

She stared at me.

"Noonsite. It's a web page that reports on pirate activity around the world. It didn't report any incidents off the coast of Cuba," I said. What I didn't say was that Jack's incident hadn't been reported yet. But she must have thought of that. "Anyway, most of the time pirates just take your boat if you're near land. And they leave you stranded." What I didn't tell her was that if you're on the open sea, they're likely to throw you overboard. And that would be a long swim home.

"You want to take the wheel?" I said, figuring it might take her mind off Jack.

She nodded and took the wheel like a skilled helmsman and aimed the Canyon toward the Straits.

I stood at the rail and watched water fly over the bow as Cynthia opened up the Yamahas. At forty miles per hour the three engines tossed great geysers off the stern, forming a wake that stretched for hundreds of yards. Then she swung the Canyon south toward the Lower Keys where we would ultimately cross through at Islamorada and emerge on the north side of the Keys that faces Everglades National Forest. From there we would head north-northwest into Florida Bay toward the Ten Thousand Islands.

Jack does a lot of fishing there, she had said before we left, still speaking of him in the present.

When I looked into the water untouched by the engines, the water far out from the Canyon, where it was smooth and tranquil, I got to thinking of Maxie once again—can't keep him out of my thoughts. When I'm looking for a missing person, I feel guilty about not finding him. As I stared into the wake, the roiling water drew me as though Franz Mesmer, the medieval mystic who developed hypnotism, was riding the wake and using the waves that rolled with an even cadence to induce a trance. He captured me and my eyes gave away to his magic.

T*he road was moving away quickly now, Muskingum disappearing into the distance. A hand was pulling the Boy away from the window. He was straining to see if a blue Volvo was following—that would be me. But he didn't see any cars at all, just the road falling away, a hand rougher on him now, forcing him into the seat. He had never seen them before— the man who was now removing his hand, saying, "That's a good boy now" --or the man driving, "Not to worry, boy, we're friends of your dad." He's lying! I was trying to tell him—the Boy could hear it in the driver's voice, that sound that made his stomach hurt, and I knew he was thinking of our warning, "Never get into a car with strangers,"—and these men were certainly strangers—the people I warned you about! They were driving faster now, past fields that he had watched on so many Sundays, past barns that sat back in the fields, past telephone poles that*

were flying by way too quickly, and remembering, "Don't get into a car if someone you don't know tells you to. Run. Don't get in whatever happens."

"But they shoved me in," he was thinking to himself. "I didn't have a choice!"

And I knew Maxie would be worried about what we would say when he got back home. He would wonder if we would be mad. And I heard the phone lines sing in the wind as the car headed south-southeast.

Cynthia was staring at me. "You okay?"

I shook my head. *Damn dreams*, I thought. I wondered if the years of searching for my son were just piling up, like the accumulation of drugs might do to the body, like Xanax might do to the brain.

Cynthia guided the Canyon carefully into Snake Creek at Islamorada, past the Snake Creek Marina on our left, and past a series of peninsulas with houses lining each strip of land reaching out toward us and eventually traveled at idle through the No Wake zone into Florida Bay. From there we headed north to Madeira Bay—that's on the southern end of Everglades National Park, a place where Cynthia said her father often took his clients fishing. A Coast Guard helicopter was searching the area just north of the islands, disappearing into the distance then reappearing on a line closer to the National Park, sweeping the landscape like a man cutting his lawn in a manner that no blade was left untouched.

Once we were clear of the No Wake zone, Cynthia opened the throttle and we roared into the Bay, the boat slamming into waves as it rose and fell. It's about twenty kilometers to the first island group and then another twenty to Madeira. I had brought a pair of Barska Zoom Gladiator binoculars. With a variable magnification of 20 to 140 times, the glasses gave me an up-front and personal view of objects that are a long way off —like the islands that we were searching. I was looking for signs of wreckage that could easily have been missed by the helicopter. Huck had found a pair of binoculars that Jack had stowed below. He was searching the starboard side. I was at port.

"Jack loved to fish the Islands, but we're sure as hell not going to find him here," Huck said, dropping his glasses and looking up at the copter now directly overhead. We were approaching the first island group.

"You knew...I mean, know... my father?" said Cynthia, catching herself.

"Yeah, Miss Hayward. Fishing buddies," he said, picking up his glasses and keying in on an island over starboard.

"I don't remember him talking about you?"

"Jack didn't talk much about his friends, did he?" More a statement than a question.

Cynthia nodded. "It seems like the Ten Thousand Islands would be too far to get there and back in one day."

"When did Jack leave?" Huck said.

"Sometime around 4:00 a.m.—according to the dock master."

"Plenty of time." He paused and adjusted his binoculars. "No. Ol' Jack's not here," his glasses sweeping the Bay.

Cynthia looked my way, puzzled.

I waited for Huck to put down his glasses.

"No signs of Jack here," he noted, sounding like a tracker. "We need to take this bronco to the Ten Thousand Islands. That's where he did most of his fishing..." and he turned to Cynthia, "...and not to worry. We'll find him, missy."

Huck's father and his grandfather were both trackers. Early on, Huck trained with the Shadow Wolves, members of the Sioux and Navajo tribes. He learned a method of tracking that involved "cutting for signs." The "signs" being something as indistinguishable as a misplaced stone or a wisp of smoke from a campfire or a tree scarred by a knife. Signs would be more difficult to spot on the water—easier on hard ground. There are signs invisible to the naked eye of a normal man but visible to a skilled tracker and it is perhaps those that Huck now saw in the waters of Florida Bay. Then there is instinct. And maybe that's what was guiding Huck as he decided we were in the wrong place.

"All right," Cynthia said, shaking her head.

"I trust Huck," I said. "Let's go with what he says."

"Shark River," Huck said.

So, Cynthia turned the Canyon about and headed west-northwest toward the Ten Thousand Islands.

The best route to the Islands is the open sea around East Cape, the southernmost point of Everglades National Park. The direct route would be tricky and dangerous, trying to dodge the crab traps that line the waters along the western shore of the Park. There would be some in the open sea route as well. But they would be fewer and spread further apart.

Cynthia steered the Canyon around Triplet Keys and Club Key and out into the open water of the Bay again, then west-southwest around a series of smaller keys until we reached the open waters of Florida Bay again. Then she headed for the Gulf of Mexico. There's a line on the map that separates the Bay from the Gulf. You can't see it of course. But along this imaginary line, the two bodies of water merge like lovers in an embrace.

Once we caught the open water, we headed north passing Sandy Key on our right and steered directly for East Cape. It was mid-afternoon by the time we were even with the Cape having been slowed by a web of crab traps that laced the waters off the Capes. And it would be late afternoon before we would hit the Little Shark River Inlet where we could anchor for the night.

"A storm's brewin', buckaroo," said Huck, pointing to a line of black and charcoal clouds piled high on the horizon. They were moving in over the Gulf from the west.

Huck is proud of his ancestry as a Florida cowboy—thus greetings like 'buckaroo'— as well as his Seminole heritage. *My great granddaddy was in the Seminole wars, as is betokened by the totem in my living room, Cooper, which we have talked about on many an evening*, explained Huck one night when I was drinking with him at his Everglades City house.

The clouds moved in from the Gulf more quickly than I had expected, the storm now about a half-hour away. It looked like we would be entering the Little Shark River inlet about the time it would hit.

"You ready to spend the night aboard?" I said to Cynthia.

"There's provisions in the refrigerator. Jack always kept the boat well-stocked. You like rum?" she said, gripping the wheel more tightly as waves began to build in front of the approaching storm.

I nodded. "Rum and Coke or a good, dry white."

"We have both," she said.

The darkness was spreading toward us.

CHAPTER EIGHT
SHARK RIVER

By the time we hit the Little Shark River inlet, I could see that the bank of rain that had been far out over the Gulf was now closing in, the first drops already hitting me in the face. I had taken the wheel. Waves were beginning to build so I cut the throttle as the Canyon struggled with the rough surf. On my right was the green marker that signaled the mouth of the river—it's lighted and so easily spotted in the dark. We would anchor at Marker 5 at mid-river about half a kilometer away.

As the boat began to heave in the waves, Huck came topside to check out what was going on. "Better stay below," I said. "It's getting rough."

And just as I said it there was a deafening bang and I watched a huge ball of flame roll across the inlet toward us no more than a hundred yards away—a tumbling, silent wheel of fire, rhythmic in its movement, spinning like a whirling dervish, like part of the sun broken loose—a hell-on-wheels come to burn us alive.

I never thought to turn the Canyon away, and it grew in size as it got closer—too late to get out of the way—and it was like a house on fire, and huge, and the heat—it boiled the water and it cooked the air—and this oven in motion headed right for us. It dropped when it was only a few hundred feet away, this ball of fire, this wheel of enormous flames. And I felt the heat of it, and the draft of it, and I smelled things burning and I hoped it wasn't me. Then, I saw fire on the boat, and looked up, and just as quickly as it had appeared, the wheel was gone. But its effects were not: the hair on my arms and head was singed. I rose up in time to see the rolling ball of fire sweep onto the shore, and into the mangrove forest—already burned from another fire—and the skeletons of trees, still black from the last conflagration, were lit up again, as well as the forest undergrowth that had turned green but was now aflame—but the fire would soon be extinguished by the hard rain.

"My God!" yelled Cynthia, who had just come topside with Huck and had come over to see how I was. "What was that?"

And I told the two of them to look at their hair, and theirs was singed and frizzy like mine. And the fiberglass surface of the prow was blistered, and the flag that had been flying there—Jack's flag of Ireland—was gone, the post it was hanging from, black.

"The gods have spoken," said Huck.

We continued to check the boat for damage. But there wasn't much—mostly surface stuff. We were like a house that was in the way of a forest fire but had escaped major damage, with only the paint blackened from the heat of the fire and the soot that filled the air. The temperatures of a forest fire can reach 1000 to 1500 degrees. I wondered what the internal temperature of that wheel of fire that had just missed us was.

What we had seen, I'm convinced, was a ball of lightning. Something that sailors talk about but is rarely verified. The lightning ball is the stuff of mythology. To us, it was a reality.

And the people we would relate it to would probably nod and say, "Uh-huh."

"The Thunder and Lightning Men are showing us where to go," said Huck, wiping the rain away from his eyes. "The *Bed-day yek* (thunder) caused this," he continued, pointing to where the ball of fire disappeared onto the shore. "The Thunder Boys have picked up the *Bed-dags k'chisousan* (the thunder bullets) and thrown them." He paused. "Maybe Jack was caught in their play. Maybe he has been Thundrified. And maybe they will bring him back to us as a man on fire."

Cynthia just stared at him. I didn't say anything. Better to let Huck opine. Who knows? Maybe he's right.

∾

I steered for Marker 4. It was just after 5:00 p.m. The rain, coming down in sheets now, made visibility nearly impossible. We were about 100 yards from anchorage when a wave crashed against the boat, ripping me from the helm. I tried to hang on but couldn't and was swept to the side of the boat, hitting my head against the gunnel.

"Cooper, you all right?" yelled Huck over the wind, slipping and falling on the deck as he reached for me.

"'This is one hell of a storm," I said. "Fireballs, killer waves. What the hell...?" and I stared at my hand. My head hurt like mad and I had reached up to feel where it hurt.

When I brought my hand down, I was looking at red water.

"You're bleeding, Coop," Huck said, and called for Cynthia, who had gone below. He took the wheel. "Go below and take care of that cut."

I slid my way across the deck and started down the ladder. Cynthia grabbed my arm and helped me to a cot.

"You've got a serious gash there," she said, standing over me and checking my forehead. "Head wounds always bleed a lot and look worse than they are." She had me hold a towel to the cut while she rose and rummaged through a cabinet. "Where the heck does Jack keep his first aid kit?" she complained, like we were just borrowing his boat for the day. She found it.

Then, "Let's get that head under a shower," she said. And I stripped off my rain jacket, shirt and undershirt, and leaned into the shower as Cynthia turned on the water. I watched the blood flow into the drain.

"Remember, it looks worse than it is." Then, "A nasty little devil," she said, studying the wound after I dried my hair. "But a bandage will bring it together." And she worked quickly, spraying the wound with an antibiotic then applying a butterfly and then a large gauze bandage over that.

"How do you feel?"

"Dizzy."

"Okay. Then maybe you shouldn't lie down—just in case." I knew what she was thinking: concussion. But we had a boat to secure and Huck would need help. I paused to listen to the storm. It was quiet for a moment. Then the wind and waves were back at it. No rest.

"I'm going topside to help Huck," I said.

"Here, put this on your head," said Cynthia. "Cover that wound." She tossed a hooded rain jacket at me. I put it on.

Huck was already steering the Canyon to anchorage. He swung the boat around so that the stern was pointing against the tide and the incoming waves just like it would be if it were docked. I let out the stern anchor. When it was set, Huck shut down the motors. Several boats were already anchored around us.

In the distance a sailboat was heading our way running through the storm, trying to trim its sails. A sudden gust of wind caught it, and the crew struggled to keep it from capsizing. I watched to see if they needed help. They dropped anchor about 100 yards from us, staying clear of the shallows.

Huck had secured the wheel and was letting the front starboard anchor out. "Double check that anchor," I yelled over the noise of the storm. "I don't want the wind to drag this damn thing into the middle of the river."

"She's as set as she's gonna be," Huck replied, pulling hard against the anchor to test it.

Once the Canyon was secured, we headed below and cracked two small screened windows to let some air into the cabin.

"This feels like a tropical storm," I said to Cynthia. "You have anything on the weather?"

"No. Nothing out in the Gulf or in the Caribbean or the dock-master would have certainly said something." Then, "I hope," she added—to herself.

There were several changes of clothes in a dresser. Both of them fit Huck. I found some shorts. I was too tall for Jack's pants. Cynthia was already in the bathroom changing into dry clothes she found in a locker. When I came out of the shower, I saw Huck rummaging around in one of the lockers.

"Rum," he said, holding up a bottle of Captain Morgan— my favorite. "Got any Cokes?"

Cynthia pointed to a lower cupboard.

"Helps keep the spirits of the storm away," he said—which, by the way, was picking up again. When we anchored, the wind was at twenty-seven knots. I checked the wind gauge. It read thirty-five knots.

We scavenged a dinner of crackers, cheese, and baked beans from Jack's larder, sat in the berth and listened to the storm blow. Huck and I poured rum and cokes. Cynthia had trouble getting her wine into a glass, the boat tossing us around like a teapot in a bathtub of kids playing with the water.

After about an hour the storm subsided and the boat settled into a gentle rock. We went topside, taking our drinks with us and checked for damage. Not much—just some debris on the deck. And we hadn't drifted far from where we had anchored.

I dried off the captain's chair, sat, and stared at the stars that were visible now. My thoughts wandered back to Maxie and I wondered where he was. The rum must have reached my brain, because...

When I woke, the deck was deserted. The moon was lighting up the river like a thing of magic, and the stars were hanging over me in the millions. I pulled myself, headache and all, out of the chair and went below. Huck was half hanging out of his berth. He wasn't breathing. I poked him and he started up again, like an engine that needs priming.

It was 3:05 a.m. I heard movement around the boat. I grabbed the Gator Light that Jack kept on board and went topside. The lamp is useful for hunting gators; its warm and soft yellow beam finds the gator's eyes in the dark without startling him. A few lights were blinking over the water from boats that had anchored around us. I passed my beam over the surface, now peaceful, looking for the source of the noise, crossing through a path of silver laid there by the moon now low in the sky. I swept the beam toward the shore. About 30 feet from the shore, eyes stared back at me. I held the light steady and the eyes sank into the water, quietly. I was uneasy about our closeness to shore and our vulnerability to gators and snakes. But at the moment, I was beat and my eyes were closing. I went below and flopped into my berth, clothes and all. Huck was snoring.

"You look like you been to the Happy Hunting Ground," said Huck, when I shook him hours later. It was 7:30 a.m.

"Your fault," I said. "Your damn snoring kept me up."

Cynthia was already up, a cup in her hand. "There's coffee."

"Decaf?" I said.

She looked at me and shook her head. "At 7:30 in the morning?" Her hair was pulled back in a single braid allowing her neck and shoulder blades to stand out. "You staring at me, Cooper?" she said, smiling.

I shook my head and smiled back. "No." But I think I was.

I grabbed a cup of coffee, then added some sugar and powdered milk that we had found in Jack's provisions. I don't talk in the morning. Neither does Huck. But Cynthia seemed anxious to. So, we talked briefly about the morning and shared some dried fruit that she had found.

"So, let's head upriver," I said after we had cleared the table. Jack had a map of Shark River. So I laid it out on the small dinette table that sat in the center of the cabin.

"What do you think?" I said, studying the water depths and the smaller tributaries that ran off the river upstream. "We can break out the inflatable so we can get in closer to shore. Matter of fact, I think we'll have to." No reaction. "Anyway, let's get underway. It's early. We have the whole day to search." They both nodded.

The morning was quiet. Most of the boats that had anchored for the storm still weren't moving. Huck and I hoisted the Canyon's anchors and Cynthia started the motors and pulled into the center of the river. It was around 8:30 a.m. Several sailboats now joined us but were headed for the mouth of the river toward the Gulf, away from the rising sun. We headed right into it, toward the heart of the Everglades.

We moved slowly upriver with Shark River Island on our left and the Everglades National Park on our right. In the center of the river the depths averaged ten to twelve feet, plenty of water for the Canyon. I relieved Cynthia at the helm so she and Huck could focus on Jack's fishing spots. They swept the shores on each side, using glasses that Jack kept on board, as we moved ahead.

The sun had cleared the mangroves, blinding me. I put on my sunglasses and took off my jacket. The temperature was already close to 75 degrees and rising. I expected it to get into the 80s before the afternoon was over. The river maintained its own quiet flow beneath the low rumble of the Yamahas. Gators splashed into the water from the shore, the only other sound as we made our way upstream. As the river narrowed, I could see the brush along the shore more distinctly now. I steered the boat for a tangle of mangroves on the north side, following Huck's arm as he pointed them out.

"We fished those waters," he said. "Grouper pitch their tents over there in a hole near that marker," he added, turning to the open water and pointing to the mouth of the river. "Might get some tarpon there too. I'm figurin' Jack started fishin' in the mouth of the river and then worked his way here." Then he fell silent and scanned the forest of dead mangroves that stretched along the shore.

"Wilma kill those trees?" I said.

"Yep. Cleaned out this whole section of the island. It's just now coming back." He paused as he looked into the dense forest behind the graveyard of mangroves.

"Best way to do this is to find ourselves one of the fingers of the river that runs into the island and see if Jack got hisself hung up in there," and he looked over at Cynthia as he said it, as if to say, sorry.

"Don't worry about me, Huck," Cynthia said. "I'm okay."

I knew she wasn't, but she wasn't going to let us know that. So I suggested she take the wheel and let Huck and me look for Jack. She didn't object, took the wheel and continued to let the boat idle slowly upriver past marker #5 and toward a small offshoot of the river on our port side. Huck kept an eye on the depth marker since we were nearing the shore.

"Why don't we anchor here and explore some of this shoreline in the dinghy," I said, looking up at the sun now at about nine-o'clock. "Where does Jack keep the inflatable?"

Cynthia handed me the wheel, went to a storage unit on deck and began to pull out a large bag. I shut off the motors and went to let out the anchor when I heard Huck yell over to Cynthia. "Let me help you with that, little lady." I watched Cynthia as she stopped what she was doing, pulled her hair back away from her face, and looked his way.

"Do I look like a little lady?" she said, her eyes locked onto his. Huck froze. The two were quiet for a moment.

Then, "I sure am sorry, Miss Cynthia. You have to excuse an old tracker, raised in the swamp. I didn't mean no harm."

She nodded, obviously still pissed and went back to work on the canvas bag. Huck stayed where he was for a few moments, looked over at me, shrugged, and then went over to help. She let him, quiet the whole time.

With the anchor set I joined them. The dinghy was a Santa Cruz 10' Air Floor Tender Boat. It was designed almost like a pontoon boat only much smaller, about ten feet from stem to stern. It took about a half hour to inflate the boat and mount the 9.9 HP Johnson. After securing the Canyon, we dropped the Santa Cruz over the side and headed for shallow water that abutted a long line of mangroves that jutted into the air like skeletons, black as Halloween, their bark stripped by the winds. I watched Cynthia as she only half searched the shoreline, the glasses hanging unused around her neck.

"I don't know if I should have come," she said to no one in particular. "I don't think I could stand finding my father in this place."

I didn't say anything. The motor churned the water as I steered the Santa Cruz into a small inlet that probed the depths of the mangrove forest. There was no sound on the river, only the chug of our Johnson as we moved upstream at ten knots.

"This where you fish?" I asked Huck.

"Sure. There are some nice bass along these banks. Jack got himself a shark about 100 yards from here," he said, pointing to an overhang of mangroves up ahead. Then he fell silent, staring at the spot he had just identified.

We motored slowly upstream and I felt the day slide by. Gators lay along the shore, some drifted toward us just yards from the dinghy, egrets stood motionless in the water not far from the gators—as if they didn't exist—and the skeletons of mangroves now gave way to a forest of green, their branches choking off any path to the interior. So, we drifted, the sun dropping lower in the sky, and another hour passed, the quiet of the stream adding to the drowsiness of the day, and I thought of what Cynthia had said—that she shouldn't have come—that she wouldn't want to see her father in a place like this, and Huck gave me a break, guiding the dinghy upstream, and I drifted off...

～

The day was getting shorter, the noise of the car putting Maxie to sleep, as country towns, some of them with a hardly more than a store, slipped into the rearview mirror, the

driver, watching the Boy, seeing him nod off. Did the driver feel
sorry for him? I wondered. And he tapped the wheel as the tires
hummed against the asphalt, county roads for the most part, once
in a while state highways. They stayed off the main highways,
where the cops might be looking...and the Boy stirred. Did he
wonder where he was? And then he nodded off again, resigned to
the day, to the men, to the road as it ran by, to the destination,
wherever that might be. And I tried to read the road signs as they
flashed by—too quickly. Was that a state road? What was that
number? I strained to see. If only...but no. The landscape—it was
thick and green. Trees, full bloom, huddled together like
shivering giants, blocked any view, and the hills, they seemed to
be getting taller as the car sped into the afternoon—and I tried
desperately to keep up with it. That's my boy you have there! I
tried to scream, but couldn't, couldn't get their attention,
couldn't rap on the window to let the Boy know I'm here. Are
they in Pennsylvania? West Virginia? How long had they been
driving? I couldn't remember. One full day?

Lights were appearing in the distance—from farm houses far
off the road, from gatherings of buildings in small towns they
passed through. It was getting warmer, and Maxie was thinking,
"What did my father tell me? About being out after dark?" And
he had done two things today that his dad would be mad at. He
had gotten into a car with strangers—though they said they knew
his father, so it wasn't really his fault— and he was not going to
be home by dark. And I tried to tell him, It's okay! Just come
home safely...please don't worry. Just come home. And then...

~

Had I fallen asleep? Huck was staring at me, Cynthia lost
in her thoughts—probably about Jack.

"It's time to turn around," I said, "after an entire day of

cruising, and with evening closing in...?" Then I saw a frenzy of birds, thrashing in the trees just ahead.

"There," said Huck, as he pointed to the center of the noise. "Maybe a dead animal."

"Maybe," I said. Cynthia sat hushed.

Maybe, I thought, *and maybe not,* and Huck moved the boat toward the sound, slowly, so as not to get caught in roots, and I watched the birds land in nearby trees, waiting for us to finish our work. The forest of mangroves was darkening as the sun began its descent into the west. I used a spotlight to scan the area where the birds had gathered. A powerboat sat in a tangle of mangrove roots about thirty feet from where we were. The stern was jutting out from the underbrush. Parts of the cabin were visible through the trees. As I eased the dinghy up closer, birds cleared once again from the branches overhead. The word Canyon was painted in vivid red across the port quarter of the boat, the lettering clear even in the faded light of early evening. I wanted to warn Cynthia but she was already at my shoulder. She stared at the boat, her hand tightening around my arm.

"Did your dad name the boat?"

"No. He just called it 'my boat' because that's the one he went out in alone."

"Well, we'll have to get closer and have a look-see," I said. "But I'm not sure you want to do this."

"I need to," she said. "That's why I came. If something happened to Jack, I want to be there with him." And she was determined, but her cheeks had lost their color.

A gator slid into the water toward us. I pulled my Glock and fired in his direction.

"You can't shoot gators, Coop. It ain't the season," said Huck maneuvering the boat in closer to shore.

"Let's see if we can get up next to the Canyon, Huck. Bring

us around."

Huck pulled out into the water again and got us up next to the grounded boat.

I could hear Cynthia draw in breath, and she grabbed my arm once again, her tenseness catching hold of me.

I studied the boat quietly. Then, "Is this your father's boat?"

Cynthia didn't answer right away, but I could feel her body shake as she pulled herself next to me and I put my arm around her, holding her tightly, and asked again.

"I think it is...yes...it is..." Then, "I hope Jack is okay..." and she buried her head in my shoulder, as if to protect herself from what she dreaded, but already I could smell the foul odor of rotting flesh.

Then, "I can't take you back to the Canyon—where you should really be now—so I'm going to ask Huck to let me off here and take the boat out to the middle of the stream. There's no way you should board this thing...okay?" It was more like an order than a question.

Cynthia nodded and Huck pulled her away and I boarded the Canyon. Huck idled the dinghy into the middle of the stream away from Jack's boat.

The first thing I noticed were holes scattered along the hull and across the helm and console.

Someone shot at him. Obviously.

There was no sign of a body on deck. But the stench of death was overwhelming. I covered my mouth and nose so I could breathe. It didn't help much.

I stepped over some branches and debris that had fallen on the deck, checking for the source of the stench. My nose guided me to a hatch on the starboard side. It was ajar. The hatch provided entry to the lower level of the Canyon. The lower deck is small: a stand-up shower, a sink and a head. Not a good space to hide a body. But whoever had killed Jack made no effort to hide him. What I saw when I pulled open the hatch was a body, lying face down, wedged between a sink and some cupboards.

I descended the ladder and leaned over the body to get a closer look, holding the handkerchief hard against my mouth and nose. It was hard to tell if it was Jack or not. Nature had already begun its dirty work. There was no evidence of *rigor mortis*, meaning that he had to have been dead for at least three days. The odor was the result of cells decomposing. Bacteria had invaded the body and were wreaking their havoc on it.

The green substance that was oozing from the skin and the fluids that were seeping from the nose and mouth were the result of this end-of-life process. And I choked as my lunch tried to come up. And the maggots—they were there too—crawling out of every orifice of Jack's body. And that's all I needed. I scrambled up the ladder and over to the side of the boat where I threw up everything I had eaten this morning. Everything.

Then I called Huck to pick me up. Enough already.

When he pulled the dinghy up against the stern of the Canyon 306, a boat that had taken Jack to his last fishing trip, I said, "We need to call the Coast Guard."

Cynthia didn't move from where she sat. But she watched me, like a terrified child looking for a sign from a parent that everything was all right. I shook my head.

She didn't cry—at first. She just stared out over the water and into the mangroves that tangled their way along the shore, then turned to me and slowly her eyes began to redden and she started to cry, gently, like she knew all along what the result was going to be, and just murmured, "Oh Jack," over and over again, shaking her head and bobbing back and forth. I slid over next to her and pulled her into my arms.

CHAPTER NINE
THE BODY IN THE SWAMP

Tuesday Afternoon, November 29

When we got back to the Canyon, I radioed the Coast Guard. The guardsman who answered told me to hold on. Then, "So, Cooper, it's you again." A familiar voice.

"Cap'n Welder?" I said.

"Yes sir. I understand you have a problem." He had sent the Guard out twice before. Once when I was chasing smugglers through the Ten Thousand Islands, and another time when I tracked a Russian ship that was hauling human cargo into Cuban waters. He listened now as I explained what we had found.

"Since this sounds like a homicide," he said, "I'll have to inform the Park Police. Then, as if studying the situation by staring into the river, he added, "We'll have a chopper here in an hour or so."

Darkness settled over Shark River like a pall as we waited for the noise of the copter. Then it came. Roaring over the inlet, throwing its floods over the river like a gunship, lighting up the Everglades like the towers for a Saturday night football game. The pilot settled on an inlet about a hundred yards from us and cut the motors. I ran the dinghy over as two Guardsmen climbed out of the cockpit and stepped onto a pontoon.

"Lieutenant Dawson," said one as he handed me a duffel bag. I introduced myself and gave him a steadying hand as he climbed off the pontoon and into the dinghy.

The second guardsman followed Dawson, trying to get balanced on the rubber sides of the boat. "Phew," he said, finally settling into a seat. "Ensign Mendez, sir," he said, extending a hand. "Not much room, is there?" he added as he scooted over to make room for me to grab the steering arm.

We were back to the Canyon in just a few minutes where Huck and Cynthia were standing on the aft deck, waiting to help the Coast Guarders climb around the Yamahas.

"A Coast Guard ship is headed this way," said Dawson as he stepped onto the deck. "It'll be here in several hours. The Park Service is right behind." Then, he turned to Cynthia, bowing slightly. "You must be Miss Hayward."

After a pause, almost like he was apologizing, he added, "I knew your...sorry, know...your father," looking down then back up at her—embarrassed. "Let's hope it's not him on that boat," he said, like he was talking to the swamp itself, where Jack's boat lay like a wounded animal, caught in the mangroves.

Cynthia bit hard into her lower lip, bracing herself against crying, hope now a dying ember in her eyes.

I was about to introduce Huck when, "How's your father, Mendez?" said Huck. "I haven't seen him in...how many moons?"

"That's because he's ailing, Mr. Crow," said Mendez. "He got hurt trying to haul his boat out of the water a couple months ago—alone." He paused. "Bet he would welcome a call," and they shook on it.

"You and Cynthia follow us in the Canyon," I said to Huck, breaking in. "There's only room for three or four on the dinghy, but it's deep enough in the center of the inlet to pull in pretty close behind. The water is about four to five feet there."

Dawson and Mendez put on masks, special clothing, and booties as I steered us to Jack's boat.

"If you want to come along, put on these," said Dawson, tossing me a bundle of the same stuff they were wearing.

The two Guardsmen climbed on board first, checking out the deck, then motioned me up. I took them around to starboard and opened the hatch. The odor blew out like a hurricane of bad breath.

"Damn it, Cooper," said Dawson, holding a hand over his mask and nose.

"Body's been here a while, I would guess," I said. Dawson started down the ladder.

"It smells like it." He looked up at the sound of a boat nearing.

"Must be the Park Police," he said. "Might as well meet them," backing out of the hold, climbing up the ladder, and looking relieved.

The Rangers had pulled up to the stern of the Canyon in a Boston Whaler. It had the signature hardtop to block the sun. Not that it did much good for the ranger who introduced himself.

"Jamie Bogart," the tall ranger said. He was thin and worn and deeply tanned, like a cowboy out on the range too long. The grey mustache made him look older than he probably was. He didn't bother introducing the other ranger, he just grabbed the rail of the Canyon and climbed around the motors while his partner steadied the Whaler.

Dawson reached out his hand and introduced himself. "If you want to go below, we got some extra gear," he said.

Bogart nodded. Then, "Who discovered the body?" he said.

I told him I did.

"Okay. And who are you?"

I told him I was a PI and that Cynthia—I pointed at the Canyon where Cynthia was watching us—had hired me to investigate her father's disappearance.

"Oh yeah, right," as though he was recalling. "And this is him?"

"Maybe."

"She up to coming aboard and identifying the body?"

"I would say *no*, and for two reasons. First, this is not a good time. Too early. Second, the body is in really bad shape. I think she would have a better chance of identifying him once he's in the morgue."

The ranger nodded, pulling at his mustache. "Okay, so let's get this show on the road, gents." He made a call on his SAT phone. When he got off, "I suppose you boys been down below from the way you're dressed."

"We have," said Dawson.

"I think we'll let the medical examiner take 'er from here," he said. "We'll stand by 'til she comes. About a half hour," and he looked out over the inlet toward Shark River. "It'll be dark pretty soon. The Everglades is not a good place to be in the dark. Maybe you should take Miss Hayward back home. It's hell to pay with those crab traps along the shore. Better to take the long way." He was still looking out towards the river as he spoke.

I was anxious to get out of there. I had been in the backwaters of Shark River several times, but not commonly at night. It's never good to be on the water at night. A lot can happen even to a seasoned boater on the water in the night. So Huck and I hoisted the dinghy back up on the Canyon, and we tucked it away as Cynthia charged up the motors. I watched her pull away, leaving Jack to the cops, to the dark, to the quiet of the Great Swamp. That's where he worked and where he now lay dead.

I was getting attached to Jack Hayward and felt like I knew him. I wished I really had gotten to know him. And I could feel Cynthia's pain—it was all over her eyes. She was steering the Canyon carefully through the inlet into the deep of the river, staring straight ahead. But I could see that she wasn't looking at the river. Her eyes were on something else—probably Jack.

CHAPTER TEN
UNDER THE COPPER MOON

Tuesday Night, November 29

I t was almost a full moon. And I could see shades of copper spread along its face.

And the Yamahas roared while the moon followed us, playing hide and seek through the clouds, baiting us for a race. Thunderheads loomed in the west and I felt the edge of a cool breeze, the kind that ushers in a storm.

I nudged Huck and pointed to the sky. "No worries, boss; we'll have this baby tucked away long before that *ka'ino* catches us." Hawaiian? Huck is a wonder.

"Can you take the wheel?" said Cynthia as she steered from the mouth of the river into Ponce de Leon Bay and the Gulf of Mexico. "I don't like to drive through a storm."

And I took the wheel and watched her go below. I nodded to Huck to follow her. He did. She was going to have a hard night.

I drove with the running lights along the open waters of the Gulf, trying to avoid the crab traps that lined the shore. And I watched the moon hurrying behind me, and I took the bait and raced the moon, and raced the storm, past Middle Cape, then East Cape, until I swung once again into Florida Bay, still staying in open water, and headed south-southwest toward Snake Creek. And then the storm broke, rain lashing at the Canyon like an angry loser, and it did us a favor driving us into Snake Creek and pushing us faster than we would have moved at idle speed. I could hardly see Snake Creek Marina, the rain slashing into the windshield in steady sheets, easing up only occasionally for me to catch the lights off the shore. Not a good night to be on the water. Then it stopped—suddenly—and we were in the Straits heading north toward the Pilot House Marina and safe harbor.

"She's asleep," said Huck, standing next to me as I eased the Canyon through the canal toward the marina. The rain started up again and the moon, which a few minutes ago had appeared briefly in the Straits, disappeared once again. It was still raining when I backed into the slip. Huck hurried to tie the Canyon down.

"Let's get outta this weather," he said as he secured the lines.

I went below and woke Cynthia. She followed me up the ladder, catching my belt for balance. Then Huck helped her steady herself off the boat onto the dock, then walked her to the marina. It wasn't open so we settled on a bench that was sheltered from the wind and rain and sat there quietly for a few minutes. And I stared out into the dark of Lake Largo and thought about the photos Cynthia and I had found in Jack's house and wondered where that little rig was. And I could feel my eyes tire and my head nod, in the wet of my clothes, in the chill of the night, sitting alongside Cynthia and Huck who also huddled from the rain, and I wondered why we were not somewhere warm...

~

I t was evening now and the men weren't talking anymore and the Boy was quiet, pretending to be asleep. But he wasn't asleep. He knew he needed to be awake because he didn't really believe that these men knew his mother and his father, as they claimed, because he had asked if he could call them, and the driver, the man with the strange marks on his neck, like scars, told him there would be plenty of time for him to do that when they got to where they were going. And the Boy asked him where that would be—the destination, that is—because he wanted to be sure that they understood exactly what he was asking so there would be no misunderstanding, even though he was only seven —he was a very bright boy—and he knew it.

The road slipped by quickly into the night, heading to wherever they were going, and he wished he knew where, but he didn't. He knew this wasn't right—that these men, whom he didn't know, knew his father—and he was now pretty sure that these men whom he had never seen before, were the bad men that his mother and father had warned him about. And that thought frightened him, sent funny feelings through his stomach, made it hurt. Then he looked back—through the rear window— through the darkness—to see if a blue Volvo was following. He hoped it was. But it was too dark to tell, and the lights from the following cars prevented him from seeing anything. And he had that urgent fear that there was no Volvo behind him—at all.

Then, he took a deep breath, stared through the side window, and saw himself—staring back. He watched himself and studied his face—the boy in the window—who imitated his every movement—of his mouth, of his hand as it moved up to his face, of his cheeks, as he filled them with air and sighed the air out. He fell asleep as the face looked on. The Boy, the disobedient one. And he dreamed of his parents reminding him of what he had *done wrong, and the nightmare continued all night as the car carried him further and further away from his home, that beautiful home in Muskingum, Ohio, where he played with his baseball in the yard and where his mother and father watched him so carefully, the place he would never see again. He was sure of that now. The nightmare told him that.*

CHAPTER ELEVEN
MIDNIGHT DRIVE

Wednesday Morning, November 30

My nightmares were continuing, even as I nodded off for what was probably only moments, in the rain, outside the marina. I felt like I was reading his thoughts, feeling his fears, worrying with him in that car that was heading only God knows where.

"Come on let's get out of here," said Huck, rising and jostling me awake. "Let's go to your place," he said, pulling me up.

The rain was hell to drive through, especially since we had just come off a long boat ride. I was very tired. But I drove anyway. Had to. Cynthia had crawled into the back seat of the Volvo and had fallen asleep—we left her Jeep behind. Huck climbed up into his Ford pick-up and followed, his lights hanging over the rear of the Volvo like two angry eyes. We got to my house off Midnight Drive around 2:00 a.m., give or take. I parked, climbed the steps to the porch, holding onto Cynthia who was still not quite awake, and sat her on the swing while I reached down and scratched Sammy who was waiting just outside the screen door. Huck, who was right behind me, headed for the swing and sat next to Cynthia.

"Where are we?" she said, as she cleared her eyes with the back of her hands.

"My house. Let's get you to bed." I helped her up and through the screen door, Sammy watching us and purring. Basically, he wanted food.

Huck helped me get Cynthia into my bed. We took off her shoes. She stretched out and was sleeping, her right hand pulling a pillow up against her head before I turned off the light. I closed the door and Huck and I went to the kitchen. My home office. It's a good place to work. The wine is just a few feet away in the fridge—and the crackers and the cheese.

Huck settled into a chair across from me, shaking his head. "Poor girl. She just lost her daddy. For good."

"She was hoping he wasn't...too bad," I said.

"Jack Hayward was a warrior, Cooper. He will cross over like a fighter and find his horses waiting for him."

I must have looked confused.

"His boats, man. His horses are his boats. The boats are like an extension of his life. They live..."

I shook my head.

"What?" he said. "Animism," he continued, ignoring my looks. "We are all the same, amigo, plants, animals, humans. We're all part of the earth. Ol' Jack is just like that sawgrass," he continued, pointing out over the back porch. "Only thing is, when *Jack* talks, we understand. We don't know how to listen to the grass." Huck, the philosopher.

"Pansychism," I said.

He looked at me. Puzzled.

I didn't explain. Primitives—thousands of years before Huck—subscribed to the same thinking—saw the world differently than we do. It was a simple place. Everything shares a common soul: rocks and dirt, people and flowers. Pansychism. Everything thinks and senses.

Huck continued, "When Jacko's body's turns into turnips and strawberries, he'll be seeing us—not from the goddamned Happy Hunting Grounds that you white men think we believe in, but from the ground that he's become part of, from his toes to his nose." Then he halted his lesson.

We were silent for a while as I looked through the back door, through the darkness of the late night, where the Big Swamp stretches out for fifty miles or more and wondered how many dead had already become part of the grasses, the trees, the groundwater that flowed through the Everglades, and whether or not they sensed us as we passed by.

Huck got up, headed for the fridge, and got a beer. He looked at me. I nodded. Sammy crept into the room and sat, staring at me, like he might like one also.

H uck hadn't said a word since he said "toes to nose." I
hadn't either. It must have been five, maybe ten
minutes before I broke the silence,
"You know what we have to do, right?"

"I do."

"Just to make sure..."

"We need to go back and check out that dad-burned boat
again,"—Huck hates to swear—"check for clues." He looked
over at me to see if he got it right. Huck has been bugging me to
get him a PI badge—he wants one badly.

"Think you can handle it, Huxter?" I paused. "The boat
will be gone, you know. Evidence."

"No problemo," he said. "If it's gone, the scene will still be
there." And we both stared out the back into the darkness,
probably thinking of different things.

Then after a few moments, "Good. I'm going to drive into
Miami, visit the morgue," I said. "Check on Jack."

Huck nodded.

"Let me know if you need any help on your
reconnaissance," I said.

Huck smiled. He loves that word.

CHAPTER THIRTEEN
MEDICAL EXAMINER'S OFFICE

Wednesday Afternoon, November 30

I t was early afternoon when Cynthia and I pulled into the parking lot behind the Medical Examiner's office. Down the street was Jackson Memorial Hospital, the teaching hospital for the University of Miami. It's a tall building, steps leading circularly up to a wide set of glass doors. We stopped at reception and were buzzed into the morgue itself. I pulled out some Vick's Vapor Rub packets and offered one to Cynthia on the way in. She shook her head. I told her she would need it. She took it.

It was Jack Hayward all right. The entire five-foot ten inches of Jack, naked under the white covering, waiting for Cynthia—who was still in the hall outside the morgue—not wanting to enter. Cynthia, tearing at first, then, braving the room, walked steadily—almost steadily—through the door into the morgue. She stood next to me, gripping my arm. Dr. Wann, hesitating, waiting for a sign that she was ready—which she gave with the same hesitation—slowly pulled back the sheet. She passed out. I grabbed her—like in a game of trust—and struggled to hold her up. Wann lunged forward to help, and the two of us guided her to a chair outside the room.

"It's okay, Miss Hayward," Dr. Wann whispered, bending over. "It happens to everybody."

She sat for a few minutes, then looked up and nodded.

Wann motioned me aside. We walked into the hall away from Cynthia who was lost in her thoughts.

"It's good to see you, Cooper. How are you?"

Wann and I had known each other from my time as a homicide detective with MPD. He was a thorough, meticulous, careful, and a maddeningly slow analyst. But he was good. So I got to like him, even though he would take weeks where others would have results in days. It was for that very reason—his thoroughness—that made him world famous as a pathologist. But he also had a lot of advice for me—more than I needed most of the time.

"Say, when you gonna get married again?" Like I need a woman to keep me living a long life. Advice like that.

I shrugged. "I'm not ready."

"How about that Detective Delgado? She's a very pretty woman. I think she might be good for you," nudging me.

I shook my head.

He threw up his hands like *I'm just trying to help.* Then, "So..." Wann began, as if he were going to tell me something else I wanted to know. "I will be doing an autopsy soon on Mr. Hayward. I suppose you are wanting me to fill you in," he added, leading me on.

"I would," I said, taking the bait.

"Interesting," he continued. "I did a prelim—"

"And...?"

"Funny thing. I found some oily residue on his skin."

I gave him a look.

"You found him in the Everglades," he continued. "Where is there oil in the Everglades?"

I nodded, checking on Cynthia who was now looking our way. "Maybe he was working on his motors. Gas...oil...you know, spillage."

"Maybe. You check it out. You're the detective, Cooper. Meantime, I'll have this crap analyzed. Maybe two weeks."

I nodded. Oil in the Everglades?

I asked Wann to let me know when he had the results.

"Always," he said.

We walked back to Cynthia who was now standing and watching us. "Anything I need to know?" she said, worry sneaking across her face.

"No. Just catching up," I said.

"We need to get some breakfast somewhere," I said to Wann. "Know someplace close?"

He was checking his cell phone. Then, as if realizing I had just asked a question, he said, "Yeah. There's a Wendy's just across the street from the hospital—on Northwest 10th Ave." I must have looked unsure. "Look, you can almost see it when you walk out the door—cross the street and bingo—you're there. Okay?" He was playing with me.

"Okay," I said, "thanks for the advice," hoping he would take the hint.

"Not advice, Coop. Directions."

I shook my head and sighed. "Um-huh. Call me..." and he cut me off with a *no-problem* wave. Cynthia and I headed for breakfast with Dave Thomas.

She was still in semi-shock. So we walked in silence along a palm-lined stone pathway that skirts a large parking lot and toward the traffic and noise of NW 10th Avenue, the heat of the autumn sun picking up. We passed young men and women in blues as they were heading to and from the hospital and over to

Wendy's where I figured we could get some coffee and something that was close to breakfast—a muffin maybe. It was late afternoon—but I hadn't eaten yet today. So, breakfast had to come first.

"I'm not hungry," she said, as she settled into a seat.

"Coffee?"

"No," she said. I didn't get any either. I just watched her. She began to cry, quietly, her head in her hands. We were sitting behind a wall that screened us from the counter. Then she looked up and stared out the window—in the direction of the Examiner's Office.

"I can't believe Jack is in there." She paused for a few moments. "I can't believe I left without him." She shook her head and began to tear up again. She looked around to see if anyone was watching. Then she wiped her eyes with her sleeve and settled into a stupor, staring out the window at the parking lot across the street where a steady stream of cars filed into the hospital lot and circled, looking for a spot.

"We need to search your dad's house again. We may have missed something," I said, breaking into the silence. She didn't react. I waited for a few moments, then, "Problem?"

She shook her head. "But, why bother? He's dead. We're not going to bring him back. It's like we're stirring up his spirit. Maybe we should just let him rest and be done with it," she said, looking back into the direction of the morgue.

I didn't blame her. She was right. The problem was Jack was murdered. No way to let that go.

"Jack was trying to help you, Cynthia," I said. "I think we owe him."

She nodded, reluctantly. "Yeah. Maybe so." After a few minutes tiptoed by silently, she spoke. "And those pictures— they're bugging me. Why and where?" she added. Just like a reporter.

"There's an important story here—one that Jack was working on. Think of it as part of his legacy," I said.

She was nodding like maybe I was convincing her.

"Come on. Let's check his house again." I started to rise. "See if we missed anything."

We left Wendy's. No pancakes, no rolls, no egg sandwiches, no Big Burger, no fries, no Cokes, nothing. For once in my life, I had eaten healthy.

CHAPTER FOURTEEN
THE HOUSE THAT JACK BUILT

Early Wednesday Evening

It was dark when we pulled off the Ocean Highway onto Transylvania Avenue and then left onto Shoreland Drive. It was even darker there. No porch lights. The moon was hiding behind some clouds. I pulled into the driveway, gravel scattering under the tires as they dug in.

I jumped out and opened Cynthia's door. "Let me go in first," I said, looking at the darkness behind the windows. My ever-cautious nature.

"It's not locked," she reminded me. I ducked under the small overhang that protected the entry, opened the door and felt for a light switch.

"It's on the right," she said just as I found it. I flipped the switch. Nothing happened.

"Light must be burned out," I said, feeling for another switch.

"There should be one next to the porch light," she said, as a noise echoed from the right side of the house, toward the water, then the sound of a motor turning over. I pushed past

Cynthia, cleared the porch steps and rushed toward the water. The outline of a small motorboat emerged from the dock, a lone driver pushing it into Largo Sound toward the channel that would take him into the Atlantic. No way to catch him.

Cynthia was next to me now, breathing hard and looking out over the Sound. "He was in the house. Whoever it was unscrewed the porch light and tossed it," she added, hanging on my shoulder and struggling for air.

I shook my head. "At least we didn't run into him," I said, thinking back on the time I walked in on two guys ransacking my house in the Everglades. One of them fired at me and hit his buddy.

"So, what does Jack have that somebody wants?" I mused, mostly to myself. Then, "Let's go back and see."

We headed into the house through the lanai since that was the closest way to the den and Jack's office. The screen door was hanging on its hinges—probably broken free by the guy who had just fled. The door to the house was open. When I hit the switch, an interior light went on. From the remnants of that light I could see the debris scattered over the carpet: paper, envelopes, stamps, all the stuff that you might find in a desk and then more. Most of the drawers had been ripped out of the desk and thrown into the middle of the room, the contents scattered. The middle drawer was there also. At least he didn't get the pictures.

"What else could he have been looking for?" I searched the room while we both thought about that.

"Maybe someone knew about the pictures and was looking for them," she said. "I've been writing about drilling in the Everglades as well as in the Gulf. Jack has been helping me— scouting around. This is dangerous business, you know— writing about things that happen in the Everglades. You never know who you're going to piss off—including the people who live there."

"Uh-huh. They're a breed unto themselves."

"That's right. There's not much of an industry there, but they've got to make a living—some of it isn't legal. There's a code of silence among them. You don't break it if you value your life. Jack has lived in the Keys and fished the swamp all his life. So, he's one of them.

She paused. Then she said, "You know about the large tract of oil under the Great Cypress I imagine."

I nodded. "You mean the Sunniland Trend?"

"Right. It's one of the largest oil fields in the country you know, and it runs under the Everglades—all the way from Fort Myers to Miami." I knew all about it. But she was going to tell me anyway. "That's a lot of oil—and that means big money. Jack's been pushing me to get involved in the public inquiry about drilling—you know fracking, poisoning the ground water —that kind of thing. I haven't done it. Yet.

"Then of course, there's the drilling that's going on in the Gulf—right off the coast of Florida, maybe fifty to sixty miles from Key West, where a foreign country is drilling in waters where US companies are not allowed to drill. And that has wreaked holy hell with the locals—especially since they are suspicious of anything that's not American. And, as I told you before, Jack is one of those."

I nodded and let her talk. She needed to.

She told me again about how she took Jack out into the Straits to see the big rig and about how mad he got when he saw it—couldn't control himself, wanted to get himself a gun and *show them foreigners a 'what for', blow them the hell outta U.S. of A. waters*—his words," she added. "I just hope to hell he wasn't messing around with that rig."

"Obviously was," I said, thinking of the pictures. "Why

aren't more people covering this story?" I said. "I mean, besides you."

"I don't know. Seems like nobody cares. I mean our own leaders in Congress seem to care. And the President, of course," she added quickly. "But nothing is being done about it." She took a breath. "So, I figure I'll keep telling the story," and she was nodding her head, reinforcing what she had said. "I'll be visiting that big baby—again—soon."

"Ouch," I said. "There's some trouble there. That's foreign waters."

I pulled out my cell. She looked at me with a question but didn't ask.

"Calling a partner," I said. I dialed Louise.

CHAPTER FIFTEEN
DETECTIVE LOUISE DELGADO

I left a message. *Call me.*

Louise Delgado is a Miami PD detective in charge of the gang unit—actually she *is* the entire unit. We became friends when I was working a case that included a double homicide involving two children. A lead took me into Gangland, a section of Miami where cops don't go. It's controlled by the 55th Street Boys—a gang that originated from Chicago. Since there are usually over 400 homicides a year in the Windy City—many of them gang-related—Miami cops figured it wouldn't be long before those figures began to show up in the Magic City. So, Louise went with me into that miserable piece of crap real estate and we got shot up—badly enough to send us both on an extended visit to the hospital. We've been friends ever since. Great way to build a friendship, isn't it?

My cell rang out a new sound. I had dropped Pachelbel's Canon. Got tired of it and found a chime that drove everybody crazy but me. So, I stuck with it.

"You called?" said Louise.

"Yeah," I said. "I need some help."

Silence.

"How about, I need some help, partner?"

"I like the sound of that," she said.

In the heat of the last case, chasing down some crazy Russians who were chopping up people for their parts, I had told Delgado that I needed a partner and that she should think about it. That was a month ago. She said she would do that and get back to me. She never did.

"So...?" I said. "Does that mean...?"

"Maybe later, partner. I got too many bills to pay and we've gotta get to know each other a little better." She stressed the *little* and dragged it out.

"We already know each other." I didn't add in the biblical sense—which we already did.

"That's funny," she said. But she didn't mean it.

"Anyway, see you tomorrow?" I said.

"*Mañana*," she said. The moon rose in front of the Volvo as I cleared the rise on the bridge that connects Key Largo to the mainland. Cynthia was already sleeping the deep sleep.

CHAPTER SIXTEEN
DONUTS

Thursday Morning, December 1

I was frying eggs and bacon when Louise came over the porch of my Everglades house with a box of Dunkin Donuts and two cups of coffee. Once a cop, always a cop.

"Hey, partner," is all she said as she let the screen door slam behind her.

"So, we're partners?" I said.

"Only in the biblical sense, buddy," she said quickly, then came over to where I was cooking the bacon. We kissed and I saw stars even though I knew they weren't out for another twelve hours.

"Wow," I said. "That seals it." The grease from the bacon was snapping in the pan like popcorn gone crazy. I shut off the burner, shifted the pan to a cool spot on the stove, and began forking the bacon onto a paper towel to sop up the grease.

"Behold the chef," she said, watching me. "And you made a nice table!" she added, studying my handiwork with the place settings.

"I did," I said. "I learned from the best. My mom was a

Home-Ec teacher. Have a seat." I used the flipper to fold the eggs onto her plate. I laid four pieces of almost burned bacon next to the eggs. That's the way she likes them. I do, too. No fat.

"Where's Cynthia?" she said, coyly.

I shook my head. "In the guest bedroom, sacked out," I said. "Like I said, she's a client."

"Uh-huh," she said, eyeing the toaster.

"Cinnamon bread...with a brown sugar frosting," I said.

"Ouch. There goes my diet," she said.

"*Vita brevis, ars longa,*" I said.

"That's Italian for...?"

"Latin. Be happy." I thought of the Bobby McFerrin song:

> *Don't worry, be happy*
> *In every life we have some trouble*
> *When you worry you make it double*
> *Don't worry, be happy.*

I was lying in bed in Pompano Beach with Jillie one night—on our honeymoon—and this song was playing on the radio. I heard it that night and every night after that until Jillie finally made me change the station. *It's driving me crazy!* she said. I loved it. But I turned it off. One of the many compromises that you make in a marriage. Too bad we couldn't make them after Maxie disappeared.

I saw Louise staring at me. She changed the subject.

"Your case made the headlines in the *Herald* this morning," she said. "You see the paper?" I said I hadn't. "I got a copy in the car. I'll get it for you," she said, rising.

"After," I said, motioning for her to stay. I sat down across from her, broke off a piece of crispy bacon, and told her all about Cynthia and Jack Hayward. It took about an hour.

Sammy came prowling in while we talked, pacing from one end of the kitchen to the other.

"You fed him today?"

"Nope. Breakfast is in the fridge. It's chicken and gravy."

"Yuk. Who eats chicken and gravy for breakfast?"

"Sammy does."

Sammy's a stray cat that I adopted a year ago. He just washed up from the Great Swamp one day, showed up on my porch and gave me that hungry and lonesome look—like a baby left on the stoop. He keeps me company and watches the house when I'm gone. There's an old gator that hangs out in the back yard. He keeps him company, too. Just far enough away so he doesn't get eaten.

When we were finished, Louise spooned some cat food into a saucer and placed it on the front porch, opening the screen for him. He stood there for a moment, stretched, and slowly made his way out, rubbing himself against the doorjamb. That's the way he makes his exit every morning.

"How's your mental health?" Louise said, coming back and sitting down next to me.

"I'm okay," I said.

She took my hand. "You'll find him," she said.

I nodded and took her hand in mine. I didn't know whether she was talking about Jack's killer or my son.

"I've been having nightmares again."

"About Maxie," she said. A statement.

"Yeah," I said, resting my head in my hands. "It's like I'm actually watching his kidnapping. Two men pick him up in front of our house and I watch them drive away and..." and my head hurts as I tell it. "The worst part is I can't do anything about it!" I felt sweat building in my palms.

"I'm so sorry, Coop," she said, gripping my hand more tightly.

"Yeah. The worst part of it is, it's so real. Like I'm there." I paused, trying to explain the next part. "The weird thing is I'm looking for clues—you know, road signs, landmarks, geography, kinds of trees, vegetation, anything that would tell me where they're going," and I was thinking back even as I talked, trying to remember, "and then I wake and realize that it's all too crazy —that it's just a nightmare—and yet..."

"Go ahead. Talk about it," she said, her head tilted as she watched me.

"I see his face in the rear window, Louise," I said, my stomach turning as I said it. Because I feel responsible. Because I'm the father who didn't take care of him. "I just need to find him." I felt my eyes begin to water. "I just need to find him."

"You will, Coop" she said. "You will."

We sat there for a few minutes, Louise trying to comfort me, and me not wanting to be comforted. Finally, I checked the clock on the kitchen wall, and we both got up.

"Okay, sunshine, let's get the hell out of here and check out that rig." Then, turning as she started for the kitchen, "Better wake up that journalist girlfriend of yours," she said, smiling sideways at me. "And by the way, *you're* supposed to be cleanup," she reminded me as she began to clear away the dishes.

"She's a client," I said.

"Uh-huh." She threw a towel at my head.

CHAPTER SEVENTEEN
THE ITSY-BITSY SPIDER

Early Afternoon

"Watch out for them afternoon storms," said Jimmy as I filled the tanks on Jack's boat. It was going to be an expensive trip: three 350 Yamahas with a fuel capacity of 390 gallons. I watched the pump pass $669.00 and continue climbing.

Louise and Cynthia were already on board, prepping the boat and getting acquainted. I could hear Louise asking her about her work at the *Herald.*

"You keep an eye, Cooper," Jimmy said, as he watched the numbers on the pump climb. "Things blow up pretty quick out there. This here's a big boat, but it's a piece of wood in a storm." I nodded. Jimmy likes to give advice.

"What's your last name, Jimmy?" I said.

"Johnson."

"Jimmy Johnson?"

"That's right."

"Any relation?" Referring to the Dolphin's former coach.

"Wish."

"Wouldn't have to work," I said, smiling.

He smiled, too.

"I don't know about this weather," I said, looking at the skies, uneasily.

"Afternoon storms. Nothin' big coming. Maybe. But then this here's the dry season..." Like I didn't know.

"It is that. Still..." and I looked at the clouds in the south over the Straits. The sky was patchy blue from the dock to Cuba with drifting pillows of white scattered here and there, some piled high like mountains of snow. I hate going out on the water in a storm.

"You be careful, hear?" he said for the hundredth time, as he watched me board.

Louise and Cynthia cast off the lines and gave me the go-ahead to crank up the motors. They roared, even at idle, like an Indy 500 car pulling into the starting line-up on the track. I throttled ahead and eased the Canyon away from the dock and into the channel. It would be about a two-hour ride to the rig. It would be getting dark when we got there. That was good. Dark is better. And no moon. It would be hiding behind the clouds. Good moon.

"You want to drive?" I asked Cynthia as she gazed into the wake thrown by the three Yamahas.

She shook her head. I think she was preparing herself mentally for whatever we would find and wanted no part of getting there.

It was 2:30 when I steered the Canyon past the canals that fed the channel, each canal lined with houses and docks. Each dock with boats hanging from davits or floating in a slip. No one was out as we passed, though I could smell the smoke from someone's Bar-B-Que. Maybe later we would stop and get some fish at the Caribbean Club. I would call Huck. Tell him to meet us there. He knows all the nightlife that hangs around in the Club and even those that don't—if you believe Huck.

We were free of the channel and heading into the Straits around 3:00. Clouds had started to pile up. They were stacked across the horizon, mostly white and non-threatening, some with grey spread across the lower edges. I asked Louise to take the wheel while I checked the weather.

Actually, the journey across the Straits should be a short one in terms of mileage. The shortest point between the U.S. coast, Key West, and the coast of Cuba is 90 miles. But then there is the current that travels through the middle of the Straits northward to the east coast of Florida at about five to six miles an hour. Then there are the sudden storms, and the tropical depressions, and the tornados that blow out of the hurricanes that track the waters of the Caribbean and cross the Straits into Florida, crushing what gets in the way like so much paper. So, it's a short trip really but a dangerous one as well—as so many Cuban refugees who fought the current to get to U.S. soil will testify. That same current that makes it possible for them to use rafts to get to this country might also kill them. The sword of Damocles.

But no threat of weather yet—and no sign of rain on the weather channel. There were the clouds, but the water was gentle against the boat. We were about twenty miles offshore when Louise pointed to a boat off starboard, U.S. Coast Guard colors across the bow. They sounded a horn and we waved back. Friendly? Or a warning? We were nearing the International Boundary that delineates the Exclusive Economic Zones of Cuba and the U.S. Maybe that was making them nervous. I wondered what they were doing out here so far from the station in Miami. Looking for illegals maybe.

It was 3:50 and we were already over the Pourtales Terrace, a narrow undersea ridge that follows the curve of the

Keys for 213 kilometers. The reef stretches southwest from Key Largo to the Marquesas Keys that lie between Key West and the Dry Tortugas. In a half hour we would be over the Pourtales Escarpment where the Terrace drops sharply into the depths of the Straits. I care about that drop because after a gentle slide from 180 meters to 450, the reef plunges into an abyss. I didn't like the thought of sinking there. Once we crossed the Pourtales, we would be about thirty miles from the rig.

"The wind's picking up," said Louise. It was blowing in from the starboard side.

Clouds, dark ones, had gathered quickly over the Straits. Where had all those white clouds gone? By the time we spotted the outline of the rig it was 4:45 p.m. and the sun was nodding off in the west, sinking into the clouds like they were pillows. I was at the helm and Louise had her glasses on the rig.

"Big," I said.

"Fifty-three thousand tons," said Cynthia. "It's a ship—on stilts."

It sat on the water like a giant spider, its large body raised high in the sky on four massive legs. A city of iron, with a maze of metal beams, scaffolding, derricks, and exhaust pipes sticking out of the deck. Tubes that were at least twenty feet in diameter ran along the vessel's topside. A massive grid-work rose from the center of the deck that I assumed housed the drill that dove into the sea. Across the side of the rig, in letters as large as those on the Empire State Building, were the words:

ZHI ZHU NU

They were also spread broadside across a large structure on one corner of the ship. It's hard to describe any part of the monstrous machine as being aft, port, or starboard because it was, after all, a square. I assumed there was an engine somewhere that drove it.

"Strange name," said Cynthia.

"It is that," I said. Maybe Chinese.

We were several hundred yards away when its lights went on. Dusk was already settling over the Straits, throwing red from a dying sun across the waters. I pictured Jackson Pollack striding over the Straits, dipping his brush and snapping it over the surface. The colors were changing from red to orange to yellow, as the rays of the sun hit the surface and disappeared into the waves. Nearer the rig they washed over its legs and up over its massive sides, coloring it like a massive kaleidoscope.

It wasn't until I could distinguish the colors of the setting sun from the lights of the rig itself that I realized that the red flashes emerging from within those colors were coming from a boat headed our way. A shell smashed into the Canyon's windshield, throwing glass everywhere. Cynthia screamed. I turned around and saw her staring at her shoulder. It was turning scarlet. She pushed her hand against the blood trying to stem the flow that was seeping through her fingers. She looked up at me.

"Louise!" I yelled. She had gone below just moments before. "Get the first aid kit, now! And grab a towel!"

"I've been shot," Cynthia said staring at her shoulder, but like she couldn't be sure.

Louise was topside with a large first aid kit, yanking it open as she came. A towel was draped over her shoulder.

"I'll take care of Cynthia. You get us out of here," she yelled as more shells hit the hull of the boat.

I pulled myself back up into the captain's chair, swung hard around and pushed the throttle forward. The Canyon lifted up like a bronco bucking against its rider and tore into the waves that were blocking us from the mainland. The boat that was chasing us fell behind and the Yamahas screamed as we reached fifty-five miles per hour.

"You're going to kill us!" yelled Louise.

"Better than them killing us," I said, then eased back on the throttle. We fell into a steady thirty miles per hour and were over the Pourtales in a half hour. Louise had called in an SOS and the EMTs said they would meet us at the marina. The shell had passed through the fleshy part of Cynthia's shoulder, just beneath her armpit. Louise had applied pressure to the wound with a tight bandage and had finally gotten the bleeding to stop. Cynthia was now resting across a leather pull-down bench aft.

"You doing okay?" I yelled over the motors. She just nodded and stared at her bloodied shoulder.

"It hurts," she said as loudly as she could, and didn't look up.

Lights from the mainland blinked through the darkness like friends. I breathed a sigh of relief as I cut the motors back and entered the No Wake zone. The Yamahas boiled the water like eggbeaters as I steered the Canyon into the channel that cuts through to Lake Largo and the Pilot House Marina.

CHAPTER EIGHTEEN
THE ER

"You callin' cause you wanna know what I want for Christmas," said Richie. Louise had called him while I was helping the medics offload Cynthia at the hospital. She had the phone on speaker. A medic looked over at her. She turned down the volume.

"Planning early," I said, leaning into the phone and following Cynthia into Emergency. Then Louise told him we would call him later.

The ER team hooked Cynthia up to an IV and rushed her through the double doors leading into the recesses of the hospital.

"Don't leave me, Cooper," Cynthia called anxiously from the stretcher. I took her hand and then lost her as they wheeled the gurney away.

Louise sat. I paced. About ten minutes later, a doctor, who looked like Doogie Howser, swung through the doors where Cynthia had disappeared. He must have skipped grades on his way to medical school. Brown hair, soft face, glasses, and a smile that made you like him.

"Family?" he asked as he approached.

"No," I said. "Friends." Then, "Actually a client."

He nodded and motioned for us to follow him back through the swinging doors. Cynthia was wired with tubes. They ran up both arms. An oxygen mask blocked her face.

"Uh-huh," said Doogie, examining the shoulder. Then, without looking up, "How did this happen?" I knew what he was asking. The bullet wound.

It was a long story, but I told it in about two minutes. The doc then called for the nurse to wheel Cynthia into surgery and asked us to go back to the waiting room.

We were the only people there so I pulled out my cell to call the Key Largo police. Before anyone answered, a cop car pulled up, lighting the entryway outside the ER. Two plainclothesmen came through the door and looked our way. Good detective work. We were the only other people there.

"Cooper?" said the lead cop. He was tall—maybe six-three or -four, his skin dark from the sun and smelling like a cigar.

"That would be me," I said. Louise got up and was standing next to me now.

The cop looked over at Louise.

"Delgado," she said—clipped, like a cop.

He hesitated. Thought. "Delgado. Miami PD?"

"Yeah." She paused. "Do I know you?"

"Kelly," he said. Then added, "Joe. You came down for a gang-related a couple years ago." Louise was nodding. "I was the cop reported the case," he added quickly, looking at Louise like maybe she remembered him now. She didn't seem to, but acted like she did. "I got promoted to detective two months ago."

"Congratulations," said Louise, nodding again. Silence.

Kelly coughed. Then, "This is Detective Monday," he continued, turning to the man standing next to him. "He doesn't work on his name-day. Lucky this is Thursday, I guess, huh?" Smiling like he enjoyed his humor. I stared at him. Monday didn't laugh.

"So, tell me how this happened."

"How'd you hear about the shooting?" I said.

"Doc told me. They gotta report shootings."

I nodded. "That was fast."

"If nothin' else, we're fast," he said. "So, fill me in."

Louise and I took turns recounting the events of the evening. Briefly.

"Why were you out there?" Monday said, asking like I was a suspect. He was chewing on a fingernail.

"The victim—" I began.

"Miss Hayward," Kelly added. "Family's good people down here."

I nodded. "Our client. She hired us to investigate the death of her father—"

"Jack Hayward." Kelly broke in.

I felt like asking him if he just wanted to tell the whole damn story. But instead, I just nodded.

Kelly was staring at me. Then, "You used to work homicide, right?" Studying me as he asked. "Miami PD?"

I nodded.

"No longer, huh?"

"Um-huh. Left a year ago."

"Worked a case about a priest running a prostitution ring in his school?"

"Seminary," I said.

"Fuckin' crazy story," he said.

"That it was," I said. He shook his head.

He turned to Louise. "Well, since the vic's here in our hospital, this case is technically ours. In reality I should kick it over to the Coast Guard. Only they don't have fuckin' police authority. So...it looks like we're stuck with it." He turned to his partner, who was now smoothing a fingernail with his teeth.

"Aaron, what the hell you doin'? It's not healthy. Germs!" He shook his head and turned to me. "Good meeting you guys," he said, hurrying, as if he was embarrassed for either himself or Monday. "Okay, we gotta get to work," he said, looking over at Monday, nodding to the double doors that were quiet now. I watched him set those doors swinging as he banged into the Inner Sanctum of the ER.

Monday was just behind him but stopped short of the swinging doors and turned. "By the way, we're going to need you to come down to HQ and file a report," he said. "You know how it works."

"On Monday?" I said.

He actually laughed this time.

Louise and I followed him into Emergency.

A woman at the nursing station just inside the door was talking with Kelly mostly, Monday leaning in. I heard her say Cynthia was in surgery and the doctor would talk to them when he came out.

Louise and I hung out near Cynthia's room, watching Kelly. He pushed his body off the nurses' counter, looked our way, and must have decided we had something else to tell him. The look on his face.

"Pretty crazy," said Kelly, finding a place close to Louise. She edged away. He noticed. "I mean, given two members of the same family are involved in a shooting." He thought for a moment, then, "Who caught the homicide?"

"Park Police," I said. "They're Sharing it with MPD."

Kelly nodded. " Needed the forensics lab, right?"

"Right you are."

A doc had come to the Nurses' Station. Louise murmured, "Be right back."

Monday cocked his head toward Louise who was walking away. "She working it?"

"No. Tony DeFelice. She's off duty."

"Nice," Kelly said, looking over at Louise. "Lucky you."

Lucky me, I thought, watching her talking at the nurses' station, pulling back her hair, even blacker in the dim light of the hall, her features, angular and perfectly formed.

Lucky me.

CHAPTER NINETEEN
THE FLY TRAP

I thought about the oil rig as we waited for word on Cynthia. Louise settled into the chair next to me. "*Zhi Zhu Nu*. What does that mean?" she said.

"Damned if I know." I Googled it on my phone.

"It's Chinese. *Zhi zhu* means spider," I said, reading from Wikipedia. "A special kind of spider. From the Araneidae family," I added, scrolling down. "They're orb weavers." Louise was staring at my screen.

"An orb weaver?"

"Yeah, they make webs shaped like wheels. You know, like the ones you see in your backyard."

She nodded.

"They trap their victims and then eat them. The spider and the fly." I paused. "Like that," I said, working my fingers like a mouth chewing.

"Ugh!" said Louise. "Stop that." I had irritated her. "You know they were trying to kill us," she said, locking onto my eyes. Then she stared off into empty space and mused softly, "Maybe the ones who killed Jack."

Maybe, I thought. *Maybe.*

"Chinese," she said, and shook her head. "They're everywhere."

"Easy," I said. "Your bias is showing. They're also buying up our debt."

"Why would they shoot at us?" she muttered, now more to herself than me.

"We were in Cuban waters. Maybe they thought they had a right."

"But that rig's run by a private company."

"Good point."

"So why does a private enterprise launch a boat to fire at an unarmed vessel? No warning. Like pirates, only they don't chase us."

"Another good point. But there aren't many pirates in that part of the Straits."

"Maybe this boat is the first wave of the Chinese invasion we've been waiting for," she said, getting up and heading for the candy machine. "What does *Nu* mean?" Her back was turned to me now.

This time I went to Google Translate.

"There was a movie. It was made in 1996, called *Zhi Zhu Nu.*" I paused, still reading. "*Nu* means woman. So, *Zhi Zhu Nu—The Spider Woman.*" Louise looked back at me as she fought the machine for her purchase.

"I never saw it," she said, impatient with the machine's knob. "This damn thing owes me a dollar." She hit it hard with the palm of her hand.

"No one else did either," I said, pulling out a dollar, walking over to the machine and sticking it in the slot. The candy dropped into the tray.

She glared at me. "Don't be a wise ass."

"Jade Leung played the part of Spider Woman."

Louise looked at me curiously.

"She's a beautiful woman. Made most of her films in Hong Kong. She has a kind of cult following," I added.

"And you're one of her fan boys," she said, sitting back down next to me. She broke off a chunk of her Milky Way and handed it to me. My favorite candy bar. Hers too. "So why are you telling me this?"

"I find it interesting that a Chinese drilling company would call their rig *The Spider Woman*. Do you know what the female spider does to her mate when they are done...uh...mating?"

"She gives him a cigarette?" Shrugging.

I smiled. "That's really good." I paused. "She kills him."

"That's one for women," she said, almost cheering.

"Uh-huh. But on another note," and the wait seemed eternal as I watched the clock move on the waiting room wall, "it's interesting that the rig has *Zhi Zhu* on its hull." I kept reading. "Zhi Zhu was an assassin—for the Black Lotus Tong. Interesting huh?" I thought about it as Louise watched me.

"And...?" she said.

"And it's interesting that an oil rig would have a Tong allusion on its hull. The only thing that was missing is the Black Lotus below the name. But, hey, maybe it's no different than the name Enola Gay on the plane that dropped the bomb on Nagasaki."

Louise stared at me as if to ask, *What the hell are you talking about?*

"Enola Gay Tibbets was the mother of the pilot who captained the plane."

"You're saying a Chinese gang is running that rig? That doesn't make sense."

I shook my head. "Just saying. Probably not. But interesting anyway."

Louise nodded.

The Kiss of the Spider Woman. We felt the sting of that spider tonight. Zhi Zhu, the assassin, was killed trying to strangle Sherlock Holmes. But *Zhi Zhu Nu* is still alive. Maybe on that rig. Maybe Jade Leung kissed Cynthia tonight. A chilling thought.

CHAPTER TWENTY
THE NEWS

The doctor came back into the waiting room about two hours later. "She's out of surgery," he said, leaning over to talk with us like we were family. "She's lost a lot of blood. But she'll be fine," he added quickly seeing the concern on my face.

"How long?" said Louise.

"The bullet passed through her shoulder. I cleaned out the wound and patched her up. She should have full use of her arm when she heals. In the meantime, Dr. Kopf—he's the orthopedist on staff—will see her in the morning." Then he read my mind. "Not to worry. He's good. But if she has her own doctor, she should follow up with him when she's released. Okay?" He straightened up.

I nodded.

"Can we see her now?" said Louise.

"She's in recovery. We'll be assigning a room shortly. When she gets settled, you can visit her." Then he smiled, shook our hands, and headed back through the double doors. Doogie Howser. Up late.

CHAPTER TWENTY-ONE
BACK HOME

Friday Morning, December 2

I t was after six in the a.m. when Louise and I left Cynthia. The cops had left hours ago. Before they did, Kelly had reminded me that PIs are not cops—*We got a shooting here and...* I said thanks for the reminder and darn I had forgotten that and turned to Louise—and she said wow she had forgotten that too and thanks. Kelly didn't appreciate the humor.

I headed back to the marina to pick up Louise's car. She was driving an unmarked.

I jumped out when we got there and opened her door. She flipped down the mirror on the visor and studied her face.

"You're beautiful even when you're tired," I said, leaning in and kissing her.

She shrugged. "You're biased," she said.

"Nope. Just honest," I said. She smiled.

We held each other in the darkened parking lot of the marina for a few minutes.

Only a couple of cars there. It was 6:50 a.m. and the early

rays of the sun were just appearing over the Florida Straits. No clouds at all.

"What are you going to do?" she said, as we held hands and stared at each other.

"Go home and sleep till I wake. What about you?"

"Same thing, I think. Call me when you get up."

Louise has a condo in Oceanside. On the water. You have to be there in the early morning. It's hard to describe the rising of the sun over the ocean. I always think of the people who live across the water who are losing the sun at the same time that we are gaining it. They're going to bed while we're rising. And when we go to bed, Asia is rising in the East.

I watched her pull away and felt a strange loneliness.

Sammy was waiting on the porch when I pulled into my drive, gravel flying away from the tires. It was late morning.

"Seen any bad guys lately?" I said.

He stared, made his way slowly down the porch stairs, stopping several times to rub himself against the railing supports. I waited for him. When he got to me, he pushed himself against my pant leg to let me know he missed me—but I knew it was because he was hungry. Sammy would make a great politician. So, I went to the fridge, pulled out an open can of Friskies Tuna, spooned some into a dish and microwaved it for five seconds. Then I placed it on the porch rail—to keep it out of Herman's reach—not that the old gator would go for Friskies. Sammy purred his way to his breakfast while I headed for the bedroom. But first I propped open the screen door so he could get back in.

CHAPTER TWENTY-TWO
DESTINATION

He fell asleep when the sun drifted behind the trees and darkness crept into the car. The men were talking in a drone—low enough so he couldn't hear what they were saying. And then he finally fell off the earth. And he dreamed of a stream that ran near his house, or somewhere near the house—he wasn't entirely sure—filled with shiny stones of varied colors that shone in the sunlight, and he reached down, picked several up, and felt them, as if they were precious, and tossed them back again, wondering at their brilliance. Then he stepped among them, in bare feet, and gazed about, at the woods, at how the stream wandered through the woods, and at the cool of the water as it washed over his feet. And the peace, the quiet of the woods, the absolute quiet bathed him.

And then he woke. The trees looked different from the ones he was used to in Muskingum, Ohio. They were thick and covered with hanging plants. And the road was lined with heavy underbrush, the fields all dense and green and smelling sweet. Another odor came through the car—like rotten eggs. He didn't like it and the smell made him feel bad that he wasn't home. It made his stomach hurt. And he wondered why his dad wasn't

following him. To make sure he looked through the rear win.
The road was empty.

"You awake, eh, young fella?" the man in the passenger seat
said, turning around and smiling. His teeth were bad, the Boy
thought. And he felt his heart beat against his ribs. And his
hands worried themselves as he watched the man.

"We're almost home, boy." the driver said, looking at him in
the rearview mirror. "You're going to meet your new family in a
few hours." And the trees and the brush blurred for the Boy as he
thought about what the driver had told him. About the new
family. And he had lots of questions that rushed through his
mind as he stared at the face in the rearview mirror, the face that
never left him and never changed how it looked at him.

The Boy thought that he might have to run away to get back
to his family, and that these men were the ones his parents had
warned him about—and how was he to know? He hoped that he
wouldn't get punished when he got home, and he worried about
that as he watched the trees falling away behind him and the
distance narrowing between the car and where he was headed.
Then he saw a strange looking tree, one that looked like trees he
had seen in a book about Florida, like a palm, and he thought
maybe he was in Florida.

He fell back into the seat and wondered what his father
would have told him to do. And he had no idea.

CHAPTER TWENTY-THREE
THE MESSAGE

W hen I'm alone—which is most of the time—I have trouble sleeping—which is most of the time. And those dreams...! This morning was no different. So, I stared at the clock on my dresser—red numbers, so I can't miss the time. And I hate that part of not sleeping—seeing the minutes and hours go by and I'm still awake, sometimes not knowing if I'm awake or sleeping. I tried to empty my mind and my eyes must have closed because when I opened them again and checked the clock, it read 8:01 and I knew it was in the p.m. because it was dark. I had slept for ten hours straight.

I could hear the noises of the swamp in the darkness. There were no lights. I had only sounds to guide me. And my feelings. And the sound of Sammy sleeping next to me. He does that. Curls up and squeezes as close as he can to my head. Someday I expect to wake up and find Herman curled up next to him.

I heard a noise. In the kitchen maybe. I lifted the sheet off my body as quietly as I could and slid off the bed. No sound. Then I heard it again. Like the murmur of slippers against the floor. I froze half way off the bed and wondered where my gun was, then remembered it was in my nightstand. I opened the drawer quietly and felt the cold of the Glock. I pulled it out, checked the load as quietly as I could, then slipped into a corner near the bed. There was no light anywhere.

Sammy stirred and jumped off the bed and purred next to me. I was too tense to tell him to keep quiet. I held the Glock at my side and felt for the furniture that stood between my bed and the door. My dresser was on my left. I skirted it and slid alongside so that I was now directly behind the open door. I still couldn't see anything.

I heard someone breathing near me—in the room! Then that someone hit me from behind. The gun slipped from my hand and I heard a pop as I landed on the floor, my brain whirling, a brilliant white light spreading everywhere. And then it all went away and darkness spread over my world...

Sammy woke me, his breath against my mouth. Everything was still black, except for the red numbers on the clock that read 3:33. I guessed that it was in the a.m. because the moon was framed in the window. If that's the case, I had lost about six hours or more. And some blood too—if the sticky stuff on my head was what I thought it was. I reached up and found a lump on the back of my head that felt as large as an Idaho potato. It hurt like hell. So did my ribs.

I crawled to the bed, reached for the lamp and turned it on.

The room was tossed like a storm had hit it. Every drawer in my dresser was on the floor. And in the middle of the mess was my gun. I stumbled into the bathroom and looked in the mirror. I was hoping the person I saw wasn't me: my hair stuck to my forehead—sweat and blood all mixed together—my right cheek bruised where I must have hit it when I fell. And the back of my head—when I held a hand mirror up to the mirror on the medicine cabinet—it looked...well, just nasty. Whoever hit me was quick, quiet, and deadly. But clearly if he wanted to kill me, he would have.

I stripped, got in the shower and watched the blood run down the drain. After I dried off, I stood in front of a full-length mirror on the back of the bathroom door and looked at the damage. Besides needing a new face, I had survived. If some ribs were broken there wouldn't be much an ER doc could do. So I voted on whether to go to the hospital or not. It was one to nothing not to go. Then I sat down on the bed to think about what to do next. One thing at least, I had gotten sixteen hours sleep—maybe more. Hell of a wake-up call though. I could have slept longer.

Then I noticed it. On the night stand. In plain sight. How had I missed it? An Origami. In the shape of a Black Lotus.

I called Richie. His voicemail picked up: "We ain't here. Leave a message." I did. And I lay back down to think and let my pain seep into the mattress.

∼

The Boy woke as the car hit ruts in the road. He looked out at trees that hung over the road and ahead was a house. A large one. White with several floors. The second floor was mostly hidden by the trees and by the moss that hung from them. Some of the branches snapped at the car even though the man driving tried to avoid them. Then he saw him: a man waiting in the drive, in front of the house.

"You're home, kid," the man in the passenger seat said, turning around, and the Boy's stomach gave way to fear. His heart was beating faster than he ever remembered and his mind was confused. 'Home'? This was his home? And he couldn't talk. He just sat frozen in his seat as the car drew nearer, his eyes locked on the man who stood in the driveway, in front of the big white house, with a smile on his face, his hand raised as if to say you're here. The Boy couldn't breathe, and a mist covered his *eyes so he couldn't see the man anymore, nor hear the voices of the men in the front seat talking, though their lips were moving and they were turned to him. And he went dizzy and heard himself call out—for his mother and father, knowing all the while they were too far away. Don't get into a car with strangers. His mind faded with the mist, and the Boy fell back onto the seat. He felt as though he had died.*

CHAPTER TWENTY-FOUR
RICHIE

Early Saturday Morning, December 3

I heard chimes in the distance. They were coming from the dark. I slid out of bed, holding my side to ease the pain—those ribs. My cell was on the dresser and still lit up from the call. There was a message from Richie.

We had grown up together on the near east side of Cleveland. Richie, Tony DeFelice, and I. In those days—in the mid-70s—the streets of Cleveland were rough. So every day was fight-day. Richie used a baseball bat. I used my fists. DeFelice had a gun. He carries a gun today—only it's legal. And Richie? Today, he's got every gun imaginable. But his weapon of choice is still his Louisville Slugger. "Larry Doby signed it—right here," he would brag, pointing to the scrawl on the thick end.

"So, what's up with you, bud," said Richie when I called him back. "Ma wants to know where you been. You ain't been back to the neighborhood. For what? A year?"

"It's only been two months," I reminded him. "Remember? The Russians?"

"Yeah, yeah, I know. It seems like a year. You know you got a friend here. You gotta keep in touch you wanna keep your friends," and before I could jump in, "so what's goin' on?" he demanded.

I filled him in on Cynthia and her father and saved the latest episode for last.

"Holy fuck, Coop!" Then silence. "You okay?"

I told him I was, but figured I needed his help.

"I'm on my way," and before I could say anything more, he was gone. I wanted to tell him, *Take your time*. But...anyway.

CHAPTER TWENTY-FIVE
CALL WONG

That Same Morning

Then I called Cleveland Wong, a friend of mine who works in Homeland Security. Actually, he's the Deputy Secretary of Homeland Security with an office in D.C. and one in Florida as well. But I didn't call either. I called his personal number because...well, because it was early.

"Cooper! What do you want? You realize the sun's not up? That means I'm not either." Obviously not happy. Cleveland wasn't happy very often. His father gave him his name because of where he was born. Cleveland, Ohio. Wong has never liked it. "Don't call me Cleveland," he told me when I first met him. "My name is Wong."

"So okay, you got me, what do you want?" he said, still irritated.

I told him about the oil rig in the Gulf, to which he responded, *Sure I know about that and so what?* I said the "so what" is that the rig sent a boat after us and shot one of our crew.

"Jeez, Cooper. Why didn't you tell me this before?"

I told him it just happened.

"But, wait a minute, what the hell you guys doing in Cuban waters anyway. You're breaking International Law."

I told him briefly about the case: Jack Hayward's disappearance, about finding his body, about the pictures of the *Zhi Zhu Nu* and the small rig, and about the shooting of Cynthia in the Straits and that the shooting took place *outside* Cuban waters. "So, I'm figuring this *is* a Homeland Security issue," I said.

"And," I continued, "someone came into my house this morning..."

"Yeah?"

"They were looking for something—I don't think they found it."

"What do you think they were looking for?"

"Beats the hell out of me—something about the case I'm working on—maybe the pictures of the rig."

"Yeah. But why are you telling me? You need to tell the locals."

"I figure it's all related."

"Uh-huh." He paused. "You okay?"

"Yeah. But the reason I'm calling is that the person who beat the hell out of me left something behind," I added, pushing him.

"Come on, Cooper. Tell me what you want to tell me, for Chrissake," he shot back, growing impatient.

"He left an origami shaped like a Black Lotus." I paused for few moments.

"A Black Lotus?" More a statement than a question.

"That's right. And you know what that means, right?"

"It means someone is trying to deliver you a message,

Cooper. Maybe you ought to listen. But why're you calling me about this?"

"Because I think the Tong is involved in Jack Hayward's death. I think they shot him."

Silence for a while.

"The Tong!" He paused for a moment. "You're kidding. Why would the Tong be involved with the killing of Jack Hayward?"

"Let me explain. It's a Chinese rig, right? The *Zhi Zhu Nu.*"

"Right."

"A group of guys attacked our boat in international waters—not Cuban—and shot at us, actually hitting Jack's daughter."

Cleveland was silent. But he was still there. I could hear his breathing.

"Then right after that someone breaks into my house—how the hell they knew where I live, I don't have a clue—hits me over the head and leaves a Black Lotus origami on my bedside table." I paused again. "I think they're guarding the rig."

"That's crazy. The Tong? Guarding an oil rig?"

"You know about the rig, right?" I said.

"Yeah. Sure. It was built by a Finnish company for a Chinese oil exploration outfit. The project also has some serious Venezuelan backing. But it's all private stuff. Our people know all about it. They don't like it because the American companies say *Why can't we drill, baby, if the Chinese are drilling?* We say because they are drilling in Cuban waters. Hey, the Chinese bought the drilling rights from Cuba. And—to make your day even better, Cooper—the Russians are trying to get into the same game."

"Okay. So that takes us back to the Tong. Do you know the story about the Black Lotus Tong?"

"Oh sure. Sherlock Holmes. Famous story. About Zhi Zhu and General Shan and the Black Lotus gang. Very good story."

"Do they really exist?"

"The Tong? Of course."

"No, I mean the Black Lotus Tong."

"Of course. All very secret. That is one of the problems with Chinese gangs. Secrecy is very important. Very difficult to get into the gang. Impossible to get out. Very dangerous people," he warned. Then, after a pause, "So, Cooper, what do you want from me?"

"I need you to make a phone call." Maybe he nodded. I don't know. I didn't care.

I told him who and why. I heard a grunt. Figured that for okay, and signed off.

I was tired. No, beat. I sat back down on the bed, dropped my head in my hands, turned off the lamp, and fell back, pulling a pillow over my head. Just for a few minutes, I thought, until the rising sun chases away the demons and peeks in my window. And the minutes turned into hours and the hours into a deep, deep sleep.

~

The house was big. A big living room and big bedrooms. It was not like the Boy's house back home, not like his bedroom there, which was small and had a bunk in it—in case a little brother or sister came along, his mom had said. There was no bunk bed here. No mom or dad here. Just the Man in the driveway.

He had slept through most of the day and was exploring the house. The Man didn't know he was awake. The Boy had thought about running away but he didn't know where he would go. He didn't know where he was.

"There you are," said the Man from the driveway, coming through the front door. "I was looking for you. How do you like your room?"

But the Boy didn't know how to answer that question. It wasn't his room. It didn't have his games, or his books, or his baseball cards, or his guitar, or the buckeyes he had been gathering for the past year to make a chain he planned to take to school and show his friends. They all had one—a buckeye chain. You would wear your chain around your waist and other kids would try to break yours and you would try to break theirs and then you would throw at each other. And yes, it would hurt when you got hit. But that was part of the game: not to be afraid of getting hit by a buckeye.

So, the Boy didn't understand why the Man would ask him if he liked his room because there was nothing there that he had back home. He was afraid to tell him that, so he just said, "Yeah, I guess." And the Man nodded.

He was tall and had a short grey beard. But the Boy didn't think he was much older than his dad because his hair wasn't very grey—just his beard—kind of grey—and his face didn't look old and he didn't act old—not too much. And he had a little stomach that stuck out over his belt buckle. And he wore glasses that made him look serious. And he looked like a nice person, though the Boy didn't understand why he was here and he was afraid to ask him. Don't go with strangers....is all he could think of.

The men who took him were strangers. So, they definitely must be bad men. But then he didn't know for sure whether the Man was bad. After all he didn't personally take him. "I'm a friend of your parents," he said as he stood in the doorway. "They told me, if anything happened to them, I should take you. And I'm sorry to say that something bad did happen to them." The Man seemed to think carefully about what he was saying, "and *now I will take care of you. You will be able to go back home if they get better. But until that time, you will be staying here with me. You won't be able to call them because they are not at home now. Maybe later when they return. I will let you know when they do. Do you understand?"*

The Boy had nodded even though he didn't understand. And he wondered—no worried—about what bad things had happened to his parents and he searched through the Man's face, the Man from the driveway, the tall, thin Man with the beard, the Man who looked to be about the same age as his father, the Man who was looking kindly at him now, who said he would take care of him. The Man said all this to him as he came through the doorway into the living room where Maxie was standing.

And the Boy looked around the room with the large overstuffed couch, and the piano under the bay window, and the twin chairs with the shiny wood arms and backs with blue cushions as seats, and the large fireplace with a wooden mantle across the top covered with glass decorations, and a picture of the Man in a long black gown, holding a round hat that was green with a gold tassel hanging over the side. The picture hung on the wall over the center of the mantle.

And the Boy fought back his tears, because he didn't want the Man to see him cry. But he knew he would cry later...in his room...the one that was not like his room back home.

CHAPTER TWENTY-SIX
THE VISITOR

Saturday Afternoon, December 3
It was late in the day. The sun succumbing to the early December chill that settles over the marsh in the night this time of year. And I heard it again. The noise. I reached for the Glock that I had laid on the floor next to my bed. *Fool me once...*There's no safety on a Glock. Touch the trigger and it shoots bullets. So, I laid my finger on the side of the gun and raised it as I got out of bed so that the barrel was level with my eyes. And I heard a voice.

"I know you got a gun, Cooper. Drop it." and the door flew open as I lowered the weapon. I recognized the voice. And there he was. All six feet two inches of him, filling the doorway with his bulk and his bags, smiling. It was—and I checked the clock—5:14 in the p.m. The red numbers too large to miss. I had slept through the entire day.

"Rise and shine, bud," and he tossed his bags on my bed, in case I had any thought of lying back down. "Uncle Richie's here!"

CHAPTER TWENTY-SEVEN
CHINATOWN

Around 6:00 p.m. Louise showed up. I had called her shortly after Richie arrived and said we had a trip to plan.

"So, what's this trip you've got in mind, Coop?" she said as she settled at the table in the kitchen which also doubles as my dining room table. My house is small. About 1700 square feet including three bedrooms, a living room, a kitchen and my office—my dining room table. My real office is in downtown Oceanside. But I hadn't been there in a few days. Not since Cynthia had visited me this past Monday, just five days ago. It seemed so much longer than that. And now she was in a hospital, shot just like her father. At least hers wasn't fatal.

"We're going to Boston," I said. Richie and Louise stared at me. "Chinatown," I added. "There's a man there I need to talk to and I think—"

"It might be dangerous. Thus, you need protection," said Richie. "Why I'm here. And you need some firepower," and he reached into the bag that he had dragged into the kitchen and pulled out a Browning HP JMP 50th and handed it to me. The Hi Power Browning holds 13 rounds of 9mm shells and is capable of cock and lock carry. Meaning you can cock the hammer and lock it down until you need to use it. One less motion. It has ivory grips and a polished blue metal finish. I turned it over to check out the Browning signature. Black against a gold scroll background. I handed it to Louise who turned it over, inspecting it with obvious admiration while carefully avoiding getting prints on the blue metal. She knows how obsessive Richie is. She handed it back to him.

"Try this one out," he said, reaching into his bag and handing me a Glock. "It's got fixed night sights. Remember?" I nodded. I had used it in the Russian kidnapping case. It's a small, easy-to-conceal weapon, with a black metal finish.

Then Richie looked over at Louise and like Santa Claus peeked into his bag again. "Let's see what I got here for the little lady," he said.

Louise kicked him. "I told you, Richie..." and before she could finish, he held up his hands. "You guys are so goddamn macho," she said, looking at me also. "You think these guns are an extension of your dicks."

Louise pulled her Glock and laid it on the table. "Does that make me part of the club, boys?" And she got up to refill her coffee. She was wearing jeans. She looked good. Richie noticed, too. Just a couple of macho guys.

"I got the tickets for later this evening. We fly out of Miami and land at Logan."

"Stopovers?" said Louise fixing her coffee. I shook my head. "You want a refill, Richie?" Not asking me. Must be mad. Richie nodded. I did, too. She put the pot down next to me. I looked at her like what did I do now?

She gave me that *just playing with you* smile.

～

We packed fast, Richie complaining about the travel— *Man, two flights in one day! Fuckin' crazy.* But I knew he was excited. We got to the airport by 7:40, checked one bag that held the guns and boarded the American 9:00 p.m. non-stop flight to Boston, landing at 12:17 a.m. Louise and I had two seats in the third row from the back, Richie was in a seat in front of us. He was asleep by the time we lifted off. No more complaints.

CHAPTER TWENTY-EIGHT
THE GODFATHER

Sunday Morning, December 4

It was late when we landed. After 12:45 a.m. Bad weather had us circling Boston's Logan International for about twenty minutes. I was beat and Richie was grouchy (what else was new?) as we stood around baggage claim and waited for the red light to go on and the bags begin to show up from the hole in the wall. Louise was getting a rental. A half hour later we were loading a Ford Explorer and heading out of Logan through the tunnel to the mainland and over to Copley Square where I had booked two rooms at the Copley Plaza Hotel, one of Boston's finest —and that was clear from the price. It felt like two-week's pay.

Louise was happy. "Vacation," she said.

"Why not?" I said.

The Copley shone in the night like a newly lit European hotel, its massive front overlooking the Square brilliantly illuminated against the black of the early morning sky.

"Geez," said Richie as we checked in. "Just like the Breakers." He was referring to the old hotel that dominates

Cedar Point, an amusement park on Lake Erie built in 1905. I think it was the richness of the carpeting at the Copley; the deep plush red of the furnishings; the domed lobby, ensconced in dark hardwood and supported by marble pillars. I wondered which hotel was vying with the other. The Copley was built in 1891, fourteen years earlier than the old hotel on Lake Erie. Your call.

Chinatown is only a mile or so from Copley Square. But I was up early. Louise was still sleeping. So, I dressed quietly and went to the living room of the suite. I was anxious to follow up on information Cleveland Wong had given me about Chinatown and about whom to talk to about the Tong.

You be careful, Cooper, he had said. *Chinatown is closed to outsiders like you. They will smile and tell you nothing. Maybe get you into trouble. You have any Chinese friends to go with you? You,* I said. *Nice try, Cooper,* he said. *We're not friends. We know each other. Need to read* I Ching *about friends. Anyway, good luck.*

∿

I called Richie and invited him for breakfast—"Coffee, toast, orange juice and Danish—in our room," I said. He was over in fifteen minutes.

"The sun ain't up yet. Can't eat," he said, "but I'll have some coffee," and he scrubbed his fingers through his hair, still a natural black, and then picked a chair near the desk, complaint all over his face. He hadn't shaved. That's not like Richie. But he did have on a white shirt and black pants, pressed; black shoes, tied; and gold cufflinks. Richie doesn't know informal. "Idiots don't know how to dress," is what he says about people in jeans or shorts. "Fuckin' hillbillies."

Louise stirred in the other room and turned over. I put my finger to my lips and shut the door.

"Sorry," he said, studying his black socks and pulling them so they were tight all the way up his leg.

Louise opened the door and popped her head out. "I'm up. I just need a shower and I'll join you." Then she was gone.

She opened the door ten minutes later, her hair still wet, but dressed in jeans and a sweater. The towel around her head made her look like a middle-eastern cowgirl.

So, I spent the next half hour laying out the plans for the day as they drank coffee and Richie broke down and had some Danish with us. Nobody touched the toast and orange juice —except me.

It was after eight when we set out, on foot, for Chinatown. The weather was warm for December, about 45 degrees, but clear. Boston is funny that way. Warm and clear one day, a nor'easter the next, bringing in gales of wind and torrents of snow filling the streets with white stuff. It all makes you grit your teeth as you steel yourself against the burn of winter chill. It wasn't that kind of day. But I felt an undercurrent of anxiety as we headed south on Trinity—some birds still in branches, brave sons of bitches to try to last a Boston winter—and then east on Stuart, past the Castle at Park Plaza and on to the Revere Hotel—it didn't look old enough for Paul Revere to have stayed there—and at that point we were just 400 feet or so from the Boston Common.

We turned north for the Boston Common. In late spring, Swan boats would be loading people for a ride on the lake, now frozen, that centers the Common. But families were still gathering there, catching what might be the last of the winter sun. I stared at some boys who were kicking a soccer ball around in a field—in tee shirts. I opened my leather jacket. And closed it soon after. I'm from Florida. My blood's still thin.

Louise had brought a long black overcoat. Richie had a Burberry raincoat on over his suit jacket. I was glad I was wearing a sweater under my jacket. I pulled the collar up around my neck. The wind was blowing stiff and cold off the Harbor.

Just east of Boston Common is Chinatown. We knew we were there when we caught a glimpse of the Paifang, the gateway to Chinatown: a massive structure rising about fifty feet into the air over Beach Street and Surface Road. It consisted of two large white columns on either side of Beach, topped by a pagoda-style roof stretching over the street and extending about eight feet beyond the pillars on each side. The roof curled over the columns, the green tile snaking across like a living creature, morphing and rising into a head as it reached each side of the structure. If that weren't daunting enough, two lions, white and heavy, guarded the entrance, their teeth set on edge.

"Fuck's that?" said Richie, staring at the lions.

"In case we have bad intentions," said Louise. "There are probably cameras in the statues looking for weapons."

Richie felt for his gun. It was tucked under his arm.

"You know where we're going, Coop?" said Louise.

"A tea house on Beach Street and Tyler," I replied, looking at the street signs for Tyler. "Wong said someone would meet us there."

"Uh-huh," is all she said, taking in the shops that lined Beach.

Ads for restaurants hung over the street, large Chinese lettering running from top to bottom on the signs. We passed a bakery at Hudson and Beach: Hing Shing Pastry. Richie nodded toward it. *Later*, I signaled. We passed fruit and vegetable stands with baskets filled to overflowing. The vendors didn't pay attention to us. They were busy arranging their displays and adding to them. A newspaper dispenser crowded the curb. The title of the paper was in English: *The Epoch Times*. The articles were in Chinese.

Two phone booths stood next to each other near the curb, bright red and decorated with a Paifang style green roof. A miniature pagoda with a phone—a relic of early America—in Chinatown. We came to Tyler.

"There's a teahouse," said Louise, looking down the street to her right. It was easy to spot. Teahouse read the sign hanging over the sidewalk, Chinese lettering below the English.

"About time," said Richie, glaring at the sign. He's never happy outside his comfort zone, Cleveland's Little Italy. "Fuckin' people should learn English," he said, looking around at the confusion that was growing in the streets and stepping away from a bicycler who wheeled past him and yelled at him in Chinese—or Vietnamese—or something.

Chinatown has the densest population in Boston—about 2,800 people per square mile—and they push cars through narrow streets already pinched by vehicles parked on both sides. But it's a sign of business. So the traffic, and the congestion, and the honking, and the bicycles are all good.

"Come in!" smiled a small man standing outside the teahouse, his arm directing us toward the entrance.

The place was busy. Some students—their backpacks on the floor—were listening carefully to a grey-haired Chinese man drinking tea. In a far corner, young men were standing around a table watching men playing checkers. They were quiet—showing respect.

Richie and Louse made space at a long table where some people were already seated. I ordered green tea, Louise something called Boba—*a bubble tea with tapioca pearls*, our hostess explained. She also ordered some pastry (*Charge it to Cooper Investigations,* Louise whispered): puff biscuits with cream filling and egg tarts. Richie had the same reaction to Louise's order as he did to the lions: "The fuck is that? Don't they got toast?" He ordered coffee.

Two young men appeared at our table. One was tall with black hair. The other about a foot shorter. Both were dressed in black jackets, white shirts, and black pants. They looked like they were going either to a wedding or to a funeral. Interesting how the dress is the same. I moved to share the space as is the custom in a Chinese restaurant. They didn't sit.

"Mr. Cooper," said the tall man, "you will come with us," reaching to take my arm. Richie rose quickly, knocking over his chair, and blocked his arm. Some of the people around us pushed their chairs away and the noisy cafe became the silent cafe.

"Mr. Lung Li said you wanted to meet with him," the tall man spoke quickly, bowing apologetically and looking around. He was embarrassed. "He has sent us to bring you," he explained in both Chinese and English—obviously for the onlookers. The shorter man had backed away, his smile gone. He was watching Richie and Louise who were both standing. Louise had her hand on her gun.

"We walking or driving?" I said to the tall man.

"We are walking."

"Then let's walk," I said, and turned to Louise and Richie. They both nodded. Richie patted his shoulder where his JMP was obvious. Louise was her usual quiet self. She leaned over and whispered, "I would feel better if one of us followed. I'll keep my cell on. You two stay with them." I nodded.

I recalled an AP story about the arrest of a gangster in Chinatown. An American—a rare thing in Chinatown's closed community. For two decades he was the leader of a powerful gang, following in the shadow of the brutal and one-time violent Ping On Gang. I remembered what Wong had said: "Chinatown can be a dangerous place."

Richie and I stayed behind both men as they led us back to Beach Street where we turned right. We followed them past the sellers of fruits and vegetables that lined the street; past the bakeries; around a woman pounding drums on the sidewalk— the Spring Festival was coming; around racks of clothes choking what little space there was on the sidewalk; down a narrow street where the signs for stores rose thirty feet or so overhead, identifying shops on the second floor; and finally to a restaurant hidden from Beach Street, inside a courtyard and to our left. Two men stood at either side of the entrance, like the two Foo lions at the gate of Chinatown. They were tall and heavy in the shoulder. Their faces had seen hard times—beaten like a boxer's face—and they ignored us as we passed. Richie paused for a moment, looked at both of them, snorted, and followed us in.

From inside the restaurant I watched a bus pull up to the curb, *Lucky Star* printed in large letters across the side. I had heard about the Chinatown buses. They run every hour between Boston and New York. They are the glue that bind the Chinese communities—like a spider web.

I was surprised that someone hadn't checked for guns, that is until I heard a voice from behind a screen that sheltered the dining area from reception. A woman in a dark purple dress that fit her tightly with a neckline that rose to her throat nodded and smiled. She reached for my briefcase. "Please," she said. I handed it to her. She opened it, pointed to the origami, and asked what it was. I told her it was a gift for Mr. Lung. She smiled and nodded in approval. "It is very beautiful," she said. "He will be very pleased."

"But now, you must leave guns with us," she continued,

smiling as she held out her hands. The soft approach, yet just as effective. We did as she asked.

"Your ankle guns as well," she continued. The same smile. I shook my head in surprise and looked at her like *How did you know?*

"I saw when you came in," she said, still smiling. Then, after we were relieved of all our hardware, "This way, please," she said, and we followed her into the dining room.

It was dark, the room lit only by candles on the tables. Silk lanterns, decorated with Chinese characters, burned low. They were hanging on the walls, some from the ceiling. It was an expansive room, large enough for a dance floor, and empty of people, except for the two men in black, Richie, Louise, me, and —at a table near the back of the room—a man sitting erect awaiting us, his face without emotion, sitting alone. Two men, one on each side, stood just behind him, their arms crossed. Behind them, partially lost in the shadows cast by the lanterns, stood a young woman who looked very much like the one who led us into the room. I looked behind me to see if she had suddenly changed places, but the hostess was already on her way back to the front and the woman in the shadows was still there.

Then, "Mr. Cooper, please sit down," said the man at the table, a thin man, pointing with a very thin hand toward a chair. He didn't invite Richie to sit.

And so I sat, the silk lanterns flickering, creating an interesting pattern of light and darkness, so that the faces of those seated fell in and out of shadow. It was hard to tell how old he was, except that his hair was silver, combed straight back from an unlined face.

"I understand from Mr. Wong that you have come to talk with me." No pleasantries, no bows, no change in his expression. Straight out. I heard a bus pull away from the sidewalk outside the restaurant.

"And you are...?" I said into the silence.

"He is Mr. Li Lung," said one of the men behind me. I bowed. And so did Mr. Li Lung.

Several delicate, gold embossed teacups and a matching teapot, embellished with green leaves, sat on the table between us. Mister Lung poured for both of us. He studied me for a moment, then...

"Mr. Wong is a very good friend, otherwise we would not be sitting here. He tells me you are concerned about an attack on you and your friends and are wondering if I might help."

I bowed again.

"Let me just say that I know nothing about those events." He focused on my eyes.

I told him about the intruder in my house, about the pictures of the *Zhi Zhu Nu* in Jack's office, about the attack on our boat when we approached the *Zhi Zhu Nu*, and finally about the origami that was left on my nightstand.

"All that is very interesting," he said. "But what is that to us, Mr. Cooper?"

"My question to you, sir, is this," I said, pressing on. "Is there, as far as you know, any connection between the Tong and the *Zhi Zhu Nu*?"

There was some commotion at the door as one of the *lions* who stood guard there, came into the restaurant and whispered something to Mr. Lung. He turned to me.

"He says that there is a woman standing across the street watching our place. Do you know her?"

That would be Louise. She obviously decided to make herself visible—in case we had to shoot our way out.

I smiled and nodded. "She is a friend. She's waiting for us."

Mr. Lung smiled. "You are in no danger, Mr. Cooper."

Richie grunted behind me. Everybody turned to him.

"The Tong..." continued Li Lung, ignoring Richie, "Tong means Hall. They run our communities. They run our buses. They organize our meetings. They make sure we are financially secure. You make a mistake to think they are a gang. Or that they might be the cause of any trouble you and your people have had."

I reached for my briefcase...and everyone in the room suddenly stirred. I stopped, held up my hands and explained what I was going to do. Li Lung nodded. I opened the briefcase and pulled out the origami that had been left in my bedroom.

Everyone relaxed as Li Lung examined the piece of art. Black as onyx, formed as a concave structure and moving downwards with the sides shaped delicately as though by a fanatic of detail, each part of the bloom poignantly puffed and rising to a rounded point. I could feel the gasps rising from those around me.

"Quite amazing," Li Lung said admiringly, nodding as he turned the creation over several times, studying it like a gemologist would examine a rare stone. After several minutes of silence, he handed the lotus back to me carefully, as though he were transmitting a religious relic.

"The Black Lotus Tong does not exist," he said, no emotion in his voice. Just like that.

"Then why this?" I pressed, nodding at the gift I had received on my bedside table. "Perhaps someone is trying to say they do." And Li Lung studied me briefly, then nodded.

I was staring at the woman in the shadows. About five feet four, black hair, sharp but delicate features. She was beautiful by any standard.

"This is my daughter, Li Lang Zhu, Mr. Cooper," and he smiled as he turned and bowed toward her. "Her name means Tarantula," he continued. "And, therefore, I am Lang

Zhu de fuqin, the father of Tarantula. No?" He was still smiling.

The *Kiss of the Spider Woman*, I thought. "She looks so much like the hostess," I remarked.

"Liu Xue. She is *also* my daughter," he said. "They are twins, can you not tell?" he said, still smiling. I didn't ask the meaning of her name.

And then a deep silence fell over the room. Nor did anyone move to disturb the silence. He didn't say our meeting was over but one would have to be an Emily Post class dropout not to get the idea. Whatever else there was to learn would have to keep for another day.

CHAPTER TWENTY-NINE
THE CALLER

Sunday Afternoon, December 4

I heard my phone ring as we left the restaurant and searched my jacket for the cell. I looked at the number —Jillie.

"Hi Coop. Busy?"

I told her where we were. She was quiet for a moment thinking, I'm sure, of asking why in Boston, but she didn't. So, I waited. She hesitated.

"Had a call last night."

"Oh yeah?"

"Uh-huh. Remember the guy I was seeing at Georgetown before we got together?"

Oh boy. Did I remember. "Uh-huh," I said, kicking myself for not saying more.

"He was in Columbus for the weekend and asked me out to dinner..." I was just about to ask her when she told me, "tonight." Was she asking my permission? I was surprised at my reaction. Caught me off guard. Louise looked over at me. A question on her face. Was I that obvious? Richie was walking ahead, like a point guard.

"I told him, okay," Jillie said. That hesitation again like I was supposed to say something about it, make a comment, like say *no*, ask *why?* get upset, say we should get back together again. I didn't. All I said was *okay* and hated myself for not saying more. I never liked him. I liked him even less now. He was a pompous ass. Studying psychiatry. I remember a comment he made to me once—about my degree—PhD— nodding his head. "We all need philosophers, don't we?" Smart ass. But I got the girl. At least until now.

Jillie was quiet on the other end.

"That's great," I said. Lying. Louise was still staring at me. I mouthed Jillie's name. Louise nodded. Not happy.

"Let me know how it goes," I added, shrugging to Louise. She just turned and walked ahead.

"I will," she said. "I just..."

"No problem," I said. "I understand." My nose should be getting longer. "Anyway, thanks for calling," and I ended the call. Not wanting to dwell any longer.

"So..." Louise started.

"Yeah," I said, "Jillie."

"What's up?"

I told her.

"How does that make you feel?" I knew that was a leading question since it must have showed in my shoulders. It always does. When I'm upset, my shoulders fold over my body. I can feel them. I could feel it now.

We walked in silence for a while. "I understand, Coop. We're just feeling our way through this thing. You got Jillie you've got to work through; I've got my own problems."

I hadn't heard that one before and looked over at her.

She shook her head. "Later."

"Mr. Cooper." A voice behind us. Richie slowed down and looked back—past us—at someone coming our way. "Mr. Cooper." Again. Almost in a whisper. It was the hostess from the restaurant. In the deep purple dress. She was hurrying in high heels, having a hard time keeping her balance and looking back every few steps to see if anyone was behind her.

"Quickly," she said. "We must get off the street." She pointed to a tea room a few signs down on our left. I motioned to Richie. He nodded, came back, waited, looking around as we passed him, and then followed us into the shop. Once we settled in a booth, she relaxed, still breathing hard from running. She reached for her ankles and massaged them.

"That must hurt," said Louise. "Why I gave them up a long time ago."

Liu Xue looked at her. Puzzled.

"High heels," said Louise.

"I am the hostess," she explained, smiling, then quickly raised her hand to cover her mouth. Embarrassed.

We waited, Richie on the inside of the booth next to her. Louise and I facing her.

"Just take your time," Louise said, pulling her cop face. "Would you like some tea? Coffee?"

She shook her head, still breathing hard and looking from me to Louise. "I cannot stay here," she said suddenly, looking around. "Too many eyes for my father."

I searched the room to see if anyone was watching. I couldn't tell.

"Is there somewhere else we can meet?" she said, anxious to leave.

"Can you come to Copley Square?" I said.

She thought for a moment. "Yes. The bus goes there. I come in the morning. Where will you be?" and she glanced at some young men who were staring at her from the checkers corner.

"In the lobby of the Copley Square Hotel," I said, following her eyes to the young men. "Are they a problem?"

"I must go," she replied, rising quickly, motioning for us to stay seated. We got up anyway, exchanging some brief, modest bows—I wouldn't want to try to describe Richie's. She pushed quickly through the doors and back onto Beach Street. I walked over to the window and watched her as she headed back into the heart of Chinatown and wondered if we would see her again.

"She is beautiful," said Richie. Louise nodded.

"Like Jade Leung Chang," I said, referring once again to the exotic actress from Hong Kong who starred in one of the worst films ever made, *The Spider Woman*. A terrible movie, but Jade Leung's charisma and captivating beauty were all any of her fan-boys ever cared about—including me. Liu Xue didn't have any of Spider Woman's darkness. Her twin sister did though. Li Lang Zhu, the Tarantula, was the one I wondered

about as I watched Liu Xue disappear into the dista
become part of a crowd of tourists who had just unloadea
a Chinatown bus. *YOLBUS* in big letters across the side, *Neu
York to Boston* on the destination sign over the driver's window.
I heard that the Tong operated some of these buses. I wondered
about this one. Liu Xue appeared on the other side of the crowd
as it thinned out. The driver looked her way as he stepped
down, watching as she hurried. Watching longer than he
should have.

CHAPTER THIRTY-ONE
THE NEW BOYFRIEND

Sunday Evening, December 4

We had dinner at Boston's famous Durgin Park restaurant and got the normal verbal abuse that you could expect there. Richie gave it right back to our waitress, Kim. We all had the clam chowder (pronounced chowdah). Louise ordered a fish sandwich with fries—first time I had seen her do that. Richie and I had burgers —with fries too of course.

Richie complained about his fries, "These ain't done!"

"No?" Kim said. "How would you like 'em?" And she gave him the gesture. Richie grunted and shook his head. He loved it.

We were in bed as snow began to drift in over the Square. The temperature was dropping below 30. It was a good time for sleeping—and for other things. But Louise was already asleep. I woke several times thinking about Liu Xue, wondering what she was going to tell us, and yes, a little worried about how safe it was for her to meet us.

It was just after 7:00 a.m. when I woke. Louise was already up and out. She always jogs in the morning.

My cell rang. Jillie.

"So, how was it?" I asked, not really wanting to know. I picked my jeans off the dresser and pulled them on, holding the cell to my ear with my shoulder. She hesitated. "You liked him," I said.

Silence. "Maybe."

"So, tell me about it," I pushed on, wondering why I was doing that. See, the problem with Jillie and me was that we weren't having any problems—that is until the morning Maxie disappeared.

"He was very nice," Jillie said carefully. "We just talked... that's all..." and she let the silence hang for a while.

"I don't really want to talk about it," I said, getting angry inside. "I didn't like that guy then"—not wanting to say his name—"and I don't like him now." I was glad I said it.

"Sorry, Coop. I just thought I should tell you..."

"Because you were feeling guilty."

"I guess I still miss you," she said, almost in a whisper.

I didn't say anything. Not in a good mood.

"How's your case coming?" she asked.

"Slowly. We're still in Boston. Chinatown."

"Why Chinatown?"

"Somebody sacked my place and left a keepsake on my nightstand. An origami in the form of a lotus. A black lotus."

She gasped. "My God. Were you hurt?"

"No. But if I'm not careful someone might get hurt." She was quiet. "But not to worry, Richie is here with me." I didn't mention Louise and I have no idea why. Louise would not like that.

"Is your cop friend with you?" she said, coyly, referring, of course, to Louise. I hesitated.

"I mean Tony," she said, rescuing me. Tony DeFelice was my partner when I worked homicide in Miami for six years. He also likes Jillie. A lot. I think he hopes, consciously or unconsciously, we'll get back together again.

"Gotta run," I said quickly, as I heard Louise using the card to get back into our room.

She gave me a funny look when she came through the door. Was I that obvious?

"Jillie," I confessed. "She has a new boyfriend."

CHAPTER THIRTY-TWO
SNOW

Monday Morning, December 5

Richie, Louise and I were hanging out in the Copley bar waiting for Liu Xue when my cell went off. It was hard to hear what the caller was saying so I left the bar, Richie and Louise giving me the *What's up?* look. It was no wonder I couldn't hear, the voice was all whispers, like the wind trying to talk with me. But in a foreign language. I held the cell out in front of me to see who was calling. A Boston area code, but I didn't recognize the number. I put the phone back against my ear and said, *What?* for the third or fourth time. I had already dropped, *Excuse me?* And then it struck me. The caller was clearly a woman. Small voice. Frightened. Chinese.

Then I finally heard a weak, "Can we meet, Mr. Cooper?" It was hard to distinguish the voice from the wind that was hustling about me as I stood on the sidewalk, still wet from melting snow, outside the Copley.

"Liu Xue?"

"Yes," she said, quietly, so quietly I had to strain to hear her.

"Where are you?" I said.

"I am near your hotel," she said. "I take bus as I promised and no one following me...I think." There was fear in the air between us.

Not wanting to ask a young Chinese girl to come to my room, even if Louise was there, I suggested that we meet in the restaurant. I would find a quiet, dark corner. She said she would be there in a few minutes. I guessed she was calling from a building across the Square. I stayed outside the front doors of the hotel, the doorman asking if I needed help with a taxi. I waived him off and watched her cross, her shoulders hunched as if that would help conceal her, her eyes cast down to the street, looking up quickly now and then to make sure no cars were coming.

"Mr. Cooper!" she said, as though surprised to see me. I was waiting for her on the sidewalk outside the heavy glass doors fronting the Copley.

I nodded and took her arm, nodded to the doorman who held the doors for us, and headed for the Xhale—I assumed the name had something to do with Nathan Hale. The dining room was dark with chairs stained a glowing onyx. They were cushioned red and pushed up against round wooden tables that gleamed with glass tops. Padded benches, crimson, with a touch of purple bleeding through, were built into the walls on either side of the entrance. In a far corner a grand piano, its top catching and reflecting the sparse light cast by lamps that lined the walls on all sides, sat lonely, as though waiting for an audience. It was easy to get privacy. There was no one else in the restaurant.

My cell went off.

"Where are you?" Louise.

I told her and explained why I disappeared.

"No shit," she said. "You could have at least come back in and told me."

"Then Richie would have wanted to come." Liu Xue was watching me.

"Richie is out somewhere," she said.

"Why don't you join us in the restaurant. We're in the Xhale."

Liu Xue and I settled into one of the tables along the wall, a soft amber light against her face. She sat still, almost frozen, while I tried to flag a server. Then I focused on her and stared for probably too long. I was wondering what her name meant.

As if she could read my mind, she said, "My name, Xue, means *snow*. I am not like my twin sister. I am the soft one. I bring coolness to anger. It is my nature. And I see much anger and much danger here for you. I would like to help. And," she added looking around nervously, "I think my father is involved in your project."

Louise appeared at the hostess stand and right behind her was Richie. Interestingly Snow smiled when she saw Richie. Must be that Teddy Bear look of his.

Richie and Louise pulled out the remaining two chairs and looked expectantly at Snow and then over at me. I filled them in.

Richie cleared his throat. "How do you plan on helping us?" he said, shaking his jacket sleeves out so his cufflinks showed. She stared at him as he did this.

"Maybe more to the point," I said. "Why are you helping us?" and I watched her eyes as she considered my question. "Your father will be angry with you, no?" She nodded. "And your sister?" She nodded again. "Okay," I said. "What am I missing here?"

"Many things," she said, matter-of-factly. "First, you do not know Chinese ways. You come into our restaurant with no introduction and ask for information from my father. That's very bad manners. And you ask, of all things, about Tong. So, you embarrass my father again." She paused, thinking. Then, "My father is a powerful man in Chinatown. He runs Chinatown. Right now, he does not like you, Mr. Cooper. And my sister does not trust you." I was getting the idea. People didn't like me. So I nodded.

"But I trust you. You have a hard face. One that has seen much trouble. But your eyes are kind." I have dark hair and blue eyes. I think the blue is what did it for me.

"Because you make my father angry, he has called the Tong leaders in Chinatown and told them about you. He has also called Mr. Cleveland Wong, who you call your friend, and complained to him. And you clearly don't understand Tong," she said. "They are really part of CCBAs..." She looked at me and hesitated.

"The Chinese Consolidated Benevolent Associations," I said.

"Yes. Main job is to help Chinese families with English language and learn American cultures. So, Tong provide many services," and she paused again to see if I got it. She continued, "I know you see movies like *Black Rain* and Bruce Lee movies like *The Crow* about Chinese gangs. But that is extreme, Mr. Cooper. Like your *Godfather* movie."

"But *The Godfather* is about a real gang, Liu Xue. And I'm sure that many Tong follow the ways of secret societies in China and are connected to gangs."

Wong had already filled me in on the connection between the Chinese gangs in this country and the gangs in China. Most are organized under Triads—secret organizations which grew in China during the British occupation. They were considered a threat to the safety of the British government—which they were. Today they have spread worldwide with a structure similar to the mafia: soldiers, enforcers, and big bosses.

"No," insisted Snow. "Tong is not a gang. It started when our ancestors first came to United States to help with becoming part of American culture. Tong are not criminals, though some members did become criminal peoples. Real Chinese gangs are part of Triad, and they are in big cities, like New York and San Francisco—not here in Chinatown." She took a deep breath. "I hope you understand," she said, looking worried that I might not.

"I hear you," I said and her shoulders lost some of their slump. "But," I continued, "you still have not told us *why* you are willing to help when there is so much danger for you." I paused. "Nor *how* you would help," I added, looking at her sideways.

After several minutes of fidgeting with her hands and looking around at the empty room, she said, "Mr. Cooper. I think my friend is part of your problems."

"I see," I said. "My problems?"

She nodded. Eyes not cast down this time.

"Who is this friend?" said Louise, jumping in—softly.

Snow hesitated, looking around again. The emptiness of the restaurant seemed to press in on her.

"I think he *is* a gang member," she said, a small voice in such a large room.

"In the Tong?" I said. Surprised.

"No. Like I tell you Tong is not a gang," she insisted, impatient with me. Then she looked down. Embarrassed.

"Black Lotus Tong," she said finally. So quiet I had to strain to hear her.

"Black Lotus Tong?" Louise said, surprised and she looked over at me. "I thought the Black Lotus Tong was pure fiction."

"Yes. There are many fictional stories about Black Lotus. But they are a real gang."

"Does your father know?" I asked. Richie leaned in, his cuffs showing.

"No."

"But you said your father was involved with our project," I said.

"Only that he knows about the project in the Gulf. You see, Tong protect the *Zhi Zhu Nu*."

"What?" I said, leaning back. Then I realized how abrupt I sounded. "Sorry," I said. "Did you say they *protect* the oil rig?"

"Yes. You see, this is not unusual. As I tell you, their job is to protect Chinese interests everywhere," and she emphasized *everywhere*.

"And your friend?" said Richie, leaning in closer now. "What's his name?"

"His name Lei Sun," she said. "Lei Sun and my sister are very close. She is Black Lotus Tong Dragon."

"She's what?" I said. Again abrupt. Bad manners.

"Triads—biggest of Chinese gangs—have names for leaders. Head of gang is called Mountain Master—or Dragon Head. Li Lang is Dragon Head." She paused momentarily as if trying to decide to go further. Then, "And Lei Sun is Deputy Mountain Master," she added, now sitting up very straight as if to brace against my reaction.

This was wild. I didn't know how to respond.

"So..." she continued, trying nervously to fill the silence, "I know this is not good."

I couldn't have agreed more.

"How good a friend is he?" Louise asked, leaning over and taking her hand.

"He is *nanpengyou*," she said in a whisper, then noticed the confusion on my face.

"He is my man-friend," she explained quickly, a soft shade of pink rising in her cheeks. And she looked away, embarrassed. "Someday we will marry," she added, so quietly I had to lean in to hear and nodding as if to assure me all was fine. "But bigger problem," she said, her eyes carrying the warning, "Li Lang Zhu and Sun Lei left this morning for Florida. I think they will visit the *Zhi Zhu Nu*. Maybe."

CHAPTER THIRTY-FOUR
BACK TO MIAMI

Late Monday Afternoon, December 5

W e had just taken off from Logan International Airport on a non-stop to Miami and I was watching the Cape disappear in the cloud cover when Louise broke in.

"Black Lotus Tong. Who would've believed?"

Richie looked over. He was sitting in the seat directly across from Louise. "What the hell? Dragon Lady?"

"Uh-huh. Like a don, only female." I figured Richie would get the mafia analogy.

Richie turned away shaking his head. "Damn Chinese."

The stewardess brought our drink orders. Orange juice for me, cranberry/apple for Louise. Richie ordered a beer. *Crazy people*, was what I heard when he took his first sip. He didn't look over at me.

"So, what's the plan," said Louise, staring into her cranberry/apple juice.

"He don't have none," came the voice from across the aisle. Richie took another drink.

"Part of the answer is on the *Zhi Zhu Nu*. We have to find a way to board it," I said.

"It's in Cuban waters. And it's also a Chinese company. How do you plan to do that?" said Louise.

I didn't have an answer. So I shrugged.

"Part of your plan?" she said.

"Yeah," I said. "No-plan strategy."

The captain broke the silence by announcing we were approaching Miami International. Saved.

CHAPTER THIRTY-FIVE
THE NO-PLAN STRATEGY

Monday Night, Miami, December 5

Even though there's no winter in Miami, no snow on the baked tile roofs of homes in Coral Gables, no need for salt on the streets, there are still the Santas dressed in their red, heavy winter Santa-suits, white fur pulled up over their necks as though it were below zero, red-cheeked and laughing as though they were enjoying the heat in those clothes, and ringing bells outside the shops in the main lobby of the airport. It's Christmas and we'll make believe Santa is really going to drag all those toys down the chimneys of tropical homes that don't have chimneys. But who cares? It's the season.

My cell buzzed in my pocket. I had forgotten to turn the speaker back on when I powered it up again once we deplaned. I turned it back on. Richie and Louise were walking ahead of me but paused when the chimes played.

"Cooper?"

I recognized the voice. Cleveland Wong. He said my name like he wasn't happy.

I told him he had me.

"Listen," he said, in a way that reminded me of my first-grade teacher—a nun—when she was about to tell me what I had done wrong. "I completely understand your concern about what happened to you in the Florida Straits," he paused, "and what happened to you in your home. Reason I gave you Li Lung's name. But now—"

"Yeah?" I said, trying to interrupt the flow of what he was about to say.

"Now, I get phone calls from Mr. Lung, a personal friend of mine, that you are disrespecting him—"

"No way," I said. "I asked simple questions. No disrespect intended." I was confused about what I could possibly have done.

"His daughter...she met with you?"

"That's right."

"That's not good, Cooper. Breach of Chinese custom. You met with her and by doing that disrespected the father. He doesn't like you anyway, Cooper. He said you have a hard face. Not trustworthy. He thinks you are looking at him for your recent problems. And so..."

"He called you..."

"Yeah..."

"And...?"

"Some others did too. They all think you are fucking around in Chinatown business. Need to leave Chinatown alone now, Cooper. You are personally screwing things up." He hesitated. Then, after a momentary pause, he began again: "Also—"

"There's more?"

"Uh-huh. Someone from the Chinese Embassy called the State Department and complained that you are spying on them out in the Florida Straits. Cuban Embassy did the same thing. They are not happy either. Neither am I. You are in international waters out there. Did you cross into Cuban waters?"

"No, we did not. The rig is pushing the edge of the Cuban waters where it's currently located. All I did was put glasses on the boat. First thing I know, they're shooting at us. I'm not freaking happy about that either!" There was silence between us for a moment.

Then, "Okay, okay," he hurried, in rapid succession. "You freelance, Cooper—you break protocols because you're not military or police. But that has to stop."

Wong was referring to the time I had chased a ship some Russians had converted into a floating hospital. They were using it to surgically remove body parts from kidnapped women and children and sell them on the black market. Like running a parts store. I followed the ship into Cuban waters and ignored Coast Guard and Homeland Security warnings when I did it. Wong was still mad about that. I couldn't blame him.

"I'm just trying to find out who murdered my client's father." No apologies.

Wong was silent. Then, "What you need to do is back off. Right now. You're creating an incident for us with two countries."

"Where are you calling from?" It sounded like a wind tunnel.

"Helicopter. Just circling back to the Coast Guard Station."

I had an idea. "How about I get a lift from you and we visit the Chinese rig together." I spoke quickly before he could interrupt. "The boat that attacked us was in international waters. We were within our rights to be there. In my mind, the security of the United States was compromised by that action."

"No way," he said quickly. "That's a crazy idea!"

"Not crazy," I said. "Think about it. Headline: American

boaters attacked by a Chinese boat in the Florida Straits. Remember the Maine!"

"Okay, okay, that's pretty crazy, Cooper. That's not going to happen."

"Meet Ms. Cynthia Hayward, reporter for the *Miami Herald*. She reports first-hand experience with the incident. She was shot. Remember? And she's looking for a story."

A pause. "We would have to involve the Coast Guard," he said, quietly. I couldn't believe what I was hearing.

"Absolutely," I said, thinking of my old buddy, Captain Welder, charge officer for the Miami Coast Guard Station. He bailed me out of trouble two times already. He wouldn't be happy about my latest idea.

"I'll think about it," he said, and ended the call.

"Welder?" said Louise.

"Close. Wong," I said. Richie came closer. We were already in the main lobby of the airport. I nodded toward baggage. They followed as I talked.

"I think we're going for either a helicopter ride or a boat ride."

"Uh-huh. And where would that ride be taking us?" said Louise.

"To the *Zhi Zhu Nu*."

They were both silent for a moment.

"See. The no-strategy strategy's working already," I said.

CHAPTER THIRTY-SIX
THE VISITOR

Monday Night, December 5
Twenty Shopping Days before Christmas

We were back at my house in the Everglades by midnight. Richie took the guest bedroom.

"See you when the sun does," he said and closed his door. Then, "Target practice at 7:30 sharp," came through the door.

Louise threw her bags into my bedroom.

"Confident, aren't we?" I said.

"You better believe it. If you're good, I'll let you sleep with me."

"It's my house!" I protested.

"Finders keepers," she said. I loved her logic. She smiled as she said it. You've got to love her.

We closed the door and I turned to Louise. "Come here," I said, holding my arms out and moving toward her.

"You're so big and strong," she said.

I flexed my muscles. "Yep."

"Oh my," she said removing my leather jacket. "It's way too warm for that. And for this old tee shirt," and she took that off.

"My turn." I removed her blouse.

"Should I get my gun?" she said, blinking coyly and turning her face sidewise.

"You won't need it," I said. "I'm already turned on."

"Then maybe I need it," she said. "And maybe my badge too." She took off my belt.

I was sliding out of my pants when Richie started banging on the door.

"Hang on!" I said, and we both got dressed.

I opened it to see Richie in his jeans and a tee and holding his Browning 9 millimeter and the Mossberg. "Here," he said, pulling a Glock out of the back of his pants and handing it to me. "You get the Mossberg," he said to Louise. Then he nodded, "Let's go."

"What the hell's going on?" I said.

"Someone's in the back yard and it ain't Herman." Herman is the ten-foot gator that hangs out in the swamp behind my house.

We followed Richie to his room. Sure enough, you could make out the shape of someone lying in my hammock that's hung between two palms not far from the mangroves separating the house from the Great Swamp. I wondered if he knew about Herman. I heard a 'meow' at the front door and let Sammy in. He must have been hanging out with Herman.

"I'm gonna circle around. See who we got back there," whispered Richie.

"It's not like he thinks we don't know he's there," replied Louise quietly. "He's making it pretty obvious." She pulled away from the window. I had closed the bedroom door on the way in. So there was no light inside. The form didn't move.

Then I heard him. A familiar voice.

"I see you peekin' out that back window. Y'all ruined a good sleep," and Huck raised himself off the hammock and lowered his feet to the ground. "I got some news," he said, as he stretched his arms in the faint light of the moon. It was disappearing behind the cover of the night clouds.

"Idiot," said Richie banging angrily through the back door to the porch.

Louise just looked at me and shook her head. "Guys. You're all so weird."

So, the four of us pulled some chairs around a table on the back porch and sat as Huck readied himself as if he were going to reveal one of his stories from the Great Swamp.

"You asked me to check out the boat one more time, buckaroo," he began.

"Shit," said Richie, disgusted. "We on a cattle drive now?"

I shook my head. Huck irritates Richie. Deliberately, my guess. Huck ignored him, but Louise leaned in, giving him encouragement.

"The boat was still there. Crime tape all over it. Not to worry—I was careful." Richie snorted. Huck turned, annoyed this time. But he continued.

"Nothin' much really," and he hesitated like there was a 'but' there somewhere, "to the untrained eye," he added, raising his eyebrows as if there were something special about to come forth out of his mouth. "Except there was residue all over the bottom of that pony," he continued, looking over at me mysteriously.

"And...?" I said, getting impatient.

"Yeah, I found something..."

"Dammit, would you just say it!" said Richie.

"Now hold on there, amigo, I'm coming to it," he added quickly, hurt sounding in his voice. Then, "What I found didn't smell like no engine oil. Besides, the oil level was up on the Canyon. And no sign of a leak anywhere on the boat."

He paused momentarily, then continued: "If it wasn't engine oil, then maybe ..."

"Uh-huh," Louise said, "then maybe what?" Pressing.

He paused for effect.

"Maybe someone's drilling in the Happy Hunting Grounds."

PART TWO

THE BOY'S STORY

CHAPTER THIRTY-SEVEN
EIGHT YEARS LATER

I t was eight years—the Boy had counted them—since the men had brought him to his new home. The Man lived in the big house alone—except for a man-servant who seemed to double as a driver and a butler. He always wore black: black jacket and black pants, like a tuxedo. The manservant was always formal. Distant. And he had an accent, like the bad guys on X-Files.

One day the Boy spotted a gun in the man's jacket tucked under his arm. In a black holster. The Boy had watched detective shows with his dad on TCM. The cops and the bad-guys always wore guns like that. But he didn't know which one the manservant was—cop or bad guy. And the manservant always called him boy—never by his right name.

And it was this man—the manservant with the gun—who drove him everywhere, not that the Man who lived in the big house didn't want to drive him. He was "Just too busy," he always said. "My driver will take you wherever you want to go," he would explain.

Instead of going to a regular school, the Boy would go to a private home and get tutored, and the driver—the man with the gun—would always be with him—like a guard—so that the Boy wasn't sure if the man was really protecting him or if he was guarding him—to keep him from running away—or to watch him when he talked to people. And he rarely did that.

He never seemed to be alone—like normal kids—like back home. He was always with the man with the gun—except when he was in his room and playing with the games the Man had bought him when he got him the new computer.

The Man warned him not to go on the internet. He wouldn't give the Boy the password to get on the wireless— though the Boy tried to steal it. "Too dangerous for you," the Man said. "There are a lot of bad people on the internet. I promised your mom and dad that I would protect you from them."

And the Boy wondered why, if the Man was a friend...why had he never told him his name? He only knew him as Sir.

He liked the house, the island where the house was situated, the moss that hung on the oaks, how it felt so soft, even the odor that hung in the air, especially in the summer months, that smelled like rotten eggs or cabbage that had spoiled. He hated it at first. Then, he learned that the odor came from the paper mills nearby and that it resulted from the chemicals used to make pulp out of wood chips from which paper was made. He learned this from his tutor, a young woman from the local college. She was pretty. And the Boy liked her—a lot. After all he was fifteen years old now—just turned this past summer. And he still had the memories of summers in another home— far from where he was—and his mother and father—but he had trouble remembering what they looked like—no pictures—and the Man said he didn't have any pictures but he would try to find some somewhere—but he never did. Yet the Man did show him a letter from someone who said that his mother and father had died.

The Boy being older now had questioned the Man more and more about his parents: details about the accident, and things like when they had asked the Man to take him. And he wondered about his old home, his old town, his old school, his old yard where he played ball—he remembered them more vividly now—and he thought to himself, *Maybe I'll go back there sometime—maybe sometime soon.*

CHAPTER THIRTY-EIGHT
NO! NO! NO!

Early Tuesday Morning, December 6
We were all up early, Richie frying eggs and bacon, Louise, Huck, and I around the kitchen table, watching him flip the grease from the bacon over the eggs.

"Make mine over hard, amigo," said Huck.

Richie turned and shook his head.

My cell played out its tune again. Chimes. I thought about assigning rings to various people. An irritating one to Wong. Wong because that's who this call was from.

"Cooper?"

"Yeah?" Small talk.

"The answer is, no. No from me. No, from the Coast Guard. No, from everybody else. It was crazy for me to even consider it. I don't know why I did."

I didn't say anything for a moment. Then, "All right. So, no help."

"Not with any invasion force. And that means you don't go out there with your little band of commandos and attack a rig in foreign waters like you did that Russian boat. Is that clear?" That was a statement put like a question.

"Uh-huh," I said.

Silence. "Don't do it, Cooper. We've been through this before. You get into hot water this time, no one comes to rescue you." Silence. I could hear the anger.

"I got it," I insisted. "I got it." And I saw Richie, Huck and Louise looking at me puzzled, like *What's up?* I shook my head. The call was over.

"What was that all about?" said Louise.

"No deal on the free trip to the rig with the Coast Guard— or Homeland Security."

I stared at the table for a moment. The bacon smelled like it was burning.

"Shit," said Richie and hurried the bacon out of the pan onto a paper towel to soak up the grease. The eggs were already on four dishes. Then he turned to me. "So...?"

"So, we're on our own," I said.

"Meaning...?" said Louise.

"Meaning we're on our own," I said. "Detecting on the high seas. Hell, we can go where the Coast Guard can't. Wong knows that, so does the Coast Guard."

Nobody said anything. We had done this before. And I knew it was not only crazy but dangerous. But these days, I didn't give a damn. I hadn't found Maxie. And life was meaning a lot less to me the longer he was missing. So, the hell with it!

.

CHAPTER THIRTY-NINE
COOPER'S PLAN

"So, okay..." Louise started and there was doubt in her eyes as she studied me. I knew what she was thinking. Like she could read my mind. "Let's talk about this... plan..." she said, pausing and reaching for my hand. She could have said crazy plan. But she didn't. She continued, her mouth taking on a firmness she rarely shows, "Right now, you're upset. You're not going to make up for not finding Maxie by boarding an oil rig and getting us all killed."

"I've been dreaming about him," I said, quietly. I looked over and Richie had stopped cooking and was staring at me. So was Huck. Shit. Richie cleared his throat, embarrassed.

"We done everything we could. Hey, whaddya expect. We got nothin' to go on," said Richie. Trying to share the blame. "What?" he continued as I shook my head. "We had a lead on a gangbanger in Miami. That went nowheres. Some retard in Muskingum thinks he mighta seen the car. What the fuck you supposed to do with that?" Then he turned back to the bacon forked it harshly onto our plates to keep the eggs company and sat down.

"Every night. It's like I'm reliving his whole kidnapping," I continued. "I mean it's like I'm watching what's actually happening to him," and I could feel the whole nightmare and picture it all over again.

"I know," said Louise. And I stared at her.

"You talk in your sleep," she said. "And you've told me a little of this before."

"I talk in my sleep?" I had forgotten about telling her before.

Huck had a slice of bacon half in his mouth and stopped to listen, looking embarrassed.

Richie got up and pulled him away from the table. "Come on, bud." Mother Richie.

When Richie and Huck settled in the living room, Louise pulled my hands toward her. "Why don't you tell me about it."

So, I did—again, I guess: about the man pushing Maxie into the black sedan; about the two men in the front seat—and Maxie searching the road behind, looking for me. "It makes me sick to my stomach that I wasn't there—to help!" I told her. "I mean, what the hell is going on? It's crazy Stephen King stuff." I paused to catch myself. "Is this some kind of freaking revelation? I mean..."

Her grip was firm on my hands, like she was trying to hold me together.

And I wondered if I was having a kind of metaphysical experience, like one of Jung's so-called "mythic dreams" where the dreamer has a cosmic experience, tapping into what the psychologist would call the "collective unconscious." In this case into Maxie's thoughts, his lived experiences: you know, the kidnapping, the men, the house. Or was I just reliving my worst fears? Following Maxie in my imagination in a belated effort to save him? And I watched Louise—for her reactions. She looked sad as she ran her fingers across my face.

"It's all right," she said. "You've been carrying this around with you for a long time."

I nodded.

"You have to let it go and focus on the present. This plan to visit the Chinese oil rig is crazy," and she pulled her hands away.

"I know. But it's the only way."

"I'm in this with you, right?"

"Right."

"I say we don't do this thing."

"I'm in it more than you are. Got more years in," and I pointed to some gray I had found in my hair.

"I see one," and she pulled it out.

"Wow! That hurt, babe!"

"It's a love pull," she said.

CHAPTER FORTY
THE ALTERNATE PLAN

We were all back around my office desk—that would be my kitchen table, which serves as my dining room table, which serves as my office table, Richie and Huck looking at me.

"Change of plans," I said, and looked over at Louise who had folded her arms over her breasts, watching me.

"Uh-huh," said Richie. "And that would be?"

"We're going to drive out to the derrick at night and see what happens. Watch from a distance."

"We're going to do surveillance?" said Richie. I couldn't believe he got the word right.

"And if nothing transpires?" said Huck. My pals were showing their literacy. Huck actually has an excellent command of the English language. He pretends not to. An English major at the University of Miami. Got a master's degree and worked part time as a teacher on the Miccosukee Reservation. Still does.

"Then we think," I said.

"Like a fucking philosopher," Richie said.

"There are women present," I said.

"Who don't care," said Louise.

My cell went off again—a cricket sound. I had assigned an annoying ring tone for Wong.

"Cleveland," I said, sliding the bar to answer.

"That's right. You see the paper this morning?"

"No."

"Get a copy. Damn client of yours is all over Homeland Security. Didn't say anything about the Coast Guard."

"Lucky them," I said. "Cynthia is a reporter. I warned you."

"All right. You tell her we'll pay a visit. But you and your friends stay the hell away. You hear?"

"I can feel your anger," I said. Wong ended the call.

"What?" said Louise.

"Homeland Security is going to help. Without us. So…"

"So…?" said Richie.

"We're going to do some investigating," I said.

"Surveillance," Richie said.

"Uh-huh. We'll bring plenty of coffee."

"And donuts," said Richie.

"And some Captain Morgan," said Huck.

"All right. I can do this, Cooper. But surveillance is as far as it goes," Louise said.

"Absolutely," I said. "What do we do if they shoot at us?"

"Shoot back," she said. "Part of surveillance."

"Wow," I said. "Girls with Guns," and she smacked me on the arm.

CHAPTER FORTY-ONE
THE NIGHT WATCHMEN

We packed like we were going on a five-day camping trip, only on a boat instead of in a tent: cans of food, bacon, eggs, bread, and lunch meat for the sandwiches, along with pickles, mustard, mayo, beer, and wine. I threw in a bottle of. Captain Morgan for Huck and me.

We checked our guns and ammo. And I packed my night vision glasses: Armasight PVS Gen 2s. A military grade night vision goggle that can operate under zero light conditions. It would be useful in the event the moon went into hiding. I figured we would need to hang out about a half-mile from the rig, give or take, depending on the mood of the moon.

We had loaded the Volvo and were on the road to the Keys by nightfall, the moon hiding behind clouds. A good sign. By 9:00 p.m. we were pulling into the marina and heading for the boat. Huck was first on board and reached down for Louise. She was wearing khakis, her Glock strapped to her shoulder. Richie and I handed up the supplies, the guns and the ammo. Enough for a small invasion. The wind was picking up. I looked at Huck, our Native American weatherman.

"Feels like storm. Not big," said Huck, "but a storm for sure," and he put his finger in the air. "Coming from the east." I wondered if he was kidding with the finger. Can't tell. He's so straight. I don't remember him ever laughing.

I drove the boat over to the pump and filled up the tanks. Two hundred and three gallons—at 4.59 a gallon. You figure it out. I didn't want to read the numbers. My expenses were climbing.

We were in the channel leading to the Straits by 9:30 and in the open water and out of the No Wake zone by 9:45. The wind was pushing us toward the Pourtales Terrace, a platform of seabed that's about 180 meters below the surface. From there we would drive over the Pourtales Escarpment where the seabed descends slowly to a depth of 450 meters. Plenty of water to drown in. Richie knows all about it. He will be asking me about depths as we proceed, nervously watching the weather. He should have learned to swim. Water. His one fear, as I've said before.

Darkness took over the moon as the wind drove a cold spray over the gunnels. I was hoping to be in place—and no moon was ideal—before any kind of storm hit. We cleared the Escarpment around 10:30 p.m. and were heading west-southwest at about 30 knots and about 30 kilometers from the *Zhi Zhu Nu* when I cut back the motors. Tip-toe in.

The silence didn't last long. A noise—a low whine—coming from the northeast, from the Keys, and it came over the wind that had gathered force, and over the sound of the waves hitting the hull, and it was growing in intensity as it neared. I strained to see the source. But it was dark, the December Moon still in its hidey-hole behind the clouds. And the noise slowly became a roar, Richie now next to me—I could feel his shotgun nudge against my leg—and then Louise, leaning over the starboard gunnel, and Huck with her, staring into the same dark hole I was staring into. Then a faint light appeared, and I remembered that *we* were running dark, so I flipped on the lights just as a fast boat broke into view. And the moon slipped through the veil of clouds, throwing a path of silver across the water, and the fast boat skidded to our starboard side, missing us by maybe fifty feet. The men in the boat screamed at us as the fast boat slowed and crossed our bow. But their voices were lost in the noise. And then the boat turned, the prow high in the air as the driver opened up the inboards, and roared into the darkness.

"What the hell!" said Richie as he dropped the Mossberg to his side. He had raised it as the boat flew past us, blowing water over the deck—and us.

Our boat had swung around so the four of us were looking out over the Yamahas that were still purring in the water. The sound of the go-fast boat finally died in the distance. It was headed toward the oil rig.

"What was that about?" said Louise, staring into the darkness where the fast boat had disappeared.

"I don't know," I said. "A drug run? Only thing is their lights were on. Doesn't make sense."

"Want me to take the reins?" said Huck. The boat bounced as the wake from the fast boat washed against the Canyon.

The motors were still at idle as Huck swung the Canyon around, heading south-southwest once again. Then I sighted it, about fifteen minutes after the incident with the go-fast boat. I focused in with the Armasight. The powerful glasses brought the image of the rig into plain view, even with the moon in hiding. It sprawled over the water like a monstrous spider, towers rising from its back, belching light as a drill in the belly of the beast worked through the darkness punching a hole into the floor of the Straits and looking for a cache of oil where twenty billion gallons are supposed to lie. A river of oil, rolling somewhere down below. In Cuban waters. All being done with the help of China and Venezuela, no more than sixty miles from the U.S. mainland.

I handed the glasses to Louise. "The water under the rig is over a mile deep. And—believe it or not—from what I've read, the *Zhi Zhu Nu* can drill as deep as 49,000 feet—that's a little over nine miles."

"My God. How far down is the oil?" she said, her glasses still locked onto the giant rig.

"Three or four miles below the surface of the water—my guess." I paused. "I figure that's what they're doing now—trying to find out."

Huck cut the engines, and we rested in the now calm waters, waiting for something to happen. It was close to midnight, the sky completely black from storm clouds. No rain...yet. And we waited. At three o'clock I decided we should do something. The lights on the rig had been extinguished, only a few blinking on the top of the tower. I decided to take a closer look and motioned for Huck to bring us in. He brought the motors up to idle speed again and, between the drift of the water and the soft movement of the Yamahas, we soon closed in on one of the massive legs of the *Zhi Zhu Nu*. And there was the go-fast boat that nearly hit us, tied to a caged orange ladder that scaled the leg of the rig like a giant centipede writhing its way to the top,

CHAPTER FORTY-TWO
DID YOU EVER TRY
BOARDING AN OIL RIG?

Late Tuesday Night, December 6

Y ou know when you are doing something dumb, but you do it anyway. Why we persist when warning signs are there, I don't know. Well, that's what we did. Despite the fact that the go-fast boat was docked at the rig —the very boat that fired on us—the boat that probably reported the incident to those on board the rig—to the very people who might even now be waiting for us. Despite that, I told Richie and Huck and Louise that I was going to board the rig. And they all looked at me like this was not smart—more like crazy-dumb. But I eyed the ladder anyway.

Shortly after the Deepwater Horizon explosion, where eleven men were killed, engineers began to explore better ways of evacuating a rig—other than by helicopter which was the accepted method at the time. Helicopters can only carry three or four people at a time. And they don't land on rigs that explode. So... the ladder. And this ladder was built as an alternative to the helicopter and to jumping into the sea, some 70 to 100 feet below—depending on the rig.

The ladder I was contemplating climbing boasted several stops on the way—and that was a good thing. One was at a caged platform about twenty feet above me. There was another one about twenty feet above that one, and finally a larger platform that jutted to the right of the ladder and sat about fifteen feet below the gunnels of the rig. The final ladder dumped into what appeared to be a passageway that skirted a white structure. Maybe living quarters.

The only problem with climbing was meeting someone coming back down. But...

"Okay, I'm going up—alone," I insisted, as I saw the three of them start to object.

"What do you hope to accomplish?" asked Louise, showing irritation.

"I don't know," I said. And I really didn't. "Maybe find some crazy reason for why they're shooting at us. Who knows? Maybe they're running drugs out of this damn thing," and I was being facetious. But then, on second thought, crazier things have happened. "Anyway, I just want to have a look-see. Besides this rig is awfully quiet." And I wondered why. Something this costly—hundreds of millions of dollars—should be working 24/7.

"I'll signal when I get to the final platform if I want the rest of you to follow. But somebody has to stay with the boat," I added.

Water washed over the hull as a wave broke under the rig. A storm coming. It had been threatening all night, spitting rain intermittently, hanging out above the clouds, but there none-the-less.

"Me and Huck are going with you," Richie said. "No way you're going alone."

"Right. And I'm also going with you, bozos," Louise said. "This isn't a one-man show, Coop. We're in this together."

I couldn't believe what I was hearing. My friends in a full-scale revolt. *Mutiny on the Bounty.*

"Okay," I said, not really happy about the mutiny. "But somebody needs to stay with the boat," I told Louise.

"In case the bad guys pull a gun on you and you have to run," she said.

"Good point," said Richie, reaching for his shotgun and getting ready to mount the ladder.

"It's why I'm going," she continued.

"Listen, Lou..." Huck began.

"Lou?" said Louise, glaring at him. Huck looked down. "If someone needs to stay below, you stay." She pulled her Glock, ejected the magazine and checked the load. When she was satisfied, she slammed the magazine home and followed Richie up the ladder.

Huck shrugged. "Okay. I'm good with that." Then he turned to me. "I'll keep the motors at slow idle. Nobody's gonna hear this baby down here. She'll run quiet as a bobcat hunting a rabbit."

Climbing the damn thing was like working my way up one of those massive transmission towers that carry electric power cross-country. The ladder seemed to narrow as I worked my way up, and the top so far away.

After what seemed like a hike up Mount Everest, we were finally there, Richie struggling to pull himself over the gunnels and onto the passageway. He looked around quickly then reached to hoist Louise up. She slid easily off the ladder. I followed.

Off to my right and extending out over the water was a helicopter pad—empty. It was a half circle of deck and just large enough for an experienced pilot to land. God help anyone who tried to drop down in bad weather—like the kind that's threatening tonight.

There was no activity, and very little light, only the glow from the nightlights hanging off the towers, keeping the rig visible to air traffic or boats that might wander through a mist into the area. The lights threw a mysterious glow about the rig as they struggled to fight through the darkness. And it was quiet, except for the thrum of the giant drill that plunged from the top of the tower into the seabed below. It hummed while it worked, like thousands of bees swarming around a nest as it punched ever deeper into the bed of the Straits. And we kept pace with the thump, thump, thumping of the drill as we crept around the building into the heart of the rig, through a maze of I-beams supporting the tower housing the drill, and past the long tubes that held the drill extensions, and past the pipes, and around the cages for the machinery that drove the drill and housed the diesels that powered the rig, and the sound of the drill grew louder as we neared the tower, like a machine hungry for oil, a sound we couldn't hear when we were at the base of the ladder where the wash of waves against the legs of the rig drowned it out.

"So, what are we looking for?" whispered Louise as we huddled near the tower trying to stay out of the wind.

"Good question," I said. "See what they're hiding. I mean what's the deal with the fast boat? And why are they shooting at us?" I paused until a gust of wind died out. "Why don't we split up."

So that's what we did, Richie moving to the left around the tower and through the maze of pipes and metal beams, Louise and I to the right. I was hoping that the crew was asleep.

We hadn't gotten more than twenty yards from each other when I heard the sound of a chopper in the distance.

"Hey," I whispered as loudly as I could. "Come over here." Richie doubled back and we watched a light steadily grow larger. Then a powerful beam hit the rig, lighting it up like it was noon on a summer's day. The copter must have been still a quarter mile or so away.

"Let's get out of here," I said, leading the way quickly back around the passageway that skirted the white structure and back to the ladder that was just below the helicopter pad. Richie was first on the ladder, then Louise. I scrambled down right behind her, barely missing her hand

"Watch it!" she said, louder than I would have liked and just about the time I heard some hatches break open. I looked up but there was no one in the passageway above us. The lights from the copter finally found the landing pad, flooding the entire side of the rig, sweeping over us momentarily then zeroing in on the helipad. It circled the *Zhi Zhu Nu* then hovered and slowly descended. I grabbed my ball cap before the pressure from the blades blew it into the Gulf.

The copter hit the pad at a tilt at first, the blades coming dangerously close to the rig's bulkhead, then it straightened and came to a safe rest.

I had stopped on the first platform below the top of the ladder, hoping no one would spot me in the cage. Richie was still descending. Louise was waiting.

Two men had come down the passageway from the right side of the white structure and were waiting for the copter's blades to come to a complete stop. It never happened. So they stooped and moved slowly, keeping their heads well below the thresher above them.

A young Chinese woman in a black jump suit leaned out of the hatch and reached for the hands of one of the two men waiting. He lifted her away from the door and swung her down onto the deck.

"Li Lang," whispered Louise. "I would recognize that bitch anywhere." I was surprised. I never heard her use that expression before. She must have noticed. "She's a bitch—believe me!"

I nodded. Spider Woman.

And then a man jumped down. He was tall and lean, wearing khaki pants and a leather jacket. He was also Chinese.

I tried to listen to what the men said to the visitors, but their voices were muffled by the wind and the blades churning in it.

"My guess, Li Lang and Lei Sun just landed," I said, as we headed down the ladder, in the dark, in the wind, in the spattering of rain. A presage of the coming storm.

CHAPTER FORTY-THREE
JILLIE

Tuesday Night, December 6

It was late when her cell went off—after 11:00. Late calls made Jillie nervous. Someone died—maybe her mother who had been fighting breast cancer for the last four years—maybe her brother who disappeared from her life regularly and only showed up when he needed something—and he was older than she was. Yet she felt she had to take care of him. She looked at the number on the screen. She didn't recognize it.

"Yes?" she said, tentatively. *Why did she answer the damn thing?* she thought to herself. Well, because she thought it might be Cooper—hoping it might be him—with news about Maxie—about anything, she didn't care. She was still in love with him, she thought. Her friends all said, *You have to move on.* Her mother said that. Even her brother, and really just about everyone who knew her.

"It's Henry."

And before she could say anything, he continued, "Have

dinner with me." Just like that. No explanation of where he was. As though they had just seen each other last night.

"You in town again?"

"Right. Decided to stay. Tie up some loose ends."

"Oh," and she hesitated.

"Can't keep us apart," he added.

The last time had been good. A distraction from Cooper and Maxie—memories of college—a time when there was nothing to worry about except grades and where the next meal was coming from.

"How about tomorrow night?" he said, not giving her time to think. "I'm tied up with meetings during the day but am free after six." Silent then. Expectant.

She hesitated.

"Don't worry," he said. "No pressure."

"No... Not a problem," she said, trying to think. Then...*Oh what the heck*, she thought. *Why not?*

"Yes," she said. "I would love to." She thought she heard a sigh of relief, and smiled.

"Great!" he said. "How about the Worthington Inn at seven?"

"My favorite place," she said, and then began thinking about her times there with Coop and wondered why she had said that—to a man who was a rival many years ago.

CHAPTER FORTY-FOUR
RUN FOR YOUR LIFE

Early Wednesday Morning, December 7

When Huck started the Yamahas, they sounded like Niagara Falls dumping water. I could picture them: Li Lang, Lei Sun and others rushing to the side of the derrick to see what the hell was going on. Then Huck opened up the Yamahas and they blew the Canyon away from the rig and into the open water of the Straits.

I saw several men scramble for the ladder and just as quickly disappear into the darkness of the cage, but Huck had us almost a half-mile out to sea in minutes.

So we ran with the motors wide open—three Yamahas pushing us close to sixty miles an hour, the boat hitting every wave like a brick wall. And when the boat fell into the empty space after cresting on a wave, it slammed back into the water, like a hard landing in a parachute jump. I thought if I was ever going to have a concussion, it would be now. All the time Richie hung onto the gunnels as if they were his last connection to life.

I watched for the lights of the go-fast boat chasing us. But they never appeared. So, I told Huck to ease up. He backed the boat down and it slowed like a wild horse that had just been busted. Then the Canyon settled into a peaceful run. I asked Richie and Louise if they wanted a beer. And they said, *Sure!* So I went below and grabbed three Rolling Rocks and brought them topside.

"Where's mine?" said Huck.

"You're driving," I said, as I took a long drink.

CHAPTER FORTY-FIVE
BACK HOME

Wednesday Morning, December 7

S leep was something that was not happening these days. If it came, it was during the day. My nights were consumed by nightmares. And they were becoming more frequent. And my days? Well, I spend those chasing or being chased by bad guys, as happened this morning.

So all of us sacked out when we got back to my house, Richie and Huck in the guest bedroom, Louise and I in the so-called master bedroom which was no bigger than the guest room—but master sounded better.

We didn't sleep long. A couple of hours. Then I headed for the kitchen to make some coffee. Louise followed me. Richie and Huck had gone outside to check on Herman and to leave us alone. *The lovebirds*, I heard them say on the way out.

We stared at each other, and then at the wall, and then out the window, until we had no choice but to stare at each other again.

"I've been thinking," I said.

"Wow," she said. Always the kidder.

"Remember what Huck said he had found on the boat?"

"Some residue. Oil? Chemicals?"

"Right."

"So?"

"So we have to go where the oil leads us."

"Uh-huh. And..."

"The most likely place where Jack might have gone that's reachable would be Shark Island—he fishes there. But I can't figure out how oil—or chemicals—would get on his boat there."

Louise took a sip of coffee and stared off through the living room where the early morning sun was beginning to leak into the house.

"I guess that's what we're going to find out," she said. "You think he got shot there?"

"Maybe. Probably. Too hard to shoot him and drag his boat there."

"Maybe someone's drilling where they shouldn't be. Is that what you're thinking?"

"Maybe."

"So, shot him there, huh?" Like she was still thinking about the bullet holes in the hull.

"Uh-huh."

"You say that a lot."

"What?"

"Uh-huh," she said.

"Uh-Uh," I said, and leaned across and kissed her.

"What was that about?" she said.

"I just love your repartee," I said.

"I don't know French," she said.

"Neither do I," I said, and kissed her again. She kissed me back...hard...and we made our way to the bedroom and locked the door.

CHAPTER FORTY-SIX
BACK TO SHARK ISLAND

Wednesday Afternoon, December 7

The closest place for Jack to have come across drilling, except for the deep-water drilling in the Gulf, was in the Big Cypress where the Feds have allowed wells. There are about twelve in all in the Big Cypress, which is, by the way, part of the Everglades. Not part of the National Park, someone might add quickly. But hell, it's all the Everglades, the Big Swamp, the River of Grass which flows from Lake Okeechobee through south Florida until it reaches Alligator Alley which slows the flow, and then to the Tamiami Trail, which slows it again. Is that progress? Civilization chasing the tropics away, clearing the way for massive developments, outdoor malls, highways that are two, four, and six lanes—both ways—that connect the new communities, and bring hundreds of thousands of people to the southern tip of Florida, as well as culture, and education, and companies (Big Oil and Big Sugar), to a previously untouched area that a writer once described as a *land not fit for man nor beast,* but is now *civilized*—finally. And now that developers had cut large swathes of land from the

Great Swamp, it was time to begin to extract the minerals from it, and so the exploration for oil, and gas, in an ecosystem already damaged by Big Sugar and big developers, would continue the slow eradication of the Everglades and its reduction to a shadow of its original self.

When Richie and Huck came back, Louise and I were just coming out of the bedroom. Richie smiled.

"Did I interrupt?"

"Planning session," I said.

"Inna bedroom?" said Richie.

"Secret meeting. If I tell you, I will have to kill you."

"Ma won't like that," he threatened.

"I'll never tell her," I said.

Huck was staring and shook his head. "White man loco," said Huck.

Richie turned his back on Huck as he said it. Exercising patience.

Huck smiled. "So, what's the plan, Coop?"

"Louise and I are going to follow up your lead about the spillage you found in Shark River."

"Good thinking. Why don't we go with you—"

"I have an idea," I said. "We didn't come up with anything tangible in our aborted trip to the *Zhi Zhu Nu*."

Huck and Richie nodded. "Okay..." said Huck.

"So, I'm thinking you and Richie go back out to the big rig. See what you can stir up."

"Do surveillance," said Richie. He said it right and he loved it.

"That's right."

"We will be silent like *O-pa*, follow like *chen-te,* and watch like *ke-hay-ke,*" said Huck. I stared at him.

"The owl, the snake, and the hawk."

CHAPTER FORTY-SEVEN
SHARK ISLAND

And so, the four of us headed back to the marina, this time to gas up both of Jack's boats. I warned Richie and Huck about getting too close to the rig. They both nodded. Humoring me. Jack's 306 Canyon was back at the pier now. The repairs had been minimal—the bullet holes well above the water line. The only other damage was from being in the weather without maintenance for a few days.

"Hmmm," observed Louise, checking out the hull.

"Grady Whites don't sink," I said, but she still looked worried. "The Grady White Canyon is like the Boston Whalers. Holes don't sink them."

"Uh-huh," she replied, and looked at the skies where once again storm clouds were gathering. After all, this is Florida. And it rains here in the afternoon—even though it's not the rainy season. "How about we take the 376?" she said, looking over at Huck and Richie, knowing it was the bigger boat. They both shrugged, like no big deal. Macho.

We followed Richie and Huck out of Lake Largo—Huck behind the wheel—and into the waterway that leads to the Straits. When we finally broke out into open water, Huck steered directly south toward Cuba. We headed south-southwest along the Keys past Tavernier, past Plantation Key, and then toward Snake Key on Islamorada where the Snake Creek Marina is located and where there is a pass that leads from the Straits to Florida Bay.

We turned into the waterway and passed under the Overseas Highway. The marina was off to our left. I cut the motors to idle through the No-Wake zone. We finally broke into the open water of the Gulf of Mexico around 3:30 p.m. With the Yamahas wide open, it would be an easy one-hour drive even taking the long way, that is staying in the open waters of the Gulf and circling Cape Sable to avoid the coral reefs that lie close to Everglades National Park.

Louise served as navigator, spreading out the chart and checking our direction on the GPS. I aimed for Sable Key. There were relatively few islands between us and Sable Key, so I eased the throttle forward and we bounced over the waves at forty-five miles per hour.

"I'm going to need a dentist, Coop," Louise said, as we crested a large wave and came down hard on the water. "Whoa!" she said, and grabbed my arm, the maps sliding onto the deck. She wasn't laughing. So I throttled back to thirty-five miles per hour, the boat still bucking the water as the Canyon fought through waves kicked up by mid-afternoon winds. She gave me one of her *no-fun* looks and leaned over to retrieve the maps, shaking off water and arranging them back on the console.

"At least we're out of hurricane season," I said, looking up at some clouds that were gathering in the west, piled high like cushions on a bed. They were fluffy but not white, the edges grey but growing black as they climbed over the horizon.

Hurricane season officially ends on November 30. But tell that to the gods of the sea. The National Hurricane Center counted about twenty-two hurricanes or tropical storms on its official list that hit between 1851 to 2013 during the month of December, many of them in the early weeks of the month. There was an unnamed tropical storm as recently as December 5, 2013, and then there was Olga, a storm that developed in early December, 2007 and Epsilon, a Category 1 that hit in early December, 2005, one of the worst years in Florida's brutal hurricane history. Four major hurricanes making landfall in the Sunshine State that year. A killer season. So, yes, Virginia, there are hurricanes even at Christmas. Those bad boys come whenever they feel like it.

We were at Ponce de Leon Bay, the entryway to Shark River, by 4:30 p.m. No storm—so far—the sky still heavy with clouds as we entered the broad mouth of the River. I guided the boat toward the shore of Shark Island where we had docked only days ago. Great Tarpon fishing there.

The winter sun was warm as we dropped anchor. We went below to grab the sandwiches, drinks, and chips we had brought, settled into the soft captain's seats at the helm and listened to the water slapping against the boat as it rocked in the waves.

"Think we can drive the Canyon into the creek where we found Jack?" said Louise, breaking into the quiet.

"No. We'll need to anchor near the mouth of the creek and take the dinghy upstream just like we did last time. The Canyon has about a two-foot draw. That's too much for where we're going."

My cell went off.

"Cooper?" It was Cynthia.

Damn. Her ride. We had left it at the Marina. "Your Jeep..." I began.

"A friend picked it up." She sounded annoyed.

"You okay?"

"You abandoned me," she admonished.

"Hmmm," I said. "It seems you're back to your old self. Want to join us?" Kidding.

"Where is *us?*"

"*Us* is about to find out who killed Jack." I had seldom heard Cynthia call him father. It was always just Jack.

"I want to join *us*," she said. Enthusiastic.

"I was kidding, Cynthia. You must be still mending. The shoulder—"

"Is fine," she filled in quickly. I didn't believe her.

"We're anchored in Shark River. My plan is to go back to the scene and look for what Huck found—the residue on the water. I need to get it analyzed."

"What can I do to help?"

"Stir up the waters again."

Silence. "Uh-huh. And how would you like me to do that?" she said, sounding anxious to help.

"An article on drilling in the Everglades. You stirred up a bee's nest with that last series. I even got a call from Homeland. It keeps the pressure on," I added. No reply from Cynthia. "Are you still there?"

"Yeah. I was just thinking. There's a rig operating in the bay off Shark Island—about a mile out in the Gulf. You might want to check that out."

"We'll do that."

"I was thinking that maybe that's the one in the pictures we found," she added, like she was still thinking.

I nodded. She hung up—never seeing my nod.

～

When we dropped the dinghy into the water, my cell phone read 4:45. A short distance away near the shore, there was a splash. I searched the water. A tip of a gator's nose rested just above the surface, his eyes bulging, wide and dreamy, fixed in our direction. I kept the boat at a safe distance —in case the gator was hungry.

It only took ten minutes to get to the mouth of the stream where we had found Jack's boat. It was a twenty-minute slow ride from there, skirting the shallows, mangrove roots, and alligators stretched out on the banks, seemingly oblivious to everything around them. Except, if you looked closely, their eyes were alert. But it wasn't mating season so I wasn't worried. Attacks on humans are infrequent, but they do occur: to someone swimming in a lake or river alone; to a pet too close to a path. Some feed gators—*Here boy, come and get it.* Good way to lose an arm to 3,000 PSIs of jaw strength.

It was cool, this late afternoon, the sun lowering itself toward the Gulf. I watched the motor churn up a small wake and followed it to the shore. Maybe Jack did the same thing, his last trip up this stream.

CHAPTER FORTY-EIGHT
JILLIE AND HENRY

Wednesday Evening, December 7

Jillie was early at the Worthington Inn. It was dusk. The lamps that lined the street were beginning to awaken. The Inn looked even cozier than she had remembered—an old two-story Colonial with red-brick facing. It matched the architecture of this upscale Columbus suburb. The Inn fronted High Street, the main thoroughfare of historic Old Worthington, an *All-American City*, its streets lined with specialty shops and cafes; wreaths on doors and miniature firs in windows lit up for the holidays; and High Street overhung with white bulbs woven through pine. New England in the center of Ohio. She and Cooper had come here for every one of their anniversaries—all but the eighth.

What happened to us? Was it all Maxie? Or did we just fall out of love? she wondered. She hadn't been back since that time. As she pulled at the heavy entrance door, she wondered if she had made a mistake to meet Henry here.

Once inside, she was standing in a room that looked more like a parlor than a dining room. It was one of several restaurants in the Inn. This one was done in warm browns. Velvety crimson valences, asking to be felt, hung over tall grilled windows, their tops high up the walls and overlooking the town. Several of them faced trellises, green vines growing up the side of the building showing on the edges of the pane. Soft lighting gave warmth to the sandy brown walls. Complementing the whole scene were long, polished, dark wooden tables covered with light cream cloths; each table set with heavy linen napkins, dark red; and knives, forks and spoons, gleaming like real silver. Early American high-back chairs, enameled black against mahogany, were pulled slightly away from each table, as though they were waiting for guests to take their places.

She felt like turning and leaving...

"How many, ma'am?" The host said, a white shirt under a black jacket, menus in his hand. She mused at how much the Inn had remained the same,

"Just two of us," she replied, turning back to the room. "He'll be here shortly."

"Why don't I seat you while you're waiting," he suggested. "I'll have the waiter bring you something to drink," and he led her up a wide stairway, carpeted crimson, to a lounge where a fireplace burned the air, throwing an easy light into the room.

"It takes the chill out of December, doesn't it?" the *maître d'* observed as they walked.

So poetic, she thought. So much like the Worthington.

"Please," he said, guiding her past a bar adjacent to the fireplace, the wood of the bar, dark mahogany with a high gloss finish, reflecting the flames from the fire. He led her to a gathering of tables in the center of the room, small and round, with tablecloths of pure white. The chairs were more comfortable than those in the restaurant on the main floor—round backs with seats cushioned crimson.

Henry appeared at the entrance within minutes of Jillie being seated. He smiled as soon as he saw her, hurrying past the bar and over to her table.

"You look truly lovely!" he said, kissing her on the cheek. He placed a small gift in front of her. It was wrapped in ribbed linen paper and bound with a ribbon that shone like real gold. There was a bow on top almost as large as the package itself. She stared at it.

"What is this?" she said, smiling uncertainly. He motioned for her to open it.

She pulled at the ribbon, then carefully peeled away the paper.

She stared at it for a few moments. A ring. Gold with a green stone setting. Around the setting the word, Hoyas. The name of the Georgetown basketball team. She continued to stare for a few moments longer, then smiled.

"I love it," she said. He was relieved.

"Remember? It's the ring I gave you at a Georgetown tea."

She nodded. Henry was a little chubby then, a nerd. Medical school took most of his time. He was trim now, no stomach, the semblance of a beard between his chin and lower lip—it looked good on him—hair still brown, no gray, eyes still a clear blue, like the sky on a clear, sunny summer afternoon.

"You look good," she said. And then, after a silence, mused aloud, "Why didn't you ever marry?" Wondering why she was asking that question—was she becoming interested? And suddenly the waiter was there.

Henry gave him their drink orders: wine for her, a Grey Goose martini for him. Then they sat in silence for a while, Henry staring at a couple sitting near them, then...

"I did," he said quietly.

"Oh, I thought..."

"Yes, I said I wasn't married. It's a long story—"

"No, I..."

"It didn't last long. For another time, perhaps."

They waited for the drinks.

"One child," he finally added.

She nodded and didn't press him further. He looked at her.

"We have one," she said. And he seemed... something...surprised?

"I know," he said, finally. "Maxie." She looked at him, carefully, like *How would you know that?*

"It was on the news," he said.

Jillie dropped her head.

"I'm so sorry about what happened," he added, taking her hand. She let him.

"It's come between us. Cooper and me. And I just can't get past it. I don't think he can either." She couldn't look at him, making that confession like she did, to an almost stranger, even though they had been lovers at one time, but that was so long ago—was it fifteen years? Since Georgetown...since she first met Cooper...Henry making the introduction, of all things...and later she broke it off with Henry and started up with the philosopher, had long talks into the night about...what the hell was it about? Anything, and everything really. They just enjoyed each other so it didn't matter what they talked about, and they held hands and they made love, and drank wine, cheap wine, that's all they could afford, on a Fellow's salary of twelve thousand bucks. And then she got pregnant, and thank God they were both almost finished with their doctorates and Henry was angry about his friend betraying him, taking his girl, *my girl,* he had said, and he threatened Cooper, his friend, but Coop was bigger—and stronger—and she drifted off thinking about him and how they held hands, and how she and Henry never did, and the wine, and their talks into the early morning, and their kisses, and she could still feel him on her lips, even now...

"Jillian...?" Henry.

"I'm sorry." She shook off her thoughts and jumped into the conversation again. "Where are you living now?" she asked and felt uncomfortable with the artificiality of her questions.

"I have a practice in D.C." He studied her, as though analyzing her thoughts.

She felt it and shifted in her seat.

"But for dinner...?" Henry said, filling the silence.

"Oh, yes," Jillie replied opening the menu. "Do you have a suggestion," she asked quickly, just as the waiter came.

"Are you ready?" the waiter asked. The waiter was in black, tall and thin, with a mustache, neatly trimmed, and resembling Christian Bale—Jillie told him so, Henry not looking up from the menu.

"How is your Pan-Roasted Duck this evening?" she asked.

The waiter said it was extraordinary and that she should try it. "And it comes with multi-grain risotto, sautéed Brussels sprouts, butternut squash and a blood-orange, pine nut *agrodolce* sauce," he added. Then he turned to Henry.

"Is your salmon wild?" Henry asked.

"Yes, sir," he replied quickly, almost defensively.

"Good," said Henry. "Then I'll have the Scottish Salmon."

"An excellent choice. And that comes with sticky rice cake, sautéed Swiss chard, *Yuzukosho* butter, golden beets, and cucumber." *Hmmm*, thought Henry, *probably anything I choose this guy will say was excellent.*

Henry nodded. "And what pinot noir would you recommend to go with the duck?"

"I would suggest the Clos LaChance Santa Cruz Mountains," he said. "I believe we have the 2006. But I will check."

"Excellent," said Henry, and then he turned back to Jillie.

"I'm so happy you could get away. And what a great place this is," he said, looking around and admiring the decor of the dining room. The light emanating from the fireplace accentuated the richness of the colors: the draperies, a dusty crimson; the rail topping the bar, bright gold and showing off; and the polished browns of the bar and the chairs.

There were only a few other diners. It was like Henry had reserved the entire room just for them. And so the evening was theirs, the first for Jillie since she and Cooper separated—she just couldn't do it—put their marriage aside, that is. And so she enjoyed the dinner, playing with it at times, Henry watching her. *Are You okay?* from him several times. But the duck was as good as she ever remembered, and the wine was exquisite, and Henry was so attentive. And they talked—Jillie mostly interviewing—she felt more at ease that way—occasionally disappearing into her thoughts, and Henry bringing her back. And they held hands and smiled over their wine glasses. And finally, Jillie relaxed, Henry leaning back against his chair and saying he was so happy that she was finally getting out—especially because it was with him.

And so the evening went like that until it got late and Jillie felt it was time for her to leave—and so she told him that. And he said, *No problem, I understand. A first evening of many*, he promised, then he rose and took her back to her car. It was snowing now, soft and dry. And they kissed in the dark, in the cold, but it didn't seem so cold to either one of them. He kissed her hard and he held her and told her how much he had missed her and could they meet again? And she said, maybe...she didn't know if she wanted to, really. And he held her for a few moments longer, under the lights of High Street, in front of the Inn where she and Coop had celebrated anniversaries, and made love—*Why am I here with Henry?* she wondered.

Henry held the car door for her, held her eyes momentarily, then waved as she pulled away. Jillie headed back to Muskingum, to her home on the college campus, with the lawn that sloped toward the road, where Maxie used to toss his baseball and wait for his dad, and she parked near the porch, where she had leaned out that autumn morning and called for Maxie—who never came—and where she called Cooper and told him—she was so scared—that she couldn't find their son. And what ruined her mind that day was that she really felt like *she* had lost him—that it was all her fault—and that was the beginning of the end as far as she was concerned.

She cried as she stood on the porch. And then she opened the screen and entered the dark house, thinking she might have to call Coop.

CHAPTER FORTY-NINE
RICHIE AND HUCK

Early Evening, Wednesday, December 7

They had made good time in Jack's boat, breaking through the water at thirty-five miles per hour, sometimes even hitting forty. To Richie it could have been 100. *Damn idiot...almost ran us into a battleship,* he had said when Huck had steered them out of the way of an oil tanker heading for the Atlantic. Richie was never happy on the water. And for good reason, as I've told you.

"I need a fucking jacket!" he said, holding on to the rail along the gunnels as waves splashed over the bow. The nights were chilly now—on the water—in December. Even in Florida. Huck had warned of a cold front before they left the marina, but Richie had said, *What the fuck is a cold front? Can't be any worse than Cleveland.* Huck just shrugged, like *Don't say I didn't tell you, city boy.*

Richie had gone below and gotten a blanket and was now pulling it around his shoulders. "This is supposed to be Florida!" he said, as he stared through the windshield of the Canyon. "At least this thing's got a warm bed downstairs—"

"Below," corrected Huck, focusing on the sea tossing waves over the deck. He was fighting to keep her steady.

"How much longer?"

"Maybe a half hour," said Huck. "Why don't you go below. I got this bronco under control." He swung a light over the sea ahead, the beam hitting the blackness like the high beams of a car on a deserted highway. Nothing anywhere except waves beating at them and a black sky.

"Might be a storm comin', *amigo*," said Huck, looking up at the blackness.

Richie looked worried.

They were within sight of the rig, maybe within twenty minutes, the lights from the *Zhi Zhu Nu* dim in the distance—no competition from stars. They were hiding.

"I'm gonna rein it in," said Huck, and he cut the motors to a low idle, letting the boat drift with the motion of the water.

After about a half hour of staring at the rig, Richie moved out from the helm and leaned over the gunnels. He pulled a pair of binoculars up to his eyes—the ones that Jack had stored in the cabin.

"Not a fucking thing moving. Whaddya wanna do?" Richie complained, still staring through the binoculars.

"You hear that?" said Huck, silencing the Yamahas and ignoring Richie's question.

They both leaned into the sound. A slight murmur at first, a susurration, then a more distinct whine, and they stared off in the direction of the noise, riveted by it, turning into it, trying to make out what it was. The sound was like a swarm of bumble bees, then a steady, pulsing vibration that ran through the Canyon, a thirty-foot boat that doesn't disturb easily, and the vibration turned into a beat, then into a rumble, and then a roar, and with the roar, a fast boat, running straight at them...

"Jeez," said Richie. "What the hell is that?" as he stared at the lights rushing toward them.

As Huck revved the motors, the Yamahas tossed water a good ten feet high over the stern, the approaching boat now almost on top of them.

"Damn," yelled Huck as he swung to the starboard side to avoid a collision. "Hang on, buckaroo," and they bounced over the waves like cowboys on a wild horse.

Someone from the fast boat fired at them as Huck veered away and headed for open water. If there were more shots, they were lost in the wind and in the scream of the motors.

"What the hell?" said Richie, reaching for his gun beneath the wheel.

CHAPTER FIFTY
THE BOY AND THE MAN

The Man was back and the Boy, who was now fifteen, was growing to dislike him more and more. First, he was, in reality, a prisoner in the Man's house. For almost eight years now. And home-schooled. He knew that he should be in a regular school—so he could meet other kids—maybe some girls. He had seen what that would be like on television—when he was able to watch it—mostly when the Man wasn't home. And sometimes he had tried to leave the house, but he didn't know where to go and when he did get away, either the Man or his bodyguard found him—on the road, or at a gas station—because really, if you think about it, he didn't have any money, or any plastic to charge things—he had thought about that—and he didn't have any parents—they were both dead. He didn't know about uncles or aunts, or cousins, or grandparents. He wondered about the grandparents and had asked the Man about them, but the Man wouldn't talk about any of those things.

And he frequently asked the Man what he did—for a living —and the Man said he had a consulting business, and not to worry, he made plenty of money to support them both, and the housekeeper, and the goon, who looked like the Asp in *Little Orphan Annie*. And the boy thought the Man kind of looked like Daddy Warbucks in *Little Orphan Annie*.

"Don't you ever...try...to leave again!" the Man had said, after one of his escapades on the road. "Your parents have entrusted you to me and I take my job seriously!" The Boy thought he might hit him, or turn him into the police—as a runaway—he had said that once. So he didn't try again, nor did he even think of it again after that—until just a few weeks ago when the Man said he was going away on a trip—for two weeks. Then the Boy thought about running.

Again.

This time for good.

CHAPTER FIFTY-ONE
HUCK AND RICHIE

"Hang on," yelled Huck and pushed the throttle forward, aiming the Canyon at the fast boat only a hundred yards away.

Richie ducked as shells peppered the water, missing them and the boat, then he leaned over the gunnels and fired as Huck veered only yards away from the shooters, throwing a wake that almost swamped them.

"Take the wheel," said Huck. He moved quickly below, grabbed his alligator gun, took the ladder back to the deck in one leap, and fired at the fast boat as Richie pulled away. "I'm gonna sink that boy before he gets his senses back and tries to follow," and he fired four more rounds as the boat roared away.

"Let's get us the hell out of here before they come back," yelled Richie, handing the wheel back to Huck.

Huck opened the throttle and the Canyon tore through the Straits, the prow rising and falling as it beat through waves, slamming hard as it fell from a swell, rising to meet the next wave. The pounding went on like that for what must have seemed an eternity to Richie who hung onto his seat like it was the coming of the Savior.

Finally, Huck eased up on the throttle and looked behind them. Nothing but sea and a path of light thrown across the water by the moon.

"I'm guessing that was the same boat that fired on us before," said Huck, checking out Richie who was stretched out on the seat behind him like a landed fish.

"That was a go-fast boat," continued Huck, his eyes on the expanse of black sea in front of him. "Can reach 100 miles per hour, easy. They're mostly used for running drugs in and out of the Everglades." Then, "My daddy used to see them down by Chokoloskee—I seen a couple myself few months ago—"

"Why the hell didn't you tell anyone?" said Richie, sitting up.

"Hear how quiet it is in the Big Swamp at night, city boy?" Huck said, looking sideways at Richie for a reaction.

"You tell me," said Richie, working to keep his temper.

"That's the quiet you get when you have information. You talk. You get your tongue cut out—or someone takes you out into the swamp and feeds you to the alligators. Then I catch the gator and find you in its stomach."

Richie rested his chin against his fist. Thinking it over, maybe.

Huck continued, "Take Everglades City. It's a quiet city." He paused. "You talk, you're off the Res."

They rode in silence for a while—just like in the Big Swamp. The only sound, the steady push of the Yamahas against the water.

"So, you think those guys are running drugs?" mused Richie, staring into the darkness.

"Yeah. Maybe. And maybe the rig is the home of their Big Chief."

CHAPTER FIFTY-TWO
THE MYSTERIOUS SUBSTANCE

Late Afternoon, Wednesday, December 7

We were at the spot where we found Jack's boat, the branches still broken where the boat had beaten back the mangroves. The yellow tape was still there, stretched awkwardly between whatever it could catch. Who they were trying to keep out? Gators? Pythons? Panthers? There were few bugs to bother us this time of year. In the summer they will eat you alive.

"Over there," said Louise, pointing to a stain on the water off to starboard, about twenty feet from Jack's boat. It winked at us as the late rays of the sun caught it. We pushed over to it carefully. I dipped my finger into the water. An oily-like substance, just like Huck had said. I stared at it for a few moments then looked at Louise who was staring at the residue also.

"Engine oil?"

I put my finger to her nose.

"Ugh! What the hell is that?" she said, backing away and pushing my finger to the side.

I had brought along an evidence jar I had kept from the time I worked homicide. I scooped the surface of the gooey stuff into the container, trying to get as big a sample as I could, sealed it, and wiped the outside of the jar on my jeans.

"Eeeuuu! Why would you do that?"

I shrugged. "It works."

"Right. And I get to smell you all the way back. You're going to shower on the boat, sunshine."

A tremor shook the water as she was talking. "You listening to me?" she said.

"You feel that?" I said.

She looked puzzled. "No. What?"

"That," I said. "The noise." And I put my head down to the water. A thud, dull, barely discernible, but I was hearing it regularly now. "Listen," I said, my head almost touching the water, soft and calm in the late afternoon.

She strained, then leaned down next to me so that we both had our ears close to the water. I splashed a little of the gunk on her arm.

"Yuck!" she cried. "Don't get that fricking crap on me!"

"Listen," I said, wondering if I was imagining it. She listened.

A hum and thump. Hum and thump. Regular, soft, dull, as though coming from far away. But consistent and regular. Hum, thump. Hum, thump. Hum, thump.

"That's the damnedest thing," I said, more to myself than to Louise. I could feel the heat from her body as she leaned further out over the water to listen. I brushed against her breast as I did the same.

"Save that for later," she said.

"All work and no play..." I said.

"Makes for a good boy," she finished, and placed her hand against the surface of the river, avoiding the goo that slid along its top. "I can feel it," and she motioned for me to do the same.

"Yeah," I said. "Definitely. Something's disturbing the water." *As if a gator—or a bunch of them—were beating their tails, way upriver,* I thought.

"If you look carefully, you can see a few ripples," I said, pointing to a slight movement in the water. Almost like the tide moving in. And it stirred the gunk, and the gunk moved with the sound.

Hum, thump. Hum, thump. Hum, thump.

CHAPTER FIFTY-THREE
ANOTHER RIG... THIS TIME...

"I wonder what's going on down there," Louise muttered, looking into the blackness below. "We've either discovered the Loch Ness monster or the Creature from the Black Lagoon," and she looked downstream as though one of them might be sloshing toward us.

"Let's get the hell out of here," she said, and cranked up the motor.

We slid out of the narrow waterway and back into Shark River. We loaded the dinghy back onto the Canyon and headed for Ponce de Leon Bay and the Gulf of Mexico. Louise was driving and she was racing with the oncoming darkness and with a storm that was brewing out at sea. The sun was hovering over the horizon and sinking rapidly as we drove through the bay and into the waters of the Gulf of Mexico.

"I never noticed that before," I said, pointing to what looked like the tip of the Eiffel Tower far out in the Gulf— maybe two or three miles away. "An oil rig?" I wondered if it was the one Jack had taken shots of.

"I don't think the Feds allow drilling in this close."

"It's clear of the boundary line of Everglades National Park. If that's a rig..."

"There's a company that purchased the rights to drill offshore decades ago. But I think the Florida Legislature shut them down," she said.

"Yeah, but I think the President opened that door again." I began to wonder just how open that door was. The thumping, the substance we had just sampled, Jack's killing not too far from here.

"We should check it out. Another time," she added quickly and steered the boat for home.

Lightning broke over the Gulf then the distant sound of thunder seconds later. The gods were at work already. I took the wheel. Louise doesn't like to drive in the rain.

We hurried through rough water as the wind out front of the storm stirred up waves. I fought off the spray and pushed the Yamahas as hard as I dared. No rain as yet but the sky grew as dark as midnight.

"Think we'll beat it home?" asked Louise. I was busy skirting the crab traps and coral reefs off port.

"Probably not." I could see the outline of Cape Sable. A few lights gave away its location. That's a little less than two hours from the Pilot House—in good conditions.

She leaned against me, finding shelter against the spray and the beginnings of rain. It took us over an hour to slog our way through choppy water. I stayed well off-shore trying to avoid the myriad of crab traps that lie in wait in the waters off Cape Sable. They would eat the Canyon's motors. By early evening, we had cleared the Cape and crossed the imaginary line that separates the Gulf of Mexico from Florida Bay. Once we were free of the traps, I pushed the throttle forward, skirted Club Key and Triplet Keys, and then headed across the bay toward

Islamorada and Snake Key. The storm still had not hit us. It was beginning to look like it would pass over. Louise took the wheel. I went below to get us some coffee.

The storm never developed and the moon was visible once again. It hung low in the sky as we passed Snake Key Marina, a few lonely lights backlighting piers where boats were tied down. Nobody else on the water. Only crazy people are out late on the water.

"We're almost there," said Louise, leaning against the wheel, sounding tired.

"I'll take over." I put my arm around her, pulling her in close. "You're cold!"

She was shivering as though she were fighting off the cold. Her sweater and jeans were wet from the spray.

"You need to go below and get out of these clothes. They're soaked!"

"Should have brought a windbreaker." She held onto me tightly as we bounced over some suddenly harsh water.

"There's one below—in the closet near the bunks. And change into something dry while you're down there."

She ducked through the hatch and appeared minutes later with a jacket pulled up over her ears. "The Hurricanes," she said, turning so I could see the green and orange 'U' of the University of Miami on the back.

"You a fan girl?" I said.

"Nope, but it keeps me warm."

"I hope you changed."

"Nope, again. Still the same sweet girl." She smiled—wickedly—and bumped against me.

"Uh-oh," I said.

"You better believe it, dick," she said.

"Private Investigator," I corrected, and bumped her back.

She stayed with me looking out over the shore as we passed Plantation Key where lights from several hotels were visible, and then Tavernier. Key Largo was only a few kilometers away.

"I wonder if Richie and Huck are back?" she said.

CHAPTER FIFTY-FOUR
BACK HOME

Early Thursday Morning, December 8

We pulled into the dock at the Pilot House Marina a little after midnight. I called Richie—not expecting him to have service in the Straits.

He answered immediately. "Where are you guys?"

I told him.

"You missed it, bud," he said, sounding angry, out of breath. "Damn guys shot at us. Same boat!" He was breathing hard.

"Where are you?"

Silence. I figured he was talking to Huck. Then, "The cowboy says an hour away. Where are you?

"Waiting on the dock. You'll tell us the whole story when you get here."

"Yeah," he said, and signed off.

"What?" said Louise as I ended the call.

"Apparently, Richie and Huck ran into trouble. And he's mad."

Louise nodded. "Of course. They okay?"

"I guess," I said. "We'll see."

~

We cleaned up the Canyon while we waited. I washed down the hull, deck, and console, Louise worked on the cabin. When I finished clearing salt off the boat, I went below to give Louise a hand. She was stooped over the fridge and pulling out some drinks. She had read my mind. She handed me an opened bottle of Chardonnay and pulled out a couple of Sam Adams for herself.

We took the drinks topside and settled in the forward lounge. Soft leather seats there, wide enough for three or four people. That's the Grady White 376 for you. So we talked about what we had found and what it might mean, and drank. Louise went below for more beer. Pretty soon the motion of the boat and the drinks rocked us to sleep.

Someone shook me. "Hey, love birds! You guys drink all the beer?"

I rubbed my eyes and tried to focus on who it was. "Richie?" I said.

He was standing over us. My wine glass was empty. That's because it had spilled and my jeans had soaked it up. Empty bottles were lying on the deck.

"What time is it?" I said, looking around like there was a clock nearby.

"Time to rise," said Huck. "Breakfast is a-calling, ladies and gents."

I slid off the lounge and steadied myself, trying to shake off the drowsiness that came from too little sleep and too much wine.

"So, what happened?" I said, as I struggled to step off the boat.

"Same damn go-fast boat," said Huck, running a hand through his wet hair. "I'd love to feed them boys to some gators." And I didn't think for a minute he wouldn't, given the chance. He's done it before. That's justice in the Everglades.

"And no doubt, same bozos who shot at us yesterday," said Richie, shaking his head, disgusted. "What the hell. We get close to that damn rig and somebody shoots at us."

"Let's head to my place where we can get a drink," I said. "It'll be easier to talk there."

Richie grunted an approval.

We cleaned up the 306 and checked the lines on both boats to make sure they were secure. Hurricane season might be over but storms blow up all the time in the Gulf.

Then we headed for the parking lot.

~

The sun was starting to break through the clouds when we pulled onto Midnight Drive. Another long night. And we looked like it. Lucky nobody was at my house to see us when I pulled in—except...

Sammy who was sitting on the porch like a ceramic cat in a china shop, his eyes fixed on us. "Look at that guy! Should put him on TV—damn cat's got ESP," Richie said, his palms turned up like *I don't believe this.*

I'm convinced Sammy does, in fact, have ESP, that it's built into his DNA and informs him of my comings and goings. Either that or my secretary—whom I haven't hired yet—calls and tells him I'm on my way and better clean up. Anyway, he's always there—on the porch—waiting, when I get back from wherever I am. I stood there watching Sammy's routine as he carefully stepped down each of the three steps from the porch, made his way circuitously toward me—stopping momentarily when Richie piled out of the back of the Volvo, slamming the door—and rubbed against my leg. That meant food.

Louise, who has known Sammy now for over a year, jumped in. "Let me," she said, and climbed the steps. Sammy circled slowly behind her, as she headed for the fridge where I usually have an opened can of Friskies.

"Where do you keep the cans?" Louise called from the kitchen.

"In the cabinet near the fridge," I yelled back, looking over at Richie who was glaring at me.

"She don't know where you keep the cat food?" he complained. He could have said, *What kind of a girlfriend don't know where the cat food is?* Because Richie does know: on the second shelf from the bottom of the pantry. And Richie, shaking his head in disgust (because, really, he wanted to feed Sammy), headed back to the Volvo to help Huck unload our gear. I grabbed the bottle of gunk we had gathered from Shark River, brought it into the house, and laid it on the kitchen table.

Louise gave me a look.

"You don't know what kind of crud that is, and you're going to lay it on the table?" she protested, shaking her head. "Where we eat?"

Louise dug out a spoonful of tuna and placed it in Sammy's special bowl. "At least I know what this is," she said, continuing her complaint.

"Good point." And I carried the mysterious substance to the back porch and placed it on a table there where we could pore over the contents—talk about them really. No one was going to open the jar and take the chance. You know—maybe Kryptonite.

Then everybody joined me in staring at the jar—even Sammy. After a few moments Richie and Huck continued their story.

"Fuckin' Chinese almost ran us down. So, this cowboy throws the boat into high gear—last minute—and they just miss us," he said, nodding at Huck who was staring at the ceiling.

"Boat stopped about fifty feet from us, city boy," Huck said, leveling his gaze at Richie.

"What did the boat look like?" I said, ignoring their crap.

"It was dark. But it was a go-fast boat," Huck said. "Inboard motors, long and shiny-like. You know, same as the ones I told you about in Chokoloskee," and he waited for me to react. "The kidnappers...the ones we tracked through the Everglades," he explained.

I nodded.

In a prior case Huck had spotted several go-fast boats at a dock near the Smallwood Museum on Chokoloskee Bay, south of Everglades City. We traced those boats to smugglers who were running a sex-trade business from a house in Chokoloskee where they shipped their victims out to clients in South and Central America. They used the go-fast boats. And from there, God only knows where the kids went: Europe? The Middle East?

"So where was the boat coming from?" I said.

"From the north," Huck said. "Maybe making deliveries for the Big Chief. I'm thinking drug runners. I mean who else is out when the wolf howls?"

"Why don't you talk English," grumbled Richie. "But he's right about one thing," he added, nodding at Huck, "they didn't shoot at us because we were trespassing. They got something to protect—"

"I bet that's what got ol' Jacko shot," finished Huck.

So we sat in silence around the table on the porch, watching the sun push toward the west over the mangroves. It was a long night and Louise suggested we take a break.

"I got to get some sleep," she said, and headed for the bedroom.

I didn't particularly care what Huck and Richie did. They could stay on the porch and keep Sammy and Herman company for all I cared. I was just a few minutes behind Louise in falling on the bed and crashing.

CHAPTER FIFTY-FIVE
HENRY AND JILLIE

"Hi Jillian, it's Henry." The voice firm, yet casual, like they talked together all the time. But it'd only been a week or so since they began seeing each other. But what the heck, she thought, Coop is seeing someone—a cop, and she was sure they were sleeping together. So, she was lonely, missed the feel of a man, the smell. Coop was perfect—if they could manage not to hurt each other. But every time she saw him, she was reminded of Maxie. They looked so much alike, so much so it made her stomach hurt, and then she hurt for Maxie, and saw his face, that beautiful face, every day, in her thoughts, in her dreams, in every young boy she saw on the streets.

She had made a mistake several times, thinking that she saw him, and she would run up behind him—but it was not him. She remembered the embarrassment. The boy's mother would be startled, looking at Jillie like, *What are you doing?* But the mother obviously didn't know what it was like to lose a child—or to lose a husband, for that matter, because of the child—because if she did, she would understand a mother thinking she had found her child, she would understand if it had happened to *her,* and she would have hugged the mother instead of giving her odd looks—like she was crazy—*and maybe I am,* she thought.

"Jillian?" The voice.

"I'm here," she said quickly, wondering how long she had been drifting. She was doing a lot of that lately. And she kind of liked how he called her by her full name, Jillian.

"Great. I hope you enjoyed our time together last night."

"I did," Jillie said, and she really did. It was her first time out since she and Coop had broken up, and she had really enjoyed it. Henry. The Inn. The wine. The...

"What's your weekend like?" he said, breaking into her thoughts. Then, in a hurry as if to cut off any objections, "I've got some plans I think you'll love."

"Oh?" she replied, open to hearing. Why not? She dismissed thoughts of Cooper that crept in to talk her out of it. *No,* she thought. *No. This is my time.*

"Are you free?"

"Yes," she said quickly, not wanting to ask what he had in mind, willing to go along—anxious to get out—even forgetting to ask what day or what time.

"I thought you might enjoy visiting the Cleveland Museum of Art. It would be a nice drive—weather is supposed to be good —cold, but no snow. And if it does snow, I hear that the new Atrium looks magical." And he paused, hope riding on his words. Jillie could hear it.

She didn't pause. "I would love it. And to be honest," she hated herself for using that phrase, "I need to get out of Muskingum for a while. This place is driving me crazy."

"Good! I'll pick you up Friday morning... at nine?"

"It's a date," she said and almost kicked herself for saying it. "I mean..."

"I know what you mean. Either way is good with me. Tomorrow then," and he ended the call.

"Tomorrow?" she said out loud. "My God," and she checked her calendar and saw that Friday was tomorrow!

CHAPTER FIFTY-SIX
THOUGHTS OF ESCAPE

It was time. The Boy, a young man—fifteen years old, eight years now since his parents had died—had made up his mind. It was time. He would leave this home, this place that was not like his home in Muskingum, and leave this Man who took the place of his father—and his mother—who said that they had asked him to take him away. For a long time now he wondered about this Man—whose first name he didn't know—and what kind of father would leave a boy with the creep who was his valet when he was gone, a man who carried a gun concealed under his coat? This man who was more like a jailer than a friend.

The Man refused to take him anywhere. "There are a lot of bad people out there, boy," he would say. "And, you have a good life. You never have to leave here, where you are safe. I will get you anything you want. Anything!" And, strangely enough, the Boy believed him, as though maybe he was a real—though substitute—father. Someone who really did care.

But then he remembered what his dad had said, *Never get into a car with a stranger.* But he had. He disobeyed. Maybe he was being punished. Punished for disobeying. Maybe this was where he should stay—because he had disobeyed. And maybe, worse yet, because he had disobeyed, his parents had died. The thought haunted the Boy as he tried to go to sleep. This night. When he had thought of escaping. He lay awake for hours, even though the sun had gone down long ago, worrying about how he might have killed his father—and his mother. And he stared into the darkness and wondered about what he should do.

CHAPTER FIFTY-SEVEN
THE PLAN

So, the Boy lay awake, his mind running through the ways he might escape if he decided to. Hitchhike. No, take a bus—that made more sense—then get off at the nearest town and make a phone call. He remembered his home phone number—his mom and dad had gone over it with him endless times—until he got bored with it. But he remembered it now. He wondered if it still worked and, if it did, who would answer it. Maybe a relative, an aunt or uncle who had moved in after his parents were killed in the automobile accident. Sometimes he wondered if that were true—you know, the accident— if the Man was lying to him, the Man who had him taken away by two men, whom the Boy never saw again. He thought about it all until his mind got confused. Then he finally fell asleep, late in the morning, just before the sun rose, just before his tutor was due to give him his lesson. And he would be too tired to do the work, and the tutor would chide him about falling asleep while she was teaching him.

The Asp—that's what the Boy called him—woke him at 10:00 a.m. and told him his tutor was in the study. The boy called him Asp—not really, only in his mind—because he looked like an asp: sneaky, eely, oily, snaky, just like the bodyguard in Little Orphan Annie. Like a killer. And the Boy looked for the bulge in the Asp's jacket where the gun was. The black gun and it was there—always there. The Boy wondered what the Asp would do if he ran away. Would he chase him and shoot him? The Asp watched him as he got up, and he stayed with him while he dressed, and he led him to the study where the tutor was, and showed him a breakfast that he had made—that was the good thing about this killer—he was a good cook.

"So how are we today?" said the tutor who also had food in front of her. Each morning they would eat together. This morning they had crisp bacon and eggs, wheat bread, butter and jelly, and orange juice—always orange juice. It's good for you, the Asp would say, as though he were trying to keep him healthy before he killed him. Then the tutor, who looked about twenty or so, would brush back her hair—she had a lot of it, ash brown and wavy, like a movie star—and open the first book, usually English lit, saving math and science for later when the Boy was fully awake.

The Boy wanted to tell the tutor about his plans because he trusted her, he liked her, this tutor—whose name was Angelika. German, she had told him. It means angelic, she had said. Just like me, and she laughed. He liked her because she smiled when he did well on a project. But he didn't tell Angelika his plans—it would have to be a surprise. Someday I will not be here when she comes, the Boy thought. And he was a little sad at that thought—because he liked Angelika, and he would miss her. But I will be on my way home, he thought. To my real home.

After a while the Asp interrupted them to say it was time for lunch. The Boy hoped the Asp couldn't read minds as part of his many skills—and the Boy knew he had many. He looked at Asp, but there was no sign that he knew anything—nothing at all. *So*, thought the Boy, *maybe it will be this week. Maybe this week.*

At that moment he saw Asp turn around and look at him as they walked toward the dining room. The Boy wondered if he could read minds after all.

CHAPTER FIFTY-EIGHT
THE VISITS

Thursday Night, December 8

L ouise was already up when I woke.

I heard her call out after she turned off the water in the shower: "What's up next, doc? You got a plan?"

"I've got one," I said without thinking. My mind is blank in the morning, until I get my first cup of coffee.

"So...?" Louise said, coming out of the bathroom, massaging her hair with a large bath towel—and nothing else on. "Are you going to reveal what you're talking about. Or is this, *I've Got a Secret?* and she sat on the bed next to me and wrapped the towel around her head like a turban. I moved over to allow room. She snuggled up against me.

"It's time to make two visits, after we drop off our collection sample with a biologist."

"Visits?"

"To those two rigs..." I said.

"Again?"

"Uh-huh."

"Maybe overdoing it a little?" she said, giving her head a massage with the towel.

"Principle number one of Cooper Investigations..." I said.

"Do everything Cooper wants to do," she finished.

"When you don't know what to do next, revisit the scene of the crime."

"Exactly what I was thinking," she said.

"ESP," I said.

"Just like Sammy," she said.

"Okay, what am I thinking now?"

"You're going to call your friend the biologist even though it's almost midnight—and then we're going to bed." She winked. "Did I get it right?"

～

Graham Bell roams the Everglades like a hunter, only what he's looking for are poachers, polluters, illegal fishermen, in short, anyone who is threatening his precious Swamp. And he's a fanatic: never married, doesn't date—though he's only thirty-five years old—and he doesn't sleep much—which is why I can call him this late at night—and he will love to get my sample, put his PhD research degree from Duke to work and tear that sample apart with a fury that would match a man who was out to find a terrorist who's carrying around a nuclear weapon. Because the Everglades is his family, and any threat to his beautiful River of Grass deserves to be punished—or killed.

"Fuckin' midnight, Cooper!" was his answer.

"You don't sleep."

"Hey, for once I was asleep."

"Uh-huh. On the couch? Watching TV?"

Silence. "Whaddya need?" Graham wasn't happy with me. Normal for him.

"I've got something you're going to want to see."

"Uh-huh. At midnight?"

"Yeah. A sample that I took from Shark River."

"And why would I want to check out a water sample from Shark River?" he asked with a well-honed edge to his voice. I figured I had to be clearer.

"This isn't a water sample. It looks like oil or some kind of gunk-like substance, like oil. A non-biologist's assessment," I said.

"In Shark River? Probably motor oil."

"No. Not motor oil. There's a derrick up there—as you know—about a mile or so out in the Bay. I was just wondering..."

"If it might be leakage from a drilling."

"Maybe."

"Unlikely that far from a drill site, but..."

"You're going to want to see this stuff," I said.

"Okay." Reluctance all over his words. But, "What time are we looking at?"

"About a half hour."

Bell lives in Oceanside, near the University. He doesn't teach there. He never applied, even though the chair of the Science Department has bugged him about teaching ever since he moved into the city. Graham is a loner, enjoying his canoe trips into the quiet of the swamp, studying the wildlife, including the gators, crocs, and pythons. I don't think he ever shaves—his beard growing wild like the wilderness he explores.

My baby keeps me too busy, he says—his *baby* being the Everglades.

We were at his house at 12:45 a.m. He was at the door as we pulled in.

"Where is this sample?" he said, coming out to the car before I could climb out. "Come on in—got some coffee ready," and he waived us toward the open door. He seemed cheerier. "You brought your whole posse?" he said, nodding at Huck and Richie. He knew Huck. I told him about Richie.

"Protection, huh?" Bell observed. Richie gave him his usual stare when he doesn't want to reply. "No offense intended," Bell said, apologetically.

"Yeah," Richie said as he hunched through the door, checking out the room.

It was an outdoorsman's place: tropical deep green plants spread around the walls and on the sills of two windows fronting the road; a well-worn dark green leather couch that should have been replaced a long time ago; a fabric love seat that hadn't seen much love; and two bamboo floor lamps, one painted a soft aqua and the other left in its native state: a light shade of cinnamon with darker streaks running vertically from top to bottom.

Graham jumped in: "Coffee's in the kitchen. Cups, milk—no cream, gents, I mean..."—Louise waved him off—"So, honey or sugar, if you must—your choice." Graham was a real naturalist. Hated sugar. *Can kill you.*

Richie, Huck, and Louise went for the coffee. I followed Graham into his den that's in the back of his house—I should say his lab. A stainless-steel table sat in the center of the room. Cupboards with glass doors lined the walls and were filled with beakers, jars, scales, petri dishes, Bunsen burners, tubes curling in and around each other, and boxes and bottles of what I figured were chemicals. It smelled like a lab—sulfur and alcohol burning my sinuses.

I tried not to breathe in the noxious stuff. "I thought you were a biologist."

"Need chem to do what I'm doing. The fields are related.

Shoulda taken the philosophy of science," he said, looking over his wire-rims.

"Taught it, doc," I said, smiling.

"All right, gimme that stuff." He tried to look calm, but the excitement was in his eyes as he stared at the gunk in the jar. "And you found this exactly where?"

I told him about the trip to Shark River, about the unusual noises we heard in the water, about the proximity of the oil derrick out in the Gulf, just beyond the boundary of the National Park, and about what we thought was an oil slick on the water not far from Jack's boat.

"So I scooped up what I thought was a good sample," I said. I waited for his reaction.

He pulled over a microscope from a group scattered around the table and spread a small amount of the goop on a glass plate he stuck under the scope.

"Jeez, this stuff stinks!" he said, as he leaned over the scope. He studied the sample for over a minute, moving it around with a thin wooden spatula, then straightened up.

"Someone's fucking around out there!" he said, and I watched the color rise in his cheeks. His beard, bleached by the sun, shook as he said it, and the veins in his cheeks went from a fine spider web of almost indistinguishable red to scarlet. Then he hit the table almost knocking over the jar of evidence. It bounced and fell back without shattering. "Damn them!" he said, and I knew that 'them' were the demons he had been fighting his whole professional life—and they were destroying his home, the Swamp.

"Somebody's fracking with my baby!"

CHAPTER FIFTY-NINE
PLANNING FOR WAR

We were back at my house off Midnight Drive by 2:00 a.m. We talked about nothing else the whole way, except what Graham Bell had discovered about our Shark River sample.

"What the hell have we gotten into, Coop?" said Louise. "We're working a murder case and now we're suddenly looking at fracking?" She thought for a moment. "Maybe Jack was helping his daughter more than she realized."

"Uh-huh." I turned on the porch lights so we could see where we were going. Sammy was there, his tail curled around his body and sitting erect. He padded over, purring, and wrapped himself around my leg, rubbing against my jeans. That means dinner. As I mentioned, Sammy stays outside when I'm away and keeps Herman company. Sometimes he gets to eat the scraps left from Herman's dinner—I never wanted to know where Herman went shopping.

Sammy followed me into the kitchen. I opened a new can of Friskies—chicken livers this time—and spooned them into his dish. He was waiting for me by his water.

"You should take better care of your cat, Cooper. Your

baby needs attention. Just like yous would if you were left alone all-a-time." Richie, the sensitive one. Actually, Richie takes care of his mother who lives in a walk-up near his place on Murray Hill in Cleveland. *Ma wouldn't know what to do I don't take care of her. My brothers could care less,* Richie complained. But he loved it—taking care of Ma.

"Let's sit," I said, when everyone was settled. Louise had picked up Sammy and was stroking his fur, his kitty motor running smoothly.

"First of all," I looked over at Louise who had stopped petting Sammy—his motor had stopped— "we have several things going on. There's Jack...and his murder. Then there's the boat shooting at us near the big oil rig—"

"And hitting Cynthia," Louise added, "strangely enough."

I nodded.

"And the person who was in Jack's house when you and Cynthia went through it," she continued. "And the Black Lotus somebody left in your bedroom," she said.

"And the go-fast boats," said Richie, jumping in. "Probably running drugs."

"And Li Lung and Sun Lei showing up at the big rig," I added. "And now the stuff that Graham Bell initially identified as chemicals that are used in fracking—"

"That he's obviously going to have to follow up on. I mean his first look is hardly scientific," said Louise. "And the noises—"

"Yeah, the thumping. That was weird. It was coming from below us, like a—"

"Like the beginning of an earthquake, Coop. The ground was speaking to you," added Huck. *Huck the philosopher,* I thought.

"I speak from the knowledge that my ancestors received

from their fathers, and from the ancestors who dwelt in the Great Swamp..."

I closed my eyes. Huck has a way of going on, too...

"Oh, shut up," said Richie, harshly.

"I'm just saying..." said Huck.

"Hey!" I said. "Maybe the earth was speaking to us. Something *is* going on out there—or down there."

"And now we have the information from Doctor Bell," broke in Louise. "Maybe that goo we sampled is coming from a break in a pipe. But where?"

"Maybe from the rig we saw off-shore, that wildcatter rig, a mile or so out in the Gulf, near Ponce de Leon Bay," I said. *But how?* I wondered.

"How?" said Louise. More ESP.

"Maybe horizontal drilling. Extracting oil from underneath the National Park." *Maybe that's what Jack had stumbled on,* I thought.

"Don't make sense," said Richie.

"You drill straight down, say 10,000 feet, turn at a right angle and drill horizontally—a couple of miles maybe—to extract oil from an area not reachable from above—like in an environmentally sensitive area. Like the Everglades." I said.

And if a sparrow had lost a feather in flight, the sound of that feather hitting the earth would have shattered the silence of my house tonight.

"The basic technology has been around for a few decades," I continued. "But the capacity for drilling horizontally has grown. The record is over six miles."

No one said anything. I just stopped and thought.

I wondered what company owned the rights to drill just outside the boundaries of the National Park. And I wondered if there was a connection between that rig and the *Zhi Zhu Nu*. Huck had said the fast boat that had fired on them was coming from the north. Maybe running from the small derrick to the *Zhi Zhu Nu*. And if so, why? Lots of things to think about—and check up on.

I saw two visits in our future, and I didn't need a crystal ball.

CHAPTER SIXTY
DREAMING ABOUT MAXIE

Friday Morning, December 9

We talked ourselves out by 3:35 in the a.m. according to the big red numbers on the digital clock in my bedroom. Richie had taken the bed in the guest bedroom. Huck was sacked out on the couch in the front room.

"Used to roughin' it, amigos," he had said. I never thought of a couch as roughing it.

Richie was good with that. "Need my space," he said.

I was lying on my back, eyes locked on the ceiling when Louise rolled over, put her arms around me, and asked, what was the problem?

"I don't know. I'm thinking. No. I'm dreaming—about Maxie. A lot more these days. As I told you, it's like he's alive and I'm living these days with him—and he's in trouble. I swear, Louise, I can almost see where he is, feel what he is experiencing, sense his presence—physically."

I was sweating, and she held me tighter.

"You've been looking for a long time, babe." She falls into

that Colombian accent of hers when she lets her guard down, that voice when she first told me about how her father, a director of the Federales in Colombia, was assassinated by a drug lord—probably with help from the police. How he was an honest man, a good man, at war with the cartels; how she saw him shot on the steps of her own home, in front of her mother and her brothers and sisters—and she watched from behind a screen door; how he had bled to death, as her mother ran out on the steps while the car from where the shots were fired sped away; how her mother had screamed. *And I'll never forget it. I was only eleven, for God's sake*, she had said.

And it was that scene I was recalling when she said, "It's perfectly natural for you to dream about your son. He lives in your memory and he will for as long as you live. And it's okay." She ran her hand through my hair. "We will find him," she assured me. I loved how she said *we*. "And when we do, I swear, Coop, I will kill the people responsible for this thing."

And I believed her. Since she was not able to find the men responsible for her father's death, she would get her revenge— on the guys who took my son.

And so will I. I swear it! I thought.

We were all up at the smell of bacon. Richie—the cook. The Master Chef.

Back in Little Italy—in his condo, he has a kitchen to kill for. On Sundays, when he has visitors, he's up at 3:00 a.m. cooking the sauce. *Takes at least eight hours!* he says. Then there's the meatballs—*Just like Ma's,* he says. When Ma's there, she does the cooking. Her secret ingredients are pig's feet and pork. *And there ain't nothin' better than Ma's,* Richie insists.

Louise was out of bed before me and in the bathroom, probably for a half hour—minimum. She's not a girly-girl, but she likes to look good, she says. Period. No arguments. *But, I'm no girly-girl,* she insists.

Louise is tough, physically and mentally—and beautiful. You would never expect the fire that burns inside her. Probably from what she saw as a kid: the killing of her father. And that's why she understands—about Maxie. Nothing like experience to teach us about life. About evil.

A friend, a psychiatrist, and I were walking away from an encounter with a nasty clerk at a golf pro-shop. He didn't seem to be bothered, like I was. "He's got a form of autism," my friend explained. Then, noticing my surprise, he added, "There are three kinds of people in the world: those who are ignorant—they just don't know any better—those who are mentally ill—like our friend back there—and those who are evil."

"Evil?" I said, shocked at the thought.

"Yes," he said. "Evil."

"And normal people? Like us?" I said, hopefully.

"Sure," he admitted. "But I don't see normal people."

"So, what's the plan, boss?" asked Huck. Calling me boss more and more these days. I wondered what he wanted. That PI license he told me he expected, I figured. *I put in the hours, boss—working cases*, he would argue. There's that boss again.

"My thought," and they all watched me over the bacon and eggs that Richie had laid on their plates, the whites dark brown from the butter he had spooned over them while they cooked; pancakes, steaming and covered with blueberries; and bacon, crisp, almost burned—*way I like it,* said Richie—"we'll visit the derrick in Ponce de Leon Bay first. See what we can see. Somebody's fracking somewhere and that's the closest rig."

"And how do you plan to find this out?" said Louise. "Board the rig, line up the big boys and torture them?" Always the Devil's Advocate.

"Jack was killed in that vicinity. And Graham says that the substance we found near Jack's boat appears to contain chemicals used in fracking—he expects his analysis to confirm that. And then there was that noise we heard last night near Jack's boat, like an alligator pounding his tail against the ground.

"So right now, I'm looking at the derrick in Ponce de Leon Bay for some of those answers. That's why we're going to pay those boys a visit. See what we can see."

Louise nodded. "Uh-huh. I'm still not clear on how we're going to do that without boarding."

"Maybe when we get there it will come clear," I said. "Let's get there first, and then make a plan."

"Typical, Cooper," said Richie. "Best plan's no plan, right?"

I shrugged. "It's all I've got right now. So, let's eat."

CHAPTER SIXTY-TWO
THE PONCE DE LEON
DERRICK

Late Friday Morning, December 9

We were back at the Pilot House prepping Jack's Canyon 376. Its 350 HP Yamahas are enough to bankrupt most boat owners. The tank was half empty, so we added another 190 gallons of fuel. Figure it out. At approximately $5.00 a gallon, that would be about $900. I wondered how I would tell Cynthia as I watched the pump run up the bill. *No problems,* she had said. *Jack had a good business. Plenty of money to find his killers. Don't care if we spend it all! Hell with it.*

By late morning we were back in the Florida Straits, passing Islamorada and entering Snake River. It would carry us to Florida Bay and eventually back into the Gulf of Mexico. We passed Snake River Marina by 11:30 and Huck had us at full throttle heading out into the Bay and east toward the Gulf of Mexico ten minutes later. We were east of Cape Sable by 1:00 and heading north toward Ponce de Leon Bay, staying well offshore to avoid the ever-present crab traps. In another half-hour we were in Ponce de Leon Bay, storm clouds pulling down the shades on the day.

"Do you think we should head into Shark River for some cover?" said Louise, looking nervously at the black stuff piling up against the horizon.

"Yes, Ma'am," said Huck, swinging the wheel east into the bay and toward Shark River Island which lies between Little Shark River on the south and Shark River on the north. There's shallow water near the Island where we could anchor and find some shelter.

In the distance, off to the west, maybe several miles away, was the derrick. All that was visible was the upper part of the structure, lights beginning to blink on the tower as the sky darkened. No sooner had we anchored than the storm set in, rain pouring over the Canyon like a waterfall, waves pushing up over the deck.

"Jesus," said Huck, pulling the hatch behind him as a wall of water drove him forward, the noise of the storm blocked by the slamming of the door.

"Why don't you drown us!" yelled Richie, glaring at Huck.

Huck ignored him.

We were anchored firmly in about four feet of water. But waves would heave the boat up, pushing the water out from under us, then we would crash, like free-falling on a tidal wave, the anchor chain screaming and grinding as the boat descended. I worried about what would happen if the floor of the river were ever completely exposed.

This went on for several hours as we took turns in the head, trying to clean it each time for the next person. That's like riding a bronco and trying to brush your teeth.

By late afternoon we were finally able to go topside. As with all storms, there is the humidity and there is also the sun as it tries to restore the day as it was. The bay was calm again, and the rig—looking like the Eiffel Tower—hadn't moved an inch. We moved toward it as the shadows of late afternoon began to play on the water.

"Let's slow her down here," I said as the platform grew in size. We were about a half-mile away.

"What are we going to do? Knock on the door and see if they'll let us in?" Louise said, always thinking ahead.

"Yeah," I said. "That's exactly what we're going to do," and I signaled Huck. He pushed the throttle ahead, the boat jumping in the water as the motors caught the surface.

The water surrounding the rig was probably about seventy meters deep. The Gulf of Mexico is like a massive water basin whose sides slope upwards and eventually form a shelf at the very top. That's where the rig was sitting—on the shelf of that basin, where the depths average less than 100 meters, shallow by comparison to the deepest part of the Gulf, the Sigsbee Deep, where depths run over 4300 meters. That's almost three miles. Anyway, that should give you an idea of the greater challenge that deepwater drilling faces—like the *Zhi Zhu Nu* that's drilling into 1,982 meters of water.

The smaller rig would be easier to approach, its platform resting maybe ten meters above the sea, high enough to stay above the enormous waves stirred up by Gulf storms. By comparison, the platform of the *Zhi Zhu Nu* rises about thirty-five meters above the surface of the Straits. In either case you need a helicopter to climb aboard—unless you want to use the emergency ladder. Try either one in a storm and you get the idea of what life on a rig is like.

"Let's see what we can stir up," I said, and motioned for Huck to drive the Canyon up close to the rig.

CHAPTER SIXTY-THREE
JILLIE AND HENRY

Late Friday Morning, December 9

The winter sun was moving across the mid-day sky as Jillie stared out the window at fields that rolled endlessly along Route 40 toward Cambridge, Ohio. Highway 40 is the scenic route. Henry had thought that road would be more interesting—*and romantic*—his words. It was cold. Thirty-nine degrees and clouds hung in the sky—low and ponderous—like they were full of snow. The weather over the Thanksgiving holiday had been a mild, almost early fall kind of weather, a break from the normal cool, sometimes frosty, days normal for late November.

The leaves had dropped from most of the trees and were piled high against the sidewalk in front of her house, leaving the trees naked against the sky, stripped down for the winter storms that hit central Ohio regularly. Jillie didn't like this part of the year—transition time—she was looking forward to the first big snowfall when winter would really be here, and yes, when she could build a snowman on the front lawn, just like she and Maxie had done every year when he was...alive?

She had a hard time with that thought—her mind telling her he was dead. It's been how long now? Eight years? Surely... but she chased that thought from her mind and focused on the telephone poles that ran along the highway, imagining she could hear the voices carried through those lines and trying to guess at what they were saying—she did that as a kid—and she wondered if Maxie had passed those same poles when his kidnappers took him away? A man in town had told her he had seen Maxie get into a car with someone—a man, he thought. Maybe two. But the witness was Rawley Bunkers and he was crazy. Maybe not completely mad, but he was odd. Talked endlessly about nothing. Ran for public office every year—for mayor most of the time. Tried to talk Jillie into voting for him. She said she would, but didn't mean it. He always got three or four votes. Probably his mother's, his two sisters', and his own.

"Jillian?"

And that brought her out of her thoughts.

"You okay?"

"I'm fine. Just thinking."

"Leave the past to itself," Henry said. "It's been eight years. Time for you to have a life. Now I forbid you to think about anything but the good time we're going to have in Cleveland. And you...you're going to love the new art museum." Henry was glad he was able to break away from his work before the weekend. It would give them three extra days in Cleveland.

Jillie thought about what he had said—not thinking about Maxie. He should understand. He had one of his own.

Henry cut around Cambridge, a small crossroads town where I-77 and I-70 meet and then depart from one another leaving exit ramps behind them that stretched for miles. He took Route 22, a two-lane country road that ran through farm fields, bypassing the busy main street of Cambridge and connecting with I-77 on the north end of the city. In twenty minutes he was on the ramp for I-77 that would take them to Cleveland and the brand-new, world class art museum that everyone in Cleveland said was right up there with MOMA in New York City—and visiting New Yorkers would say, *Yeah, sure, gimme a break.*

Henry's rental, a black Mercedes sedan—*diesel,* he explained—sped past harvested corn fields with dead stalks rotting after the reaping; past barns painted red, some near the highway, some backed against a tree-line away from the road, some with tobacco advertisements written in big letters across the side facing the highway—the signs always worn, like advertisements from decades ago; past acres of trees that looked black now that they had lost their leaves; and past cows, some standing, some lying down. Jillie watched it all in her own quiet corner of the car.

"It's snowing," Henry said, breaking into her silence, smiling and pointing to the sky where flakes almost invisible were beginning to dance in front of the windshield. They quickly turned to water when they landed.

Jillie nodded, smiling. "Maybe it'll stick. I'll build a snowman when we get there." *Why did I say that?* she thought, confused about her feelings. But she was resentful of Cooper. He had deserted her. Or...had it been her who...? She shook her head and stared at the gathering of snow building on the highway ahead.

Henry turned on the lights. "We'll build a fire tonight." And she felt a sting in her stomach. *Oh God. I'm so happy and yet I'm not,* she said to herself. And she refused to think of Cooper.

CHAPTER SIXTY-FOUR
THE INN AND TAVERN

Friday Afternoon, December 9

Jillie looked at her phone. There were no messages. *I don't know what I expected*, she thought. A message from Coop telling me not to do this? It was noon and the snow had taken over the highway. She saw the Akron City Limits sign and knew they were just a half-hour from Cleveland. But Henry didn't take the freeway downtown. He exited I-77 and took the ramp that fed into I-271 north, Cleveland's outer belt on the east side. It runs through the Cuyahoga Valley National Park, a forest as green and lush as Saint Patrick's Ireland, and is part of Cleveland's Emerald Necklace, a ring of parks that surrounds Cleveland on all sides save the north where Lake Erie spreads out to Canada.

But today the forest, now stripped of its leaves from the fall harvest and bare to the winter winds, was lost in the snowstorm and the highway, now a brilliant blanket of white, was indistinguishable from the roadside. And that made Jillie nervous. So she told Henry that they should stop soon. He said he would.

"Where are we going?" she asked.

Henry smiled. "A surprise."

He turned off the outer belt and headed west on Ohio 422. They had only travelled a few miles when he turned again, this time left onto a small rural road that wound among hills and valleys and along a stream where water gushed over stones. The storm was less intense here in this New England style countryside with its stone-fronted houses and fenced-in barns— no farms here, just good old country squire living. And then she saw the sign.

"Chagrin Falls!" she cried, excited—and relieved.

Henry took Solon Road to the center of the town where there was a bridge overhanging a stream with a small waterfall that broke under the bridge, and next to it an ice cream store. And he stopped in front of the shop and watched as she stared in wonder at the falls and the water and the bridge.

"I just love it," she said, and stared for a few moments until...

"How about some ice cream?" he said. "Also, we absolutely have to try their chocolate covered strawberries. They're famous for them." He hesitated before opening his door to see her reaction.

"I would love it," she said, still lost in the falls. The sound of the water washing over the large, smooth stones beneath the falls consumed the silence.

And they ate ice cream and chocolate covered strawberries until they were both filled with the sweetness of it all. *We will never be able to eat dinner*, Jillie thought. She studied his face, angular and soft, partially covered with a beard, carefully manicured, and no more than four or five days old; the hunting vest that he had thrown on to block out the cold; his hands— delicate like a surgeon's. She wondered if any of his patients fell in love with him, and she wondered why he hadn't married all these years, and she also wondered who was the mother of his child—he never talked about her—or about the child—just that he had one, and she wondered if she could love him, this kind, tall, handsome man who was a psychiatrist, trying not to compare him to Cooper. But she couldn't help it—Cooper was also tall, and kind, and handsome. But she refused to go further...refused to think that she might still love him...

"What are you thinking of?" Henry said, brushing snow from the bridge's stone railing, smiling as he asked her.

"Oh nothing," and she stared off into the sky that was now clear of snow but was beginning to darken on this late December afternoon.

"Where will we stay?" she asked, hoping for something romantic.

"You'll see," he said, and he took her arm and led her back to the car.

CHAPTER SIXTY-FIVE
THE RIG

Late Friday Afternoon, December 9

They were 100 yards or so from the derrick when Cooper heard a shout. It sounded like someone calling from a megaphone. He looked closer and noticed that the one who shouted was shouldering a rifle. Huck moved the boat closer. The man pulled the rifle off his shoulder and held it high, the barrel pointed skyward.

"Hold'er there," the man on the rig yelled.

The deck of the derrick was about ten meters (thirty-three feet) above the water, give or take. There were several boats secured to the pilings around the rig.

"Shut down the motors," I said to Huck. He did, then reached for his alligator rifle he had laid on the bench behind him.

Richie went below and came back topside carrying his shotgun. I waved him off before the man on the rig could see it. All we needed.

"Why don't I talk with him?" asked Louise, waving at rifle-man.

She stood near the gunnels and called out. "We suffered some damage in the storm and were hoping for help from y'all," she said. A little southern girl?

That caught him. Men seem to have trouble with women from the south. They seem so vulnerable maybe—compared to the straight-talking northern women—and men like to rescue women who are in trouble—the hell with the rest of us on board.

"Well...what kind of trouble you having?" he yelled down, cradling the rifle in his arms.

Louise looked at me and winked—like watch this.

"The motors are not working right and my husband and his friends surely don't know how to fix a motor. I was hoping y'all could look at them—just quick like—see what's wrong."

He replied, "This here's a private rig, Ma'am. I don't have permission to let you on board," in a soft voice, but steady and sure.

I once took Jillie on a ride over a country road in southern Ohio. Near Fire Creek. I got lost and headed up a hill to a house sitting at the top of the drive, almost lost in the trees that surrounded it. About half way up, a man appeared on the porch carrying a rifle. He didn't point it at us. Just carried it across his chest. "What does that mean?" said Jillie. I told her it meant he didn't want any visitors today.

And that's the message I got from the man on the rig. So...

"Let's turn her around," I said to Huck, "and get the hell out of here. We're definitely not wanted."

He started up the motors and headed back to where we had come from. "Where we going?" he said as he pointed the boat toward the bay. The man on the deck of the rig was still watching until we lost him and the rig in the ebb-tide of the setting sun.

"Back to the crime scene," I said. "See if we can trace those sounds to their origin."

CHAPTER SIXTY-SIX
THE ESCAPE

Friday, December 9

T he Boy woke up early, almost like he had set an alarm. Only he didn't need to do that. He was excited. Nervous. Afraid. And he felt every other emotion that a prisoner would experience before he went over the wall. And today he was going over the wall, past the Asp, before the tutor came, before the Man returned, before the sun rose, before breakfast, but only after he readied his back-pack—with food, with money, with chewing gum—that always settled his stomach—and with a kitchen knife—just in case. So he packed his bag—quietly—so the Asp wouldn't hear, stuffed some blankets under the quilt on his bed—so it would look as though he were still sleeping—and then went into the fridge and got some apples, and oranges, and bananas—some peanut butter too—just for protein—and he checked the stash of money that he had been saving for eight years in his pack, opened the back door to the house, took the Man's bicycle from the garage —a cool, 12 speed, with racing tires—threw the pack over his shoulder and set off down the road that led to he knew not where.

The rising sun was at his back, so he knew he was headed east, and he knew that his home was north-northwest. He knew that from studying the maps that his tutor had let him have. The wheels of the bicycle hummed against the tarmac. The woods were silent, and the road was wet from the morning dew, and free of all traffic, this early morning. And the Boy realized that today was the start of a new part of his life, and he was excited, nervous, maybe even a little terrified. But he was determined. So, he peddled steadily and confidently toward the town at the end of the road he had seen on the map so many times, that he had never visited but would this morning. And this was the first leg of the plan that he had carefully laid out for the last few months. The plan that would take him back to his home. Or to what was left of it.

CHAPTER SIXTY-SEVEN
INTO THE WORLD

"I want a ticket to Muskingum, Ohio," the Boy said. And the man looked at him curiously, over his glasses—they were wire-rimmed over eyes that were blood-shot. *Maybe from not getting sleep*, the Boy thought.

As the man considered his request the Boy studied his face, and couldn't help but notice the hairs growing out of his nose, and the black hair that was growing out of his ears. Except for the Man who had taken him away, and the Asp, and the tutor, the Boy never really had a chance to meet people, or to study them. Once he talked—briefly—to the mailman. But the Man came out of the house and pulled him away, quickly. Another time a woman came to the door when the Man was not at home and the Asp was busy and she said she was a missionary and gave him a brochure, with angels and devils in a fight on the front cover and the word, Watchtower, written over the top. The Man scolded him for answering the door. "You can't trust people," he had said. "Bad people take children away and sell them," he warned. That scared the Boy and he was careful not to answer the door—though he still did it several more times—when the Man wasn't around—or the Asp.

"You travelin' alone?" the man with the wire-rimmed glasses said, his head down, counting the money.

The Boy nodded. The man looked up, a question mark appearing on his head, just above his glasses.

"Yeah," the Boy said, wondering if he was in trouble. "Goin' to my grandparents' house," he added quickly.

'Y'all take care, hear?" said the man as he passed the Boy the ticket, the Boy thanking him and looking out to where the buses were parked.

"Yours will be waiting just outside that door," he said, pointing to a group of people waiting in a line. "You'll have a stopover at Charlotte, North Carolina, and then again at Charleston, West Virginia," and the Boy noticed that he pronounced all the names like there was no 'r'. The Man didn't talk like that. The Asp didn't talk like that. Nobody he knew talked like that. He hoped the ticket man didn't know either one of them.

The Boy had been careful to hide his bicycle so it wouldn't be visible to the Man or to the Asp if they came looking. He didn't want them to know he had taken a bus. So he left it in a field near the road. They would think I hitchhiked, he hoped.

"How long?" the Boy asked.

"The stopovers?" the man asked.

"No, the whole trip."

"Sixteen hours and forty-five minutes, including the stops. You'll have a one-hour wait in Charlotte," and he looked behind the Boy at a small line of people waiting to buy tickets.

"Have a good trip," he said.

The Boy looked down at the ticket in his hand.

"Just give it to the driver when you get on," the man said, and motioned to the bus.

The Boy checked the big clock on the wall of the station: 7:14.

"Bus leaves in fifteen minutes," the man said. "Might as well get right out there now," and he watched the Boy over his glasses as the he walked away tentatively, then the man with the wire-rimmed glasses shook his head and waited on a woman in a fur coat that looked like she had picked it up in a trash bin.

The bus was on its way at 7:30 a.m., pulling out of the station with a full load of passengers and the odor that comes from bodies too close together. The temperature was warming up. Forty-five degrees, the gauge on the bus garage read. The Boy huddled against the window, ignoring the fat man who was pushing against him, trying to settle into a sleeping position. It was going to be about sixteen hours on the road. Lots of time for sleep.

He watched the mangroves slide by, his face up against the window, resting his cheek against the cold of the glass as he followed the scenery: trees hanging over the highway, telephone poles, partially hidden in the density of the overhang. That same smell—like eggs rotting—caught him again. He had remembered it on the way to his new home eight years ago. The driver had said it was the paper mills.

He watched the signs that announced the towns they were entering and the number of miles to the next one. When they got close to a town, the speed limit dropped to forty miles an hour, then twenty-five as the bus slowed through the downtown, which for the most part consisted of a gas station, some slumping stores, and old rusted signs in front of buildings that were leaning toward each other, gravestones for the businesses that used to be there. The bus was following US 21, northbound. He recognized it from the maps that his tutor had shared with him. He had even brought one of the maps with him so he could follow the route to Muskingum, Ohio.

The morning grew cooler. The Boy could feel the change in the window as he laid his head against it. And the landscape changed—long stretches of open countryside with few hills. He watched as the bus pulled onto a freeway— I-26 the sign read— the Boy with his cheek still up against the window, and the fat man next to him sleeping, sometimes leaning into him, and his odor, like a man who never showered. When they reached Columbia, the bus took the exit onto I-77, and the Boy knew this would be a long stretch. He fell asleep to the hum of the wheels against the concrete, and the snoring of the man next to him, and he forgot about the danger of his mission, and what lay ahead in Muskingum, Ohio.

CHAPTER SIXTY-EIGHT
THE ROAD

He slept for hours, or at least that's what it seemed. He woke when the bus pulled into a station, came to a stop in a parking lane, and the driver opened the front doors with a hiss that sounded like air being let out of a huge balloon. Then it was quiet as passengers stirred, murmuring at first, then listening to the voice of the driver announcing an hour layover and that those who were changing busses should be sure to get all their belongings—which for the Boy was just his knapsack. No problem.

The sign on the side of the bus station read, Charlotte—just like the man with the wire-rimmed glasses had predicted. First stop.

The hour layover went fast as the Boy searched for his next bus—It'll say Charleston, the driver had said. So the Boy looked for that bus first, asked the driver if he could stow his bag on board, and then headed for the restroom.

He bought a burger and coke with fries at a McDonald's nearby, hurried back to the bus, and was early enough to find a window seat in the back next to a boy who looked about fifteen who was holding down an aisle seat. He slid in, saying only excuse me, and again leaned his head against the window—this time it was warmer. The sun was high; no clouds in a clear sky and blue, so blue it seemed to go on forever.

He closed his eyes as he thought about the blue of the sky and he thought about what he would find in his old home, his old town, his old school, and wondered if he would find any of his old friends. Then he dozed and dreamed of the college campus where his father—who was dead—had taught, and of his mother—who was also dead— and wondered if any of his relatives had come to their house and wondered why he wasn't able to live with one of them? Gramps and Nana lived in the forest near the Ohio River. His aunts and uncles did, too. He wondered why none of them had ever called. But maybe they were mad at him for leaving with strange men—and maybe they blamed him for his parents' death. And the bad dreams continued until the boy next to him shook his arm.

"You having a nightmare?"

"I guess," the Boy said, wiping sleep from his eyes. Then he looked outside. It was dark and they were in mountains, the bus twisting and turning on the highway, like the driver was guiding a roller coaster down a chute.

"Where are we?" the Boy said.

CHAPTER SIXTY-NINE
DR. GRAHAM BELL

Early Friday Evening, December 9

The sun had set by the time we got back to the inlet where we had found Jack's body and his boat. Richie and I dumped the dinghy into the water while Huck and Louise dropped anchor. I started the motor and we moved slowly upriver, Louise shining a lamp to watch for debris or animals, like gators or sharks. They move at night—gators I mean.

We were almost back at the crime scene when I spotted a faint light in the dark ahead.

"Shut off those damn lights! I can't see anything," came a voice from out of the darkness. I caught the outline of a boat and a man, holding a hand against his face to deflect the light.

"Graham? Is that you?"

"Dammit!" he said. "Would you turn that thing off!" Louise did.

It was Graham Bell. He was bundled in a canvas coat and holding a bottle in his free hand.

"What's going on?" I said, as we moved in closer. He was in

a flat boat with a small motor. It looked like he had brought a whole lab with him in a large tackle box.

"What do you think I'm doing?" he said. Not a question really. "I've already checked the sample you left. What you brought me was a glob of chemicals, chief among which are some carcinogens: methanol and mercury. There is also some sodium bentonite. They are using that, I assume, to help grease the bits for the drill that's boring into my baby's belly—right underneath us, guys!" And he held up a new bottle of sample he had just collected and illuminated it with a pocket flashlight. "Evidence," he observed.

"That they're fracking?" I said.

"Right under your butt," he said. "I think we can trace the sound right back to your rig in the Gulf."

Now it was *my* rig.

"But we don't need to do that. This stuff *can't* be coming from anywhere else," he continued, as he held the sample he had collected against the glow of his flashlight. "There's some bad stuff in here," he said. The 'stuff' in the jar was dark and thick against the light, just like the junk we had collected earlier.

"So, they're fracking here now," he said. "And they're using directional drilling to get into forbidden territory. And it's not just here. It's happening everywhere." He was still staring at the jar. "And it's pissing people off—as it should! Like the people in southwest Florida. Golden Gate. And there are at least a hundred rigs in the Gulf that are fracking illegally—right now. And who's reporting it?" He paused—mostly for effect—because how in the hell would I know who's reporting? "*Al Jazeera!*" he continued, throwing his arms in the air like they were taking flight. "I mean where are our own newspaper and TV people? *Al Jazeera?* Are you kidding me? But at least *they're* reporting it, for Chrissake."

It was dark and he had turned off his light. But I could feel the blood rise in his cheeks. He needed some aspirin.

"Someone's coming," said Richie, breaking into the silence. I heard the faint roar of engines—or a single powerful engine—coming up river. It grew in intensity very quickly and sounded very much like a go-fast boat.

"Is that possible?" I said more to myself than to the others. "A fast boat at this time of night?"

"Maybe someone's coming to check up on us," said Louise. "We need to get out of here." Huck already had the motor running as she said it.

"I'm going back the way I came," said Graham, quickly loading the sample jars into his large tackle box then starting his motor.

The boat sounded like it was less than a mile away.

"I'm taking the long way back," Graham said hurriedly. "I can do it with my little buddy here." He slapped the side of his boat. "Call that Homeland Security friend of yours," he said as he moved away. "If you don't, I will! These damn guys are poisoning my swamp."

Bell quickly disappeared into a mangrove tunnel as we headed back to the Canyon.

CHAPTER SEVENTY
JILLIE AND HENRY

Friday Evening, December 9

The temperature had dropped to thirty degrees. A light snow was still falling but now it was sticking to the ground. Downtown Chagrin Falls was a winter postcard: wreaths of pine with clusters of red berries hung from old-fashioned street lamps; strands of pine, twisted and secured on a wire, stretched across Main Street; and a lone tree in the town square, weighted with bulbs, red and green and blue, rose above the street, its lights jumping and winking and playing with the snow that was trying to cover it.

"It's so beautiful," whispered Jillie—as much to herself as to Henry—as they drove slowly past stores still filled with shoppers. And the candy shop—there were lines out to the sidewalk. No one seemed to mind the cold.

Then Henry pulled into a bed and breakfast—like something out of an English countryside—a white picket fence, a wrap-around porch with a swing, a gazebo off to the side of the Inn with a built-in sitting area that watched over a fire pit.

Two gas lamps hung over a walkway that led to a porch fronting the inn. Jillie paused to see if they were real.

"They are!" she exclaimed. "I wonder if the lighting inside the inn is gas as well?" Henry shook his head and grinned. He was enjoying watching her.

They passed under a green awning and into an entry room where three chairs and a couch, upholstered in soft rose, were arranged around a fireplace. Its heat warmed the entire room.

"Hot apple cider or wine?" said a young woman, smiling and hurrying through glass doors toward them.

Henry turned to Jillie. "Let's try the wine," he suggested.

"It's a local wine made from grapes grown in the vineyards on the southern shore of Lake Erie," the hostess explained, pouring a sample into Henry's glass. "A Cabernet Franc," she added.

"Ah, very light," said Henry, letting the wine wash over his palate. "You know, the Lake Erie wineries are becoming well known. And this Cabernet Franc is marvelous! I think you'll like it, Jillian," and he motioned for the hostess to pour her a glass.

Jillie studied him as she sipped the wine, wondering how it would be later—in the room—when they were in bed, to have sex with him again, after these many years. Would it be the same? She didn't know. She worried, but she was also excited. After all, Cooper...But she put her thoughts to rest. *Enjoy these moments*, she chided herself.

They sat in front of the fireplace, trying different wines. There were five or six varieties. And they sat quietly, watching the flames throw sparks around the hearth like shooting stars in a miniature night sky.

Henry looked over at Jillie. "Are you all right?" he asked.

She nodded. "My first time after our separation. But," she

added quickly, "I want to do this," not wanting to sound reluctant, *and about time*, she thought to herself.

"And it's about time, you thought of yourself," he said, as if reading her thoughts. And then his cell buzzed. He checked a message, concerned. Then shook off whatever it was.

"Is everything okay?"

He nodded. "Just one of my patients—she was just admitted to the hospital. I was hoping..." He stopped himself. "Sorry. Nature of the job." He slid his phone back into his pocket.

"Shall we?" he said and gestured toward a stairway that twisted upwards into an open hallway. "Let's check out our room."

They took their time mounting the stairs, plush red and protected by an ivory enameled rail. And they followed the rail as it swung right at the top of the stairs and across the front of an open hall from where there was a full view of the lower level: the lights from the street blinking white through the high windows of the reception area, and the fireplace still burning and throwing its heat and light against the glass doors leading to the restaurant, now closed.

Jillie paused and leaned against the rail, watching snow filling the street and enjoying the warmth of the inn. Henry bent over next to her and put his arm around her, and they stayed like that, the only sound, the steady ticking of a grandfather clock in the lobby.

∞

Their room was the first one on the left after the open hall. Right behind them, actually.

"Allow me," Henry said and slid the plastic room key into the slot and opened the door.

"It's perfect!" said Jillie, staring at the canopied four-poster bed covered with a burnt-orange duvet and matching pillows. Then there was the nineteenth century dresser against the wall —she knew the style since it was the same kind she had seen in Anthony's Antique Shop; and the burnt-orange drapes, matching the duvet and chenille pillows—only a softer color; and finally, the fireplace! Gas. No logs.

"Let's light it!" she said. *Am I delaying?* she wondered.

Henry didn't seem to mind. He went directly to the mantel, found some matches, located the handle to turn on the jets, applied the match, and the room warmed. And Jillie? —she suddenly relaxed for the first time in a long time. And she noticed how handsome he was, the semblance of a beard—he hadn't shaved—his features sharp, his cheeks slightly drawn. It gave him a rugged, outdoor look. And she remembered his gentleness.

She could see herself actually falling for him—this substitute for Cooper—no, maybe a new person altogether. Someone who could help her forget Cooper, and Maxie, and Muskingum; and all the nights she cried away her thoughts; and her marriage; and about how much they had loved each other—she and Coop—and about how it all fell apart that morning when she was home with her son, and he got away, somehow, and she was in charge—Cooper had reminded her of that—and she had reminded him that if he were home more maybe it would never have happened. But deep down, she blamed herself, and she knew Cooper did also—and she hated him for that. Truth be told, she hated herself even more. But tonight, there was the fire, and there was Henry and maybe everything would change.

CHAPTER SEVENTY-ONE
THE NIGHT VISITOR

The boat blew past us just as we boarded the Canyon, its motors howling like a banshee. The river was wide where we were anchored, and the Canyon was near the shore. So I figured they hadn't seen us.

"What the hell," said Richie, going below for his gun. "Who are those guys?" Huck was right behind him.

"I think we're about to find out," I said, turning to Louise. The fast boat had suddenly slowed down to an idle. And then there were voices in the dark—about several hundred yards downriver. I assumed they were bent on taking the inland water route to the mainland. Avoiding traffic. A load of drugs maybe.

"What you doing out there?" A voice came out of the dark. Chinese? I didn't answer. Louise drew her gun, ejected the magazine, checked the load, and slammed it back in place—so he could hear it.

"We're in West Virginia," the boy in the seat next to him said, waking up Maxie. "There was a sign about a half hour ago. And this here's the West Virginia Turnpike," he added, as the bus twisted and turned down a mountain side. Then, "Dude, this your first time on a bus?"

The Boy nodded. "Yeah. Yours?

"Nope. Ride all the time. My Mom and Dad—they're divorced. So right now, I'm going to stay with my uncle—in Columbus."

"Ohio?"

"Of course, idiot," he said, and laughed. "Is there any other?"

"I don't know. Maybe."

"Good old Columbus of O.H.I.O." The kid paused, like he was thinking about it. He shook his head. "Can't believe it," and he turned back to the Boy. "I'm practically an orphan!"

The bus was hurtling down another chute on the highway, weaving in and out of construction barrels blocking the outer of two lanes, and the mountains seemed so high to the Boy who had never seen them before, and the night so dark and dangerous, and the way home so scary, especially as he thought of what he would find when he got there. Maybe it would have been better if he had stayed with the Man. And what the kid next to him said really got him—about being an orphan—and for the first time he realized that he was one also. The face that looked back at him as he stared out the window looked lonely to him, and sad. And his stomach hurt as he tried to shake the thought—I'm an orphan. But it persisted as he stared into the face in the window and watched the sides of the mountain rush by. High. Rough. And dangerous.

CHAPTER SEVENTY-THREE
JILLIE AND HENRY

The wine went to her head quickly. She wasn't used to drinking. Henry had brought a special wine for this trip: a Beaujolais. She had remembered a trip to the Riviera when she and Coop had been out late and were walking through the narrow streets of Nice near the beach, and it was late, dark, most of the cafes were closed. But signs announcing *Beaujolais Nouveau est arrive'* were on every corner, in the window of every shop, and on the lips of every Frenchman they passed—everyone in France, a wine lover. And they had just passed one shop that had already closed and were looking in the window at the tables, when a man unlocked the door, smiling, and announced, *"Beaujolais Nouveau, est arrive'!"* and waved for them to come in.

"Aren't you closed?" Coop had said, since the sign said they were.

"Oui!" said the man, but for you...ah lovers!" He led them into his shop, closing the front door and locking it.

She remembered how he had seated them at a small round table in a back room, walls lined with bottles of wine and smelling of Beaujolais. She could see him even now, holding up a bottle—*a Beaujolais,* he had said—*first of the season.* Then he opened it, allowed the flavor to drift into the room, placed two glasses on the table, and carefully poured, and then filled one for himself.

Pour vous, mes amis, he had said, lifting his glass and taking a sip, savoring it as if it were the last he would ever take. *Sante'. A la votre, mes amis.* And she remembered how they drank, how they wondered at the amazing good luck they had to run into this hospitable Frenchman, and she remembered the taste of the wine, the first of the season, the newest of the Beaujolais, the rich odor of it, the sting of the wine as she tasted it before swallowing, the look on Coop's face as they drank and watched each other, the indescribable smile on the face of the Frenchman as he watched them. *Sante'.* Again, he said it and poured once more. Her mind was giddy then.

It was giddy again this evening, but in a different way. Exciting. But softened. By the memories of Cooper.

"Do you like the wine?" said Henry, watching her carefully, noticing her eyes wandering.

"Yes," she said and held up her glass for him to pour again and almost said, *sante',* but she kept it to herself. And she drank.

CHAPTER SEVENTY-FOUR
WHAT ARE YOU DOING HERE?

Friday Night, December 9

"This is not good," I whispered to Louise who was standing next to me at the helm. "Time to get the hell out of here," and I punched the starter and the motors roared, as flashes of light burst out of the darkness, shattering the Canyon's windshield and blowing it outward—lucky thing—seawater and glass exploding everywhere. I ducked, spun the boat away from the shots, while Louise, waiting for me to come full circle, rested her arm on the gunnel and fired rapidly into the darkness. The damn guys were running without lights.

Both Richie and Huck were topside now and firing blindly with Louise into the heart of the dark of Shark River, the only target the sound of the fast boat screaming in the night. I pushed the Canyon after them toward the bay. But soon the only sound on the water was the roar of our own Yamahas. So I slowed as we broke free of Shark River and entered the open waters of Ponce de Leon Bay, the fast boat nowhere to be seen —or heard.

In the distance, I could see lights from the rig and I cursed it, wondering who the hell they were and what they were doing. "We're going to find out," I swore under my breath. "And we're going to shut you down."

I handed the wheel to Louise, the helm taking the full brunt of the sea now that the windshield was gone.

"Take us home," I said, "I gotta make a call."

"For some cops, I hope, Lone Ranger."

"We already have cops," I said. "We've got you."

"Right," she said. "Make your call."

Richie and Huck had dropped onto a bench aft. Richie had his hands hard against his ears. "Can't you shut this thing down for a fucking minute?" he said. "I think I'm going deaf."

Louise cut the motors back. Good thing. I couldn't use the phone anyway from the noise.

I called Cleveland Wong on his SAT.

CHAPTER SEVENTY-FIVE
NEARLY HOME

The Boy strained to see the clock on the outside wall of the Greyhound station in Charleston, West Virginia. It was 10:11 p.m. A fog had set in, blurring the lights around the station. And buses rolled in like creatures from outer space, their passengers barely visible through the fog as they pressed their faces against the windows—orphans waiting for a welcome.

"Got fifteen minutes," announced the bus driver as he pulled into one of the parking slots circling the station. There was a hiss and a rush of cold air as the driver opened the door. "Temperature's 33 degrees," he said, pointing to large red digitals on the side of the station. The Boy pulled on his jacket. It was a warm-weather jacket not one suited for the kind of weather that plagues the north in December. As he climbed down from the bus, frigid air hit him in the face forcing him to pull his hood over his head. He headed for the doors of the bus station, shaking from the cold as he swung through. Inside it was warm. He beat his hands together to chase away the chill that ran like needles through his fingers.

"Not used to this shit, huh?" said his friend from the bus.

"Just wait. This ain't nothin'. When January comes, you'll see what cold is." He rubbed his hands together like he was standing in front of a bonfire. The Boy tried to remember what it was like back then—before the men took him away. He found a cup of watery hot chocolate at a newsstand that stood dirty and dark at the far end of the station. The steam warmed his nose and his insides. A few minutes later both boys were re-boarding the bus.

The big doors hissed closed and the driver backed out of the station, his headlights penetrating the darkness like a lighthouse beam. They were back on I-77.

"Next stop, Ohio," the driver said, matter-of-fact, as he wound the bus's motor up to speed.

Home was only a few hours away, and the Boy's stomach began to hurt again. He wondered if he would have a place to sleep tonight. Maybe in my own house, he hoped. He could picture his bedroom, and he hoped that his mom had left it just as he remembered, all warm and cozy. Not at all like his bedroom back in South Carolina. Not at all like that. So, he stared into the darkness as the bus rolled past the West Virginia countryside where there were no lights except for a lonely one now and then—from a distant farmhouse—or when they came to a rest stop—there were plenty of those along the highway. Then it would get dark again as the rest stop settled in behind them, and the Boy would get to thinking again—of his home in Muskingum, Ohio. And hope. And worry.

CHAPTER SEVENTY-SIX
CLEVELAND WONG

Friday Night, December 9

Cleveland Wong doesn't have a life—or a wife. His life is Homeland Security. Assistant Secretary. But once in a while he gets away—hides out in his second home in Delray Beach, Florida. His first home, of course, is in D.C. That's where he spends most of his time. I wondered where he was tonight.

"So, where do you think I am, Cooper?" he said testily.

"I don't know," I said.

"Would you guess...on vacation?" he said.

"Oops," I said. "So, you're in Delray."

"Nice," he said. "I'm vacationing in Delray—one of my few vacation weeks of the year. And here I am talking with you," he added, turning to sarcasm.

"You're resorting to sarcasm to bug me," I said, calling him on it.

"You are right." A pause—an angry one. "So now that you are part of my vacation. What've you got?"

I told him about the drilling. I told him about Dr. Graham

Bell's lab findings. I told him about our suspicions about drug trafficking from the oil rigs. I told him about the go-fast boat. About the airboat and the shooting at Shark River. He listened —didn't interrupt once. But he was almost too quiet.

"Let me talk with him," said Louise, impatient.

"Hey," she said.

I heard him grunt.

"This is Louise." She paused. Breathing harder than normal. Upset. "We've got trouble down here in paradise and we need your help."

I heard a *Damn straight* from Richie and a *You bet your ass* from Huck, both loud enough for Wong to hear. Louise put the phone on speaker.

"You've got your gang members with you, Cooper?" Wong said after Louise handed me back the cell.

"I do," I said. "And we have an incursion into U.S. territory that you need to be concerned about," I added.

"Okay, okay, okay," he said, still impatient. "Tell you what, Cooper. I'll fly down there and meet you. Where are you now?"

I told him.

"I'll meet you at your house. Give me four hours. Okay?" The 'okay' was just politeness.

"You gonna call the Coast Guard?"

"Damn right," he said. "Four hours. And get some coffee ready—not decaf!" And he was gone.

I checked my cell. It was 10:00 p.m. and we were west of Sable Key. We had to make time to get back to the marina and then back to Oceanside and Sammy. I was trying to picture Wong landing the helicopter in my back yard, and the neighbors thinking an alien ship was landing. *Close Encounters of a Fourth Kind*, maybe.

Friday Night, December 9

"So, where you heading?" his new friend said.

The Boy studied him and wondered how old he was. He didn't have any facial hair, his face looked young, but he acted older, like maybe seventeen or eighteen. And his hair was long—kind of scraggly—like he didn't take care of himself. His pants were worn and baggy—and there was a hole in the knee. And he had a long sleeve shirt—like a grown-up—blue, like denim, and a jacket with the letters WASPS across the back, big and black. They matched his hair color.

"Muskingum," the Boy said, leaving the rest of the story alone. But Joey continued and asked why he was going there. And the Boy told him it was his family's home. And then Joey—his new friend—maybe his only friend—introduced himself: Joey Lewis.

Named after the famous comedian Joe E. Lewis, by a nun who found him on the steps of the orphanage, and she was crazy about the guy, so the nun gives him that name but—

"I'm no comedian," he said. "I'm a real orphan! And then I

find out that it was my mom who left me at the orphanage—on the steps—and she comes back later and tries to take me but I tell the nuns to tell her to go fuck herself. And the head nun washes my mouth out, see, but then she doesn't let her take me, anyways."

And then he continued—on a roll—about his father. "Forget him. He didn't know nothin' about the orphanage I was in. It was in South Carolina," he said turning to the Boy. "Or about the nuns who raised me. They were nice but one of them —the head penguin, the one who washed my mouth out, she was a bitch, and she kept on me all the time until..." and the Boy dozed off as Joey Lewis spoke and as the bus rolled through the Ohio Valley—through the darkness—and he woke and the boy was still talking—about an uncle who he learned about from his delinquent mother—who, by the way, doesn't live in Columbus, but his uncle lives there, and his delinquent mother —who gave him away—said that he should go visit him sometime. Stay close to the family, she told him. "Probably feeling guilty for being a stupid mother," the boy said, good old Joey Lewis, otherwise known as Joe E. Lewis.

"So, I called him—my uncle—and he said, 'Yeah, your mom told me all about you. And, yeah, I would love to have you stay with me.' And he told me to call him when I get into town." He stopped, breathing hard since he had been talking forever. Then, he leaned back in his seat, turned to the Boy, nodded and said, "Cool!'

The movement of the bus rode the Boy to sleep, and he dreamed of the telephone wires that lined the road when he was in the car with the two men who had taken him, and of the smell—like rotten eggs—as they got closer to his new home in South Carolina, and of the Man, and of the Asp...

And Joey was now watching him when he woke and the Boy said he was sorry that he slept and Joey, said no worries, and why was he going to Muskingum? Maxie told him about the house in South Carolina, and the Man and the Asp—and maybe the Asp was looking for him—*even now*, the Boy worried—but he hesitated, hesitated telling his new friend, Joey, about why he was in South Carolina.

Joey pressed him—of course he would. Joey was like a street kid, and he was smart. So, Maxie told him what had happened, about the men who had taken him. His new friend, gasped and said, *No shit!* And Maxie nodded and went on and told about how his parents had been killed, or something; and that he was sort of locked up in the house in South Carolina—and he didn't know just where that was; and about his tutor.

And Joey said: *You mean you never went to school?*

Maxie said: *Of course.*

Joey said: *I mean to a real school?*

Maxie said: *Well, no.*

Joey: *Did you ever go out? I mean to a movie?*

And Maxie said: *No.*

Joey: *Or to the store?*

Maxie: *No.*

Joey: *Or anywhere?*

Maxie, embarrassed to say, hesitated, but he didn't have to answer because the boy, Joey, his new friend, already knew.

"Shit!" Joey said. "They kidnapped you!"

And Maxie's world ended—right there.

CHAPTER SEVENTY-EIGHT
GOOD OL' JOEY LEWIS

J oey saw the look on his face and knew he said the wrong thing.

"Sorry, dude...."

Maxie was quiet. Kidnapped. All these years. The Man telling him his parents were dead—maybe they were; never being able to leave the house; the tutor; Asp who was probably looking for him now; it was all a make-believe story; it was all a lie. How was that possible? And Maxie shut out the world, shut out the boy who claimed to be Joey Lewis, his friend. Was that also a lie? Shut out the sound of the bus as its tires sang out the fact that they were—no he was—Maxie—on his way home.

"How do you know I was kidnapped?" asked Maxie, turning on Joe E. Lewis. Angry, not believing. How could he believe it? Everything he had lived for the past eight years—was it all a lie? "I wasn't kidnapped! My parents weren't able to keep me and then they were killed in an automobile accident and...." and it all began to sound strange to him and the story began to fall apart, like an avalanche, beginning with a single stone, then...the whole explanation, which he had accepted so easily when the Man explained to him about why he had brought him to his house: his parents in trouble, then killed in an automobile accident, it all sounded so believable, and he wanted to believe it, or else...the alternative...

He looked over at Joey, whose face was in shadows. That's because the bus driver had turned off the lights, and most of the passengers seemed to be asleep—except for the two of them, of course. And Maxie's stomach ache was now a ten. A doctor had come to the house one time and asked how much he hurt when he had bruised his knee in a fall—and he had said, *Tell me, on a scale of one to ten, with ten being the worst, how much pain are you feeling?* That was like a five. But right now, Maxie was feeling a ten.

"I'm sorry, dude. I shouldn't..." Joey struggled with the words.

"No, you shouldn't. When you don't know..."

"But dude...the men who took you, the man who wouldn't let you out of the house, the tutor you talked about, and this guy who is supposed to be following you..."

"The Asp," Maxie finished.

"Yeah." Then as though done with the argument, Joey, his new friend, the boy who was named by some nuns, a name that he thought he would change sometime, because why not? it wasn't his real name anyway, this friend, Maxie's only friend, continued, "Okay. Forget about the kidnapping thing. Let's get back to your story. You never finished it." And Maxie marveled how old Joey acted. He was probably his same age but he acted like a grown-up. "I mean you never really told me about what you're going to do in old Muskingum of O.H.I.O. I mean, who do you think is going to be there?"

So Maxie told him he just wanted to see his house, see if somebody—maybe his mom, maybe his dad—was there. Joey nodded, sympathetically, like the Artful Dodger might do in his shabby clothes and his face all dirty with soot. Then, "Hey, what if nobody is at home, dude? Where you going to sleep?"

Maxie thought, *I know*. Then, "I was hoping..."

And the kid said he would go with him to his parents' house—if it was still his parents' house—and see what's up. "My uncle will be at the bus station in Columbus. But I'll call him and he'll come and pick me up in Muskingum—no problems."

So Maxie thought about it and thought about his last days at his house in Muskingum, near the college, not far from Anthony's Antique Shop, and about his room, and the toys, even though he was too old for them now, but he wanted them anyway, and the baseball mitt, and his dad. And his mom at the screen door. His eyes watered as he fought the tears but he couldn't, so he turned toward the window again where the boy couldn't see him and he saw his face again, but he didn't see the tears, because of the darkness. And this face—in the window— looked sad to him, soft and sad. And it stared back so he turned away, but he knew it would still be watching him even when he would sleep.

Then his eyes drooped, and shut, and he slept, while the boy next to him, Joey Lewis, watched him. The Boy dreamed about the field down the street from his house and wondered if it would still be there and if he would be able to find it. In the dark. In the snow. It was so long ago.

Joey pulled out his cell as he watched Maxie sleep and made a call.

CHAPTER SEVENTY-NINE
CLEVELAND WONG

Early Saturday Morning, December 10

A winter storm was blowing into the Midwest from Canada—Canadians hate to be blamed for the weather. But the storms do develop in the north and the worst of them penetrate into Florida, chilling even south Florida, including Miami, where even the palms would wrap themselves in their branches if they could.

The temperature was dropping quickly—down to 53 degrees already—as I steered the Canyon down the waterway that led into the Pilot House. No lights were on in the houses that lined the channel. It was after 1:00 a.m. Everyone was tucked in. By the time we docked and tied the boat down it was nearly 1:30 and Wong would be landing near my house somewhere around 2:00. I wanted to get there before he did— warn the neighbors.

Wong touched down at 2:05. It was a Bell 407 with a long sleek body, built for easy egress for an assault team. The noise from the copter was deafening. If anyone in the area was asleep, they were awake now. He landed in a field nearby, one that he had used before. The pilot was a Coast Guardsman—it was a Coast Guard copter.

Richie, Louise, Huck, and I were waiting about a football field away—just to make sure we didn't lose our heads in the blades. It's happened. That's why people duck. The pilot shut the motor down and then there was silence. I waited for the sirens—neighbors complaining to the cops. Matter of fact my nearest neighbor was about a mile away. Most of the land surrounding me was Everglades. No sirens. Just the noise of the door of the copter opening and Wong climbing down. Wong is tall, six feet two at least, with black hair and a young face belying his fifty years. He crouched under the main rotor wing even though the blades were idle. Habit. The pilot remained in the cockpit and waved.

As soon as we were all clear, the pilot started the copter, warning beeps first then the whine of the turbine as the engine began the slow process of turning the blades. Then the noise grew, making me cringe as I thought of neighbors—even though the closest was a mile away—and the blades whipped the air, sounding like the world's largest lawn mower, and rose slowly, angling toward the open field. Then it dipped its blades forward and roared east toward the Miami skyline.

"Fucking better be a good reason for all this, Cooper," were the first words out of Wong's mouth as we all watched the lights of the copter disappear over Oceanside. But then he took my hand and gripped it firmly. "Good to see you again." Sign of acceptance. We started for the house.

"So, Richie, how's Cleveland these days?" he said as we followed the beam of my flashlight over the uneven ground.

"Same old, same old," he said. "Bad guys are still winning."

"So that's good for you, right?" and Wong chuckled over that.

"I'm one of the good guys. Ask Coop," Richie retorted.

"Uh-huh. And you keep the bad guys out of your territory, right?" Another chuckle.

Richie growled and muttered under his breath.

Then Wong turned to Louise. "How you doing?"

"I'm good, Cleveland," she said.

Wong had known Louise through her father, an important national police administrator in Colombia. He was working with Wong to curb Cartel operations in the U.S. when he was assassinated in front of his family home. Louise was just a young girl when she witnessed it. After that horrific incident, Wong felt responsible for the family and helped bring Louise to the U.S. He was Director of ICE (Immigrations and Customs Enforcement) at the time.

"You still shooting buffalo?" Now picking on Huck. He likes to stir him up.

"My family roamed this territory long before the white man —and your people," he said, turning to Wong, "came to our land..." That's Huck. "We had buffalo. You shot them."

Wong shook his head. "The Chinese didn't shoot buffalo. They built your railroads! Slave labor."

"Please," I said, holding up my hands. And Huck and Wong both shut up.

"Nice place you got here, Cooper," said Wong, as we climbed the three steps to the front porch. Sammy, of course, was there—inside the screen. Wong stared at him. He was afraid of cats. Sammy hissed at him. ESP. Wong skirted Sammy like he was avoiding a roadside bomb. When he had safely escaped, he fell in behind us as we headed for the kitchen where we could spread out, have a beer, and make a plan.

"So, see if I got this right," Wong began as we settled around the kitchen table. His hands formed a tent in front of his face as he looked over the tops of his fingers at each one of us. "You found a sample of some suspicious substance in Shark River where Ms. Cynthia's father was killed. And you told me that Doctor Graham Bell confirmed your suspicions about the substance. Right?"

"Right."

"And this substance is consistent with what is used in fracking and in directional drilling." He paused, pulling his glasses down so they rested on the tip of his nose.

Again, I said, "That's right."

"Uh-huh. And....there's that shooting this past evening from a go-fast boat—for no reason." Pause. I nodded. "From a boat that you saw parked by an oil rig in Ponce de Leon Bay? And—correct me if I have this wrong—you say this go-fast boat is the same boat that was parked at the *Zhi Zhu Nu*?" Nods all around.

"And you conclude that maybe our friends on the rig are not only engaging in illegal drilling but maybe also using the rig—maybe both rigs—as platforms for drug distribution. Right?"

"Right," I said. And everybody else nodded again. I wondered where this was going. Wong wasn't usually this talkative.

"You know about DTOs, right?" I did but I didn't tell him that. I wanted to hear what he had to say.

"Drug Trafficking Organizations," he continued. "You know that the greatest danger to this country" (talking only to me now) "is not terrorism but the inflow of drugs across our borders—especially the southwestern border?"

Richie and Huck were listening intently. But they looked like they were asking the same question I was: *Where was he going with this?*

Wong continued. "Smuggling drugs into the U.S. by maritime means only accounts for about one percent of all the drugs that flow into our country—I'm talking coke, meth, heroin, and *mary juana.*" His idea of a joke.

I got up and fished out a bottle of wine from the fridge. "You need this," I told Wong.

"Amen to that," said Richie. Then, "Where the fuck we goin' with this?"

Wong, ignoring the comment, went on: "So, ever since you told me about what you found about the go-fast boat, I'm thinking, you're right." He wasn't looking at me, but he was talking to me. "I think the Chinese guys are taking over the distribution of drugs in the Caribbean and using the rigs as a cover."

I saw Homeland Security written all over his brow—the Deputy Secretary at work in south Florida.

"Let's get some shut-eye, boys, and first thing in the morning I want you to show me where Hayward was killed. And I want to see where you got the sample, and then I want to go over to that damn rig and find out what the hell's going on—I mean the *Zhi Zhu Nu*. And if Li Lang Zhu is involved, then she and I are gonna have a little talk."

I had never seen Wong so wound up. I guess I finally got to him.

CHAPTER EIGHTY-ONE
MUSKINGUM OF O.H.I.O

Friday Night, December 9

The bus doors hissed and cold air rushed into the interior of the bus waking Maxie. And the driver announced that it was the Muskingum stop and everybody had about ten minutes before the bus left for Columbus.

"Come on, Maxie," said Joey, as he shook him awake and began to pull down his own bag from the overhead compartment. "You got a bag?"

"Yeah," said Maxie. "It's up there with yours. I'll get it." And he did, climbing over the seat and reaching over the people seated in front of him to grab his bag, and he was just tall enough to get it from where he stood. He was almost 5 feet 8 inches actually. Then he had it in hand and was following Joey to the door and down the stairs to the cold, to the snow, to the small station that was on the main street of where he used to live. He didn't remember this place, but of course he had never taken a bus from Muskingum to anywhere because his parents always took him places. The Boy looked down the street as he pulled his hood up over his head, Joey urging him, "Get inside, dude, it's too cold to stay out here."

Maxie looked around and didn't recognize any of the buildings that lined the street in the snow, in the cold, and suddenly he was very nervous. Maybe he had made a mistake leaving the comfort of his home in South Carolina, and his tutor, and even the Asp, even though he was a scary person—like a shadow. At least the Asp took care of him.

Then Joey grabbed him, ending the spell, ending the thoughts of returning, the rethinking of going back to the home that was really not his home and then they entered the warmth of the bus station, in good old Muskingum of O.H.I.O. and the Boy wondered what waited for him at his house on Main Street. And he wondered if Anthony might be there in his antique shop, because he lived there in an apartment upstairs. He was thinking of that—just in case. You know—if he needed a place to sleep.

CHAPTER EIGHTY-TWO
THE CALL

Early Saturday Morning, December 10

I t was 7:15 when I smelled coffee perking. Richie. He was probably up at 5:00 and ran to the all-night grocery store in Oceanside to stock up supplies. I had nothing but wine, cheese, peanut butter, and Sammy's food in my fridge.

Richie loves to cook. When he does, he starts early. If it's Italian, he begins to cook the sauce at 2:00 a.m. He puts the bread in the oven by 5:00 and starts the sausage and peppers around 7:00—that's for a 12:00 lunch. Sicilian style.

This morning the only other odor coming from the kitchen was the smell of bread baking, a rich, tempting smell, enough to make anyone lose their taste for a diet.

I was following the smell of the coffee and bread when I heard the guest bedroom door open and turned to see Wong duck under the fan and head for the living room couch.

"You look like hell," I said as he mussed up his full head of black hair and tried to wipe sleep from his eyes. Then he just sat, staring into the kitchen.

"I feel like hell," he said, then paused and looked into the kitchen where Richie was busy grilling maple-smoked ham. "But it smells like Richie is cooking up something good." And he got up and we both headed for the kitchen where we pulled up chairs and watched Richie take bread out of the oven. It was just after 7:00 a.m. and the bread was hot and risen.

"Wow!" said Louise, standing in the bedroom door. "Why didn't you wake me?"

"Wanted the bread for myself."

"You're in trouble, Coopertino," she said yawning, then struggled to the table.

"Where's Huck?" I said, turning to Wong. Louise and I had gone to bed before the others.

"I was on the couch," said Richie, opening the fridge and pulling out the butter. "Huck was in the guest bedroom with the Chinese guy," he said—not thinking.

"Fuck you, too," said Wong. He was in a bad mood already. Richie made it worse.

Then the four of us sat while Richie served hot bread and crispy grilled ham and poured regular coffee—I skipped decaf in deference to Wong. Then Richie joined us and we all feasted on the ham, the bread and butter, and the blackberry jam that melted on it, and for the moment we forgot about Shark River, and the *Zhi Zhu Nu*, and even about Jack's murder—just for this moment. And then Wong broke the silence.

"I didn't sleep last night," he said.

"Because...?" I said.

"I have to make a call."

"Uh-huh."

No response.

Then, "I better make that call," said Wong, surly. He got up from the table and walked out to the porch. Sammy followed him, rubbing against his leg. Wong pushed the cat away with his foot.

"Hey," I said. "Easy with Sammy!" He wasn't paying attention.

We all watched as Wong thumbed in a number and waited. The National Forest was quiet, as it is every morning until the swamp creatures waken, then, if you listen carefully, you can hear the life that exists below eye level, in the reeds, beneath the mangroves, in the grasses of the Everglades. But it's a subtle sound and it didn't drown out Wong's voice as he spoke—in Chinese—at first quiet as though respecting the silence of the Swamp, and relaxed, and then, ever so slowly, growing tense and perturbed, then yelling, Wong's voice disturbing the silence. And I knew why he was sour; I knew who he was talking to. It was Li Lung, the father of Li Lang Zhu, Tarantula Woman. The *Zhi Zhu Nu* named in deference to her.

Then Wong broke into English, probably so we could hear. "They have given the giant oil rig in the Florida Straits your daughter's name." (Just as I thought.) "And you, what do you know about this?" And he went on, sometimes in English, sometimes reverting to Chinese, and now and then looking back at us, then turning away, angry. And then it was over, and he walked back into the kitchen, his shoulders bent like a man ashamed of his height and shaking his head.

"*Wo hen cankui he houhui,*" he muttered, then looked up. "I am so ashamed," he said. "Li Lung denies everything. No drug transportation. Nothing to do with the rig in the bay. *Didn't know anything about that,* he said. I asked him about the fast boat that you saw at both rigs. He didn't know anything about that either. He says we are overreacting!" And Wong threw up his hands. He studied us for a few moments.

Then, "I think we have big trouble—"

"In Little China," I said.

CHAPTER EIGHTY-THREE
BACK TO SHARK RIVER

Later Saturday Morning, December 10

"Okay. We need to get on the road," said Wong. "Need us to help clean up?" he said turning to Richie. Like it just occurred to him.

"Nah. Let the little lady do that," Richie said, turning away from Louise and whistling as he picked up dishes and carried them to the counter. He turned around just as Louise was swinging at him with a wet towel. Because he had turned, she hit him in the face.

"Yeow!" he yelled, ducking, his hands over his head. "I was kidding!" His face red from the impact of the cloth.

"Uh-huh," said Louise. "So was I."

"Geez," said Wong. "You guys! Okay..." And he was getting serious. "This is the story about the *Zhi Zhu Nu...*"

Then he went on to explain how the giant rig, put together in the shipbuilding ports of three different countries, including Russia and the UK and owned by a Chinese firm with partial funding from Venezuela, had completed its drilling operation in its current western site that was offshore from Havana, and would be moving toward a new site, still in Cuban waters but further east, and that the offshore drilling activity—"believe it or not"—was "fully compliant with U.S. regulations"—as far as could be determined since inspections currently were almost non-existent ("fucked" is what he actually said) due to the tensions between the two countries— and that the present site was now non-operative, its two-hundred man workforce gone. "Just a skeleton crew," he added. "And now the only thing happening on that baby is maybe a little..."

"Drug activity." I added.

"That and some distribution—"

"That we need to curtail," I said.

"Right." A pause. "You want to finish my remarks?" he said. Testy.

"No. You're doing fine."

"Okay," (holding his temper) "then let's see if we can catch some bad guys."

We packed for a day trip and were back on the road again at mid-morning, Wong in the front seat with me, Louise in the second seat with Richie. They'd made up. Huck had crawled into the cargo section of the wagon.

Everybody was quiet. A short night—not much sleep. Wong had stretched out his legs as far as he could—which wasn't far. He tried to squirm himself into some sort of comfort and wasn't successful.

"So what else did Li Lung have to say?" I said. There was an uncomfortable silence.

But then, "I'm worried about his daughter."

"Li Lang Zhu?"

"Of course. Liu Xue is a sweet girl. Do you know the story of the Spider Woman in Chinese culture?"

"A little. I know the film *Zhi Zhu Nu—The Spider Woman.* And it was a really bad movie."

He nodded. "Yes, yes, yes. I know that film as well. And you are right, it was stupid. Yet it tells the story that Chinese people know about the Spider Woman.

"You know Zhi Zhu, which means The Spider, was an assassin who worked for the Black Lotus Tong."

I nodded, having told the same story to Louise several times. But I didn't stop him.

"In the movie Jade Leung plays two roles, Kenny and Ken, one an evil woman who kills her lovers while they are in midst of orgasm," and he paused as if to apologize, "and the other sensitive and kind. The two are in fact one person. Like your Dr. Jekyll and Mr. Hyde. Twins in one body. Spider Woman is Kenny. The final crazy part of the story is the detective who is pursuing Kenny, suspecting that she is a serial killer, is Michael Wong. Crazy, huh?"

I must have looked confused.

"You know, Wong, like the detective Michael Wong." He paused. "Ironic, no?" I must have still looked puzzled. "I, Cleveland Wong, pursuing the daughter of my good friend, Spider Woman." He was shaking his head. "It all spells..."

"Yeah. Trouble..."

"Big trouble..."

"In Little China."

"You already said that," he said, annoyed.

"I know. I liked it then and—"

"Uh-huh. Once is enough."

After a pause he continued: "Snow called me to say that Li Lang has left Boston and is now in Florida. And she's worried about her boyfriend, Lei Sun. She thinks he is with Li Lang."

Pause. "She wants us to look out for him," he added, shaking his head.

"You think he doesn't need looking out for," I said.

"That is correct," he said.

We were on the bridge that crosses the Bay of Florida and enters the Lower Keys. Key Largo was visible in the distance.

"Snow is thinking Li Lang is working with the Tong in the distribution of drugs."

"I think we saw Li Lang land by helicopter on the *Zhi Zhu Nu*. And I think Liu Xue's boyfriend was with her," I reminded him.

"I know. You told me. But I thought you made a mistake. In fact, I didn't want to believe it. I mean..." He hesitated.

"What?" I said, looking over at him. He was staring out at the Bay which runs beneath the bridge and stretches from the top of the Keys to Key West. The sun was high in the sky, but it hadn't crossed the meridian yet to reach high noon. And it was a warm sun that came through the windshield, not the burning sun of July and August.

"She is my niece, Cooper," he said, staring into the sun.

CHAPTER EIGHTY-FOUR
THE HOUSE ON MAIN STREET

The Boy and Joey walked down Main Street, in the dark, in the cold, and it was still snowing. They walked because nothing is very far in Muskingum, Ohio, nothing that a short walk wouldn't take them there. And they passed Anthony's Antique Shop, and Maxie's stomach turned as they did; and they passed the entrance to the college; and the great tree-filled lawn that fronted the administration building, behind which were the faculty offices of the philosophy department where his dad taught; and Maxie wished his father still taught there, that he wasn't dead.

Maybe he's not, he thought—but quickly dismissed that idea because the Man had said he was and why would he lie? Maxie got a headache and didn't want to think of those things anymore. And then, up ahead, there it was: on the right, up a small embankment where he had chased his baseball down the hill, where he remembered meeting a man at the base of the hill where the ditch met the road. He stopped and stared at it. Joey stopped and stared as well.

"What's the matter, dude?" Joey said. But Maxie couldn't tell him, couldn't tell him about the feeling in his stomach as he watched, about the terror when the man shoved him into the car, about the helplessness as he watched his house disappear in the rear window and about how he had hoped that his dad and mom would see him and...and he had to look up to see it, towering above the road. His house. How could he ever forget it? And he gasped as he took it in, that house that he had dreamed about so many nights in his new home that was never his home, that was a place of captivity.

This was his home, and it was still here, looking just like it did so many years ago, the porch and the swing, and the screen door, and the second story that looked out over the street, and his bedroom, up there on the second story, where all his toys had been, and his bed, and his glove and bat, and he looked for lights, any sign of life, in this house, where his mom and dad used to live, any sign that someone was still living there who could tell him what happened to his mother and father. He was frozen, staring.

Joe E. Lewis was staring at the Boy, because Maxie was standing like a zombie, his body locked in the snow and his eyes locked on the house. And there were no lights, no sign of life at all, in the dark, in the cold, and it was snowing there on Main Street, in Muskingum, Ohio.

CHAPTER EIGHTY-FIVE
THE BIG RIG

Saturday Morning. December 10

I never followed up on what Wong had told me—about Li Lang. I would never, ever have guessed it...but it is what he said. So...

We drove in silence to the marina and I never raised the issue. It was his business. And besides, it would be his to discuss and his to tell the others when and if he decided to do it. We were at the Pilot House by 11:30 a.m. The winter sun—what there was of it—had already burned off the mist from the water. Richie and Louise readied the boat while I unhooked the gas hose and began to pump fuel into the Canyon's tanks. The boat drank in the gas like a thirsty marathoner. By the time the tanks were full, the pump read $2,030.00. My wallet groaned, but Wong produced a credit card. "I get reimbursed; no problems, Coop." And just like that, the Federal Government rescued the little guy.

We cast off. Richie tossed the fore and aft lines on board to Louise and me. We tied them down while Huck took the wheel. He kicked the starter and the three Yamahas roared like hungry lions as the Canyon began to churn its way slowly away from the dock into the No-Wake zone of Lake Largo. It took about twenty minutes to clear the channel that leads to the Straits.

Okay, let's talk about where we're going," Wong said.

"Shark River, right?" I said, turning to him. He saw my confusion.

"No. Change of plans."

"What?"

"Liu Xue called to warn me about a conversation she overheard between her sister and Lei Sun about a shipment of drugs. She said it would be coming through the Florida Straits and it would be sometime today—either late afternoon or early evening." I must have continued to look confused because he continued:

"I didn't tell you because this is Homeland business."

I shook my head as Huck throttled back. "So where are we going?" Huck said, an edge to that question.

"Toward the *Zhi Zhu Nu*," he said. "I think the shipment is originating from there."

"How do you know that?" I said, irritated that he had kept this secret from us until just now.

"Because Liu Xue thought so. And she was very concerned that her friend, Lei Sun, was in big trouble with her sister. *Under the influence of Dragon Lady*—her words. She thought that's where they are now—on the big rig. Get it?" He paused. "And she wants me—Uncle Wong—to save him." And just like that, he told the others. They showed it by the looks on their faces.

"I know. I still can't believe it." He threw up his hands. "You realize I could be putting some of my own family in jail. This could cost me my job!"

I knew what he was really saying: that he would be

dishonored in the Chinese community and would not be able to face his family because of the shame his niece had brought to them.

"So, Li Lung is...?"

"My brother," he said, like he had just been caught in a major crime.

I felt bad for him—and guilty for asking. "So, now what?" I said.

"I've ordered a cutter with a copter and a fast boat to the area near the *Zhi Zhu Nu*—it should be there later this afternoon."

I was stunned. "You getting ready for an invasion?"

"Gotta be prepared, Cooper. You should know. Used to be a Boy Scout, didn't you?"

I shook my head. Good old Wong.

"So we wait in the Straits for a while. See what happens," he continued. Then, as if there were some good news, "Hey, this might be the biggest bust ever. But my family..." And the good news died there.

CHAPTER EIGHTY-SIX
THE WAITING GAME

Once we were clear of the canal, Huck eased the throttle forward and we were on our way, south-southwest toward Havana and the Florida Straits. The Canyon has about a 350-statute mile range, but at the rate at which we would be traveling, about forty miles per hour, that range drops significantly. Still plenty of fuel to get us across the Straits and back several times.

We made good time under clear skies with fair weather predicted for the afternoon. But there are always those sudden storms that rise in the Gulf. Mother Nature. She can always change her mind.

Richie and Louise were below. We joined them. Richie was pouring drinks for himself and Louise.

"Make two for us," I said, looking at Wong.

"Rum and Coke," he said.

"Double that," I said.

We sat across from each other, Richie and Louise still standing near the sink.

Wong thought for a moment, looking sheepishly at Louise and Richie. "As you now know, I got family in this gig," he said, continuing his confession. We all stared and listened. Richie took a swig of a drink that he should have been sipping.

"Hey, no need..." Louise began.

"No, no, no. I need," Wong said. He thought for a moment as Richie handed him his drink, then continued.

"For a long time, I have suspected that the family of Li Lang has been involved in the drug business. And here I am, Deputy Secretary of Homeland Security, fighting against the spread of drugs into our country. Recently, I got word that the Chinese gangs have been taking over the drug business in the Caribbean—from the Columbians. It's a war. And the Chinese are winning."

We nursed our drinks while he talked.

"So, when you,"and he was looking at me, "told me your suspicions about the rigs, I figured, yeah, they're getting sophisticated, and smart, using the rigs like a distribution center. Hey what could be better? A big base in the Caribbean, in Cuban waters, in our 'can't touch zone' and able to ship throughout southeast U.S. Get it? Make money two ways: oil and drugs. And oil is their big front."

Wong was staring into his drink. "Li Lung is the big kingpin in the U.S. He is the godfather for the Tong on the east coast. Lei Sun is his right-hand man. And..." he continued, "unfortunately," like he was apologizing, "his daughter thinks she *is* the Spider Woman."

We stared at him, in this small space, in this cramped cabin under the console, drinking and saying nothing, waiting for Wong to continue.

"And I am afraid Li Lang is involved—and Lei Sun as well," he said, still staring at me sidewise, his body slumped forward, like it was broken at the waist.

"I think she is in charge down here." The sadness in his eyes was like that of a man who had just lost a daughter.

They were huddled against the cold, staring at the house when a car pulled up in front of Anthony's Antique Shop and honked, twice, quickly—small beeps, into the silence.

"That's gotta be my Uncle Charley," Joey said.

Maxie looked at the car. It was across the street and down a block. In the dark it looked long and sleek like the car that had taken him away and he jerked back at the sight of it.

"What's wrong?" said Joey.

"Oh nothing," said Maxie. "How'd he know where we were?"

"I told him where we would be—near the antique shop across from the college." He paused. "Like you said," he added, reassuring his new friend.

Maxie nodded and the car door opened. A tall man—he was thin—stepped out and looked around. He was wearing a long black overcoat—but everything looked black in the dark. And he was wearing a hat. Clothes like the Man wore when he went out.

"Uncle Charley," said Joey, grabbing Maxie. "Come on,

dude," He started running over to the man, dragging the Boy with him. The man turned to them and held his hand up over his eyes as if to shade them from the street light that was directly overhead.

"Joey!" he yelled out as we approached. "Come on over here, boy!" He held out his arms as Joey practically ran into him. The Boy was liking him already.

"And this is…?" he asked, as Joey pulled away to introduce Maxie.

"My new friend, Maxie," said Joey, beaming as the man held out his hand and took Maxie's.

"Hi Maxie, I'm Joey's uncle. So, it's good to meet you." He shook Maxie's hand in a warm and friendly way. "You can call me Charley." Maxie noticed that the man had a mustache. A big one that ran all the way across his upper lip. It was sprinkled brown and gray.

The Boy nodded and said, "Okay." He was thinking he would like Joey's uncle. He waited for the uncle to say something. Then he did.

"So, what are we going to do?" the man continued, this man who was Joey's uncle, and Maxie was glad Joey had an uncle. And the man in the long coat with the mustache said, "Joey told me that you used to live here," and he looked around as if to find out where that was.

Maxie pointed to his house on the hill across the street, on the same side of the street as the college. It was dark, and its roof was covered with snow, and he said, "Yeah. Right there." The house seemed to take on a special life as he said it, memories flooding his mind. He was losing his breath…

"It's okay," the uncle said, as if he could see Maxie's distress. "Joey kind of told me your story." He was hesitant while he spoke, not wanting to upset the Boy.

"I think my mom and dad are dead," Maxie said.

Then the three of them looked across at the house as if there were some secret there that would unlock the way to the future, in this large, early 1900s Victorian house, whose windows were dark and unyielding of secrets.

"There's a mailbox over there," the boy, Joe E. Lewis, said, pointing to the box on the wall of the porch.

"Of course," said Joey's uncle. "Maybe..."

Then all three approached the house by climbing up the bank that Maxie had descended when he chased the ball, and across the lawn where he threw the ball high into the summer air, and up to the porch where he would bang the screen door— his mom always yelled at him when he did that —and finally, to the small white box that hung on the wall. The mailbox.

Then the man, whose name was Charley, looked down at Maxie, and said, "Here goes..." and he lifted up the lid of the mail box and pulled out some letters and other stuff, and began to look through them. But then he paused. "Is this okay, Maxie?"

And, of course, Maxie nodded that it was.

CHAPTER EIGHTY-EIGHT
JILLIE AND HENRY

Early Saturday Morning, December 10
Fourteen Shopping Days Before Christmas

J illie and Henry had stayed inside, through the cold, through the heavy snow that settled over the Inn and over the town of Chagrin Falls, the kind of snowfall that makes Chagrin look like a New England town. They had made love in the warmth of the inn's bedroom, and drunk wine in the inn's dining room, in front of the hearth—a fire burning constantly there—and then, returning to the bedroom, made love again, each time setting a new record since she had never given herself to anyone since Cooper had left. Still Jillie fretted, worrying her fingers. *But Cooper would understand*, she would tell herself—*would encourage*, she thought, and yet...

"I think I need to get back," she said, on this early Saturday morning, feeling uneasy about something, suddenly, over breakfast, while the fire was warming them.

Henry looked at her, holding his coffee carefully as he studied her, and began, "But..." And she knew what he was going to say: that they had two more days of their quick get-a-way left...

"I know, Henry," she said quickly, feeling kind of bad, but not that bad, "but I need to get back." Saying it with the finality of reasoning that only a woman can summon up, that finality that comes from an instinct as old as human memory. And Henry, reluctant, but willing to abide her decision, nodded and said, "Okay. Then we go back. We'll save the two days for another time, shall we?"

Jillie smiled at that and nodded.

C harley, the uncle with the big mustache, studied the mail—he had to bend into the street light to see—Maxie and Joey watching him closely. Then he looked over at Maxie and said,

"Joey told me your last name was Cooper."

Maxie just nodded. "Uh-huh."

"He said that you thought your parents were dead?" He waited.

"Yeah, that's right," said Maxie. "That's what they told me."

"Who's they?" the uncle continued, watching Maxie closely, his head cocked to one side.

"The men who took me. They said my parents were killed in an automobile accident." Defensive, like he was covering up a lie. Maybe a lie that somebody else told, but he was guilty somehow—maybe because he was part of the lie. He felt bad about that.

Then, the uncle, noticing Maxie's discomfort, continued. "Well, these letters here are addressed to Ms. Jillian Cooper. Is that your mother's name?" And it bothered Maxie that the man with the black mustache was talking to him like he was guilty of something—like a lie—when he wasn't. So Maxie didn't say anything right away. He just stared at the ground like he had been caught doing something bad. And if the letters were addressed to Ms. Jillian Cooper, who was she? His mother? And if she was, who were the men who had taken him? The men who had lied to him? The men who had taken him to his new home with the Man? Who might also be a liar.

Maxie's head began to spin. *My mother?* he thought. *Alive? And if it is my mother, and she was really alive all this time, why didn't she call?* It was all too much for Maxie, the Boy who had lived with a man who acted like his father, but had lied about his mother. Maxie wondered if his father was alive too? And if so, why didn't he come to get him?

Maxie stared into the darkness, feeling more alone now than ever. And confused. And frightened. And his stomach hurt now more than it had ever hurt, and his eyes began to water. But he fought against the tears, because he was fifteen years old, and he didn't need to cry, not now, not when he found out that maybe, after all these years, his mother and father were still alive. So, he made a decision to be tough.

Where that came from he didn't know—maybe from the Asp—so he turned to the uncle and said, "Yeah, that's my mother's name." Then he started to cry and he couldn't do a damn thing about it.

CHAPTER NINETY
WHAT TO DO NEXT?

The uncle put his arms around Maxie, this man who was much taller than Maxie, the man who found the mail addressed to Jillian Cooper, who was probably his mother. "So what are we going to do?" he said.

Joey and Maxie and the uncle stood on the porch—the letters still in Charley's hand—looking out at Main Street, Maxie trying not to think about what happened to him eight years ago. The snow had stopped falling. There was now about a half-foot on the ground, the white of it sparkling under the street lamps. It felt like Christmas, but not to the Boy, who was trying to figure out what the adults had done to him, to his life, for these past eight years. At least, he thought, maybe I'm not an orphan.

"Let's go to my place," said the uncle, who seemed like such a wise man to Maxie, like such a kind man, like a man who wouldn't tell lies. So—now that he was older, and with Joe E. Lewis—he could get into the car with him. Safely. He hoped.

Joey and Maxie got into the uncle's big black car, the one that looked something like the car the kidnappers had originally taken him in, and they drove in the cold of the night, without snowfall—but the highway was covered with it and snowplows were already trying to clear a path—until they came to a sign that read:

Columbus
City Limits

And Maxie knew he was in Columbus of O.H.I.O. . He looked at Joey, and Joey smiled at him like he knew what he was thinking; good old Joey Lewis, who was named after a famous star, Joe E. Lewis.

M axie didn't remember much about Columbus because the only time they ever went there was when his father had a meeting at a university, and his mom and he would go along. Maxie's eyes were trying to close as they drove through the city which was mostly dark now, the only lights at 4:45 in the morning—Maxie read the time on the dashboard—were the lamps hanging over the streets and, of course, the stop lights. Most of them were all flashing yellow because it was early morning. Maxie didn't remember being up this late—ever —as he fought to keep his eyes open.

Finally, they pulled into a kind of inner-city place, with red brick buildings, tall, lit up by gas lamps along the street. It was awfully pretty, Maxie thought, a lot of Christmas decorations hanging: wreaths on the lamp posts, and strings of lights—small white ones—over the intersections, and red and green Christmas bulbs in the store windows. He read the names on several store fronts: Schmidt's, a bar/restaurant that he remembered being in with his parents; The Book Loft; and his favorite, Max and Erma's—he remembered that one because it had his name on the sign. "Maybe someday the owner will sell it to us; it already has your name, Maxie," his dad had told him once.

Finally, they pulled up in front of a tall brick building that looked like an apartment building and parked on the street. It had started snowing again as Maxie's eyes were drooping—they had been for quite some time. The last thing he heard was Charley saying, "Well, we're home."

CHAPTER NINETY-ONE
THE CHASE

Saturday Afternoon, December 10

That sudden storm was developing—just like I said it might—and the wind and the rain were coming. The rain was coming as a wall of darkness leaning our way from the west. The wall was topped with clouds. Black. Menacing. It was moving quickly. I could feel it coming—in the coolness of the wind. Huck was trying to keep the Canyon steady against the push of the oncoming storm, the waves now rolling.

We had arrived at the coordinates that Wong had set out in the Straits, about two miles from the *Zhi Zhu Nu*. Huck had throttled down to idle—to conserve fuel. Then we waited for the Coast Guard. And after that we would wait again: for the drug run that was supposed to happen in early evening, according to Snow, where coke would be transferred from the big rig to the small one, from where it would be hurried through the hidden waterways of the Big Cypress by airboat to landfall and then to points north and east in the United States. Good plan. Using oil rigs in the Caribbean as distribution centers.

~

"That's what got Jack Hayward killed," Wong said as I went below to get out of the weather. "He got in the way of what they were doing!"

Richie was nodding off. Louise was trying to look interested. Wong had been talking all through the afternoon—he talked, and talked, and talked. I needed to go topside before I lost my mind. But he was still going when I got back.

"You better believe it," he muttered, as much to himself as to us. "Fucking drugs taking over our young people's lives. Our job is to stop the flow. You better believe it. And the worst thing —my niece..." His head was down the whole time, like a man condemned.

I tried to enrich his Coke with some more Captain Morgan. He refused. "Need to keep my head clear." He paused. "But suit yourself."

And so I did. Then I took my drink topside to check on Huck.

The sun was heading for the horizon, barely visible through the rain.

Huck. "How long we gonna wait?"

"I don't know," I said.

"Cooper's enigmatic," he replied.

When Huck wants to, he can speak very literately. He loves to play dumb. It's a ploy.

"I is," I said. I can play too.

The sound of heavy motors droned through the distance.

Wong must have heard them because he was topside and standing next to me, looking in the direction of the sound.

"The Cutter," he said. "They'll have a copter and a chase boat." He strained to see through the rain even though it had settled into a drizzle. But there was also a fog now haunting the Straits. I could only see about a hundred yards.

PART THREE

"Yesterday, upon the stair
I met a man who wasn't there!
He wasn't there again today,
Oh how I wish he'd go away!"

WILLIAM HUGHES MEARNS, ANTIGONISH,
1899

CHAPTER NINETY-TWO
THE WATCH

Saturday Morning, December 10

It was around 5:00 o'clock in the a.m. when Maxie dozed off on the soft queen in the guest bedroom. Joey stayed up and talked another hour until his uncle started to nod off, then they both went to sleep, Joey on a leather couch in the den and the uncle in his own bedroom. Charley didn't rise until almost noon at which time he woke both Maxie and Joey for breakfast: waffles, sausage and eggs. Both boys ate like you would expect them to eat, having only noshed on potato chips, peanuts, Cokes, and candy they picked up at the bus stops.

"Time to go back to your house," said Charley, turning to Maxie as he cleaned up the dishes. "Someone ought to be there by now."

Maxie's stomach was at it again, the pain rising quickly, right in the middle of his gut, but he didn't show it. There was no point. They piled into Charley's car—the black car. A scary black car.

It was late afternoon when they parked in front of the house. There was another car parked up the street. Maxie thought he recognized it. *Asp maybe,* he thought, and he became terrified, almost like when the men had taken him those many years ago; eight to be exact. And Maxie strained to see if there was anyone in the car.

Charley parked and they took the concrete steps up the embankment that led to the front porch of his house. Maxie kept glancing back at the car down the street, parked almost in front of Anthony's Antique Shop. Steam was coming out of the exhaust as it sat there. Maxie shivered from the cold—or from being scared. He couldn't tell which.

"Is something wrong?" Charley said, looking back at Maxie.

"No," said the Boy, wondering if he should have said, *yes,* and explained it all to him. But he was afraid of what the Asp might do if the uncle went over to his car, so he said, "No, everything is okay."

Keeping his eyes on the car the whole time, almost tripping as he mounted the stairs that scaled the embankment, and almost slipping on the icy walkway as he crossed to the porch, staring at the lawn where he had played. It was now covered with snow. Then he looked up the street to see if the car was still there. And it was.

Before the Boy realized it, the uncle was knocking on the door and waiting for a response—which didn't come. So Charley turned and pointed to a coffee shop down the street across from where the car was parked that might be the Asp's and said, "Let's wait in there and see if your mom comes home," and Maxie wondered if this woman whose name was Jillian Cooper was really his mom, or whether she was someone with the same name who, maybe, bought the house. *There might be lots of people with that same name,* he thought—*because my mom is dead. The Man who took him said she was—and he said his dad was dead also—both killed in an automobile accident.*

And Maxie had seen that crash so many times in his head that it had to be real.

So they set out for the coffee shop, and as they crossed the street in front of the car that might be the Asp's, Maxie looked quickly at the car to see...but the windows were fogged, and he thought that maybe...maybe it wasn't Asp. They entered the warmth of the coffee shop where Maxie had come often with his dad and mom, and they sat at a booth in front of a window overlooking the street so they could watch the house where Maxie had grown up.

They had sat there for over an hour, when a black Mercedes pulled into the driveway and parked in front of the garage of Maxie's house. And the Boy's breath left him as he watched a woman get out of the car. She was so bundled up he couldn't see her face. Then a man climbed out of the driver's side and helped her up the stairs. Maxie stared at the man who was with the woman who might be his mother. The man and the woman hesitated at the front door, and they kissed for what seemed an eternity to the Boy.

As the man turned away and began to descend the steps, the uncle began to rise. But the Boy had an uneasy feeling as the man started across the sidewalk to his car, because he turned and looked their way. And the Boy's stomach dropped through the floor as the man took off his hat, brushed hair away from his face, and looked straight at Maxie in the window of the coffee shop, then hesitated, like he actually saw him. Then he turned back to the house, climbed the stairs once more, and opened the door.

The Boy pulled Charley back down to the table. "Not yet," he said.

Then, moments later, the man—now Maxie was sure it was him—came back out carrying a scarf that he was wrapping around his neck. Then he got into his car, pulled around in the drive so he wouldn't have to back into the street, and headed in the direction of the black car. As he passed it, the car pulled out and followed him.

Maxie was frozen, just like the lady in the Bible story, and Charley, the uncle whom Maxie trusted now, the man who had rescued Joey from the orphanage, this same man, stared at Maxie who was white with terror, and asked him what was the matter and Joey asked him, "What's wrong, dude?"

But Maxie just stared at the two cars moving down the street, almost in synchrony, and said, "That's the man who kidnapped me!"

,

CHAPTER NINETY-THREE
I MET A MAN WHO WASN'T THERE

axie wondered why he, the Man who had kidnapped him, was with his mom—if this was his mom—and now he was hoping it wasn't, and if she was his mom really, what did it all mean?

Charley said, "Shit!" Maxie had never heard him swear before and Joey said, "No way, dude!" Then all three of them were silent for a few moments. Staring at the house where Maxie had lived out his childhood. And both the uncle and Joey must have been wondering the same thing Maxie was— why was his mother with this evil man?

But the uncle, a man of determination, rose quickly, turned to the boys and said, "Stay here," and headed toward the house on the hill. Maxie and Joey watched him ascend the drive, being careful not to slip; and then mount the stairs covered with snow; and knock on the door. They watched the woman who was supposed to be Maxie's mother, Jillian Cooper, open the door. They watched him talking with her. They saw her put her hand over her mouth as if in a scream. They watched as she fell forward into Uncle Charley's arms. He caught her, and held her.

The uncle looked back at the coffee shop, nodded for the boys, and then waved them over when he was able to free an arm from the woman, who must be Jillian Cooper, Maxie thought. Then the woman began to right herself and stood frozen on the frozen porch of the big home on the hill, where Maxie grew up, and waited for the two boys to come up the drive. And they did.

The woman, who was Maxie's mother, Jillian Cooper, the woman who had thought that her son was dead, ran off the porch almost slipping and screaming as she hurried to them—for a moment stopping and glancing at both Joey and Maxie, as if to choose between them—then quickly rushed ahead, threw her arms around Maxie, and cried and pulled him into her body, smothering him against her breasts until the snow melted around them.

"Yes, yes, yes, yes, I knew you were still alive!" she screamed, loud enough so everyone in Muskingum, of O.H.I.O could hear, and a few people on the street, walking toward Anthony's Antique Shop, did stop and stare, and Charley, the man who had come to his rescue, and Joey Lewis, his new friend—maybe his only friend—smiled and laughed and cried a little, and then, finally, Jillian held Maxie away from herself, looked into his face, into the face of the boy she had thought was lost, forever, wiped his tears away, brushed his hair away from his face—some blond still in it—and then wiped the tears from her own eyes and took a deep breath, and said, "My God, I can't believe it! You are home! After all these years!"

Jillie and Maxie, and Joey and Charley stood on the front lawn of Maxie's home, all of them still disbelieving, Jillie thinking, *I have to call Coop. He won't believe this!*

CHAPTER NINETY-FOUR
OH HOW I WISH HE'D GO
AWAY!

Then Maxie said, "Who was that Man you were kissing?"

Jillie started at that question. "The man? You saw...?"

"Yeah," Maxie said, a little embarrassed. "We were across the street at the coffee shop." He turned and pointed to it.

"Oh," she said, and tried to begin to explain—hurriedly—thinking that Maxie might think she was being disloyal to his dad. So she said, "Oh, that man is just an old friend from Georgetown." She paused, then started up again, nervously, explaining that his dad knew the man and that it was okay with him, because..." Then she realized that Maxie wouldn't know they were separated, so she added quickly, "Well, because your father and I are no longer together." She felt funny about telling him that—so soon—so soon after Maxie had reappeared so magically—after eight years of pain and worry—but Maxie was just staring at her. And she wondered why.

Then, "That's the Man who kidnapped me," Maxie said, dead-voiced and quiet.

A silence fell over Jillie, over all of them, and could have extended to all the people in Muskingum of O.H.I.O. who might be standing around them, as if to celebrate, you know, like in the movies made in Hollywood, when the main characters, the man and the woman, who are in love, finally get together and the people surrounding them on the set start clapping, just like they should be now, except...

Upon Maxie's news flash, instead of clapping (from this imaginary crowd), there was only a stunned silence. Jillie didn't know what to say, so she just stared at Maxie, afraid to ask about this Man. She was thinking, *No, that's not possible, he...*

Her mind was confused at this news from her son who had just returned to her after eight years of torture. If there had been onlookers from the town, like on a movie set, if there had been that crowd, they would also have been confused and the clapping would have stopped. And the booing and the anger would have started, just like it was starting in Jillie as she began to incorporate this new information into her brain, about *this man—whom I had been dating; this man*—and she was frozen like the wife of Lot in Sodom and Gomorrah—*whom I have slept with!*

The horror of it struck her as she realized what had happened. *This man who had wooed me in Georgetown and who has for the last eight years destroyed our lives, and contaminated our home, and taken my son away from me, and driven my husband from me; this man who dared to kiss me on the porch, in front of my son...*and she knew that Cooper would be like an erupting volcano when he found out.

She screamed and then cried and grabbed Maxie and held him tightly to her body and said, "I am so sorry. I am so sorry." And sobs shook her body as she spoke under her breath into his ear, trying to console him. "I had no idea. I had no idea!"

She looked into the winter sky and raged inside at what Henry had done to her. And to Cooper. And to Maxie. And she vowed revenge as the snow fell on them and the afternoon got colder. *I have to call Cooper,* she thought. Once excited, but now...

She looked at Charley and then at Joey, as if to thank them, but also as if to say, *I'm so ashamed.*

Charley put his arm around her and pulled Maxie in as well, and Joey tried to put his arms around them all. Then Charley whispered to Jillie, "It's going to be all right. Your son's back. That's the main thing."

Charley and Joey followed Jillie and Maxie into the house, the one that sits on a hillock in Muskingum, Ohio, where Maxie used to play, that is before someone took him, eight years ago, a man who had retrieved a baseball that Maxie had been playing with, that had rolled into a ditch at the bottom of the hill that abutted the street, muddy that morning with rain from the night before, a man who had helped him clean off his baseball, luring him to his car, a long black one, with the promise of finding a rag to "clean it up better," then pushed him into the car and drove away with him, leaving that house on the hill behind, as Maxie watched. That very house that Maxie was now entering again—for the first time—in eight years. And Maxie would be telling Jillie—and Cooper—all about it. All the while his stomach would hurt, and all the while Jillie's heart would be near to shutting down, and all the while Cooper would be raging inside. But that would be later. When this was all over.

As soon as they were all in the house, Jillie excused herself and hurried to call Cooper. But he wouldn't answer because...

PART FOUR

THE BATTLE IN THE FLORIDA STRAITS

CHAPTER NINETY-FIVE
PLAN OF ATTACK

Saturday Afternoon, December 10
Fourteen Shopping Days Before Christmas

We were in the middle of the Straits, twenty-five miles or so from the Keys, and sitting in a bank of mist, when I saw it and was transfixed by it. The ship I mean. It came out of the fog. A beast of a ship. Long and menacing in the mist that surrounded it. The words U. S. COAST GUARD in big black letters on its side. The number "910" across the prow. The ship itself was all white, a large red stripe running at an angle down the hull, white and blue stripes chasing along the side of the wide red stripe. The ship had come prepared. A big gun was mounted on a turret in the center of the foredeck and the blades of a helicopter emerged on the aft deck as the ship was now only a few hundred yards away. A small chase boat was riding in its wake.

"You brought out the Navy," I said, leaning into Wong's ear.

"The Coast Guard is part of Homeland Security, Cooper.

Been that way for a few years now. You need to study up," he added, watching the vessel approach.

"How'd they find us in this stuff?" I said.

"You kidding? I'm Deputy Secretary. Got my ways."

I watched with him as the cutter began to bear down on us, its motors quiet as it cut the waves like a sharp knife through a meringue pie.

"We going to invade the *Zhi Zhu Nu?*" I said, admiring its massive size.

"You crazy?" he said, turning from the cutter to me. "We go into Cuban waters, we could start a war."

"But you are the Deputy Secretary," I reminded him. "Maybe you can declare war on the *Zhi Zhu Nu.*"

"Yeah," he said, turning back to the cutter now only about a hundred yards from our port side, "and you would be looking at the former Deputy Secretary."

Then he pulled himself up over the railing to watch three seamen board the chase boat that had been dropped from the stern of the cutter. The seas were rough despite the passing of the rain, and the men struggled to keep their balance in the boarding maneuver. Then the chase boat wheeled away from the cutter and pulled in tight to the Canyon and three Guardsmen climbed on board through the transom door that's located next to the Yamahas. Two were in their working gear: blue cap, shirt untucked, and blue pants tucked into black boots. The third Guardsman was a woman. She had commander's insignia (resembling a Maple Leaf) on her shoulders. She was tall, maybe six feet one or two, thin. Her cheeks were chapped red from the wind and rain. Some hair had escaped from under her cap and hung over the left side of her face. She took off her cap, pushed the hair, black and wet, into place, and saluted Wong. She looked like a young Lucy Liu.

"How was your trip from Key West, Commander?" asked Wong.

"I've had better, Sir, the weather slowed us. Captain Welder sends his best." Turning to me she added, "And to you, Mr. Cooper," the trace of a smile crossing her lips. She must have known.

Welder had bailed me out twice before. The first time Richie, Louise, Huck, and I were pursuing smugglers through the Ten Thousand Islands. The second time was in international waters about twenty miles from the coast of Cuba. Chasing bad guys again.

"Third time's a charm—I hope," I said.

She smiled. She knew.

Wong jumped in. "Commander Sykes, this is Cooper." She was still smiling when she held out her hand. "Frances," she said.

"So, what have we got here, Sir," Sykes said, turning back to Wong.

The fog was dense now, but the rain had stopped. Wong was staring out at the sea toward the *Zhi Zhu Nu*.

"We can't go into Cuban waters. Need President's okay to do that," he said, still staring at the sea as though he were studying it—the waves, the rain and the fog—all working together to make his job more difficult.

"Like the Bay of Pigs," I said.

"No shit," whispered Richie from behind. Louise must have poked him in the ribs because I heard a grunt.

"My idea," said Wong, "you guys can do what we can't," turning slightly in my direction. "You do a little reconnaissance —I stay here and wait," he turned fully around now, "for your call." He paused while he had my attention. "Some danger for you and your crew," he warned.

"Understood," I said, looking around at Louise, who was

next to me (she nodded), and Richie who was leaning against the top rail, watching us (he nodded as well) and then at Huck who was minding the wheel, just listening, but then finally announcing, "We'll ride with you, buckaroo." It's hard not to love him.

And I thought of what I had just agreed to: putting the lives of my friends in jeopardy, not to mention my own. I wondered if I would ever live to find out about Maxie. But this was all about him anyway: finding missing people, like Jack; tracking kidnappers; and chasing people who make a living selling body parts. What a world. But that's been my life. The good part is I'm hoping this job will help me track down my son, the bad part being that I'm afraid of what I'll find if I ever do.

"My informant (and I knew who that was) tells me there will be a transfer from the *Zhi Zhu Nu* tonight—to a smaller rig in the Ponce de Leon Bay area," Wong continued. "My guess, this fog will give them the cover they needed." He paused, staring at his feet. "The transfer could happen any time," he added, breathing deeply, looking out at the cutter and the nasty seas beyond.

"Your fast boat's good for a chase," I assured him.

"Right," said Wong. "But we don't know when this is going to happen or precisely where. So..."

"You're suggesting we get things started early," I said.

"My thought," said Wong. "Only thing...if you guys get caught with your hands up someone's skirt, you're on your..."

"Whoa! Can't you think of a better analogy?" interrupted Louise. She was standing by Huck at the wheel. "Up someone's skirt? How about up your pants?" Talk about PC.

"Oops, so sorry. Old Chinese saying," Wong added quickly, using the cultural divide as an excuse.

"Uh-huh. Like you're old *and* you're Chinese," said Louise, getting him back. Wong looked uncomfortably at Sykes. She shrugged. But I could see a smile creep into the edges of her mouth.

"I get it," said Wong, obviously trying to end the conversation. Sykes was enjoying it.

"Never insult white woman," said Huck. "Old *Indian* saying." Louise smacked him in the arm.

In the meantime, the rain had started up again. At first, soft against the fog. Then harder.

"Good luck," Wong said. "Call me on the SAT when you get near the rig."

Then he, Sykes, and the two Guardsmen boarded the chase boat.

I watched them fight off waves through the hundred yards to the cutter. I stayed in the rain long enough to feel the misery of it and wondered what the rest of this day would bring.

CHAPTER NINETY-SIX
THE RAIN AND THE FOG

Saturday Afternoon, December 10

The fog was growing denser. Huck strained to see through it, fighting to control the boat in a sea made rough by the wind. I offered to take a turn at the wheel.

"I can break this bronco, pardner," Huck said, as the waves tried to tear the wheel from his hands.

Richie was standing next to me in the helm.

"You okay?" I said, turning to Richie. There was no blood in his cheeks.

"Yeah, yeah. No problem." He was not taking his eyes off the water. It roiled like a cauldron about to spill over.

See, since Richie can't swim, his nightmare is not about getting shot. It's about drowning. But he'll never admit it.

"How do we you know where the hell we're going?" said Richie to no one in particular.

"The boat's compass," said Louise. She was leaning over the gunnels on starboard, probably looking for lights from the rig. "Too far away yet," she added.

We were headed south-southwest toward Havana. The *Zhi Zhu Nu* was about ten miles off shore, directly north of Havana.

"Hang in there," I yelled to Huck, as a wave suddenly swept through the helm.

Richie didn't say anything, but I knew he got religion when he was on the water.

I figured we were only a couple of miles from the big rig so I told Huck to slow down. "We should see some lights soon," I said, hoping for the best.

But it was black on the water, and black in the sky and the rain kept coming. And waves were pounding the boat with more ferocity, and Richie was breathing hard against the wind and rain, and Louise—well she was being stoical through it all— and I, well I was with Maxie—as I always was when I had time to think. And that's been my life, ever since...you know...

It's like someone picked up my watch and smashed it—and my life stopped there.

At 9:45 a.m. Eight years ago. In Muskingum, Ohio...

CHAPTER NINETY-SEVEN
THE GO-FAST BOAT

The fog was thick on this Saturday afternoon, fourteen days before Christmas and we were soaked—but nobody wanted to go below to get out of the weather. We were all too tense.

"We gotta be close," Huck said, and he eased back on the throttle, bringing the Yamahas almost to idle. We had been searching for a little over half an hour for the rig.

"There!" said Louise, almost whispering. Voices carry on the water. She was pointing to lights that barely penetrated the fog. It was thick and heavy, like in a late-night London back street.

Huck eased the Canyon toward the lights. They couldn't have been more than several hundred yards away. Slowly the rig emerged, its lights outlining it like the starry points of a constellation, in the fog, in the rain. Then the ladder appeared, fastened to the side of a massive support pontoon like a centipede on a flower stem. And right beneath the ladder and lashed to its lower rung was that very same go-fast boat, sitting there like a bad luck penny. Huck pulled in close. Tucked under the sleek prow of the boat were a number of plastic bundles, pushed in tightly against each other as if to make room for more to come. I stepped onto the boat, leaned into the prow, and pulled out one of the packages. It was shaped like a brick—only slightly thinner and wider, like a thick pancake—and white. It was packaged in a simple, crude Saran Wrap kind of covering. I handed the package to Louise. She flipped it over, inspected it, and nodded. "Yep, this looks like the real deal." As she was speaking, I heard the clank of metal against metal above me.

"Pull back," I whispered to Huck, climbing back into the Canyon through the dive-door. "Quietly."

He did, backing the boat away from the ladder and into the open space beneath the rig, and sliding in behind a pontoon directly opposite the ladder. He kept the boat at idle, the noise from the motors covered by the wash of water against the rig's supports. From behind the pontoon we watched as four men descended the ladder, each holding several bundles under his arm. The first man down climbed into the fast boat and grabbed the bundles from the man behind him. The next did the same. I was so intent on watching the exchange that I missed the last man on the ladder. He was staring our way.

"Kan!" he yelled, pointing at us. One of the men in the boat picked up a rifle and fired, a shell hitting the pontoon. I ducked involuntarily and then looked up at the support to see if it was deflating. Apparently, they are sturdy little monsters.

Huck fired back with his alligator rifle but it was like trying to shoot from a running horse with the waves breaking around the pontoons and rocking the Canyon violently back and forth.

"Damn," said Richie trying to get off a shot with his Browning.

Then spray from a wave breaking over the pontoon washed over the Canyon, swamping it, the force of the water washing me across the deck and into Richie. We both slid into the boat's hull.

"Jeez," Richie complained, "what a fuckin' mess," as he struggled to his feet. He was still hanging onto the Browning. He tried to dry the gun by rubbing it against his pants. That was useless. They were both completely soaked—gun and guy. He shrugged and gave it up. His baby—all wet.

The fast boat had spun away from the rig and into open water, throwing up a tidal wave in its wake. So, all I could see was mist and rain, the sound of the motors the only sign that there was a boat out there.

"Everybody okay?" I said, checking around. Huck nodded. He was still at the wheel.

"I'm good," Louise said, massaging her arm. "That console is damn hard!"

"Do we follow?" Huck said.

"No," I said, and got on the SAT phone Jack had outfitted the Canyon with. It uses a system developed by Globalstar that routes phone calls from out-of-the way places—like this one—through a constellation of Low Earth Orbiting (LEO) satellites that cover most of the Earth's surface, including where we were. With very little delay in the voice transmission.

"Yeah?" said Wong.

"They're on their way," I said, "headed directly north. A go-fast boat. It's loaded with product."

"You following?"

"We're going upstairs," I said, assessing the ladder that disappeared at the top in the mist.

"No way!" yelled Wong. "You don't have..." and I ended the call.

The phone went off again.

"Yeah?" I said.

"Before you do anything crazy, your wife..." he hesitated, "I mean, your former wife, has been trying to call you."

"Why'd she call *you*?" I said, growing concerned.

"She didn't." He paused. "She called your buddy, DeFelice. *He* called me. She didn't say what about. But said it's urgent!" He caught his breath. "Now get back here. We'll chase down the drug boat, nothing for you to do on that rig."

I stared at the phone...wondering...then looked at the ladder, no one coming down to check, and I knew we had to go up.

"What?" asked Louise, wiping water from her face.

"Jillie. She's been trying to call me."

I wondered...and I thought about my dreams lately...and shook it all out of my head. "No, it's not possible..."

"What's not possible?"

"That it's about Maxie."

"About Maxie?"

"I've been having dreams again. I wonder—"

"Coop," she interrupted. "Don't..." She looked at me sidewise.

"I know. It's crazy."

"It's crazy." But she put her arms around me, holding on tightly. "I understand," she whispered.

Huck and Richie stared like they didn't want to interfere, but...

Louise, pushed away, faced me directly, and said, "So, let's do what we gotta do here and get the hell back to the cutter so you can make that call."

I heard an *Amen* from Richie.

CHAPTER NINETY-EIGHT
ON BOARD THE ZHI ZHU NU

Huck idled the Canyon back to the ladder. We secured it against the rising wash. There was no evidence that anyone had seen us, no sound of someone coming down the ladder, no sign of men looking over the gunnels, no shouts of alarm. There was a helicopter sitting on the deck, its blades jutting out over the edge of the helipad, turning slowly, powered by the wind and rain.

I grabbed the bottom rung of the ladder and climbed, wondering if someone would pick us off when we cleared the hull and dropped to the deck. An easy shot.

Louise was breathing hard behind me. The wind and rain penetrated the cage as we climbed onto the first platform. No movement anywhere on the rig. Even the drill was silent. *Maybe Wong had it right*, I thought. Maybe just a skeleton crew left behind.

"You ready?" I whispered through the wind. Louise nodded. I began to climb again, the rungs of the ladder hard to grip. They were wet and cold. When we reached the last platform, we finally had a clear view of the copter.

"I'm gonna take a closer look," I said and began to climb the final fifteen feet to the top. I dropped onto a passageway. It was empty, but I heard voices, indistinct and distant in the darkness. The copter was just fifteen feet to my right, a large commercial helicopter, fire truck red and big enough to carry eight to ten passengers. An EC 155 Eurocopter. One of the most expensive on the market—probably ten million or more. Good money in the oil business I figured.

The cabin door was open. I stepped under blades still moving in the wind and looked in. And there they were, neatly stacked under the seats of the passenger section, pressed bundles of white powder, the same size we saw in the go-fast boat, and room for more. I leaned in, knifed into a bundle, and fingered a sample onto my tongue. It numbed me within seconds. Bingo. I called the others up.

"Shit we got here?" said Richie, noticing the open bag.

"I sampled it. Want to try some?"

"Hell no. I don't do that shit."

"That one bag is about a million dollars, street value," said Louise. Then, "Looks like they're still busy," and she was pointing to the open spaces under the seats.

"My guess, too," I said.

The voices were closer. "How many do you think?" I said to no one in particular.

"I'll let you know," said Huck. "Give me a boost," he said, pointing to the wall of the rig that rose about ten feet over the deck.

"You're fuckin' crazy," said Richie, following Huck to the wall. "They'll be here in minutes," he warned. But he grabbed Huck's foot anyway and hoisted him up against the wall, like a power lifter in the Olympics, until he was able to literally throw him onto the roof with a burst of energy that exploded like a cannon. Richie's face was red when he turned and faced us. "Damn right," he said.

Huck was back in seventy-five seconds.

"Five," he whispered, holding up his hand. "They got bundles." Huck looked over his shoulder as the voices grew louder. "Maybe two minutes. I'll stay here."

Richie walked his alligator gun over to him. Then we split up. Richie crouched behind the oversized wheels of the helicopter; Louise climbed down the ladder, just far enough to be out of sight; I waited near the left corner of the building. The voices grew more distinct. And they were arguing.

It was raining harder now and a mist was settling on the deck. An advantage for us.

Four young Chinese men—three in loose black, karate style clothes, and a fourth, in jeans and a long shirt, rounded the corner, still arguing. I recognized the boyfriend, Lei Sun, immediately, and of course, Li Lang, the Dragon Head, wearing jeans and a black leather jacket. Each of the men was carrying a stack of stuff we saw in the fast boat and the copter. Product wrapped in plastic and ready for shipping. No one noticed me, even though I had stepped out into the open. Maybe it was the rain and fog, maybe it was that they never expected anyone else to be there. Whatever. They were surprised—stunned—when I said, "Hey!" I followed that up with "We got you surrounded."

But the woman yelled, "Shoot him!" And that did it because the guy closest to me dropped his stuff, pulled a gun and fired. He missed. Shot too fast. Unlucky, because Huck shot him in the head. And blood spattered on his black shirt, red on black, just like a checkerboard, and he was thrown into the two men next to him who immediately dropped what they were carrying and threw up their hands, screaming indecipherable things. Again, the woman screamed, "Kill him!" looking around for someone to do it. But the two guys with their hands up sure weren't going to do it, because they looked up and saw Huck on top of the building with his big gun pointed at them, and they saw Richie emerge from behind the helicopter with his Browning, and they saw Louise swing up from the ladder leveling her Glock. The man in the jeans had thrown up his hands also, so the only person who was still fighting was the woman. And she was all alone now.

"Li Lang," I said, stepping toward her, and she spat at me. But the wind stopped it mid-air. I moved in closer. "You've been a very bad girl," I chided, and she tried to spit again. But I shut her mouth by grasping her head with one hand and her jaw with the other, leveraging her mouth open by forcing her cheeks into her teeth with my thumb and forefinger and pushing her up against the hull with my body. Then, I leaned into her face and yelled over the wind and the rain, my voice rising with the intensity of the storm, "Your Uncle Wong is very angry with you. And so am I!"

I pushed off, the back of her head striking the metal frame of the hull. "Shoot him? Really?" Then, "And don't try to spit again, or I'll reach into your filthy little mouth and pull your tongue out." And she tried to look really pissed off. But her eyes worried. She knew I was serious.

Then I turned to Lei Sun who still had his hands raised, "Snow was worried about you. I guess she should have been," I said, shaking my head. "You've been a bad boy." But I don't think he knew what I was saying. He looked confused.

I turned to the two men in Karate gear. They still had their hands up.

"Jump," I said. There was a fire inside me, burning. And I had to put it out.

They stared at me.

"Jump into the fucking water!" I said. Was I taking it out on them? The fact that I was angry about Maxie? Probably. They didn't move.

"Jump!" I said, "or that man up there will shoot you!" pointing at Huck.

And they stared over the hull and down into the sea, the water boiling against the pontoon supports and waves throwing the Canyon around like a toy in a bathtub. And there was the rain, and the fog.

"Jump!" I screamed again. One man shook his head.

I nodded at Huck, and the two men stared at the man who was shot, whose blood was running with the water across the deck, and they looked up at Huck who motioned with his alligator gun, and I guess they figured they had a better chance jumping than sticking around with us. So, the man nearest the hull hoisted pulled himself up on the wall, looked down for a few moments and leaped out over the sea, feet first, and he blew out his breath as he did and I watched him hit the water and disappear. I didn't see him come up again.

The second man, hesitated, then looked at me. I nodded at Huck. Then he did the same. But this guy let out a yell, like he was on a roller coaster. And I watched him hit, and he disappeared into the foam around the pontoons. And already I felt better. Two overboard. One dead.

"Kill the helicopter," I told Richie and Louise. "I don't want those clowns climbing the ladder and taking off in this damn thing—if they survive." The two of them disabled the helicopter, shooting out the tail blades. I figured that Wong would want to check out the product while it was still on board the rig.

"You got any cuffs?" I said to Louise, after she and Richie had wasted the tail of the copter.

"You bet," she said. "Always." She pulled out some Tuff-Ties—they're light, compact and sturdy, made of braided nylon.

"We're going to deliver them to Uncle Wong," I said. I was fed up with Wong's niece.

"What do you wanna do with this guy?" Richie said, staring at the body on the deck.

"Throw him overboard," I said. "There's a lot of fish out there and they're hungry."

And that's just what they did.

"Let's get down to the boat," I said, on the chance that one of the two who went overboard found their way to the Canyon. Huck hurried ahead of us, just in case. Richie and Louise followed him, keeping Li Lang between them. I pushed Lei Sun down ahead of me.

And the rain kept right on, like it would never stop. And the fog—it was denser than before. It must have taken ten minutes or more to navigate the ladder, but finally we boarded. No sign of the two jumpers. No sign of the dead man.

"Let's get out of here," I said. Then Huck, who had the motors idling, opened the throttle and the three Yamahas churned the water like a giant egg-beater, spinning the boat toward open water. And the Canyon, like a funny car on a thousand-foot run, raced into the rain and mist that was blanketing the Florida Straits.

~

It was late afternoon, but dark, the nasty weather casting a pall over the water and my mood. After the rig disappeared in the fog, Louise and I took Li Lang and Snow's boyfriend below. Richie stayed topside with Huck. I had some questions I wanted answered.

We sat together, Louise and I, on one side of the cabin on a wide berth I was able to convert to a couch by pulling down a backrest. Li Lang and Lei Sun were opposite us, Lei Sun sitting on the head—it was covered with a blue leather pillow. Li Lang sat against the hull under a TV attached to the wall above her. It should have been hot in the cabin but a cold front had blown in from Canada—they hate being blamed for our bad weather—bringing temperatures in the low fifties.

Li Lang was sulking.

"Hey," I said. "Tell me about Jack Hayward."

"Who?" she said, looking up at me, puzzled. Then she muttered something in Chinese.

"I know you know about him," I said. "Don't pretend you don't."

"I didn't have anything to do with his death," she said in perfect English, continuing to sulk. I looked over at Lei Sun.

"He doesn't understand English," she said. "Why are you doing this?" Angry.

"Well let's see...Drugs for starters. Then there is the illegal drilling from the rig in—"

"I don't have anything to do with that rig—"

"Uh-huh. But your go-fast boat is running drugs back and forth to that rig."

She didn't say anything.

"Then there's the invasion of my home—the Black Lotus...and don't tell me you had nothing to do with that. You warning me?"

"I—" She stopped.

"You are the head of the Tong," I said.

She tried to say something.

I stopped her. "Oh yeah. That's what you are. So don't tell me—"

"I don't have to tell you anything," she said. "You have no authority to—" and she stopped herself.

"No? But I do have you. And the coke from the *Zhi Zhu Nu*. And your uncle, who's waiting to talk with you."

She began to speak but again stopped herself.

"You don't need a lawyer," I said. "I'm not a cop."

She looked at Louise.

"She's off duty," I said.

Louise smiled. "But I bet you're going to wind up in my jail," she said, pausing and looking over at Lei Sun who was still sitting on the head, fidgeting, "you and your boyfriend—"

"He's not my boyfriend."

"Uh-huh. So, you're screwing your sister's boyfriend."

She turned red but didn't say anything.

"I guess I nailed it," said Louise, nodding at me.

"And then there are the shootings. Your boys shot at us several times. Why?" I asked, but before Li Lang could answer, I continued, "On one of those occasions they shot my client, Cynthia Hayward. You know the name. Your boys killed her father," and before she could reply, I hurried on. "That's why I'm here. No other reason. So, if you hadn't done that, you'd be home free."

"But—"

"Uh-huh. But what? Because he had taken some pictures of something he shouldn't have? Because maybe he found out about the cocaine? Or maybe it was about the drilling? The fracking? In the Everglades of all places? Is that why you killed him?"

She shot back, "But I—"

"What? Didn't do any of those things?"

Lei Sun looked confused as he watched—and worried—and he shifted on the toilet seat. Too hot, I guess.

"Well, tell you what—you'll get time to explain all this to your uncle, Cleveland Wong, in just a little while.

And as I was saying that, Richie opened the hatch and yelled down. "The Coast Guard cutter. We're there, bozos."

CHAPTER ONE HUNDRED
CLEVELAND WONG AND
THE SPIDER WOMAN

H uck maneuvered us in close to the stern, where the lower deck was about twelve feet from the water. Boarding was not easy. The seas were choppy and the rain made the transfer slick and dangerous. Four Guardsmen, whose arms were larger than my legs, tossed a rope ladder over the side. I pushed Li Lang up first. She slid over the gunnels into the arms of one of the Guardsmen. Then Lei Sun scaled the ladder—easily. Louise followed him, then Richie, slipping on several rungs but keeping his cool, and last, I climbed up the ladder and over the hull and onto the deck. Huck hung the bumpers over the side then tied off the Canyon, tossing the lines to the deck hands. Then he climbed the ladder like he could do it in his sleep.

We stood around on the deck, looking at each other, soaked and shivering—the temperature must have been in the high forties—and we watched the Guardsmen pull up the ladder.

"I thought I was goin' in!" Richie whispered to me, staring out at the Straits. "Fuckin' water."

Then suddenly the Guardsmen came to attention as someone yelled, "Officer on deck," and Commander Sykes came down the ladder from the main deck with Deputy Secretary Cleveland Wong.

"Welcome back," said Sykes, holding out a hand and smiling. "Well done."

"How about the bad guys in the fast boat?" I said.

"Still out there. The copter spotted them and radioed the chase boat. I told the pilot to disable the boat if they didn't stop."

"Nice work, Coop," Wong said.

"There's a ton more on the rig," I said, "they can fill you in," nodding to Li Lang and Lei Sun.

Wong had been eyeing the two the whole time. He started toward them, looking like he wanted to get this thing over. Two Guardsman were standing on either side of the prisoners. Li Lang's eyes, filled with anger and rebellion, were focused on Wong as he came toward her.

"You should not look at me, niece," Wong said and when she continued to do so, he slapped her across the face, so hard it sent her reeling to catch her balance—which she couldn't do because of the cuffs. So, she lay sprawled out on the floor, looking up for help. None came.

Wong turned to Lei Sun who had witnessed what was in store for him. He spoke to the boyfriend in Chinese, in low tones, angry. Lei Sun said something back, got in Wong's face, and then pushed him away with his head. One of the Guardsmen hit him in the back of the head with the butt of his M4A1 carbine. The blow knocked him to the floor. He wasn't getting up anytime soon.

His face scarlet with anger, Wong turned to Li Lang. "You have disgraced your family," pausing, "and your country!" as if the first was not enough. "You are criminals and you will pay..." He stopped. As though at a loss for what else to say. Li Lang did not move.

It was foggy on deck and still raining, and I felt bad for Wong as I watched him trying to keep his anger below the surface.

"Take them below," he ordered, as if there was nothing more to do, "and lock them up."

He was furious, but it didn't show in his demeanor. It was in the way he held himself, the tenseness in his hands, the straightness of his back, his eyes forward. And he wouldn't look at them when he talked. He stared through them, or past them, as if they didn't exist to him.

And, after a few moments, he broke the silence, "I'm turning these two over to you, Detective Delgado," he said, disgust riding his words like he was turning over vermin to a pest control person.

And as the Guardsmen began to lead them below, Li Lang looked over at Louise and Louise smiled and nodded. *I told you so,* she mouthed.

"You will confine them in your jail until Homeland Security decides where they should be held," Wong added, his mouth tight against his teeth.

He turned to the four of us, his face glacial, yet the sadness, hidden deep in his culture, leaked through. "You guys should all get medals," he said, "but..."

"Yeah, I know. This thing never happened," I assured him.

"I'm afraid so. But I know what you did today," he said, "and I will never forget it. Never."

I knew he wouldn't because of how his niece had screwed up her life, disgraced the family—for which there is no forgiveness—and shamed him on a day that he should be celebrating.

"And now, Cooper, call Jillie!" Wong urged, almost as if he had forgotten everything for the moment and moved the mountain of family treachery aside. "She's called DeFelice several times. She upset. Let's find a private place for you," and he led me up the ladder to the upper deck. "This way," he said as he pointed to a hatch off to my left under the wheelhouse. I followed him below into a lounge area where a few Guardsmen were sitting at tables, drinking and talking. They stood and saluted when they saw Wong. They sat back down when he passed.

"You need privacy," Wong said, taking my arm and leading me toward one of the cabins off the lounge. It was a small room with a bunk, a chair, and a desk.

"Just a minute," he said, and headed quickly back to the lounge. When he returned, he had a glass with ice floating in an amber liquid. "Here," he said. "Drink this." Then he gave me his SAT phone and headed for the door. "Call," he said, as he closed the door.

CHAPTER ONE HUNDRED ONE
THE PHONE CALL

S he picked up on the first ring. "Coop?"

"Yeah?" I said. "You called." And I was uneasy because I could feel the tension in that single word, *Coop*. "Is everything okay?"

She doesn't call generally, except lately—about her new friend. And the urgency... Had somebody died?

"I've got some news."

"Okay," I said. "Good or bad?" Now I *was* nervous.

"It's about Maxie..." and for a moment I thought I must have misheard what she was saying.

Someone opened the hatch and looked in. It was Louise. *You okay?* she mouthed, looking worried. As it turns out—yeah, she should have been.

I nodded, shrugged, and then mouthed, *I think.*

She nodded and closed the hatch.

I jammed the phone against my mouth, excited and edgy at the same time. "Go ahead. You were saying? Something about Maxie?" I asked, the words tumbling out of my mouth like marbles in free fall.

"Yes, Maxie," she said. "He's home." I heard her voice break, and she began to sob, violently, and I was stunned.

"Did you say Maxie...?" And my heart almost came through my chest.

I repeated it again, "Maxie?" trying to make sure I heard it right. "He's home?" I stared at the phone. "How...? Where..." and I stumbled around for words.

"Yes," she finally said.

"Yes? Maxie's home?" I wondered if my mind was playing tricks. "There? With you?" Still not believing.

"Yes, Coop. He is. He's home." She was crying and I wanted to hear the whole story, immediately. Where he was. How he got home. What he looked like...all of it in one minute, my heart pounding so fast I couldn't talk, so I looked for a place to sit, and dropped on the bunk. And my head—it hurt, like a stroke was coming on—but after a few moments I settled into the quiet. And then she asked, *Did I want to talk to him?* I was shaking and said, *Of course*, and I sat, as rigid as a brick wall, waiting to hear his voice. My hand was shaking so badly I switched the phone to the other. I heard voices in the background and then, a young voice, but mature. *Oh my God*, I thought, *he's grown!* I expected the same voice I had remembered when he was a kid. I forgot to add the years...

"Hi Dad," just like that. All those years gone by, wondering if he was dead, and now...

And then Louise came back into the room and sat next to me—she must have been listening right outside. She looked worried. And hardly a minute later Richie and Huck came in, Richie holding out his hands, like *What's up?*

"Hi Maxie!" I said, watching the shock on their faces—I mean complete and utter amazement—and Louise took my hand and squeezed it—hard.

"You're home?" I said, still not believing it—making sure this wasn't another dream.

"Yeah, I'm home," he said. A small voice, not much affect.

I wanted him to tell me all about it, but didn't want to ask: his trip home and I tried to picture it—his coming home—but I couldn't. And I wanted to ask *Where have you been?* I mean, all these years? Eight. Long. Years. *What happened, Maxie? You know, you were here one morning and then...? Were you hurt? Did somebody take you? Or did you just run away?*—but I didn't believe that...and yet...*we didn't know anything, Maxie,* I wanted to tell him*, nothing about what happened to you that morning—when the Dean told me, and I came home, and your mother...she...and we didn't talk much after that— except about you.* We measured everything as before Maxie and after Maxie. And *How have you been?* I wanted to ask. What a crazy question would that be? But still, I wanted to know.

So I didn't say anything about all that, just, *How are you?* And he said, *Fine.* And I thought on that. I heard Jillie say something to him in the background—and then there was a silence and I really wanted to ask, *Where were you,* but that was a deadly question, not like the one most parents ask when a kid goes missing and they search frantically for hours—with neighbors—and then he comes walking in the door, like no big deal, and they say, "Where were you?" And maybe he was at the movies, or maybe he went off with some friends into the woods, or maybe he was at a neighbor's house watching TV, or whatever. No. With Maxie it was different. We're talking eight years! We were almost sure he was dead. Wouldn't anyone be? We split up over it.

And so I was afraid to ask, *Where were you?* Yet inside me a voice cried out, *Where were you?* Did he hear that? And so I did ask: "Where were you?" trying to make it sound normal, so as not to unsettle him too much, and I heard him take a very deep breath, then...

"Some men took me." And even though the phone wasn't on speaker, the room was so quiet that his voice filled it. I could feel the tears trying to leak from his eyes. Louise gasped and gripped my hand so tight it hurt. She had heard him. Richie and Huck had heard him. Wong had come back and was in the room, and he had heard him. I think the whole world must have heard him. And I felt guilty—before all of them. That some man came to our home and took my son and I didn't stop him. I tried to remain calm.

"Kidnapped?" I couldn't help it. The word slipped out. And I hoped the word would get lost on the way. Get caught up in the billions of words that go out into the universe every few seconds.

"And they—"

They now?

"—lied to me." He paused, "And they kept me, the men who took me, and the Man who never let me out of his house...I couldn't..."

He's apologizing! I thought.

"...and I'm so sorry for what I did..."

Still apologizing.

"...I got into a car when you told me never—"

"Stop, Maxie," I said softly—sick that he should feel he had to apologize. "You didn't do *anything* wrong." I heard Jillie say the same thing in the background.

Maxie was crying now, and I was horrified at what I was hearing, his voice coming in and out, "I thought of it all the way to the house in South Carolina..."

South Carolina? I cringed at what must have been going through his mind—my poor son—

"How you and Mom warned me, and I hoped you wouldn't

be mad—you know, that I didn't listen." He stammered through most of it. "And I caused so much trouble..."

I wanted to kill them.

"...and I was hoping that maybe you had seen me..."

Oh my God—I could picture it—Maxie looking out the window of the car, back at the house. Had I dreamed that?

"...or Mom..."

I could see her at the screen and Maxie looking for her...Had I dreamed that as well?

" ...and that you would find me..." His voice was shaking, fighting off tears, "and I'm sorry, Dad, that I got into the car..."

I was fighting off tears, but I didn't want him to know, to get upset.

"...and sometimes I thought maybe your car was behind us..." He was sobbing now, "but then I fell asleep..."

I said, "Yes, you fell asleep, Maxie. That was good." My heart skipping beats.

"I did," he continued, "then first thing I knew..." He hesitated...catching his breath, maybe, or wiping tears. "We were there..."

I could picture it—this place in South Carolina—his new home.

"...and the Man said that you said that he was supposed to take care of me because something had happened to you and Mom, and then later he said you were both killed—in an automobile accident..."

An automobile accident! What kind of insanity was that? It was a horror story. But it was my horror story.

"It's okay," I said, knowing that it wasn't, and I wanted to reach out and hug him. Eight years. I had counted every day, of each year, and the hours, and the minutes and sometimes, when it was dark, and I was alone with my thoughts, even the seconds.

I waited for more...

"And the Man who took me was here—"

"Here?" Cutting him off. "Where?" Then realized that I was loud and probably scared the hell out of him. Richie and Louise pulled back.

"Tell me that again?" I said, more softly. Then Jillie got on the phone, talking in a quiet voice to Maxie, *It's okay, honey*. I could picture her running her hands through his hair—he had such thick hair, curly, with a summer sun color of blond—at least back when he was just a boy. I wondered what it was like now.

"He was here," Jillie said, sounding strange. "But he's gone now." But I couldn't imagine what she was talking about.

"Who?" I said. "Tell me *who* was there."

I paused to make sure I understood. "You mean, the man who took our son?" And I tried to be calm. But I couldn't. "So... who?" I yelled into the phone. "What the hell are you talking about?"

"Henry," she said—then a long pause—and the line went quiet, and Richie, and Louise, and Huck, and Wong were all staring at me, and all I could do was stare at the phone, as if that were the culprit. Finally, she continued, "The man who dated me in Georgetown."

In case I didn't know which fucking Henry.

"The man who has been calling me these last few weeks for dates, the man I talked to you about, Coop, and I'm so sorry..." She was stumbling around and getting hysterical, "And now I find out he's the one who's had our son, Coop, our Maxie, all these years... That's who. The bastard!" She started crying, so hard, but I couldn't do anything...

So finally, when she became quiet, I said, "It's okay," but I really didn't mean okay, what I really meant to say was *When I kill him—that bastard—then it will be okay.*

I could picture Henry, and I wanted to say, to Jillie, *How could you be so stupid?* But I knew that was wrong—and I wanted to say, *Are you sure?* but that would be dumb because she had just said it was Henry, the guy I knew from Georgetown, the guy studying medicine, the guy that had dated Jillie—before I met her—the... He took Maxie? I pulled the phone away from my ear and stared at it, ran my hand through my hair.

Richie said, *What?* and Louise too. I was staring out over the room, like it was empty, wondering if I was just dreaming all this. I *had* dreamed of Maxie's kidnapping. The car. The road. I could picture it. And now here it was: the man, the man who I knew from Georgetown—he dated Jillie back then—before I met her. This is the guy who took our son?!

"Why would he do that?" I said, when I finally got back on the cell. More of a statement than a question. And a dumb one, I knew.

"I don't know," she said, trying to answer. She was still crying, but softly now. I had scared her. Made her feel guilty. I had done enough of that.

"It's okay," I said. "It's not your fault." But she thought it was. But I was not going to blame her for anything. Not anymore.

I glanced over at Richie, and maybe he saw the rage in me, or maybe he overheard Jillie talking, or maybe he was a mind reader...but there was that look in his eyes, like the one when we were kids, when someone in our neighborhood got fucked over, and we had to go out to wreak our kind of justice. Richie with his baseball bat. And in those days I had a gun I had stolen. See, I'm not such a nice guy. I never used a baseball bat. Too messy. But now...

"I'm on my way," I said to Jillie.

CHAPTER ONE HUNDRED TWO
MUSKINGUM OF O.H.I.O

Saturday Evening, December 1 0

It was about a half hour after the phone call, when the Boy had learned his father was alive and the Man had lied—all those years—that we find Charley and Joey sitting in Maxie's old kitchen, where Jillie had put some biscuits in the oven (the Boy remembered the smells) and had made some coffee, and Maxie was thinking back to the coffee shop.

And, the Boy knew, the moment he saw the second car pull out and follow the Man's car, he knew it was the Asp. He wondered how he had found him. Maybe seeing his bike near the bus station, or maybe asking the agent about a kid who purchased a one-way ticket to Muskingum, Ohio, or maybe he just figured *Where else would the kid go?* Home, of course. And that would be Muskingum, Ohio. Running away from home to go home.

And if the Boy had followed Henry, he would have seen both cars parked tail-to-front, and the Man would be talking to the Asp, both standing on the side of the road, face-to-face, talking with great animation, on US Route 40, one of the 1926 national highways that at one time crossed the entire country, east to west, but today the place where the Man got the news that Maxie had run away, and guess where he had gone? To none other than Muskingum of O.H.I.O. And he is at the house of the woman he had just kissed, and dated, and slept with, and just now left. He learned this on the side of the road, just east of Anthony's Antique Shop.

"I think he's coming back," Maxie blurted out, like an announcement on TV that an alien craft had just landed, and they all turned to him, but no one spoke, not Charley, not Jillie, not Joey. They just looked at him, awaiting further explanation. So he went on about the black car that had been sitting down the street from their house, almost directly across from Anthony's Antique Shop, and about the man in the car who had followed him from South Carolina, and about how the car pulled out when the Man's car passed it, and that the Asp was probably telling him everything right about now—which, in fact, he was. And that, in further fact, the Man would probably be coming back.

It was almost as if Maxie hadn't stopped speaking, which he had, because no one spoke. Like it was time to meditate on all this crazy talk, about this strange man who followed Maxie —if he really had—about whether the Man would risk coming back now that they knew he was the one who, eight years earlier, on a summer morning, had taken Maxie. And Charley and Joey were still trying to absorb this whole thing.

So Charley said, "Why would he come back? That's crazy. He should be running."

Maxie said, "Oh, he's going to come back," *and maybe kill me,* he thought.

The room was silent as they all listened to Maxie's words.

And if a sparrow had returned from Florida in the dead of winter and was sitting on the roof of Anthony's Antique shop, just down the street from where the Asp had parked, if that bird made the slightest sound at all, it would have echoed through the room.

"The Coast Guard helicopter will drop you off at the airport," said Wong. Then, noticing my concern, he added quickly, "And your bags are already on board the copter—I noticed that you brought some hardware with you," he added, smiling like he knew our little secret.

"But—" I began.

"No buts. I'll take care of everything from here. Your plane will be waiting for you on the tarmac when you get there. So, gotta hurry," he urged. "You got problems with your son to deal with." He took a breath and grasped my shoulders firmly. "Be safe, okay?"

I nodded.

"About Miss Hayward, I'll contact her, tell her what's happened." He paused. "Li Lang is awake," he continued. "We talked. And it looks like we got Jack's killers. Her fan-boys."

"What are you going to do with her?" I said, not sure I should press.

"She disgraced her family. She disgraced me. It would have been better if you had let her die." He spat out those last words.

"But now..." He floated away in his thoughts. I wondered what he would do with his niece.

"But now you go!" he continued, suddenly, pushing me topside. "Louise is already on board."

The copter was chopping away at the wind like a giant reaper. And in the open door, Louise was waving for me to hurry.

"You take care of your family," Wong yelled, as he gave me a boost up through the hatch.

I felt like I was leaving one war zone and driving into another. Then I saw Richie sitting across from Louise. "Hey buddy, Uncle Richie's gonna take care of tings." He slapped an empty seat next to him.

"Where's Huck?" I said.

"He and Wong are doing cleanup," yelled Louise as the chopper began to lift off the cutter. "Said he would see you on the other side of the night."

I fell against Richie as the copter angled sharply and left the cutter behind. It was half-past five. I was a prisoner of time. I wished I could stop it until I got to my son and Jillie.

After what seemed an eternity, a mass of light began to creep over the eastern horizon like a sunrise. It was Miami, coming to life as the evening began to settle in.

We were hovering over Miami International at 6:25 p. m. "Secretary Wong has arranged for your flight and your transportation when you arrive at Port Columbus," said the pilot as he dropped the copter on the tarmac next to a small turbo-jet. The ladder was down, and a flight attendant was waiting at the door.

"Have a good flight," the pilot yelled over the noise of the copter beating away at the air as it began to lift off the ground.

We grabbed our bags and hurried up the airstairs of the jet, the attendant checking the bags at the door.

"Welcome aboard," he said, taking our bags and stowing them near the exit. "There's plenty of room. I'll serve some refreshments when we are in flight."

There were eight plush, light tan leather seats in all. Four on each side of the aisle facing each other, a serving table in the middle. Richie sat alone, Louise and I faced each other across the narrow aisle from Richie. *Geez*, is all I heard from Richie as he settled in, leaned back in his seat, and closed his eyes.

I called Jillie again as we got seated. Still no answer. I wasn't surprised. Probably busy with Maxie. Yet...? I thought about calling the local cops but dismissed that, figuring Jillie would have done that if she needed to. And we would be there in a few hours anyway.

We were in the air by 6:45. I couldn't wait to see the sea of light from the city disappear. As we circled away from Miami and out over the Atlantic, the pilot cut the interior lights, and that left only the dim illuminations, outlining the aisle. I stared out the window and watched the lights from the city fade into the darkness. Soon the only thing visible was my own reflection. I leaned in to study it more closely. The person I saw there was no one that I knew.

The pilot announced that we were at 20,000 feet and out over the Atlantic. I continued to worry about why Jillie hadn't answered her phone.

"Guess what?" said Joey, pointing out the front window toward Route 40. "I think they're back," and they all crowded the window to see. Two cars had pulled up and parked on the highway, just below the house.

"Oh, God. That's the black car I saw," said Maxie, his eyes wide as he stared at two men climbing out of the cars.

"You have a gun?" said Charley in a whisper, pulling Jillie away from the window and away from Joey and Maxie.

"Yes," she said, "under the bed in the master bedroom," pointing toward a door off the living room. "It's a shotgun," she said, and then grabbed Maxie and Joey and followed Charley into the bedroom. "You two stay in here!" she ordered.

Charley was down on both knees searching under the bed. He reached in and slid out a black case and opened it. Jillie knelt next to him and lifted the shotgun out of the case while Charley pulled back in surprise. Then she grabbed some shells that were loose in the case and began punching them into the chamber.

"Five shot," she said, breathing hard, looking every bit like a woman who would kill to protect her child.

"Let me do this," said Charley, reaching for the gun.

"No way!" said Jillie, as she got up and headed for the living room.

She opened the front door, then the screen, and planted herself on the front porch, to the right of the swing where she and Cooper and Maxie would spend summer nights watching the traffic (there was never much) and listen to the sound of the cicadas. Then she raised the shotgun, a 16 gauge Mossberg, pump action, with a long barrel and scope, and pointed it at the two men who were coming up the embankment. They both stopped and raised their hands, Henry saying *Take it easy there, I just want to talk*, the Asp edgy, staring hard at her, and Jillie not changing her stance, the shotgun still leveled at them and Henry and the Asp drifting slowly apart from each other—divide and conquer—and Jillie shouting out *Don't move!* and then both of them freezing, Henry calm, thinking, and then...

"Let's go inside and talk," he said. She knew he was buying time, that he knew she hadn't called the police—there were no sirens and this is a small town; knew that she must be scared—and this is where they were wrong; knew that he could have his way with her—they had slept together, hadn't they?

Jillie, surprising him, said, "Sure, let's go inside."

A little too quickly for Henry's comfort, but he started forward anyway and told the Asp to stay outside, let him take care of this. The Asp nodded, lowered his hands, and stayed where he was until Jillie opened the front door, Henry following about twenty feet behind.

Then the Asp moved.

Once Jillie was inside, Charley asked for the gun and went into the bedroom, closed the door. He and Joey went to the window to watch where the Asp was going. Joey acted the commentator, whispering, *Uh-oh, he's moving to the back of the house.*

Charley putting his finger to his lips, *shhh*, and nodding.

In the meantime, Maxie had retreated when Henry mounted the porch stairs. He heard each step as the Man crossed the porch and he heard the screen door open and then the inside door, and their voices—Jillie's and the Man's, Jillie angry and threatening and saying that he will spend the rest of his *goddamned life in prison* for what he did, and so on and on until Maxie could take it no more and hurried up the stairs before Henry came through the door, and sealed himself in his bedroom on the second floor, his very room, and all the toys were still there! His Lionel train set—the tracks taken apart now and sitting in a box in his closet, the door wide open as if waiting for him, each car lined up on a book shelf his dad had built into the closet to hold all of his stuff: the tracks, the buildings, the men, the lights, the switching stations, the two tunnels. And his bed. It was the same one he had slept in eight years ago. He could hear their voices in the living room, loud, his mom shouting at times, Henry arguing, but he blocked his ears. Downstairs, Henry was explaining to Jillie why he had done what he had. But Maxie didn't hear any of it. He had stuck his fingers into his ears.

"See, I didn't hear about your baby—actually my son—"

Jillie drew in a breath like a vacuum cleaner just starting up, but the Man ignored it.

"—until a little over eight years ago, and I counted the months and yes, even the days, from the time Maxie was born back to our dating, and our love making, and you were with me, Jillian, you had not met Cooper yet. Then you met Cooper and both of you left town with your little PhD degrees and my baby!" His voice was rising to a crescendo. And as his face grew redder his voice got louder, so much so that Charley and Joey charged out of the bedroom, Charley, carrying the shotgun across his chest. What they saw was Jillie, visibly upset, angry, shaking, and Henry screaming at her. Then Henry turned, saw Charley with the shotgun, pulled a revolver from his coat pocket—small, silver, short-barreled—aimed at Charley and shot him.

CHAPTER ONE HUNDRED FIVE
PORT COLUMBUS

Saturday Night, 9:05 p.m.

I tried calling Jillie again as the plane touched down at Port Columbus. No answer.

"Still not answering?" said Louise.

"Nope," I said, my concern rising. "I don't get it."

Louise started to rise to get our bags when the pilot said, "Please stay seated and keep your seat belt on until we come to a full stop." She did.

"And when you deplane, please go easy down those steps," he cautioned.

The pilot turned and smiled as we began to disembark. "Take care."

I nodded and thanked him. He smiled. "Thank Secretary Wong. I hope all goes well." Then, "Your car is here," he continued, pointing at a black SUV that had just pulled up at the bottom of the airstair.

The driver was out of the car as Richie and Louise stepped onto the tarmac, taking their bags and loading them into the cargo space.

"I'll need to drive you off the airfield," he said, taking my bag and loading it with the others. "After that, it's yours," he continued as I opened the door to the passenger side.

We ducked around several large commercial planes taxiing to take off as we headed for the exit.

"You do this often?" I said.

"More than I would like," he replied, shaking his head. "Those boys are bigger than me."

In fewer minutes than you can count to fifty we are off the airfield and I was behind the wheel of the black Accord SUV. Louise was in the front seat.

"I'll call the cops," she said.

"Not yet," I said. "I want to see Jillie and Maxie first. I know Henry. He's not going any-fucking-where," I added, wanting to handle this one myself.

I checked my cell. It was 9:20 and no messages from Jillie.

It was cold. No snow falling now. No clouds. A sky full of stars. Crisp and clear. And the moon: I looked for signs of copper along its edges, but there were none. It was full and huge, and it lit up the fields, now long past harvest time, that surround Columbus, Ohio.

A sign outside the airport advertising a hotel sported a gauge that read 29 degrees—unusual for this time of year, even in Ohio. I took the exit toward I-270 South, dug the phone out of my jacket, and hit favorites for Jillie's phone number.

"You oughta let me drive if you're gonna use your cell," Louise cautioned. She was watching me fool with the phone and drive with my knees. She reached for the cell. I handed it to her. She put it on speaker and held it up so I could hear: "The party you have called is not available. Please leave a message at the beep."

"Want me to call the cops?" Louise said again. I shook my head.

Richie grunted in the back. "Fuckin' cops. What are they gonna do?"

It's seventy miles from Port Columbus to Concord College, a little over an hour's drive. I took the I-70 exit off I-270 toward Zanesville and hit darkness almost immediately: no lights, anywhere. It's all farmland stretching from central Ohio through a vast belt that encompasses most of Indiana, Illinois, southern Iowa, northern Missouri, and Kansas, where the farms turn into mountains in Colorado and California. It's over a thousand miles of corn and wheat and potatoes. And if you would drive it, you would see irrigation machines stretching for miles and throwing water like cannons over potato crops, and you would see barns sitting far back in the fields and farm houses barely visible from the road, and you would see silos, the high rises of rural America, and long lines of telephone poles that link the people living in those vast farmlands of the Midwest to civilization.

Snow began to fall again. A light snow. Disappearing on the road as quickly as it hit. I worried about the silence from Jillie, and it was accentuated by the silence of the night, by the silence of Richie, fooling with his gun in the back seat, by the silence of Louise who was staring out the passenger window, out at the Great Midwest. I reached for the phone again. But Louise picked it up for me and hit the speed button.

Nothing, her eyes said, and I saw sadness leaking there, like she was worried also. I knew she wanted to call the cops, but they would be the same guys who screwed up Maxie's case eight years ago when someone said they thought they saw Maxie get into a car—a black one—and the detective that caught the case said there was *not enough detail to follow up, no more witnesses, no tag number, and besides, the witness,* a local guy, whom everyone saw as the town clown, *I mean look at him —who would really believe him?* And I thought, *I would now.*

Angry. Now after eight years, it looks like the *clown* knew what he was talking about.

In twenty more minutes we were passing through Zanesville, the only town in America to boast a Y Bridge.

About twenty miles past Zanesville, we exited the freeway at US Route 40, otherwise known as the West Pike (west of Muskingum, that is) and we were only a few miles from the city limits of Muskingum, Ohio, and from my old house which would be on our left, just before the college, just before Anthony's Antique Shop, just before the Post Office, and just before the cemetery. Just a few miles away from seeing my son who had been missing for eight years. So I hurried the car, through the snow that was now swirling on the road like in a dust storm, and through the darkness of Route 40, little used now that the interstate highway had been built. Now I was only minutes from the center of town. Streetlights began to appear through the snow, through the darkness, and I was praying...

And then I saw it. My old house. Just ahead. On the left. I slowed down and reached for the phone.

CHAPTER ONE HUNDRED SIX
THE HOUSE ON US 40

Some windows were lit up. I looked for shadows of someone passing through. No sign of life. Where was she?

I was going to call again when Louise stopped me.

"She's not there," she said, "or..."

"She's in trouble."

The street was deserted except for two cars parked east of the house, near Anthony's Antique Shop. Two cars. One parked in front of the other. Otherwise the street was deserted. And I drove very slowly.

"I don't like it," I said, and slowed down as I passed an old, two-story that had been moved by the owner from a farm a few miles outside of town to the lot next to my house—I should say what used to be my house. It cost him as much to move it as it did to purchase it. Twenty-five thousand dollars.

I paused at my drive. It was a steep climb from the road to the house, made even more difficult now by ice and a thin cover of snow. The ice was black and threw off a reflection from a streetlamp that rose above the road about twenty feet away.

Trees played with the light, casting shadows that floated over the street as the wind caught their branches.

"You sure?" said Louise, studying the icy drive.

I took the hill quickly, sliding only at the very top and coming to a halt in front of the porch, next to the garage, an unattached building about ten feet from the house. I sat idling for a few moments, staring at the porch, trying to be calm, trying to decide what to do, and you might ask why not jump out, bang on the door, and grab Maxie, who should be waiting there—for me—inside the house, after eight years, eight long years, the boy whose disappearance had turned our lives inside out and upside down, the boy whom I had nightmares about almost every night since he disappeared, who I thought was dead, about whom I had the most horrendous thoughts—like how did he die? Was he abused? Was he was sold to some pedophile? And don't think it doesn't happen every day—my heart beating hard as I thought about it.

And so I sit in the car, idling, and you wonder why and I tell you, it's a father's instinct—an inner sense a parent has of danger. I've had it before—and that's the feeling I have now—that there is danger here—inside the house. And the 100 billion neurons in my brain that control my thoughts, and my consciousness, and my planning, and my decisions about what to do, and my blood pressure—now at an all-time high—all of those neurons are pouring messages into my unconscious about how to process the unanswered phone calls, the nervousness in Maxie's voice, the fact that Henry had just been there, the oddness of the two cars on the street, the quiet of the house now, sitting in my lights like a giant sleeping thing that feels dangerous—and that's why I don't go rushing up to the door, pound on it, and look for Maxie, the son whom I ache so much to take into my arms...

Then, suddenly, the lights inside the house went out.

CHAPTER ONE HUNDRED SEVEN
HENRY VS. JILLIE

Late Saturday Night, December 10

Charlie had lost a lot of blood. It was a shoulder wound. The impact had knocked him flat on his back and he had dropped the shotgun immediately. The Asp, who had come in through the back door, picked up the Mossberg, ignoring Charley—like he wasn't there—or like he didn't matter, which was worse. The room smelled of gunpowder. The odor of fresh blood already in the air, like the smell of iron. Jillie was kneeling down next to Charlie, checking the wound. She peeled away his jacket, its front filling up with blood. Charley moaned as she worked.

"Easy now," she urged, smoothing his forehead as a mother would. There was blood on her hands, and it followed her touch to his brow, and then to his face.

Jillie looked back at Henry. "We need to get him to a hospital."

Henry ignored her. And the man who was with him, the one Maxie called the Asp, walked over to Maxie and to Joey, who was standing as still as an ice carving at a winter show and grabbed them both by the arm, neither resisting, their eyes locked on the Asp, and he said, "What are we going to do with this kid?" referring to Joey, pushing him toward Henry.

"Lock him in the guest bedroom closet. Key's in the door."

"My husband will be here," said Jillie, warning him and watching Asp drag Joey up the stairs, the kid kicking, Asp stopping mid-stairs, getting a handhold on Joey's belt, dragging him easily the rest of the way up the stairs, Joey choking and kicking and trying to scream but...

"Don't hurt him," Jillie pleaded with Henry, and she wondered who this man was who had only hours before dropped her off at her home after a Chagrin Falls holiday.

Henry smiled. "Your husband?" pausing, "Cooper?" like it was some kind of joke. And he thought for a while. "We won't be here, Jillian, when he comes," he replied, almost distractedly, as he looked out the window, through the dark. And out of that dark, two beams of light swung across the front, as a car accelerated up the steep incline of the drive. Its lights swept over the porch as it swung toward the house and parked. And then it was quiet except for the low murmuring of the car's engine, and the lights stayed on, illuminating the porch. Henry threw an arm in front of his face with a *damn it*, then turned, and he and the Asp quickly doused the lights in the living room of the house on US 40 and stared through the front window at the car that was sitting there, its exhaust pushing clouds of white into the air and its lights, like two large eyes, staring back at them.

J illie watched Henry as he studied the lights in the drive outside, wondering if it was Cooper but not daring to say anything. Instead she focused on Charley.

"He's going to bleed to death if we don't get a doctor, Henry," Jillie warned, hoping to call on the person she thought she was with for the last few days.

Henry ignored her, watching the car pull back into the shadows of the garage, watching the driver kill the lights. And now the entire place was in darkness except for the light from streetlamps that danced with the shadows thrown by the naked trees and played around telephone poles and power lines that crossed the empty field between the house and college, through which Cooper had run when he heard about Maxie's disappearance. And the macabre scene played itself out over a hill behind the house.

"Do you want me to circle around behind the car?" whispered the Asp, leaning into the window with Henry.

Henry nodded and Jillie heard. A whisper travels further than a normal voice. But there was nothing she could think of to do. Maxie was now on the floor beside her, tearing off strips of cloth from his own clothes to help stem the blood from Charley's wound.

"We need to get out of here," she whispered to Maxie.

Henry turned around, and raised a finger to his mouth, then turned back to the window. "There's a gun under the bed upstairs," she said in as hushed tones as she could muster. "We need to get it."

"I have to go to the bathroom, sir," Maxie said. He had never called him by name, never by anything else but 'sir', for to Maxie he was just the Man. He existed for Maxie without a name, with no history, with no friends—that he knew of—and no girlfriend in his life—except for his mother it seemed. And his patients. He wondered if he really had any patients at all.

"I have to go to the bathroom," he said again.

Henry turned. "So? Go!" and then he was back at the window. "Come right back," he added, his back to Maxie. "Your mother's here," his voice rising in a warning.

The Asp had already disappeared into the dark. Jillie heard the creak of the floorboards in the dining room and then in the kitchen as he made his way out of the house. She wished she could warn Cooper.

CHAPTER ONE HUNDRED NINE
THE PLAN

"Fuck is that about?" said Richie, leaning over the front seat and sticking his head between Louise and me. We all stared at the front porch that was now lit only by the Honda's headlamps.

"This is not good," I said, staring into the front window, now completely dark. "Those cars on the street...I wonder..."

There was not a movement from inside the house. I watched carefully for the slightest stir of a curtain, for a face in the glass, for anything.

"Someone's there!" said Louise, excited and pointing to the window. She was trying to keep her voice low. It came out as a hoarse whisper.

"Maybe two somebodies," said Richie, echoing Louise's ragged whisper.

I saw them also. Faint outlines against the glass. Like spirits playing with us.

I backed into shadows about twenty-five feet from the porch and out of the way of the light from the highway.

Two cars in the street, I thought. *Someone is in there with Henry.*

"Okay. We need to call the locals," whispered Louise, placing her hand on my knee, trying to persuade.

"Hold on," I said. "I want to talk with Henry myself—first."

"That's a mistake, Coop," cautioned Louise. We need to..."

And just then there was movement in the brief space that separated the house from the garage. "Did you see that?" I said.

"I got this," Richie replied, and began to open the car door.

"Wait!" I whispered harshly as the interior lights came on. He quickly eased the door shut, killing the light.

Louise pulled the covers off the lights and disabled them.

Maxie headed upstairs for the guest bedroom. He was surprised that the Man had allowed him to go. "Better hurry back, boy," Henry warned from downstairs. And Maxie hurried all right, hurried to the closet where Joey was, and he found the key still in the door, and he unlocked it, and out came Joey. *Thanks dude, that man's crazy!* And Maxie told Joey about the gun...

"Time's up!" The voice from downstairs again. The two boys, scrambling like crazy for the gun under the bed, found it —a black case, small, with clips on the side, which Maxie quickly snapped open. Inside was the gun, black, the magazine next to it. He had seen the gun before. His dad had shown it to him and told him never to touch it, and here it was the same gun, so he picked it up and Joey said, *Cooooool dude*, and reached for it, turning it in his hands like he was lucky to be handling it...

"I'm coming up, Maxie," called Henry and Maxie ran to the bathroom, flushed the toilet and yelled he was coming. Joey handed him the gun as he came out. Maxie quickly jammed the magazine into the gun, tucked it in his pants, under his shirt, and hurried back down the stairs. Joey watched from the bedroom door.

CHAPTER ONE HUNDRED ELEVEN
THE ASP

Richie was out of the car and lost in darkness quickly.
"I should help," said Louise. "He's going to need it."

I nodded. "I'm going into the house."

"You think that's smart?" she warned. "You have no idea who's in there."

"Jillie and Maxie are in there."

"Right." We both exited the car quietly.

"Stay away from Richie. He might shoot you," I whispered as she slid away into the darkness.

We went in opposite directions. Louise headed toward the opening between the garage and the house, I headed left toward the street, trying to stay in the shadows. My plan was to circle the house and come in through the coal-cellar that faced US 40. I retreated behind the car toward a field that was completely dark that separated my house from the college. The embankment was snow covered so I decided to slide down on my rear rather than risk falling.

I crept below the embankment where I would be concealed from anyone watching from the front window. From a side window...well that would be a problem. In a few minutes I was climbing back up the embankment and standing over double doors whose base met at ground level and ran up at a forty-five-degree angle to the side of the house. They were old-fashioned cellar doors installed in homes built in the 20s and 30s (mostly rural) that had coal chutes and dumbwaiters and servants' quarters. The doors were made of hardwood and rested on a concrete structure that rose gradually from ground level toward the house, striking it about four feet from ground level.

I had to kneel and lean across the doors to reach a padlock located in the center. Lucky for me, the lock was sitting open. I removed it quietly from the hasp, stood back, and eased the doors open. What I faced was blackness. So, I stepped carefully into the opening, descended a short set of concrete steps, feeling my way blindly until I came to another door at the base of the steps that opened into the basement. The hinges let everybody know they needed oiling. I stopped and listened. No one was hurrying across the floor to check. I eased the door shut slowly and was now standing in my old basement, pitch black and smelling of mildew. I tried to remember where the stairway to the upper floors was. Directly ahead? To my right? As my eyes accustomed themselves to the dark, I started to remember. To my left was the coal room, long empty since we converted to gas. And directly in front of me—I could discern its outline now —was the furnace. I knew there was nothing else blocking the way to the set of stairs that led to the main floor of the house. The only problem was I had to feel my way to get there, like playing a game of Blind Man's Bluff.

As I tested the bottom stair, I heard someone call Maxie's name. I hesitated. Nothing more. So I started up, counting each stair as I went, moving slowly and carefully from step to step, pausing at each one, hoping to find solid footing—no squeaks or creaks—remembering that there were what? Fifteen steps in all? Wondering at each step if someone would open the door, turn on the light and see me. I pulled my gun as I moved up. Near the top step I paused and put my ear to the door.

Someone was coming. So I pulled back, pressing against the wall, holding my gun below my waist so I could raise it and shoot quickly if I needed to. Whoever it was walked lightly and came right toward the cellar door. Then suddenly the noises stopped and I could hear whoever it was breathing. Then I heard a voice call out. It was Henry, and he was only inches from me—separated only by a thin sheet of plywood.

"Better hurry back, boy." Then a pause. "Get down here!"

I heard a stirring upstairs. It must be Maxie.

"Time's up!" He shuffled away from the door, then back again, checking the bolt I had installed in the door years ago, sliding it out and then slamming it back into place again. I could have shot him if I knew exactly where he was, if I knew that no one else was in the house with Maxie and Jillie, could have ended it right then. But there was no way to be sure. I waited and held my breath. Then he left. I heard him retreat through the kitchen, through the dining room, and back to the living room where my son and wife were being held hostage.

After a few moments, I tried the door, even though I had heard the bolt slide into place, a bolt I myself had installed just in case...you know, just in case some bad person tried to gain entrance to our house via the basement, never realizing, of course, that that person would be me.

"I'm coming up, Maxie!" That voice again, but now from the front of the house. And I heard someone running. Across the second floor.

Then, "I'm coming," and I heard someone bang down the stairs. Maxie. Just a room away.

But...the door was locked.

CHAPTER ONE HUNDRED
TWELVE
HENRY

Henry stared at Maxie as he rounded the foot of the stairs and hurried to his mother who was applying pressure to Charley's wound, trying to stop the flow of blood. She grabbed Maxie with her free arm, staring nervously at Henry, and pulled him in close to her.

"You took a long time," Henry said, watching the two of them, then he turned back to the window and stared into the darkness. *Where are you?* he wondered, thinking about the Asp. And then he heard a car start—from a distance—and he looked hard into the darkness toward the highway, looked for the origin of the sound, wondering, and then, a flash of light, from where he and Turker (the Asp's real name) parked earlier in the day. Headlights swept across the highway, did a full turn, and headed east on Highway 40 toward...

What the hell is he doing? Henry wondered. And just then his cell phone went off.

Disappointed that I couldn't open the door, I made my way back down the stairs, quietly. And then across the basement to the stone stairs leading up to the cellar doors still partially open. *Had I wasted valuable time?* I paused once I closed the doors, turned and gazed back at where I had just been—at my house, dark and quiet—and considered if I should I have stayed.

Then a cell phone rang while I stood there. Deep from inside the house. I could hear the murmur of a distant voice. It must have been Henry's. I wondered who had called him. Then I slid back down the bank, covered with snow—now wet —and into the ditch that edged up to the highway. I beat the slush off my pants and made my way along the ditch, staying low and out of sight. I crossed the drive at street level and continued until I was well beyond the house and then struggled up the bank and worked my way back to my car where Richie and Louise were waiting.

"Did either of you call Jillie?" I said, still wondering about the phone call I had just heard.

They said they hadn't.

"Well?" Richie said. "What happened?"

"The cellar door was locked."

"Probably just as well," said Louise. "What were you going to do, shoot your way in?" She paused. "I called Wong."

"You what?" I said. "I thought I told you—"

"It's time," she said. Just like that. Matter-of-fact.

"Hey. That guy has two hostages in there—and they just happen to be your son and your ex. Don't give me that," she continued, now pissed off. "By the way, he's sending in a bird with a TAU...that's a Tactical Aviation Unit," she added, noticing the question in my eyes. "It's coming from Cleveland."

I knew Wong would do that. It's why I didn't want the cops called.

"Somebody's gonna get killed," I said. "Don't say I didn't—"

"The units gonna include a SWAT team and HRT," she replied, completely ignoring me. That would be a Hostage Rescue Team. They'll come in like an invasion force. Not what I had hoped for.

"And he said don't try anything stupid. That means do not try to gain entrance to the house before they get here." She paused, for effect. "In case you wanted to go in yourself," she continued, "like you just did, you being the Lone Ranger, big boy.

"You find the person who left the house?" I asked, ignoring what she said.

"Didn't find no one," said Richie. "That being if there was someone," he added.

I heard a car start on the street. We looked at each other.

"Only a couple of cars were parked there," said Louise.

"Uh-huh. Maybe that's our man."

I stayed in the shadows and headed toward the bank just in time to see the parking lights of a car come on. I watched it make a U-turn and head east, toward Cambridge—its headlights dark.

Yeah, that's him, I thought, and wondered where he was going.

Louise and Richie were right behind me.

"What's he doing?" Louise said. "Getting outta Dodge?"

"I doubt it," I said. "I wonder..." and we stared at the taillights fading into the distance. Then the headlights came on as the car passed Anthony's Antique Shop that's right across the road from the entrance to the college. Then they disappeared entirely. And we kept staring in silence for a while.

"Weird," said Richie.

"Wasn't Henry," I said. "He was in the house just a few minutes ago. Couldn't have gotten out there that fast. Besides—"

Louise interrupted, "Yeah. Besides, he's not leaving your son and Jillie behind. No, he's still in there."

"Then who in the fuck was that? And where's he going? I mean, assuming there was somebody else in the house with them guys," said Richie.

"I don't know," I said. "A neighbor?"

"Yeah, but what about the headlights? Who drives at night without headlights? Suspicious at least."

"Yeah. Suspicious." It was bugging me. If there was somebody in the house with Henry, then maybe he came out with a plan in mind. If a neighbor...then...well, then no big deal. But it probably wasn't a neighbor. So, either that person took off and won't be back, or...

Louise jumped in again. "Thinking what I'm thinking?"

There's an alley behind the house that parallels the highway and runs behind the homes that face the road. It gives the houses that were west of mine access to their garages located in their back yards. It dead-ends at my back door.

"Uh-huh. It's possible that whoever was in that car might be doubling back. Right?"

Louise responded, "I'm thinking yeah."

"There's a street at the far end of the college," I said, pointing east past the Antique Shop. "It runs through the campus to a street that would eventually take him to the alley behind my house." Funny how I thought of it as my house. It was really college housing built or bought to keep the profs on campus—easier for them to meet up with students.

It had been about ten minutes or so since the lights of the car disappeared down the highway.

"Might as well check it out," I said, and the three of us headed around the garage. It gave us protection from the front window but made progress difficult because—well because of all the crap that's behind the garage and because it was dark. I tripped over some logs that I remembered stacking there years ago.

"Jeez," said Richie, almost tripping over me.

My shin hurt like hell.

When we finally rounded the back of the house, I couldn't believe it but there it was: the black car that had been parked on the street, that looked more like a limo than a car. And the driver had done just what I had thought he could do but didn't think he would—find his way through the campus, connect with just the right street and find my alley! Two people were getting in from the passenger side, one in the front—a man— and one in the back—a woman. The driver's door slammed and the tires tore at the cinders in the drive, the car roaring away, throwing a cloud of dust at us. But through it all I could swear I saw a face in the rear window—and it looked like Maxie—at least I guessed it did, because...well because that's what I saw in my dreams—Maxie pulling himself up to see if I was following. And I wasn't. That's the way my dream went. But now I would. This time I would be following.

Richie took off running to the front of the house to get my car, Louise right behind him. I hurried over to the road, hoping to catch a glimpse of the fleeing vehicle as it pulled out of the alley and onto US 40. And I did. It was heading east, toward Cambridge, maybe retracing the route they took eight years ago when they kidnapped my son.

But this time, Maxie would not see an empty road behind him. No. He would see headlights. And those headlights would be mine.

PART FIVE

THE RECKONING

CHAPTER ONE HUNDRED FOURTEEN
WHAT DREAMS MAY COME

My dreams were playing out in front of me— Maxie's kidnapping. And Henry and whoever was with him were headed south-southeast. Maybe on the same highway. Maybe passing the same farms and the same small towns. And I'm watching the telephone poles, counting them, wondering if Maxie had watched those same poles fly by years ago, wondering if he was watching them now.

Richie was driving and we were staying well behind them so we could see their taillights, bright red against the darkness, and redder yet if the driver braked for a curve in the road. And they weren't speeding. So they must not be aware that we were behind them.

"This is good," I tell Richie. "Don't get any closer."

I called Wong. He answered on the first ring.

"Cooper! The copter should be over your place in less than an hour," he yelled before I had a chance to speak, the noise from the copter trying to kill his message.

"Problem," I said.

"Tell me about it," he replied sharply over the noise.

"You're not going to believe this but the damn guy has slipped out of the house with Maxie and Jillie. Right now he's on Old Route 40 heading east—and we're right behind him."

"Does he know you're behind him?"

"No. I don't think so."

"Good. Keep it that way. He finds out you're following, he might run. Better he doesn't know." Then, "You check the house? Make sure nobody's there?"

"No. I jumped into the car so we wouldn't lose them," I confessed, realizing now that one of us should have stayed to check. "Any chance you...?" I started.

"No problem. I'll call the locals..." Static. "You still there?" He finally came through again.

"Where are you?" I said.

"Somewhere near Columbus. We got an early flight to Cleveland. FBI got us a copter at the airport.

"We?" I said. "Who's we?"

"Me and Huck," he said and I lost him for good in a storm of static.

CHAPTER ONE HUNDRED
FIFTEEN
MAXIE

He watched the two men in the front, Henry driving and the Asp next to him. He felt the tension in his mother's body as she pulled him against her just like when he was small—to protect him from whatever bad thing was out there. He felt like telling her she didn't need to do that now. Because he was fifteen—a man.

He felt for the gun in his belt. It was loaded. He had done that in the bedroom upstairs, with Joey Lewis watching. Maxie felt the coldness of the gun. Then he turned to his mother and whispered, "Everything's going to be okay." She nodded and leaned into his ear, whispering that she knew it would. And she patted his hand as she did and tried to smile.

The Asp, turning and catching Jillie's smile, smiled back like he was in on the little secret the two of them were sharing. And Maxie felt the comfort of the gun pressing against his ribs.

CHAPTER ONE HUNDRED
SIXTEEN
CRISIS

The word, crisis, comes from the Greek word, *Krisis,* meaning 'decision.' And it describes the moment I'm in right now. Our two cars, pretty much alone and now on back roads which makes it hard to remain undetected— and maybe we shouldn't try that anymore, maybe we should get on their tail, hug their bumper and stay there, forcing the issue until... But then again, maybe we have an edge by hanging back, seeing where they go...I didn't know. See what I mean? Decisions. Crisis.

So I let Richie alone, keeping our distance—on a highway that I figured mirrored the way they took Maxie eight years ago —running by farm lands that were now just a wildernesses of darkness—at this late hour of the night—and running by small towns with populations of 300 people—or less—or sometimes just a store and a run-down building that used to be a store and no houses at all, anywhere. I wondered where in the hell Wong was—it's been an hour now—and he should have caught up. I had given him our route: Old Route 40 out of Muskingum and through Cambridge.

We jumped onto the Interstate (I-70) at Old Washington

and stayed on that for a while. The driver was doing exactly the speed limit. *Don't want to get any tickets here gentlemen, you with two hostages in your car. Try explaining that one.* Then he got off the Interstate where Old Route 40 picks up again just west of Morristown, Ohio, a small village of 303 (what did I tell you—small) as of the latest census (according to the sign), a town that wouldn't be looking for hostage-takers and where they could slip through in the darkness—which is where we were now, in Morristown and heading west, and Richie, keeping the right distance where we can see the tail-lights, barely. Nobody else out this time of the morning. And I'm wondering again where the hell Wong is with his rescue helicopter. And I'm wondering how this rescue is supposed to take place. And I'm anxious. And worried. And frustrated. Because I need to get Maxie back in one piece.

See what I mean? Crisis.

Then I heard it. The sound of a helicopter beating in the distance. Wong!

Moments later my cell went off.

"I see two sets of tail lights on the highway," Wong said, static in the background, again. "You hear me?"

"Loud and clear!" *And about time*, I said, under my breath.

Richie leaned back in his seat and took a large breath. "Got that right," he said. "It's about fucking time."

CHAPTER ONE HUNDRED
SEVENTEEN
MAXIE

The Man turned to the side so he could still see the road ahead, and asked the Boy, who was now fifteen and no longer a boy really, "How are you doing, son?"

Now that was shocking, because the Man, who had claimed that his father had asked him to take care of him, had never called him *son* before. He only called him by his first name and never that. Never son. And he didn't say it like older people say *son* to a younger person. No, he said it with a different tone of voice. Like he was referring to Maxie as *his son*. His mother squeezed his arm when the Man called him that and turned Maxie's head toward her and whispered, "Ignore him."

"I'm not your son," the Boy who was no longer a boy said. Quietly but firmly.

But the Man, who Maxie saw kissing his mother, said, "Oh, but yes you are, Maxie. You are."

Maxie noticed that the man whom he called the Asp, looked at Henry, puzzled—then he looked back at Maxie, as if he had heard this for the first time. Then he turned to the Man and whispered something—as if he were trying to confirm what he had just heard.

The Man's neck stiffened and he whispered something back to the Asp, like he was mad. But the Asp pulled back from Henry like he was mad too.

But the Boy who was no longer a boy was angry also. Not only had this man, Henry, kidnapped him and lied to him, but now was saying he was his father. Then Maxie felt for the gun to make sure it was there. His mother noticed. She looked worried and shook her head. So Maxie took his hand away from the gun. The very gun that his father had given to his mother and shown her how to use—in case she had to. And here he was —carrying it—maybe having to use it—just like his mother.

Just then Maxie heard the sound of a helicopter in the distance. His mother squeezed his arm again, harder this time.

CHAPTER ONE HUNDRED EIGHTEEN
WONG

The helicopter was keeping pace with our car, maybe a hundred yards behind, its lights blinking, dodging trees and phone lines. Then it roared ahead and almost sat on the car ahead that swerved like it was a living thing trying to avoid a predator. Then suddenly the helicopter veered off to the right, its long slim body disappearing over the fields, its motor belching out a hellish noise.

It reappeared in the distance—the sound of its beating rotors growing louder as it came straight at the car, low over the road, its floodlight bursting like a flash bulb over the car, and over the highway, and over the fields on both sides of the highway, and a loudspeaker blared at the car, Wong's voice, loud and warning, "Pull over and stop! Now!"

The car swerved against the blinding light, Richie braking hard so he wouldn't hit it, the helicopter hovering and blowing up a windstorm. Then Henry's car hit a ditch on the right side of the road, coming to rest against a fence that lined a pasture, and it sat there for a few moments, its motor running, its lights burning into the field.

The door opened—partially—and a man got out and yelled

something, through the noise of the copter overhead, and shook his fist, and then climbed back into the vehicle and closed the door. The car continued to sit there, in the ditch, against the fence, its motor still running, its lights burning a hole into the darkness.

CHAPTER ONE HUNDRED NINETEEN
WHAT HE SAID

W hat he said—the Man—is that he would kill his son, he would kill his wife, if the helicopter didn't leave, if Cooper didn't leave, but it seemed as though the only people who heard him were Maxie, and Jillie, and the Asp. And that wasn't good, the Boy thought. Because...well because no one was going to leave and then the Man would kill them both—that is if he had heard him correctly. That Henry, the man who had kidnapped him, who was saying that he was his father, who was saying that Jillie was his wife—*and that was crazy*, thought Maxie—was going to kill him and his mother in the end.

Then the Man got back into the car, his face red and angry, and turned toward the Boy and toward Jillie, and there was a look there, like he was now not thinking anymore—he had always seemed reasonable before—but not now—and he had a gun in his hand. Maxie had seen it before. It had a brown grip.

The Man was waving it at them, yelling at the top of his voice like a cop into a megaphone, "I meant what I said. If I can't..."

Jillie said, "You wouldn't!" and the Man slapped her

across the face, his eyes full of rage, and the mother felt for the place where he had slapped her, and fell back into the seat, gripping Maxie's arm so tightly it hurt, and then the Man turned away from them, and Maxie felt for his own gun again. It was poking him in the back, but it made him feel safe, against this man whose name was Henry, who had kidnapped him for eight years and lied and cheated him of his parents— this Man who had been with his mother—Maxie had seen him kiss her—he must have lied to her also—this Man who tried to take his mother away from him and his home away from him —who had said she was dead! And now he had the nerve to slap her—his own mother—in front of him. And the Boy, who was now a man, who was no longer a defenseless, small boy kidnapped by two men and taken to a stranger's house in South Carolina, far from his home in Ohio, this Boy was angry and he now had a rage inside—this Boy robbed of his family, and of his childhood, and of his friends, and of all the things he had back home in Muskingum, Ohio—even his bed and his toys!—this Boy was furious with the Man, with this evil person, who was sitting in front of him and even now planning to kill them because the police weren't going to go away and his dad wasn't going to go away—not this time—so Maxie raised the pistol to the back of Henry's head and Henry saw him do it in the rearview mirror—but it was too late—and the Asp saw him do it—out of his side vision—but it was too late—because Maxie put the gun up against the back of Henry's head—where all of his intelligence was—against his skull—which was hard against the gun—and he pulled the trigger—and blood, and skin, and bone, and one of Henry's eyes, blew out and covered the windshield, and the bullet carried through the windshield and out into the night, and under the helicopter that was hovering overhead, and it buried itself in a distant field after it was spent and took Henry's blood and his skin and his bone and dove with it into the ground.

Then Jillie screamed, and the Turk, moving quickly, snatched the gun from Maxie who seemed shocked by what he had done.

And the Asp took Maxie roughly by the back of his head and leaned into his face and said, "I shot him." Then the Asp put the gun down on the seat next to him, took Maxie's face in both hands and looked into his eyes. "You did the right thing," he said. "I should have shot him myself."

And about that time, Cooper was trying to break into the car and he was yelling.

CHAPTER ONE HUNDRED TWENTY
COOPER'S VIEW

I watched it happen, the helicopter bearing down on the car in front of us, the driver swerving, then losing control and slamming into a ditch, sliding side-wise about fifty feet and finally coming to rest against a wire fence. It stayed there for a few moments, the only sound the chop-chop of the copter as it circled overhead. Then the screeching and grinding of metal on metal as the driver wrestled the door open and climbed out and, yes, for sure it was Henry. He yelled out but I couldn't tell what he was saying and he stood there for a few moments maybe to see if we had gotten the message. He was strangely cool. Strangely relaxed. Like you would figure a psychiatrist would be when he was with a patient.

Then, satisfied maybe, he climbed back into the car, pulling the door shut, metal against metal, screeching and shrieking its resistance.

Behind us the helicopter was landing on a strip of open highway, its blades narrowly missing trees and telephone lines. The pilot skilled—like he had been in combat. And as soon as it was on the ground, the SWAT team leaped out of the copter, one by one, in full combat gear, and headed our way.

Then a shot from Henry's car. I froze. Wondering. Had Henry shot Jillie? Had he shot Maxie? I threw open my door and sprinted for the car, like in a hundred-yard dash, making the distance in seconds. Richie and Louise far back. When I got close, I slowed, and approached the car from behind. In the glare of the headlights from our own car I could see what looked like blood on the windows and I saw the shadows of movement within. I banged twice on the rear passenger door window and then yanked at the door, pulling it open, and Jillie almost fell out. In the front Henry was slumped over the wheel, his head hanging to the side. A big hole at the base of his skull and blood and something that looked like brain matter leaking out.

I climbed in next to Jillie and Maxie. Then the SWAT team cleared the driver's door and screamed at the Turk in the front seat to remain in the car as he was. "Hands over your head!" the lead man yelled. "And do not move!" The Turk did as he was told, hands locked together, his head bowed.

Wong was there, right next to the agent who had yelled. He leaned down, and put his hand on my shoulder: "Are you okay?" And I said I was. And then he looked to Jillie whose head was buried in my shoulder, now wet from her tears. But she didn't see him. Neither did Maxie.

It's over, I whispered as I took her hand. Maxie was holding on to her like a Velcro monkey. I held them in my arms, thinking of the time before the kidnapping. In Muskingum, Ohio. In the Fall. When the trees were just beginning to turn. When I was teaching Intro to Philosophy. And Jillie was home with Maxie. And then the Dean came to my door and...

But you know the rest of the story.

PART SIX

AFTER THE WAR

MONDAY, DECEMBER 12

Twelve Shopping Days Before Christmas

We flew back to Florida—I mean all of us: Louise, Richie, Jillie, Maxie, and Joe E. Lewis. Charley stayed behind.

Charley would need more time to recover from his wound. He was shot at close range. His shoulder showed it. I visited him at the hospital and thanked him for what he had done and said sorry about what happened to him. He laughed.

"No problem. Damn lucky to be alive. Glad I was able to be there for your son and Jillie."

"I'll always be grateful," I said and shook the hand of his good shoulder.

"Take care of Joey," he had said, wincing as he tried to raise his hand to shake.

And that's why Joey was exiting the plane with us in Fort Lauderdale, Florida, where there was no snow on the ground, the temperature was eighty-one degrees, and palm trees were bending in the afternoon breeze.

The six of us piled into my Volvo and headed for

Oceanside, Louise driving, Richie and Joe E. Lewis squeezing in the front with her, Jillie, Maxie and I in the back. I rode all the way back to my Everglades house with my arms over the shoulders of both. Louise was watching us in the rearview mirror. She gave me a silent okay with her eyes.

It's hard to describe what happened after we got home. Sammy was waiting on the porch. Richie went to the fridge to feed him. Louise hugged me for a good minute. I knew this was hard for her. She held tight, probably unable to gauge her part —here—tonight—in this reunion. Jillie watched. And then...well then Maxie and Jillie and I went to the back porch, opened up several deck chairs and began to get caught up on eight years, Maxie telling us in detail about the men who had taken him, about the ride to South Carolina and the lies they told him, about how sorry he was that he got into the car and Jillie and I—each taking one of his hands—telling him it was okay—that the thing was, he was back, and that's all that mattered.

Then I looked up and Richie and Louise were standing in the doorway. Richie came over. "Give your Uncle Richie a hug, Maxie," and Louise came over to Maxie also, her arms out, and Maxie hugged her, and then Jillie did, too.

The reunion went on like that all afternoon and into the evening, catching up on Maxie's last eight years—including Joey, the orphan, named after Joe E. Lewis.

"Dude," said Joey, "look what you did! You shot the psycho who took you and who shot my Uncle Charley. Man! How'd you do that?" he exclaimed, like he wanted the whole story, all the details.

"I don't know," said Maxie, looking down and away from Joey. "I just did."

He was quiet after that. He was quiet that way for most of the day. He had that far-away look of someone who wasn't really back, yet—still in that house in South Carolina, still trying to figure out what had happened to him these past eight years. I figured it would take a long time before he would be back to the Maxie I knew—if ever. But at least he was back home, safe, and that's a hell of a lot more than many kids who go missing ever get. Like the girl in the car wash in south Florida who was videoed being led away by a stranger who took her hand and she followed him into the street, away from the cameras, and away from her parents who were inside, completely unaware, and the girl never knew, until...And that's when I shut down my imagination. Because I don't want to think about what goes through the mind of a child who has been taken, like the child in the carwash, like Maxie, who will never be able to share what went through his mind as he was shoved into the car and as he watched out the window on that long trip to South Carolina, because he really couldn't or wouldn't want to share that.

Children are such innocents in this cold, cold world.

CHAPTER ONE HUNDRED TWENTY-TWO
THAT SAME NIGHT

Richie was barbequing in the back yard, Herman watching from the wooden walkway that leads to the dock, when a call came in. It was Cynthia Hayward.

"I've got Cleveland Wong with me, Coop. We're only about twenty minutes away. Can we drop over?"

"Why are you asking?" I said. "Of course! You like barbequed ribs?"

"Wow!" she said.

"Stay overnight," I said. "We've got room."

They were in my drive at 5:35 just as the sun was disappearing. Sammy came around the house with me. Part of the welcoming committee. Herman stayed put.

"I'm so happy for you, Coop," said Cynthia as she climbed out of Wong's black SUV and gave me a hug. Wong came around the van and held out his hand. "Cooper," and we just shook—Wong doesn't hug. But he was clearly moved, holding my eyes for a few moments then hurriedly looking around as though embarrassed.

He finally broke the silence. "Where is your son? I must see this boy!"

"He's in the house," I said and motioned for them to follow

"You call DeFelice yet?" he said as we headed up the porch. I realized I hadn't. Too fast, too crazy. *Gotta call him tonight*, I thought. *Damn.*

Cynthia was shaking her head. "Who would've thought? Maxie's back." Then, "There's a story here, Cooper," Cynthia, the journalist. And I knew she was right. And I knew she would tell it along with the story about the murder of her father.

Maxie was talking with Jillie and Louise as we came into the living room, Richie listening intently from my favorite Lazy-Boy lounger, catching up. As I watched Maxie, I couldn't help but wonder where he would eventually decide to live. Columbus or the Everglades. *All in good time,* I thought. But I couldn't help hoping that...

Then Wong and Cynthia hugged Maxie—I had never seen Wong do that—hug, I mean. And they didn't shoot questions at him about his experiences—thank God. But I knew Cynthia was already writing her feature article about a boy who came back after eight years—how often does that happen? And a second article about the killing of Jack Hayward, a local, popular fishing captain.

"Where's Huck?" said Cynthia, turning back to me.

"He was with Wong the last I knew," I said.

"I dropped him at his house in Everglades City," Wong said quickly. "Florida Fish and Wildlife gave him a permit to hunt gators—him and ten other hunters. He's getting his gear together. Should be here—soon.

"We need to talk, Coop—the three of us," Wong added quickly, looking over at Cynthia, "some place where there's some privacy." I knew what he wanted to talk about—Li Lang and her boyfriend for one. And Jack's death for another.

"The back porch," I said and led them both through the kitchen and out the screen door. There was a loud rustle in the mangroves near the dock.

"What's that?" said Wong, looking nervously into the dark.

"Probably Herman," I said.

"Herman?"

"Cooper's pet alligator," Cynthia explained. And there was a silence.

"I hope it's in a cage," Wong said, looking around as I pulled over some deck chairs.

"He's by the dock," I said. "Alligators are more afraid of you than you are of them."

"Uh-huh. And that's a line I never believe," Wong said. "Kinda like sharks—they don't bother you if you don't bother them," he added, shaking his head.

We settled in the chairs around the table, Wong still watching through the darkness nervously. "You never told me about Herman before, Cooper. Why not?"

I shrugged. "You never asked."

Then, "How you doin', Cleveland," said Richie, barging through the screen door. Right behind him were Louise and Huck, who was newly arrived and looking like an old Florida cowboy, buckskins and all. There went our private talk.

"Where's Herman?" Huck said, his alligator gun slung over his shoulder.

"Not even funny," I said. "Herman's over by the dock, and he can hear..."

"Didn't mean to offend," Huck whispered, taking a seat next to me. "Herman is a friend of mine. I respect him."

"Good," I said. "Cause if you don't...."

He smiled.

"What about the men in the fast boat?" said Louise, pulling her chair closer to Wong. "Did you catch them?"

"I did. And they're both sitting in *your* jail," he replied. "Incidentally Rodriquez was wondering where the hell you were. I covered. Said you were working a case for me."

"I told him I needed some R and R," Louise said, crossing her legs.

Then Jillie and Maxie and Joe E. Lewis came through the door carrying a bottle of wine, an eight-pack of beer, and some glasses.

"You old enough to serve alcohol?" I asked Joey.

"You bet," he said. And he poured for me and himself.

Sammy was there also, moving from chair to chair and rubbing against legs. He stopped and looked up at Richie. Richie picked him up and put him on his lap. Sammy curled up and purred like a lawn mower.

"So..." began Wong, "thanks to your heads-up, our helicopter was able to spot the fast boat. It was running north toward the Everglades..."

"Probably heading for the rig in Ponce de Leon Bay," I said.

"They didn't stop at first—then we shot out their motors. The chase boat engaged them in a firefight—one of them was shot and killed, the other two surrendered." He paused for a moment. Like he was waiting for questions.

"You not going to ask?"

"About what?" I said.

"About what we got?"

"Fuck yeah," said Richie. He was petting Sammy.

"Language," I said, nodding at Maxie and Joey. But they didn't seem to notice—or care.

"About one hundred and fifty million dollars of coke—street value."

"Wow!" I said. Wong smiled.

"But—and this is the difficult part for me—one of the leaders of this whole damn thing is my niece, Li Lang Zhu."

Wong took up the glass of white wine that he had been sipping, swirled it several times and then continued while he studied the wine.

"But I can tell you this, those we have taken into custody, including my niece and that young man with her, will be fully prosecuted." I wondered if he knew of Snow's involvement with Lei Sun.

Then Wong raised his glass to me. "I thank you, Cooper, *and* your friends," he said, nodding at Richie and Louise and Huck, "for what you have done." He drained the glass, then watched the last drops gather in the bottom. "Because of you we will bring these criminals to account."

He paused then said. "And about the rig in Ponce de Leon Bay, the Coast Guard confiscated over a thousand pounds of cocaine. They also boarded the *Zhi Zhu Nu*..." He hesitated. "I know that rig is in Cuban waters, but we treated it as a threat to the safety of the U.S., so we boarded it anyway and confiscated more than a ton of cocaine." He paused again, smiling. "They also found two young Chinese men, members of the Black Lotus Tong. They had armed themselves with M4A1 rifles but dropped them when the Guard landed. They claimed some bad people killed one of their members and then made them jump into the sea. You know anything about that?" He was looking directly at me.

"Hell of a fish story," I confessed.

"Huh. I thought so. Anyway, we got them and they're in the same jail as the other guys. Only thing worse than a Miami jail is another Miami jail, right Louise?" I think he meant it.

Louise nodded. "Uh-huh. Good place for them."

"Anyway, guys..." he caught himself then continued, "I mean guys *and* Detective Delgado, the total we confiscated—on the fast boat, on the *Zhi Zhu Nu*, and from the Ponce de Leon rig—amounted to over three and a quarter tons, a street value close to three hundred and fifty million dollars. And that's no fish story!"

"No shit!" said Joey. Jillie nudged him.

"No shit," said Wong, winking at Joey—which made Joey grin.

The wine was getting to Wong but he continued anyway. "Did you know that cocaine is an eighty-eight billion dollar a year business world-wide?" He let that sink in. "And forty percent of the drug is consumed in North America?" and he let *that* sink in. "And you guys just helped us stop some of that action."

We had been sitting and listening to Wong for about half an hour so I went into the kitchen to bring out more wine. We were down to four bottles of white and a six-pack of Sam Adams. I brought it all out.

"What about the drilling?" said Louise. "Did the Guard check out the small rig for illegal drilling?"

"Yes, they were doing horizontal drilling and we found the stash of..."

"And you shut the bastards down, " said Richie.

"Damn right—and we arrested every one of those guys. And they are also in your jail," he said, nodding to Louise.

Then he turned to Cynthia and said. "About your father, several of the guys in jail were responsible for his murder. Nobody confessed yet, but our guys..." He hesitated, "you know..." We all knew.

He continued. "Unfortunately, the organization behind all this, the Black Lotus Tong, is still operating. We got their leader (it was clear he didn't want to mention his niece again) but we didn't get the big boys. And, more bad news, the Tong is expanding their territory from the South China Sea into the

Caribbean. *And* adding to their product line. It used to be only heroin, now it's also coke and marijuana. Eighty percent of it coming through the Caribbean."

A quiet settled over the porch when Wong quit talking. No one wanted to break into it. Except Huck, who said that the ancestors were with us and that the evil spirits that had robbed us of our peace these last days were running from the spirits of the wind and the moon and the stars. I believed him as I watched the moon grow big in the sky over the Everglades. It shone brightly on the River of Grass. I was grateful for that light, and nodded a silent *thanks* to Huck. I knew that he was talking not only about drugs and illegal drilling but also about the return of a young boy to his father and mother.

I signaled Maxie to come over and sit by me, Jillie giving him a gentle shove. So, he came over, sat, and pushed up against me. Then, we all watched the moon, falling under its magic. And I drank and held Maxie close and got numb from the wine.

Tony DeFelice showed up around 10:00 p.m. "Shoulda called!" he said. Pissed, storming onto the porch.

"I..."

"I mean, right away!" he continued. "We was partners, remember! I'm the one brought you down to Miami for the job. I'm the one told you about a lead I had on a kidnapping ring—sweat it out with you for all those years while you looked—jumped in when you needed help! Remember?"

And I did. "I know I should have called right away—but..."

"Damn right. But you were too busy. Too busy to call your old partner. Hey, Richie and Louise you called, right?" Looking over at Richie and Louise who were now standing. "But you...? So, what am I? Chopped liver?"

I shrugged and nodded, like I knew he was right.

"Easy, Tony," said Louise. "Nobody meant any disrespect. You and Coop are good friends. He woulda called if he had the time."

"Maxie's like my own son," he continued, now sounding hurt. That made it worse.

Then, "Come over here, Maxie. Give your Uncle Tony a hug!" and Maxie did just that and DeFelice gave him the same bear hug that Richie gives. Then he pulled back and looked at him. "You got more handsomer since you been gone, son. Now you look better'n your old man," and he just stayed like that for a few moments, looking Maxie up and down, then, "Damn, son, it's great to have you back."

DeFelice and I made up, I promised to call him. He said *Sure, I'll believe that when it happens.* But that's his way, with Richie telling him *Shut the fuck up and get over it,* like he did back in the day when we grew up together on the streets on the East side of Cleveland. And DeFelice telling him to pound salt.

Around midnight, Wong collected his sunglasses and hat from the porch and said he was going to drop off Cynthia at her home. "This lady has got a real story here," he said, nodding at Cynthia. "Father and mother get son back—after eight years. A headline. National story!" Then to me: "And you...you not only got Jack Hayward's killers, but you uncovered illegal drilling in the Everglades and helped us make one of the biggest drug busts in history, and..." he paused, "the President said he wants to thank you personally for what you did. He's going to call you."

"The President? Of the United States?" I said, not sure I heard him right. "He's going to call me?"

"Of the United States. He's not going to meet you. But he is going to call you," he said, grabbing my hand and shaking it. "Congratulations—to you and your friends." He was looking around at all of us. "You made big news today—here, and in Washington."

"I don't believe it," I said. "I'm shocked." And I thought I might say that I accept this in the name of all my friends who helped...but decided, nah, that sounded like a speech at the Oscars.

"Believe it," Wong said. "Maybe you should buy a lottery ticket."

"And thanks, from me and Jack," Cynthia whispered, as she leaned in close and put her arms around me, squeezed like she would never let go. "It's all good now," she said. "I know what happened to him, and that makes it okay." Then she pulled back to look at me. "I can write that story now—thanks to you."

I nodded. "You should. You're a good reporter—and Jack would want you to."

I walked them out to Wong's unmarked and watched as they pulled onto Midnight Drive. I couldn't help but think of the young woman I had seen on the street below my office just a few weeks ago. We had both grown a lot older since then.

DeFelice packed it in around 1:00 a.m. *Got an early morning*, he said. *Some of us are still working*—he was really hurt when I retired from the Department. "I'm gonna leave you to spend some time with your son," he said, leaning in and whispering. And I gave him a big DeFelice kind of hug and said, *I love you, bud*. I could see him trying to stay cool—trying to stay macho—DeFelice and Richie—same kind of people—they don't cry. Matter of fact, neither do I. So we hugged and pounded each other on the back and things were back to normal with us—everything forgiven. And he said, "I love you too, bud."

Then, "You really deserve this," he said, gesturing at everything around me. "Your son back, Jillie and you able to make peace with it (he said wit it) and you know…" and he ran out of words, or was getting too choked up to talk. His eyes reddened as he looked away pretending to clear something from them.

"Dammit, Cooper, you almost got me cryin'." He paused, trying to get back to his old macho self. "I wanna know all

about Maxie's story, okay? So, call me." Then he shrugged his
shoulders through the door, like a tough cop would, turned one
last time with a thumbs-up and headed for his car. I didn't
follow him out. He wouldn't want me to. But I watched at the
door as his lights disappeared into the trees.

By two a.m. my wine supply was down to a few bottles. I
planned on drinking at least one myself. Richie and Louise had
already turned in. *I gotta catch an early flight—and don't worry,
Lou will take me,* Richie had said. All three had gone to bed
before DeFelice left, Louise in my bedroom, Richie in one of
the two guest bedrooms. Sammy followed him into the house.
My guess, he sleeps with him.

Huck was still hanging out on the porch. He rose when I
came through the screen door, and I knew he was going to say
something deep. He took my hand, grasping me by the arm and
said: "I knew that Maxie would come back to you. I would like
to bless you and this house so that no bad things can come to
you in the future." I was glad Richie was gone. Then he began:

> *"May the Warm Winds of Heaven*
> *Blow softly upon your house*
> *May the Great Spirit*
> *Bless all who enter there*
> *May your moccasins*
> *Make happy tracks*
> *In many snows*
> *And may the rainbow*
> *Always touch your shoulder."*

I determined that I would have it printed and framed and
that I would mount it over the screen door on the front porch.

CHAPTER ONE HUNDRED TWENTY-FOUR
THE FULL COPPER MOON

Early Tuesday Morning, December 13
Eleven Shopping Days Before Christmas

So, now it was just Jillie, Maxie, and I, and, of course, Joey Lewis and we were sitting on the back porch. I had opened a bottle of 2012 Liberty School, Pinot noir. We were all drinking, even Maxie and Joe E. Lewis.

Jillie put her arms around Maxie. "We are so lucky, Coop. To have our son back." And she hugged him tightly.

Joey tipped his glass but didn't say anything. I knew what he was thinking about—his own past. But Joey had his Uncle Charley. And he must have been reading my mind, because he tipped his glass again, like a real grown-up. "Here's to the former orphan," he said, smiling, and we all smiled with him and drank to that.

Suddenly a light flashed across the side of the house. I looked at my phone. Two-thirty a.m. and wondered, who the hell...?

A car door slammed and we all turned to see who was

coming around the house. The moon was now low in the December sky and it was out full. Native Americans call it the Full Cold Moon. It's when winter descends over the hunting and growing fields and one has to depend on what he has stored up from the harvest of buffalo and deer and wheat in order to live through the snow and the cold. It's sometimes called the Long Nights Moon—because the it leads us into the darkest evening of the year. We were only six days away from that night.

A lone figure emerged from the shadows and walked slowly, tentatively towards us.

"Hello," he said, the man in the shadows.

"Asp!" whispered Maxie. No fear there.

Jillie gasped. "My God, what's he doing here?"

"Hi Maxie," said the figure walking into the light cast by the dim porch lamp. He was holding up his hands in a peace gesture and said, "I wanted to make sure you were okay," in a sharp voice, a clear voice, but with a distinct accent. He hesitated at the bottom of the steps. "May I?" he asked. He was looking at Maxie.

He was dressed entirely in black—I mean entirely—black pants, a black shirt, black shoes, and a black fedora.

I waved him up.

"What happened?" I asked, my last image of him being carried away by the FBI in handcuffs.

"The Gendarme arrested me. Took me to Washington in a helicopter. Then questioned me for hours about how Doctor Henry died. I told them, simple, I shoot him!" He was holding his hands up like it was a simple explanation.

"But...?" I said.

Maxie leaned into me. "I shot him," he whispered.

"You what?" I said, loudly.

"I shot him," Maxie said again, this time so everybody could hear.

"The boy is not telling the truth," insisted the man whom Maxie called the Asp.

"That's right," said Jillie, "because I shot him."

And the five of us stared at each other.

"You are all lying," said the Asp again. "It is not necessary."

"How did you get out?" I said, totally confused.

The man who was interrogating me was replaced by a Chinese man. I think he was the same man who was at the scene." *Wong!* I thought. "What did he say?"

"He said, *Are you left-handed or right-handed?* And I said I was right-handed. And he said, *Then, you didn't shoot Doctor Fowler.* I ask him why? And he asks how could I reach behind Doctor Henry's head from where I sat and shoot him?"

"That makes sense," I said. "So..."

"He said I was free to go. I ask him who did he think killed Doctor Henry if I didn't. I was worried about what he would do next."

"You mean about Jillie or Maxie?"

"That's right."

"And he said?"

"That the gunshot was self-inflicted."

"You're kidding!" I didn't really expect him to reply.

"I am not kidding, Mister Cooper. He was serious. So, I ask him why did he think that?" He paused waiting for me to ask the question. But I didn't. I was anxious to hear what Wong had said. Then, he continued. "He said the medical examiner said the evidence points to self-inflicted wound."

"But the gun..."

"He said it had Doctor Henry's fingerprints on it," and the Asp shrugged, like *What do I know?*

There wasn't a sound from Maxie or Jillie. "You never told me what happened in the car," I said to both of them. And then added quickly, "And I think it's better if you don't."

The Asp nodded while Jillie and Maxie just stared at me, probably not knowing what to say. I shook my head, stopping the discussion at the pass. I sent a silent thanks to Wong.

"I thought you were going to kill me," said Maxie, in a voice tentative and soft, as the Asp pulled up a chair next to him.

The Turk leaned in and laid his arm over Maxie's shoulder. "I have only love for you, cocuk (child)," he said. "When you disappeared, I feared for your safety. Doctor Henry was very upset." He paused. "You see, I thought you were his true son. I did not know you were not." He looked at me and at Jillie and held up his hands. "I hope you understand that I did not know."

Then, "And Maxie, do *you* understand?" he said.

Maxie just sat there staring into the table and a long uncomfortable silence followed. Then after what seemed an endless amount of quiet, Maxie turned to the Asp, nodded his head, and said, "Okay. I understand." He paused. Then, "But I really did think you were going to kill me," he said, almost in a whisper. A sheepish smile crept over his face.

The Asp replied, "Never, *sevgili arkadasim* (my dear friend). Never." He put his arms around Maxie and hugged him. "I would always protect you." Then holding him at arms-length and staring eye to eye, he added, "My job was *always* to protect you. I was your bodyguard, *sevgili oglum* (my dear boy)," he insisted, shaking Maxie gently.

"And I feel like I must still be that." He paused, dropped his head, and thought for a moment. "But now you have your father and your mother and you won't need me anymore." He looked sad as he said it, this man in black, this thin, middle-aged, sharp featured Turk, this man with no gray hair, no sign of age other than his mature behavior, this man who looked like a shooter for the mafia. He seemed so vulnerable now.

What was there to say? So I thanked him and told him that he had actually saved us. And that we owed him. He shrugged, as if to say, *What else was I to do?* Then we sat in the quiet of the Great Swamp, and stared at the darkness of it, and listened to the noises of it, and watched the moon cast its spell over it, and said nothing for what seemed hours, but was only a few minutes.

"So, what are you going to do?" I said to the Turk. "And what is your real name, by the way?"

"Turker," he said. "I am from Istanbul. Maybe I will return there."

"Maybe you could hire him," blurted out Maxie. Joey nodded.

I stared at Maxie.

"As a private detective!" Maxie said, too loud for the quiet.

"Maxie!" said Jillie.

The Turk didn't say anything. But he smiled.

"I don't need money, Maxie," he said. "But thank you." Then suddenly, "*Cocuk,* come here!" he commanded, his arms stretched wide, and the fifteen-year-old Boy took him up on that and embraced the man whom all these years he thought was his enemy.

The moon was sitting over the mangroves, and over my dock, and it threw its light into the Great Swamp where I had fished these past seven years to fight depression, whose quiet had drugged me to sleep, and whose wildness had distracted me from my nightmares. Then the Turk got up, the man Maxie had named the Asp, and said he was leaving. I told him to find a place in the house—maybe in the living room—camp out until morning—everybody else is—and he hesitated—and I said—no arguments—go. He smiled, thanked me and said, "Maybe another time, *arkadashlar*." He left the way he came in, back around the corner of the house, into the darkness. I heard the car start, and watched the headlights sweep over the swamp.

The Asp vanished as quickly as he had appeared.

CHAPTER ONE HUNDRED TWENTY-FIVE
UNDER THE COLD COPPER MOON

Joey was asleep at the table. Jillie woke him and said she would put him to bed in the third bedroom with Richie. I told her she and Louise could share my bed — strange as that sounded—but she said, *okay*, yawned, and headed through the screen door, guiding Joey through the kitchen toward the bedroom. She looked around as she passed the kitchen window, and smiled. And I knew what she was thinking—it was a good time for us—and a good time for a father to get to know his son again.

I got up and went into the kitchen to get the last bottle of Liberty School. I brought it out with two fresh glasses and poured a little into Maxie's glass and some into mine. We leaned back in our chairs and sipped wine and listened to the sounds of the Swamp that never sleeps.

"Come on, let's try out that hammock," I said. Maxie looked toward the mangroves. "There," I said, and it was swinging in line with the palm branches under which it hung. So, we took our glasses, the bottle of Liberty School, and headed for the hammock, my favorite part of the house. We climbed up onto the hammock—or tried to—Maxie almost flipping us over, and laughing as he did it, balancing the wine glasses, until we finally found a steady seat, and then we talked, and watched the moon, now full, its edges tinged with copper. It was floating through the clouds, moving quickly as if in a race with them.

My head was dizzy with the wine and dreaming. I murmured to myself, *My race is over. Finally!*

I put my arm around Maxie. "*My* son," I said. "You're home." And I squeezed him—hard. He smiled, crowded in against me, and buried his head in my chest. I eased the wine glass from his hand and set it on a circular table I had built around a palm next to us, then put mine there and the nearly empty bottle of wine, and settled back into the hammock.

"Hey, Dad," he said, his eyes drooping.

"Yeah?"

"Can we put up some Christmas decorations this year?"

"Absolutely," I said.

"I haven't celebrated Christmas since..."

"Sure, Maxie," I said. "We'll get a tree and some lights— tomorrow. Okay?"

"Okay..." he said, and his eyes were already closing. Gone for the night.

I realized for once how much he had grown, his head now against my chin, and looked up at the moon as it chased through the clouds. It seemed to have lost its coldness.

Fifteen, I thought, *Wow!* And my eyes were closing, too.

AUTHOR'S NOTE

A Cold Copper Moon is a work of fiction. Some of the places exist only in the mind of the author. For instance, there is no city south of Miami named Oceanside, nor a town in Ohio named Muskingum, nor a college by the name of Concord. I switched the names of town and university to protect the innocent. Other places, streets, and restaurants are for the most part real, although the details may have been changed to suit the author's fancy. You must understand, writers love to tell stories.

ACKNOWLEDGMENTS

It's time for me to acknowledge the people who made it possible for me to write and publish *A Cold Copper Moon.* First, let me thank my readers: Karyn Conrath, who reads and serves as my chief editor; John and Stephanie Coburn; Ryan Conrath, PhD, who reads and edits with a deft hand; Scott Nelson; Jane and Glenn Trout; James and Helen Conrath; Jack and Melissa Conrath, who read and comment with great insight and whose constant support is magic in this lonely business; Christine Bohanan, who fills me in on Cleveland and environs; Ron Mutchnik who read the work, word by word, and provided valuable comments; Helene Naimon, my backup for details about Boston and Robert Parker, one of my favorite authors. Thanks also to others who have supported me in my writing efforts: Robert Freedman, Raymond and Susan Imbrigiotta and the entire clan. You have all been so marvelous!

A special thanks to Jack Driscoll, a PEN/Nelson Algren Fiction Award and Pushcart Editor's Book Award winner, and the author, among other notable works, of one of my favorite books, *Lucky Man, Lucky Woman.* Jack has not only guided me in my early writing efforts but has continued to help as I work on my skills. Thanks, Jack. It never ends, does it? Lois Driscoll is also a vital reader.

Thanks also to a fellow author, David Harry Tannenbaum, who has penned, among other works, the remarkable Padre Island Series. It stars two of my favorite detectives: Jimmy Redstone and Angella Martinez.

Special thanks also to other fellow writers for their support and advice as I try to put it all together correctly: Randy Rawls, Victoria Landis, Micki Browning, Nancy Cohen, Ann Meier, Gregg Brickman, and Dana Sommers among others. And, of course, Dee Tenorio, who not only designed *A Cold Copper Moon* and its cover, but also offered significant insights as she read through my manuscript.

Tristram Coburn, who originally served as my agent and is now in the publishing business (Tilbury House Publisher) and who continues to help, has been key in my development as a writer. Thanks, Tris. My books would not be what they are today without your insights about the content and your editorial direction. Thanks for hanging in there.

There are others to whom I owe a debt of gratitude. Randy Wayne White, one of my first reads when I came to Florida, has continued to encourage me with his constant and important reminder to "Persist!" And thanks also to another famous Florida writer, Tim Dorsey, who continues to inspire with his great stories about the myriad of characters in the Sunshine State that make writing about Florida such an interesting adventure.

A special thanks to J. Michael Orenduff, author of the Pot Thief Mysteries. I enjoyed my time with you on your "Talking Books" radio show. And to Julie Glenn, host of Gulf Shore Live on WGCU, an NPR affiliate. Thanks for making my appearance on your show a comfortable and delightful one.

Kathleen Donaldson, a former law enforcement officer, continues to help me with the complexities of police procedure. And a tip of the hat to David Berilla (host for book signing in Rehoboth Beach, MD) as well as to Susan Pittleman who has an editor's eye. Thanks also to Dr. Phil Jason, reviewer extraordinaire for the popular, *Florida Weekly*. I appreciate his insights into my writing. He should know about writing, as Professor Emeritus of English at the United States Naval Academy and a poet. Martin Lipschultz has been a constant with his remarkable photography. He rendered the first photograph on my website that makes me look remarkably like one of my idols: Leonard Cohen. And what can I say about Ryan Conrath, the one responsible for the website at www.richardconrath.com, for his editorial insights, and his help with rendering my books into Kindle. And thanks to Dee Tenorio who designed the latest website as well as this book and its cover.

OTHER SUPPORTERS:

The Women's and Men's Cultural Association of Collier County; Lee County Library; Collier County Library; Palm Beach County Library; Collier County Sheriff's Department; Mystery Writers of America, FL; and the Council for Critical Thinking, Naples, FL.

Some local Indie Book Stores have also been so supportive. On Sanibel Island, FL I am grateful for the help from Gene's Books, MacIntosh Books, and a special thanks to Bailey's General Store and its book manager, Rudola Richards. On Rehoboth Beach MD a special nod to Browse About Books.

And finally, last but surely not least, a deep bow and salaam to my lifelong partner, chief editor, muse, and constant inspiration, who has spent endless hours, days, and months listening to the reading of my books, editing them, commenting on whether the lines are true to the scene, and without whom *A Cold Copper Moon* would not be what it is today—and I guess, by now, you must realize that I am talking about my wife, Karyn Marie. A simple 'thank you' is just not enough.

Here is a preview of the newest novel from
Richard Conrath:

THE BLOOD MERCHANTS

Prologue

It was cold outside. It should be. Providence. In the winter—in the middle of the winter actually—with ice hanging on the eaves like tinsel on a Christmas tree, waiting for the man in red pajamas to deliver presents to the kids who were sleeping— even though the houses didn't have chimneys. A crazy feast. He was thinking he wanted to be that man. The one who climbs into peoples' homes—no danger of being arrested—when everyone is in bed. Isn't that when the Clutter family out in Kansas was murdered—one by one—in the night while they were in bed? By Perry Smith and Richard Hickock? You would think people would learn.

This is what he was thinking as he watched a man—a young man—coming out of the house across the street, his face lit up by the street lamp laced in ice and by a porch light that the girl had turned on. She looked familiar. And they kissed. In the moonlight, in the shadow of the trees that over hung the porch. But even in the shadows he could see them clearly. And then they parted, she closing the door—but not before taking one more look back as he took the stairs to the ground one-at-a-time, probably slick from ice. And then he found the gate at the white picket fence blocking his way to the street and opened it, looking back to see if she were still there, but the lights were out now—in the house—but the porch light was not, and the street light was not, and he headed the short distance to his car which was parked on the street, directly across from the house, hard up against the curb, nestled snugly against the curb, well out of the way of cars that might drift off the straight path of the street, and away from the protection of the street light, and lost in the shadows of the late night. But he crossed the street in a relaxed way, the collar of his coat pulled up against his cheeks, his stocking hat pulled down over his ears—it was close to zero this winter night in Providence, Rhode Island. He tried to open the door on the driver's side. But the key stuck in the lock and wouldn't turn.

That's when he looked up and noticed the man standing in the shadows of a large oak and watching him, not ten feet away.

ABOUT THE AUTHOR

Richard "Connie" Conrath is a former Catholic priest who left to teach philosophy at a small college while freelancing for newspapers like the *Cleveland Plain Dealer* and *Sunday Magazine*. He left teaching in 1984 and began a series of three-year stints in administration as a college vice-president,

president, and then as headmaster of an American school in southern Turkey. It was there, during the darkness of the Turkish winters that he began to write his first mystery. He now lives in south Florida with his wife.

A Cold Copper Moon is the final in the trilogy, The Cooper Series. Book two, *Blood Moon Rising*, won several awards including The Royal Palm Literary Award, The Clue Award, and The Silver Falchion Award.

Made in the USA
Columbia, SC
28 April 2021